DAWN OF DELIVERANCE

THE APOCALYPSE : EPISODE FIVE

I0584092

DAVID O. BULLOCK

Black Rose Writing | Texas

ISBN: 978-1-68513-083-1
PUBLISHED BY BLACK ROSE WRITING
www.blackrosewriting.com

Printed in the United States of America
Suggested Retail Price (SRP) $23.95

Dawn of Deliverance is printed in Calluna

*As a planet-friendly publisher, Black Rose Writing does its best to eliminate unnecessary waste to
reduce paper usage and energy costs, while never compromising the reading experience. As a result,
the final word count vs. page count may not meet common expectations.

To my Uncle Millard Warren a.k.a. Duncka, a.k.a. Shade
They always told me
I look a lot like you
And I act just like you
I wear that banner proudly
You taught me to love sports
Turned me into a Reds and Bengals fan
I work hard and play hard, just like you
I drive like you
(which may be a questionable trait)
From childhood, you have been my hero
And always my second dad
I love you, Shade, and thank you
for everything you have done for me
–David

ACKNOWLEDGMENTS

Jeanne Lose, my very capable editor who helps ensure all my books are well written and grammatically correct. Without her able assistance, I could never accomplish my mission of writing books which change lives.

Joe and Karen Rayl for allowing me to write at my favorite place when I experienced a period of writer's block and struggled to move forward. Those days in Tennessee were miraculous. When I returned home, this book was well underway again.

My wife for always supporting my writing and allowing me to pursue my dreams, even realizing how difficult that can be. She is my rock. I could never be who I am or do what I do without her.

"Then I heard a loud voice from the temple saying to the seven angels,
'Go, pour out the seven bowls of God's wrath on the earth."
–Revelation 16:1 NIV

"Hallelujah! For our Lord God Almighty reigns!
Let us rejoice and be glad and give him glory!
For the wedding of the Lamb has come,
And his bride has made herself ready."
–Revelation 19:6-7

He who was seated on the throne said,
"I am making everything new!"
Then he said, "Write this down,
For these words are trustworthy and true."
–Revelation 21:5

DAWN OF DELIVERANCE

The Smyrnians sat silently in the ruins of their new *safe* place, darkness concealing the horrifying scene from their sight. All hope faded with their extinguished lights, leaving them under the blackness of a cloud-covered midnight sky. The only thing darker than the night was the agony languishing in the depths of their souls.

They had frantically dug through the rubble, searching for family and friends who may remain alive, to no avail. Their voices calling out names were met only with eerie silence. Grief overwhelmed them like a rushing torrent, their sobs the only sounds piercing the night.

Gone. Teammates, comrades, wives, husbands, children, all perished in a brutal attack, doubtlessly ordered by Messai himself. Sure, they were all with Jesus, but how could this remaining group continue without them? Would morning never come? The darkness seemed to deepen with each passing minute.

Aissa Messai rejoiced in his luxurious mansion. This was his most victorious night yet. Of course, he wanted to see Smyrnian heads roll, but a fireball of exploding Chinese bombs wreaking mutilation would suffice. *Dismemberment is even better than decapitation*, he mused aloud. Tonight called for a celebration.

"Levi!"

He relished controlling these Jews who served him, forcing them to obey his every command. The chef rushed into the room.

"Yes, Master?"

Oh, how he loved hearing that word come from the mouths of these subservient Jewish slaves.

"Prepare a feast at noon tomorrow for twelve guests, besides myself, and spare no expense."

The man departed quickly, knowing better than to stay after receiving his orders. He understood breaking that rule led to certain punishment. His boss's voice thundered as he neared the door.

"Did you forget something?"

"I apologize, sir," Levi mumbled as he ran back and bowed low before the Secretary-General.

"That's better. Now, leave my presence and begin preparations for tomorrow. *Chana!*"

The meek, yet incredibly efficient and trustworthy secretary entered as Levi exited. Messai did not give her an opportunity to speak.

"You may stand," he said to the woman already kneeling at his feet. "Contact the ten *New World Order* leaders, Caiaphas, and General Chen, and tell them we will meet here at 9:00 a.m. tomorrow, ending with a feast at noon. Inform them we have something very important to celebrate, and remind them their presence is mandatory."

Chana bowed again, then hurried away. What was so newsworthy her boss would throw a party for his leaders? Why was General Chen invited? Whatever it was, Messai would announce it before the 3:00 p.m. executions. She knew that because his ego required it. Chana hated the man and feared what she and the world would hear tomorrow afternoon. Only one thing would bring him such joy: a tragic day for his most despised foe, the *Smyrnians*. Her heart broke for them.

CHAPTER 1

Approaching daybreak brought the first hint of morning light to what remained of Lifta. The exhausted Smyrnians began searching again the moment they could see what lay before them. Nothing appeared better than the night before. Piles of concrete and stone covered the place, intermingled with gaping holes created by detonated explosives. The latter looked hauntingly like graves which held their comrades' bodies buried alive.

Ahmad's condition deteriorated as Hala sat with him throughout the night. Omar stopped searching and helped her carry him under the few remaining small trees where they could care for him. The search continued, yielding no positive results. Not only had they found zero survivors, but they had discovered few bodies. They would not stop until they uncovered every teammate lying beneath the rubble. That changed with the sound of approaching vehicles. The group raced for a large wooded area and ducked inside, hoping they had not been spotted.

From the trees, they watched AMPP personnel spill from trucks and SUVs, then spread out in all directions, combing through the rubble. The men's loud voices and noisy clatter provided cover for the Smyrnians and soldiers to creep farther into the woods without being heard. Survival instincts took over despite their grieving hearts.

"Can we make it to the truck?"

"We can't take that chance, Trey," said Ollie. "Our best bet is to stay in these trees. We can figure something out later, but let's stay out of sight, keep moving, and get as far away as possible."

"How are we going to do that without the truck?" Trey's frustration was showing.

"What good is a truck without fuel, Trey? The fuel truck blew up, remember?"

"Everybody calm down so we can think," said Blake. "We all know we're trapped if they find us here, but this is our only option for now. Let's keep going, but walk quietly."

A sound startled them, and a man stepped out around a tree right in front of them. Magnus lunged at the man, tackled him face down on the ground, pulled both arms behind his back, and sat on him. Bruno rushed to help, but the American soldiers beat him there. They took over and rolled the man over on his back. Blake arrived and stared in amazement.

"Steve?"

"Let me up; we have to hurry. Magnus, now I understand why you were one of Messai's thugs. You may have broken some ribs."

"Steve, you're alive! Are the others...?"

"Dead? No, most of us survived. This was the only place we could go, but we can't stay here. They will come looking for survivors, although if someone else sees us first, they will turn us in for that huge reward. I have a plan."

"Mila and the boys?" Bruno asked, his voice trembling.

"They're safe, Bruno, but we can talk about that later. Follow me to where they are, then we'll all get away from this place before they find us. It also looks like you have a few who need serious medical attention. Let's get them where I can take care of them."

The big man hugged his daughter and wept. "I don't want to stand around here waiting. Let's go!"

***

Aissa Messai's phone rang as he prepared to meet with his leaders.

"Thank you for calling, Captain. Give me a full report before our meeting that will allow us to celebrate with full assurance of what happened there."

"The place is a mess, sir. Chen's bombers certainly did their job well."

"The place is not my concern, Captain. What about *them*?"

"There is no sign of life, sir. We found bodies, most of them unrecognizable, along with many body parts. I cannot imagine anyone survived this attack."

"Are you sure? I detect a hint of uncertainty in your voice."

"Oh no, sir. I have no doubt they all died instantly when the bombs hit. I suppose you could say, at least they did not suffer."

"I appreciate your humor, Captain. If only we could identify some of those *parts* as belonging to Thompson, Baldwin, Barton... you can imagine all the names I want to see on that list."

"Yes, sir, I can," the captain replied, chuckling. "But trust me, there is no need for that."

"Excellent! We will celebrate accordingly. Scour the entire area, just to be sure."

"We plan to do exactly that. I divided the men into ten teams of three each and instructed them to search every square inch of this place and the surrounding area. The *stones* are already turned, but we will check the *trees*."

"I caught what you did there, Captain. Never lose your sense of humor. I need a good chuckle now and then, and you always give me that. If you do the rest of your job well, you and your men will receive a nice bonus."

"Thank you, sir. Give my regards to General Chen and the team."

The call ended as Chen arrived at the mansion, followed shortly after by leaders of the *New World Order*, now known simply by the acronym *NWO*. In the ruins of Lifta, AMPP men dispersed into a wide circle and began their search. On a nearby mountainside, a group of Jesus' followers who survived the general's attack hid among the trees. Anything could happen before this day ended.

***

Steve led his friends through the peaceful forest of stately evergreen trees. Its beauty made them feel safe from the danger outside, but each realized staying was impossible. They needed to keep moving or be captured.

"We came here under cover of darkness, but daylight changes everything," said Steve.

"It doesn't seem very light to me," Blake said. "The cloud cover and all these trees make it seem more like dusk."

"I know where the clouds came from," said Anders.

"So, you're going to give us a lesson in meteorology?"

"No, I'm giving you a lesson in *theology*. Jesus put the clouds there, allowing us to travel through this forest unseen. He is both our provider and protector."

Steve stopped. "We're here."

"Where?" asked Trey. "I don't see anything, or anyone."

He forced his way through a patch of dense underbrush, and they had no choice except to follow with branches clawing their skin. They popped out into a clearing which seemed centrally located. Surrounded by thick pines, shrubs, saplings, and vines, it looked like a house enclosed with walls and reminded them of a farm in Missouri which provided them shelter for nearly three years.

But the clearing was not what claimed their attention. Around the perimeter sat their comrades. Bruno sprinted toward Mila and grabbed her in his arms, lifting her off the ground and twirling about like a dancer, although not nearly as graceful. Ally and her brothers joined them in a tear-filled reunion which brought moist eyes to all the others, too. Steve interrupted them.

"Everyone move back. We have medical emergencies which take priority over everything else." He motioned to Omar, Hala, and the troops to bring their wounded friends to him.

"They are critical, but I don't have any supplies. What do we have that I can use?"

One American soldier said, "Tell us what you need. We're all carrying rucksacks, so we have first aid kits and knives, plus some others things which may help."

"Give me the kits and knives. I assume you all have underwear, socks, and extra clothes. I can use the underwear for sterile cloth and the uniforms to lay them on. Trey, do you remember helping me with Rickie's surgery? Linda, I need your help too. All three have gunshot wounds, so the bullets have to come out. Then we pray there is no further damage."

"The rest of you move over there and turn your heads. Someone needs to watch for AMPP because you can bet they'll come looking for us. Trey and Linda, come on, this can't wait."

They spread the uniforms, then lay Ahmad and the two wounded soldiers on them. Steve removed the bullets without either man moving. Blood loss weakened them and rendered them unconscious, making anesthesia unnecessary. The first aid kits provided antiseptic, gauze, and bandages. The procedures were successful, leaving nothing except waiting to see if they survived without transfusions. The group gathered and prayed for them, but were soon interrupted by excited voices outside their circle... AMPP.

***

"Gentlemen, our primary foe was removed last night, thanks to General Chen and his troops," Messai proclaimed. "He dispatched bombers which flew over Lifta where the Smyrnians hid. They dropped multiple explosives and destroyed both the abandoned city and its occupants. Our patrol reports utter devastation and no survivors. This night deserves great celebration! I preferred they face the Capital Punishment Device, but the opportunity to eliminate them all at once was too tempting to pass up."

He raised his glass and said, "A toast to the general and his men!" Everyone else raised their glasses too, and raucous festivity ensued until Messai ended it.

"Levi prepared a feast for us, and we will eat at noon. Until then, let's discuss plans for eliminating all the remaining rebels and ruling the world! I will announce the Smyrnians' demise, along with decisions we make today, prior to tomorrow's executions at 3:00 p.m. Now, who wants to begin our discussion?"

***

In Rome, a meeting occurred at the same time. The pope called his cardinals together to discuss their position in the One World Religion. All remaining cardinals had now taken refuge in the Apostolic Palace, turning more of its rooms into apartments, and making it their official residence. Pope Gregory opened the conversation himself.

"Brothers, we voted to join the One World Religion and align ourselves with the vision of Aissa Messai. That decision restored our prominent position among the world's population. I also find it difficult to deny the Secretary-General's promotion of peace and prosperity. Since we united with him and took his mark, then replaced our former images with his likeness, our affluence has surpassed its former glory. He has blessed us far more than we imagined possible."

"His Majesty's power became evident when he rose from death, revealing the likelihood of his messiahship. I affirm our choice to align with him for both political and religious reasons, his name be praised. Most Roman Catholic followers have joined us and now worship him, too."

"However, I have become concerned with our lack of involvement and inclusion in decisions which affect us and the world. The secrecy surrounding him and his entire organization disturbs me greatly. We are left outside, while decisions are made inside. His position remains, if we follow him, he will continue to bless us and cause us to prosper. But at what cost?"

"The Secretary-General has taken over Vatican City and the palace, and relegated me, and you, to positions of low estate. I fear his intentions are misguided and do not have our best interest in mind. My opinion is, we should seek to regain our worldwide position of influence and authority. He must treat us with the utmost respect and grant us leadership ranking among his hierarchy."

"When he returns next week, I plan to sit down with him and make these requests known. If he refuses to honor them, I recommend we form our own movement, while continuing to worship him. I hope he realizes how valuable we are to him and the advancement of his goals. But if he rejects our wishes, we must rise and stand our ground. What do you say?"

The discussion moved rapidly toward agreement with the pontiff's words. These proud leaders in the former religion, known as Catholicism, had no intention of relinquishing their authority. But they failed to consider the powerful man in control. A confrontation was not in their best interest.

***

"AMPP," whispered Blake, causing the military guys to shoulder their weapons and surround the perimeter. One motioned with his gun, asking whether they should take them out. The three men laughed and talked, obviously thinking no Smyrnians hid anywhere nearby because they all died in Lifta. That made them easy victims for the soldiers, but Blake motioned, *wait.* Gunshots could bring others.

Inside the tree-lined enclosure the group sat barely breathing, careful not to make a sound. Outside, the men continued walking, now several feet away. Inside, Ahmad roused and groaned in pain. Outside, the AMPP men stopped, spun around, raised their guns, and crept back toward them. Inside, the troops faced an immediate decision. The armed men tore open the brush, aimed, and fired. Outside, three AMPP personnel dropped dead.

"We have to leave now," said John. "Their buddies won't waste any time getting here."

"But this place is our fort," Steve replied. "I feel safer in here than out there."

Ollie's mind never stopped, meaning he always came through with plans when they needed them. "Drag those guys in here, and cover the blood with pine needles, moss, or whatever you can use. Do it fast because the others will come soon."

They all rushed out, leaving Beth and Hala caring for the wounded. Six lifted the dead men and carried them to keep from dragging their bodies and leaving a trail of blood. The rest gathered moss and spread it over the blood where they had lain, then covered that with pine needles.

"Quick," said Ollie, "three of you soldiers walk that way and leave boot prints to make them think their buddies kept going." They sprinted several yards, occasionally shuffling their feet. One hundred yards away, they heard a loud voice.

"Bakir, are you guys okay?" No one answered. He yelled for the other patrols to join them in the woods. The Smyrnians raced toward the enclosure and dove inside, praying no one heard them.

"Don't we have something to cover them?" asked Beth, whispering. "I can't stand looking at dead men lying there."

"We didn't bring anything with us, Beth," said Kathie, just as softly.

The soldiers turned the men over so their faces would not show. Beth expressed her gratitude, but still refused to look at them. The Smyrnians huddled together while the troops encircled the inner perimeter, listening for anything which called for action. Twenty-seven excited voices soon filled their ears as the remaining nine groups converged to search for the missing men.

"We can't let them give us away," Blake said, pointing toward the wounded men, then glancing toward Steve.

"Don't look at me," said Steve. "I have nothing for that. We left so fast there was no time to grab my medical supplies. Cover their heads loosely with clothes, and someone sit with them. Do your best to keep them comfortable and quiet."

The voices grew closer until the patrol stood right outside. Everyone inside sat quietly, their faces showing concern, which bordered on fear.

"They came this way because there go their footprints. They avoided the heavy brush and walked through that opening. It clears on down the hill. We'll follow these steps, and see where they lead."

Those inside heard them moving away without speaking until one voice rang out: "Wait!"

The sound of men returning and the captain's voice increased the anxiety inside the enclosure. Every soldier slowly moved fingers to triggers, sweaty palms gripping weapons, while the others sat wide-eyed, listening to the conversation taking place outside.

"Sir, look at this."

"Blood!"

"Lots of blood! I moved a pile of stuff until I uncovered this wide area. Several people lay here bleeding, and it hasn't been long because it's still warm."

"And someone tried to hide it. But if this was our guys, where are they?" He yelled again, "Bakir!" but still no answer came.

"Our men weren't the only ones here. You can see where others shuffled all around this area. I think they killed them, carried their bodies, and hid them nearby. The steps lead toward that thicket."

Those were his last words. Ten American soldiers kneeling inside the cramped space did not ask for permission. They shoved their guns through the thick brush surrounding them and fired until all twenty-seven men lay dead on the forest floor. It ended within seconds, leaving the rest sitting in shock, their ears ringing from the loud gunshots. That woke Ahmad.

"What happened?" He tried to sit up, then groaned, and lay back down.

"Shh..." Hala whispered. "Steve, he's awake!"

Before Steve could get to him, the wounded troops also roused, and their buddies rushed to them.

"Great work, Doc," one said. "It looks like you saved their lives. Thank you."

"Don't thank me," Steve said, kneeling beside Ahmad. "I did all I could with what little we had, but Jesus took it from there!" He couldn't contain his excitement seeing the Americans now sitting up and talking. Neither was fully healed, but all would survive to fight another day.

"We can't stay in here. Search parties will cover this place when they discover those men missing. I have an idea, but Steve, I want to hear your plan first."

"No, you don't, Ollie, because you're standing in mine. I thought we could stay in this hideout, but you're right, it won't work. Your plans always seem to turn out well, so let's hear it."

"Okay, we need to move fast. The longer we stay here, the greater the danger. Messai thinks we're all dead, so we'll use that to our advantage, and hide right under his nose."

"I hope you're not talking about Jerusalem."

"That's exactly where I'm talking about. I know Jerusalem like I know London, my hometown."

"Where can we hide in Jerusalem that AMPP can't find us?"

"Zedekiah's Cave."

"Solomon's Quarry?"

"Whichever you choose to call it, John, it's the perfect hiding place."

"But isn't it still a public place where anyone can go? That doesn't sound private to me."

"I've heard no one goes there since the Tribulation began, and I imagine that is especially true since Messai took over. But I'm not talking about the *cave proper*. The other section provides much better protection."

"*Other section?* I didn't know there was another area besides the main cave, which is *huge*."

"No one is allowed in the lower chamber. We'll have to navigate our way in, which includes dropping through a hole that will make things interesting for Bruno and Magnus." Ollie glanced in their direction and grinned. "We'll have tight quarters, but I think there's room for us all."

"That's the right place," said Anders. "I saw us underground in something like a dungeon in the scroll. It looked exactly like the place you just described."

"Okay, I'm willing to run with Ollie's plan, if everyone else is," said Blake. They all raised their hands in agreement. "Before we go, we have to hide those other bodies too, then leave after dark. We can't take a chance on being spotted."

"Messai will start searching when he can't contact his men," Magnus said. "That won't happen until tomorrow, but they will begin at daybreak. We can get there tonight. It is normally an hour-long hike, but we'll be carrying three wounded men and taking routes away from high-traffic areas, so we should plan for three hours. We'll travel at our pace and should make it with no trouble."

"I think you're right on target, Magnus," said Ollie. "Let's take care of those bodies, so we'll be ready to hit the trail when the time comes. Then, since we have a few hours on our hands, will you please tell us what happened at Lifta last night, and how you guys survived?"

One of the American soldiers spoke softly. "And we want to know about our comrades who didn't make it." The group became somber as celebration mixed with sorrow over the loss of their friends.

***

"A toast to those who carried out this mission!" Messai said, raising his glass aloft. "General, you must share details with us from last night. We cannot wait to learn about the Smyrnians' demise."

"Well, sir, I appreciate the toast and your kind words, but my men simply did their job. You said bomb Lifta, and they did so using the full firepower of the PLAAF."

"Excellent! Details, General, give us details, and describe everything that happened."

"I can do better than that, Mr. Messai; I can *show* you. We have videos of each bomb hitting its target, and they are beautiful sights to behold. If we can retire to the theater room following lunch, I will play them for everyone to see. That will be an exciting way to top off today's celebration!"

"That's perfect, General! Nothing is better than a little entertainment after a great meal! It will not be easy to wait, but we must finish our feast and enjoy each other's company before we watch. After lunch and a movie, I will check back with my men and ask how their search went. Based on your success, I suspect they found nothing, except those few body parts." He laughed out loud.

"I assure you that is correct, sir. You will understand what I mean when you watch the videos. With your permission, I will go get everything ready then we can watch when we finish here."

"You may do that, General, but come back soon so you can finish celebrating with us."

Chen left the table and went to prepare their *entertainment.* He could hardly wait to display his handiwork on the large screen. *A thing of beauty*, he said to himself as he walked away.

***

After the group carried the AMPP bodies into the enclosure, creating a real space problem, they all sat down to hear about the events of the previous night.

"We spent the day getting Lifta's remains habitable," said John, beginning his explanation. "But we also took breaks throughout the day to pray for you guys. We got so concerned Kathie and I called everybody together and encouraged them to focus on facts, not fear, while Robert and his troops stood guard outside. That strengthened our faith and ended in laughter, which also relieved our tension. But it wasn't long before the stress returned and we started praying for you again."

"The entire day went like that: work, pray, then work some more. When darkness came, we were concerned, but we kept working on our living spaces and prayed while we worked. The generators provided the light we needed to see what we were doing. Robert's men suddenly ran to every place, shouting at us to evacuate. They said we didn't have time to take anything and yelled for us to go right then. So, we ran, and didn't look back."

"The soldiers stayed behind, sprinting and yelling to make sure everyone got out. When we cleared the perimeter, we heard the planes. It was like reliving what happened at the Shelter in Missouri. I screamed for the soldiers to follow us, and told them we were all out, but it was too late. We heard the bombs hit. The explosion knocked us down, and we felt the heat from the flames. We must have been far enough away it didn't kill us. All we knew to do was keep running."

The twenty-five men and women who had gone to Banias with Ally and Anders sat and listened.

"We all made it, but the troops never came," Steve said. "Bradley and Paul stayed with them, all doing their duty and making sure our lives were spared. We knew there was no way they survived the explosion. I am sure it was the Chinese, and Messai ordered the attack. The bombs were so powerful they surely obliterated everything in their path. The soldiers gave their lives to save ours."

"They must have heard the blasts in Jerusalem, but no one came to check them out," John said. "Messai must have prevented that. You can't believe how many bombs they dropped. My guess is he thought you were there too, and took no chances on anyone surviving. We ran to these woods and found our way to this place using the flashlights on our phones. Then we turned them off and sat all night in the dark so no one would see our lights. Besides, we needed to conserve battery life. None of us even knew you guys came. We just prayed you were alive."

"My heart breaks for your comrades who died to save our friends. I'm sorry," said Blake, looking at the troops who traveled with them to Banias.

"They left no one to die or fall into the hands of the enemy. We live by that creed. Sergeant Major Clark reinforced it until we grew tired of hearing it. He not only taught it, he lived it to the end."

"We found him, Bradley Clarke, and a few others deceased," Blake said. "I hate to tell you this, but other than that, we only saw body parts scattered here and there. Nothing remains of Lifta."

"None of that matters now," said Trey. "They're with Jesus, but we're still here fighting. We need to get away from here and go to the cave. Let's start by cleaning up the mess outside."

***

The party continued in the theater room. Chen had everything set up and was ready to show the videos. Messai ordered Levi to bring popcorn and drinks. The Jewish chef hated the man, knowing drinks and snacks were not needed after such a huge meal. But he reluctantly obeyed.

"Well done, Levi! Gentlemen, this is Levi, my Jewish chef. He answers my every beck and call, and always does what I command. Isn't that right, Levi?"

"Yes, Mr. Messai," Levi said, and turned to leave the room.

"Levi!" the Secretary-General thundered. "How many times must I tell you not to forget? I am losing my patience with you."

"I apologize, sir." He nearly tripped over his own feet rushing back in, then bowed low before his boss briefly and rose to leave.

"Did I give you permission to rise?" his boss asked in a threatening tone. "Never stop bowing until I say you may leave! On your knees before me, Levi, now!"

The chef wanted to attack the man or walk away, knowing he would face the guillotine for his disobedience. Fear caused him to come back and fall on his knees, face down, at the feet of Aissa Messai, Satan incarnate during the Tribulation. If only Levi understood who his boss really was.

"You must learn your lesson, so stay there until we start our movie." He loved enforcing his authority, especially in front of these men who needed to see it, too. They had witnessed what it meant to cross him, but reinforcing that never hurt. "Okay, Chen, you may begin."

"Thank you, Mr. Messai. I assume an introduction would be in order before I do?" Chen glanced at the kneeling man and smiled.

"Certainly!" Messai said, picking up on his hint to leave Levi bowing longer than expected. He recalled the times he kneeled before the dragon, bone on stone in Banias, before the beast allowed him to stand. Now he enjoyed watching others experience that same anxiety and pain.

"Gentlemen," Chen began. "You have heard about it, now you can watch for yourselves the reason for our celebration today. I believe you will find it entertaining."

He droned on for another five minutes, signaling the others so they understood why he took so long. The men savored each minute at Levi's expense. Chen finally stopped and nodded at Messai.

"Okay, Levi, you may go now. But never make that mistake again." The humiliated man rose and hurried from the room. The Secretary-General waited until the door closed behind him, then nodded at Chen, who started talking again without hesitation.

"Mr. Messai called yesterday evening to inform me the rebels hid in Lifta and requested we bomb the place an hour after dark when they were all present. It pleased me that he would entrust us with such an important task, so I immediately assigned the mission to our best men. They were precise as always and dropped enough explosives to destroy the place and obliterate every person. The captain reported earlier that their search yielded only a few bodies and many body parts."

"That reminds me, General, I must call Bakir and get a follow-up report on results of their search. I will do that later tonight. He is very thorough, and I trust him to do his job well. Please continue."

"Yes, sir. If I am not out of line suggesting this, ask him to get photographs, including shots of deceased individuals, and scattered body parts. Perhaps he can send those to us so we can witness the results of what I am about to show."

"I will instruct him to do that. Thank you for the suggestion."

Chen showed videos of the bombing, revealing what appeared to be sufficient explosives to blow the entire mountain apart. The men applauded and heaped praise upon both Chen and their leader.

"Let's call Bakir before you leave so you can hear his report for yourselves," said Messai gleefully. He ordered his voice assistant to call the captain, and the group heard the phone ringing. No answer. "It is highly unusual for him to ignore my call, but I will try again soon."

"Sir, those wooded areas are dense enough to interrupt phone service. I feel certain everything is fine and the captain will return your call the minute he realizes he missed it."

"Let's hope you are right. But I will send another patrol to ensure they are okay. I hate to end our meeting so abruptly, gentlemen, but this situation requires my immediate attention."

The men took their cue and left quickly. Messai called his AMPP director when they were all gone. He would dispatch a patrol at once to search for Bakir's team, while continually trying to reach him by phone. Their most pressing problem was the approaching darkness.

It required searching the woods during the remaining daylight hours before nightfall. They would waste no time.

***

"Are you sure we can find our way to the cave in the dark, Ollie?"

"Absolutely, Blake, but we have to stick close together and walk carefully. There's no reason to hurry, but every reason to be quiet."

"Maybe we should make our move now," John said. "I'd rather walk in the woods while we have light instead of bumping into trees when it's dark."

"We can't take that risk, John. If we're going to get there unseen, we have to go when it's dark."

Trey, Rickie, Anders, Ally, Omar, and Hala popped back in. "We got everything cleaned up," said Trey. "You can't tell anything ever happened. But we heard voices coming this way when we finished and headed back in here fast."

"Quiet, everybody," Blake said, holding a finger to his lips, shushing them. They sat in silence while the soldiers stood guard around the inside perimeter again. The voices got closer. It was clearly another fully armed AMPP patrol searching for their missing colleagues. The troops prepared to fire and looked back at Blake for permission. He shook his head *no.* The patrol passed them by, noticing nothing unusual. They let them go without discharging their weapons.

"What now?" John asked in a voice no louder than a whisper.

"They won't stay long," Magnus whispered. "It's getting dark in these woods, so they'll stop searching for tonight and come back tomorrow."

"We'll leave exactly at midnight and be in the cave no later than 3:00 a.m.," Ollie whispered.

"Can we do that carrying our wounded?"

"I can walk," said Ahmad, sitting up.

"Me too," said one soldier, and the other agreed.

"You're all too weak to walk," said Steve. "You've lost a lot of blood and undergone surgery."

"Ahmad can lean on Hala and me," said Omar. "We'll carry him, if we must." Their friend's look told them he could walk with their help. The same was true for the troops.

Darkness closed in as the group hunkered down in blackness. They must save phones to use for light later. In four hours, they would begin the treacherous trek to Zedekiah's Cave where they would hide from Messai and AMPP less than one mile from his *office.*

CHAPTER 2

"Sir, we could not locate them anywhere. We called Bakir's phone multiple times and searched the woods and surrounding area, but nothing. It's like they dropped off the earth."

"I assure you they did not, Captain. Bakir was second in command only to Magnus, and his patrol is more experienced than any other. He would neither give up the search nor fail to contact me. So, we will not quit on him and his men now. Set up camp near Lifta and stay alert for any sign of them. I will dispatch more patrols at daylight to assist you and cover Jerusalem, as well."

"Jerusalem, sir?"

"Yes, Captain, Jerusalem. Something is not right, and we must determine what is going on. Just perform your job diligently until we discover what that is."

The conversation ended, but Aissa Messai would not sleep this night. While he sat alone at midnight, he heard voices again in his mind. It sounded like his most despised enemy, the Smyrnians. But it was not them, because they were all dead. The voices came softly so he couldn't understand what they were saying. Surely it was Bakir and his patrol. They must have discovered something the captain could not report right now. But he must know.

"Beelzebub! Belial!"

The two monstrous demons appeared within seconds of his call and bowed before him.

"Command us, Master, and we will obey."

"Find my patrol, and ensure none of *his* followers remain alive. If you find any hiding away like cowards, extinguish them. The time draws near for us to attack and assume control. We cannot let anyone or anything stand in our way."

His servants left without another word. They would call others to assist them with this task. Within minutes, a multitude of demonic creatures buzzed like flies searching for Bakir's patrol and any followers of Jesus who remained alive. They would begin their quest in the forests around Lifta.

***

Ben Abramson roused from sleep in Petra, sensing something in his spirit. He stood quietly trying not to wake Miriam, but she spoke before he could take a step.

"Ben, you're getting the same impression I just got, aren't you?"

"Something is happening with the Smyrnians. I can feel it."

"Me too! Let's wake the others and pray for them. This is urgent!"

They moved fast to bring Alexander and Elizabeth, Michael and Hadassah, Mordecai, and the leaders from the Kibbutz together. But they did not have to awaken them. They all met each other near the Treasury entrance, arriving at the same time with the same concern. After a few brief words and learning their instincts matched, they hit their knees and prayed for their friends.

***

The group emerged from their thicketed enclosure at exactly midnight, leaving the dead bodies inside, covered with pine boughs topped with moss and grass. They moved stealthily, using light from only one phone to show the way. They had nothing with them except the clothes on their backs, no food, no way to charge phones... nothing. Hunger already gnawed at their stomachs, yet they had no means of getting anything to eat. Figuring out how to survive would have to come later. For now, their only concern was reaching Zedekiah's Cave safely.

Ollie and Amelia led the way, followed closely by three soldiers, with six troops in the center, and three others bringing up the rear. The central group assisted their wounded comrades as they walked along. They comprised a large group, making evading AMPP a difficult assignment. The twenty-five who had traveled to Banias joined Steve and Linda, Mila and the boys, and John and Kathie's families. Ollie gave instructions when they reached the woods' edge.

"We've gone *down*, now we're getting ready to learn what they mean by going *up* to Jerusalem. It's a tough climb, so you may need to carry the three injured men when it gets steep."

"That's no problem for us," said a soldier. "We've carried heavier stuff in rougher terrain than this. So, Omar and Hala, let us take care of Ahmad for you."

"I can carry him myself!" said Omar, determined to take care of his friend.

"Okay, okay, we're all tired, but calm down, and keep quiet. Here's the plan: we'll separate into three groups, making us harder to spot, with soldiers accompanying each group. Plus, once again, if one group gets captured, they won't get us all. My group will lead the way with the other two following twenty yards apart so we don't lose sight of each other. We'll communicate by phone, but only the leader of each group should turn theirs on."

"My man has this all figured out," said Amelia with a grin. "What about the route, Ollie?"

"We will work our way through side streets and alleys until we get to the Old City. The cave's entrance is a short distance north of the Damascus Gate, then it goes under the Muslim Quarter. That's the closest route, and we don't go near the Temple Mount. My group will wait for you a few feet inside the cave, then we will all enter the lower area together. Questions?"

"Won't that route take us right past the Garden Tomb? It's closed now, but it still reminds us of the *real* resurrection!"

"You're right, Blake. That was a cave, and Jesus stayed in it three *days* before he rose, right? We're going to a cave, so maybe we can live there almost three *years* until he returns!" They all smiled at his thought, even knowing the unlikelihood it would happen. Ollie's group began their walk.

***

Perched on a boulder atop the tallest mountain in Petra, Michael and Hadassah sat processing events since the second half of the Tribulation began, and discussing things yet to come. The reign of terror had proven worse than anyone could have imagined, but it paled compared to the horror coming soon.

"How many have died, Michael?"

"Far too many, Hadassah, but I would rather focus on those who are still alive. This very moment, our friends face a crisis that may claim all their lives, and once again, I am forbidden to intervene."

"Michael! We have to do something! Yahweh let us fight for Ally and Anders, so why not now?"

"He didn't give me any information. All I know is it happened last night and danger still exists."

"Isn't there some way to find out?"

"No, Hadassah. I only understand it was tragic, and many may have died."

Tears rolled from her eyes, and he placed his arm around her, holding her as she cried.

"However, Yahweh gave you permission to attend a glorious celebration with me!"

"You mean...?"

"Yes, where you thought we were going before we arrived in Banias."

"Don't play games with me, Michael. That would be cruel."

"I'm not kidding! We will watch from a distance, but you will hear and see everything!"

"When can we go? I am ready this time!"

"Right now!"

He grabbed her arm and lifted off, this time soaring straight up. She gasped, then he released her, and she followed, gaining ground and flying alongside him. They rose higher and higher. Hadassah was unaware how far they would travel, but her elation overrode any fear or concern she may have had. She experienced the same thrill she felt when they flew to Banias. The spirit of Esther filled her once more, and she realized this day would bring the most special moment of her life.

***

Other than the occasional barking dogs, all three Smyrnian groups arrived safely at Zedekiah's cave. Ollie picked the entrance lock, and his party waited a few steps inside where they would meet the others and guide them to the cave's lower level. It was an ideal place to hide, but if AMPP found them, they would be trapped like caged animals with no way out. Coming and going would need to occur late at night. It was the best survival plan they could come up with on short notice.

"Follow me."

Ollie used his phone for light as they walked through the cavernous open area where people previously toured and groups hosted events. Now the place was vacant. "Here is the access to our new home," he said, as they reached the small opening leading below.

"Let us check it out." Two American soldiers quickly dropped through the hole and landed on the floor below. A few minutes later, they climbed back out.

"That's not habitable, and I'm not even sure we can all fit inside that space. Many areas are sealed off, and others have a low ceiling. There is a house which appears to be from the Crusader period where a family might stay. But we cannot possibly survive long down there. However, we want to make a suggestion. It appears no one has visited this place in a long time."

"You are correct. Messai ordered it closed after the earthquake. Even though the quake didn't affect East Jerusalem, he deemed it unsafe for anyone to enter."

"That's perfect, Ollie. The gate was locked, but you got us in."

"Ollie can pick any lock!" Amelia said, with obvious pride.

"Yes, ma'am, that seems obvious," the soldier said. "If you keep it locked, why can't we live up here in this big old house? Should the need ever arise, we can hustle down there to our hiding place. Our unit is fully armed, so we'll rotate shifts standing guard close enough to the entrance to hear any intruders."

"I like his suggestion!" said John. "From my studies about this place, I wouldn't want to stay down there. We can find separate living quarters and bathroom space up here and use the Freemason's hall when we all meet together."

"That has my vote," said Blake.

"It makes sense. I don't know why I hadn't thought of that."

"You can't think of everything, Ollie," said Beth. "You've come up with every idea so far, and you were the one who thought of this place. It's about time you gave someone else a chance."

"I may have done that on purpose," he said with a grin. "Come on, Amelia, we're wasting time. Let's choose our spot before someone beats us to it." He grabbed her hand, chuckled, and ran.

Their excitement rivaled that of new homeowners moving into the home of their dreams. This cave certainly fit that. There were logistics to figure out, but they had no reason to hurry. The biggest question was whether they could avoid Messai, living so close to his headquarters.

***

Hadassah felt something she had never experienced. Her heart filled with such ecstasy she feared it would explode. Something pulled her forward like a gigantic magnet she could not resist, yet she did not want to resist it. Overwhelming joy drew her in and increased as she and Michael got closer. To her left, he looked her way and smiled.

What was that? An ocean? It looked like liquid, but smoother than glass. Fire! The water was ablaze! *That is impossible*, she thought, yet it became obvious the nearer they got. She moved right beside Michael, her heart bursting with joy, and her mind awestruck, while her body trembled with holy fear.

"This is where we stop. It provides the perfect view, don't you agree?"

"Yes," she said, her voice shaky and soft. Further words refused to come. Her heart raced from nervous anticipation of what she would soon witness. She had no idea what it would be, but could hardly wait for it to begin. "Is this *heaven?*" she asked him in a voice filled with wonder. The look on his face revealed the answer to her question.

Then she saw *them*. Who they were, she could not tell, but they stood en masse beside the sea, leading to her next whisper. *"Who are they, Michael?"*

"Just keep watching, and all your questions will be answered."

Wait! She recognized some of them! Robert Clark and Bradley Rodgers stood near the front. What are they doing here? The realization hit her: they had died at Messai's hands. Did they face the Capital Punishment Device? Momentary anger flared inside her but quickly disappeared. The looks on their faces could only be described as *rapturous*. Her anger turned to happiness. Most of Robert's troops surrounded him, but a few were missing. How had Messai killed so many at once? Michael said something bad was coming. Whatever he referred to must have caused their deaths.

Others stood among them she had never met, but she recognized them instantly as they looked directly at her. Did they see her? There was Evan Ryles. None of them would have believed in Jesus without him. Johnathan Baldwin... Malachi... John and Mary... Doc Sanderson... Hans and Heidi Meier. They were all Tribulation martyrs. This was amazing! She longed to run and embrace them, but knew she could not. Her emotions ran wild. Anger... joy... anger... elation... anger... jubilation! Moshe and Eliyahu appeared standing apart from the others. Her anger vanished, and she rejoiced for these servants of Jesus. Michael sat beside her smiling and enjoying the moment.

***

In Petra, Ben Abramson and Mordecai Chaim missed Michael and Hadassah again. Both had learned to never question them when they returned, although Mordecai still worried about his niece. However, their curiosity was always piqued every time they left for a while.

"Where do you suppose they are, and what are they doing today, Ben?" Mordecai asked his friend.

"I wish I could answer that, but neither of us can. I assume Yahweh had a special task for them."

"I also cannot help but wonder about our colleagues out there," Mordecai said, waving his hand toward the world outside their haven. "We all felt the urge to pray for them, so it would be good to find out if they are safe. I'm up for climbing the mountain and calling them, if you are."

"Of course, I am. But it isn't daylight where they are, so we can't call them yet, can we? No, you're right, this is important. Let's go."

After ascending the peak, Ben placed the call to Blake. No answer. Call after call went to voicemail until they finally gave up and left a message, asking Blake to return their call.

"I don't have a good feeling about this, Ben."

"Neither do I, but what can we do? That's the only bad thing about being here and unable to leave. When our friends need us, we're useless to them."

"You are wrong, my friend. You have always reminded me, now I will remind you. We can pray for them, and that is the best thing we can do, whether in here or out there."

"Thank you, Mordecai. I must remember to trust God and know it won't be long before we no longer have to worry about times like this."

They prayed together, then descended the mountain, separated, and walked to their dwelling places, both committed to praying more, and hoping to hear from Blake soon.

＊＊＊

Hadassah looked closer at the throng standing beside the glassy, fiery sea and noticed they were all holding something. The instruments came into view as she squinted to see: *Harps!* This was a heavenly orchestra made up of martyrs playing nothing but harps! What would such an enormous group of harpists sound like? There was no doubt they would play the most beautiful music she had ever heard. No maestro conducted them, but Hadassah expected an amazing performance.

"Michael," she said softly, "thank you for bringing me here with you."

"Don't thank me, thank Yahweh. It was he who invited you and wanted you to experience this."

Tears flooded her eyes realizing the Creator loved her enough to include her in this moment. More than an orchestral presentation, this was an ominous, yet glorious introduction to coming events. The martyrs began playing, the melodic sound gently floating into her ears and calming her spirit. After a pleasant opening number, the tone shifted, and tempo increased. Moshe cried out louder than the times he confronted Messai. *The song of Moses and the Lamb!* The dramatic effect caused her heart to pound and her body to tremble. The martyrs' voices blasted forth, powerful and strong, proclaiming Yahweh's authority and kingdom, and causing Hadassah to jump.

"Great and marvelous are your deeds,
Lord God Almighty.

> *Just and true are your ways,*
> *King of the nations.*
> *Who will not fear you, Lord, and bring glory to your name?*
> *For you alone are holy.*
> *All nations will come and worship before you, for your righteous*
> acts have been revealed."
>
> **–Revelation 15:3-4**

***

She had not heard those words before. She knew Moses' song from Exodus Chapter Fifteen. Her uncle read and taught her the Old Testament stories many times, and she could quote many. But this was neither the song Moses sang, nor one she read in The Revelation about Jesus, God's sacrificial lamb. Then the truth hit her like a tidal wave of understanding.

Moses was the Old Testament redeemer who led God's people from Egyptian bondage to the Promised Land. She celebrated that every year during Passover. Jesus was the New Testament redeemer who redeemed these Tribulation martyrs by his death and resurrection and brought them out of the seven-year *reign of terror* to the Promised Land of heaven! He also did that for her! Thankfulness overwhelmed her, and grateful tears streamed from her eyes.

***

Anders and Ally stood in a selected alcove of Zedekiah's Cave, which would afford them privacy when he suddenly stiffened, his face pale, staring straight ahead without moving.

"Anders, what's wrong?" she asked, grabbing him with both arms. He did not move or respond. She took a step to run for help when he spoke.

"Something just happened."

"I saw that! Are you okay?"

"I'm fine, but what I just felt hit me hard, so I know it's important."

"What do you think it means?"

"Something big is coming, the beginning of the end, the dawn of destruction for Messai and the dragon, the *dawn of deliverance* for us who follow Jesus. We will recognize it when it happens."

He started walking, and Ally followed, both inviting all the others to a group meeting as they went. They soon gathered in the large open area where Freemasons had once met.

"What's up, Anders?" asked Blake.

"A major development just took place. I couldn't tell what it was, but I think it kicks off the final days. We need to check the news daily and stay abreast of current events."

"That won't make any difference since we can't do anything about it, anyway."

"We don't need to just sit in here and wait for Jesus to return, John," Bruno insisted. "There must be a way to go out and fight. You don't have any idea what's coming, Anders?"

"I wish I knew or could remember it from the scroll, but I can't. My gut says Messai will face attacks from heaven, but I can't be sure. Bruno has a point. We can't sit around and do nothing."

"I agree with my partner, too," said Magnus. "We can't change whatever is coming, but we can still stop believers from dying in Messai's Capital Punishment Device."

"All we can do is pray, Magnus. You all need to stop this foolishness, because if you try that, AMPP will capture you, and Messai will enjoy watching your heads roll."

"Call it what you will, John, but Bruno and Magnus are right," Blake said. "It may cost us our lives, but every believer we save will be worth it. Who wants to help with that?"

The American soldiers walked forward in unison, followed by Omar, Ahmad, and Hala. Bruno and his family joined them along with Ollie, Amelia, Anders and Ally, and Blake and Beth. The trio of Trey, Rickie, and Magnus came last.

"Well, you're not leaving me out. I may not think it's wise, but I refuse to sit here while my brothers and sisters go fight. Kathie and I are with you one hundred percent." She walked to the front and joined her husband, taking his hand in hers as a sign of solidarity. Their families came and stood beside them, and soon the entire group united as one, no longer merely a team, but an army ready for battle against an evil regime. Let the war begin.

***

Aissa Messai sat in his temple *office*, knowing something was not right with his missing patrol. Bakir would never fail to contact him nor refuse to answer a call from his fellow AMPP members. Neither would he follow Magnus' unforgivable move and defect. The demons would locate them soon, give a report, and lead his men to any Smyrnian escapees. He now realized the undeniable truth: not all had died in Chen's attack. He summoned the general to a meeting where only one other would join them. That one would accept no excuses from the Chinese military leader.

Beelzebub and Belial had put aside their differences and faithfully served Messai as the dragon's top demon princes. Both sensed the end drew near and anticipated the great battle, which would finally give them victory over Yahweh's forces and their despised enemy, Michael and the Host. Each led teams of hideous, buzzing demonic creatures in their search this night and would not fail.

General Chen arrived and entered the office, sensing something was wrong. His fears became reality when he saw the beast standing beside Messai's impressive desk.

"Thank you for joining us, General. We appreciate your promptness in arriving so soon."

"I remain at your disposal, sir, and will always respond when you call."

"Since you use the word *disposal*, Mister Chen, let us talk about your potential failure to dispose of our primary enemy."

Mister? The Secretary-General had never called him anything other than *general*. Fear pulsed through his mind as fire seeped from the dragon's mouth, and sparks floated toward him. He instinctively stepped backwards as heat touched his face.

"My men carried out the attack exactly when and how you asked, sir. You saw the videos yourself and witnessed explosions powerful enough to annihilate the entire compound along with everyone, and everything, there. The thought of anyone surviving is unimaginable."

"Your orders were to destroy the city, including its inhabitants. A half-completed task equals failure, and failure is unacceptable, *Mister* Chen."

The dragon moved toward him just as two more grotesque-looking creatures appeared and stood before Messai.

"A report will come soon, Master, but it will not bring good news," the most gigantic one uttered.

When the words left Beelzebub's mouth, Messai's phone rang and he answered, giving Chen slight hope. But the demon made it clear any forthcoming news would not be positive. Any rebels surviving the bombing seemed impossible. He longed to run, but realized such an attempt was futile. The phone on speaker, his only option was to stay and listen to the conversation.

"We located all the men, sir."

The general perked up as a glimmer of hope returned. *They found them!*

"Put Bakir on the phone, Captain, and let me hear from his mouth what he found."

"I would love to do that, sir, but there is a problem."

"Don't leave me waiting, Captain! I have had a long day. Let me speak with Bakir *now*!"

"Bakir and his men are all dead, sir. We discovered their bodies inside a thicketed enclosure in a wooded area outside Lifta. They were all shot to death and placed there by someone."

Messai erupted, his rage spewing forth, aimed at the one he held responsible. "*Chen*, the Smyrnians did this, and *you* told me your bombs killed them all!"

The general froze in fear and watched the dragon amble toward him until he stood face-to-face with the beast. The sulfuric odor entered his nostrils and nauseated him, leaving him fighting to keep from throwing up. Sparks flickered from the creature's long nose burning his face as each tiny ember made contact. He had listened to others scream as the dragon incinerated them before his eyes. Now his time had arrived. Chen steeled himself and prepared to die a horrific death, then watched the giant red creature back away and yield his position to Aissa Messai.

"We need your services for an upcoming battle, General. You will lead your country's military against our enemy and deliver the final blow, which gives us ultimate victory. To ensure you do not fail this time, Beelzebub and Belial will observe your every move. If you disappoint them, you will face him, and next time you will not escape his wrath. Do I make myself clear?"

"Yes, Mr. Messai, I understand fully and will not let you down," Chen said, his voice trembling. He maintained eye contact with the two massive demons flanking him on each side. They would be his constant companions from this point forward. Pride slowly replaced panic as he realized the lead role he would play guiding his army to battle. He met the dragon's glare, and his eyes glowed yellow, then red. Chen threw back his head and howled, sparks now shooting from his body, too. The beast possessed him, and he would obey the creature's every command. He was ready.

***

Brief silence followed the martyrs' song, as Michael and Hadassah maintained their gaze upon the powerful heavenly scene. The throng faded from their view, causing her momentary sadness. The pause felt like it lasted for hours. *Who knows how long this lingers in eternal time*, she wondered, then chuckled at such a ridiculous thought. Michael chuckled, too.

A brilliant light flashed, and another glorious scene appeared. *This is like watching a play shifting from one act to another*, Hadassah whispered to herself. She spoke softly but could tell Michael heard and understood. His continuing smile showed he enjoyed experiencing this with her. Once again, she strained to see what was coming. A curtain opened slowly, revealing a small portion each time it moved. If only she could run and pull it back herself, but she waited *impatiently.*

A building? Yes, a tall building, but she only saw doors. When the curtain moved farther, it unveiled a glorious structure she recognized at once. *The temple of Yahweh!* It looked remarkably like the one Messai constructed and resembled pictures she had seen of Solomon's temple. Yahweh told Moshe to construct the tabernacle exactly like his temple in heaven, and Solomon followed the same pattern. Now she saw it with her own eyes!

Hadassah watched as the doors flung wide open. Someone was coming out! Her mind raced with thoughts of who it might be. *Yahweh?* No, because no one can see God and survive, unless she would die right here and stay with him, and the Tribulation martyrs. A mighty figure came into view. *Jesus?* Please let it be Jesus! She longed to see her Savior.

An angel! Was this one of the Heavenly Host she met before the battle at Banias? He wore spotless white linen, the whitest garment she had ever seen, with no speck of impurity, and a golden sash across his chest. She waited for him to speak but no words came. Instead, other angels dressed like this one followed him as they exited single file and stood side-by-side outside the temple.

She counted them as they came... seven. Of course, seven is God's number! Whatever they represented signified completion and perfection, the completed work of God. Hadassah spoke louder than she intended: *The end draws near, and Jesus will soon complete his work!* She blushed, hoping she had not interrupted this heavenly scene. It appeared no one heard her, so she breathed a sigh of relief, and looked more intently, trying to determine what this meant.

The angels stood unmoving, majestic, celestial beings, portraits of pure holiness. A magnificent creature appeared, nothing like those she encountered in her previous dream. He moved to each angel and placed something in their hands. Hadassah saw them clearly: *bowls.* She recalled reading about bowls holding prayers, but these were different. Dark, foreboding vapor emanated from them turning her delight to fearful anticipation. Something bad would come soon.

***

Omar and Hala slipped through the open gate, leaving the safety of the cave at 10:00 p.m. The large group of believers hiding there must eat but had no way to purchase food without Messai's mark. The others stayed, praying the two young Palestinians could find Muslim Quarter residents who would welcome them into their home. Since Omar and Hala knew no one there, they needed guidance to find the right house and avoid capture while they searched. When they returned after midnight, their looks revealed all attempts had failed.

"What are our options now, Blake? We can't buy anything without his mark. Will Jesus let us die of hunger and this cave be our tomb?"

"John, after Messai came back to life, I thought you promised Jesus you would always trust him from now on. How many times must I remind you of that promise?"

"I'm sorry, Blake. You're right, but we're all hungry and need an answer soon or we'll starve."

"I may have your answer," said the soldier who helped rescue Ally and her group from AMPP, the same one who suggested they live in the main cave instead of the lower level. He assumed the leadership role among his peers now that Robert was gone.

"We're all ears," said Ollie. "I loved your last suggestion, so I'm willing to hear another one."

"By the way, I am Gabriel, so you can start calling me by my name. I'm sorry I haven't told you before now," he said smiling.

"Thank you, Gabriel. I apologize for not *asking* before now. Your name comes as no surprise. It makes sense that Jesus would send someone named Gabriel to help us when we need him most."

"I believe he sent me to help, Mr. Thompson and want to do whatever I can. Sergeant Major Clark involved me in his decision-making processes. I learned from the best and have known Jesus would use me during these years before he returns. The Israeli soldiers who helped us rescue our friends have taken the mark, but they don't care for Messai, and are sympathetic with our cause. All three of them said they will help us however they can and proved that when they put themselves in danger to save our comrades."

"You're right!" Ollie said excitedly. "They were amazing that day, so it would be great to have *them* helping us again!"

"Sergeant Major Clark gave me their number. With your permission, I will call them right away."

"Please do. We have little time to wait. And by the way, you can call me Blake."

Gabriel walked toward the cave entrance where he could get phone service and placed the call. His IDF counterpart answered but was much more guarded this time. He told Gabriel the IDF was on high alert searching for rebels, especially Israeli military personnel who defected to their cause. Major General Mordecai Chaim was their most highly prized target. Thus, the man said his help must take place in another way, one the Smyrnians would not have considered, but Gabriel was not surprised. When he returned, his look warned the group the news was not what they had hoped.

"He turned us down?" asked Ollie. "I thought sure…"

Gabriel held up his hand. "He didn't exactly turn us down, Ollie, but neither are *they* helping us."

"Stop confusing us, Gabriel, and just tell us whether they told us how we can get food."

The soldier's frustration showed. "We are, and I will explain that, if you let me." They remained quiet, so he continued. "All three soldiers have Arab comrades with families living in Jerusalem. They live here in the Muslim Quarter, *and* they all own restaurants. Their businesses boomed so much under Messai's New World Order they started giving away food to anyone who needed it. But with such prosperity now, most people have plenty."

"Messai's New World Order," growled Bruno. "I know what I would like to do with his *NWO.*"

"I understand no one can change that until Jesus comes. But this can work to our advantage and provide us with food. They cook extra every day and leave containers where people can pick them up. Much has gone to waste since they started, so they considered stopping. But the soldiers will tell them they heard about several families who desperately need food and didn't know about their service. They will cook extra and leave it where we can grab it without being seen."

The group was blown away by such miraculous provision. They awaited further word from the soldiers and hoped it would come tomorrow. Until then, they would spend their time planning how to collect the food, and who would handle that responsibility. They took time to give thanks, not only for food but also for the electricity left on, which kept lights shining in the cave and allowed them to charge their devices. Jesus again proved himself faithful to meet their every need.

CHAPTER 3

Hadassah watched the angels take the bowls, their muscles straining and bulging under the weight. Something heavy and foreboding would come, possibly like nothing the world had gone through before, and it would continue until Jesus returned. The thought saddened her.

"It won't affect us," Michael said, his voice so soft no one else could hear him.

"Then who *will* it affect?"

"Messai's kingdom and his followers."

"What's in the bowls?"

"Yahweh's wrath. The angels will pour it out, bowl after bowl, the greatest outpouring of holy anger people have ever seen."

Another sight caught her eye. Thick smoke filled the temple, stopping anyone from entering or looking inside. It forced her to her knees, even from a distance.

"Yahweh's glory," said Michael, also bowing toward the temple.

Hadassah continued kneeling, eyes closed, face downward. Memories of another place and time flooded her mind. Esther sat inside Susa's palace staring westward out a second-story window toward Jerusalem, as images of Yahweh's temple passed before her, so real it seemed she could walk into its courts. She had never seen that temple, but Mordecai had told her many stories, painting indelible images on a blank canvas in her mind.

The structure now appeared before her creating a longing to enter Yahweh's presence there. But Esther lived eight hundred and fifty miles away in Susa making the newly rebuilt temple off-limits for her. She received word it was completed forty years earlier and yearned to visit it just once. What her heart craved, her eyes would never see. Words from Psalm 137 came quietly from her lips. *If I forget you, Jerusalem, may my right hand forget its skill. May my tongue cling to the roof of my mouth if I do not remember you, if I do not consider Jerusalem my highest joy.*

The vision faded back into present reality. Here before her was the temple for which she longed! Looking to her left, she saw Michael still bowing and realized she was Hadassah again viewing this heavenly scene. Yahweh allowed her to share this moment with Michael, fulfilling her heart's desire from millennia earlier. She now enjoyed bouncing back and forth between time periods. But time would only last a little while longer. She now witnessed events which would bring the end.

Esther, no, Hadassah, raised her head and looked toward the temple, which was still full of smoke. But something else claimed her attention. The first angel took a step. She gazed at him, trembling with anticipation, realizing the action was beginning! Michael rose and beckoned her to come.

"We must leave now, Hadassah."

"No, Michael! I can't leave until Yahweh shows me what is in the bowls!"

"That will happen, but not here. They will become clear in the days ahead when each one rocks the earth. But for now, we must go."

She knew there was no debating this decision. They rose and soared away from the heavenly scene, her heart already crying out to return. That day was not far away, and Hadassah could hardly wait.

The Smyrnians decided Omar, Ahmad, and Hala should go out and get the food each day. Their Palestinian descent and appearance would convince anyone they lived in the Old City's Muslim Quarter. However, if AMPP captured them, or someone turned them in, their deaths would come quickly. So far, things had gone smoothly, and the group ate well. Conversation now centered on rescue missions for those facing Messai's Capital Punishment Device.

"Our Special Ops training prepared us for this job," said Gabriel. "We'll handle rescues so everybody else can focus on other things."

"If you think you're leaving us out, you're barmy! Amelia and I own that one!"

"We heard about your escapades, Ollie, and saw them ourselves. We welcome your help."

"How do you propose we free people Messai holds captive?" asked John. "That sounds impossible, or perhaps you will get yourselves killed too."

"I don't have a plan, John," Blake said. "That's why we're meeting and discussing it. We need to hear from the one who knows how AMPP and Messai operate. Magnus, do you have any input?"

"I've thought about this and put a few ideas together. Despite Messai insisting executions occur the same day AMPP captures believers, that seldom happens. They almost always hold prisoners overnight until 3:00 p.m. the next day. Darkness is a good time for rescues, don't you think?"

"A jolly good time, Magnus, old chap!" said Ollie. "We have no reason to wait, especially when every day more followers of Jesus die. Let's plan our first rescue attempt tonight and see if we can pull it off."

"I would say let's not jump the gun, Ollie, but you're right. Believers will die tomorrow if we don't act tonight. We can't afford to wait."

"I agree, Blake," said Gabriel. "Ollie, if you and Miss Amelia will join us right over there, we will devise a plan. We welcome any others who want to join us."

They moved to one side and began their work. Trey and Rickie united with their military comrades, along with Magnus and Bruno. All four had significant experience with the Smyrnians, which prepared them for this task. Anders and Ally opted to avoid these dangerous missions and focus instead on listening to Jesus and deciphering events from the scroll before they happened, rather than afterwards. Blake and Beth, John and Kathie and their families, and Bruno's family opted out, as well. They all agreed the original Smyrnians should stay away from AMPP.

**

"Don't tell me anything, and I will not ask," said Ben as he greeted Michael and Hadassah upon their return to Petra. "You have been gone a long time again, so I'm certain it was good."

"Ben, you and Mordecai speculate too much. You don't want us to stay cooped up in Petra every day, do you? We love exploring the universe!"

Universe? Ben thought. What did Michael mean by that? Why didn't he say world or planet? But *universe?* Curiosity drove him crazy, but he understood answers would not come until after Jesus returned. He noticed something else, prompting further discussion, or one may call it *interrogation*.

"Hadassah, have you seen your face?" Ben asked shielding his eyes. "You are a beautiful young woman, but I have never seen you glow like this. I can hardly look at you!"

He suddenly realized what he said and stood with a blank stare. Mordecai walked up, stopped, and stared at his niece, too. He shielded his eyes and took a moment before he spoke.

"My niece, what has happened to you? You look more radiant than you have ever looked."

"Yes, Hadassah, *much* more radiant. I have only seen that one other time." Ben paused, then whispered, "On Anders' face when he talked about visiting heaven."

"Michael, where did you take my niece? Hadassah, I demand answers right now!"

She felt it herself now and glanced to Michael for help.

"You two crack me up," he said, drawing Ben's and Mordecai's looks away from her. "You said no questions, and now you're both losing your minds. Turn around, Hadassah, and face away from the sun. Now, turn back around and look at us."

She turned, sensed the warmth leaving, and knew the glow disappeared with it. Michael came through again, as he always did. She obeyed and turned back toward them, her face normal again.

"There, you see? This *glow* you thought you saw was nothing more than the sun shining on Hadassah's face. The angle caused that, but when she turned, it left. Hadassah, turn back toward the sun again."

She did, and could tell the warmth flooded her face again. How did he do that? She smiled remembering what brought the glow and wondered if everyone would experience it in eternity.

"Once again, gentlemen, her glow has returned! Turn back, Hadassah." The glow left her face. "Now, turn again," he said, and it returned. He laughed like a little kid playing jokes.

"That's enough, Michael," Mordecai said. "We can do without your little games. Don't worry, I won't ask again where you were today. Until Jesus returns, those things will stay between you and him. I promise you we will ask after he returns and learn the truth."

"His return draws closer every day, and I assure you time will move fast," said Michael. The conversation changed, and he and Hadassah walked away, leaving the two men standing alone.

Hadassah wondered what that time would bring, but knew whatever came she wanted to continue her journeys with her friend, Michael, the mighty Warrior Angel of heaven.

***

Magnus dreamed, like he had many times before. He found himself inside a room with beautiful stone walls, and people huddled in the center. They kneeled shoulder-to-shoulder forming a circle. Magnus heard them speaking but couldn't tell what they were saying. He realized from previous experiences like this they couldn't see him, so he walked over and stood outside the circle. They were praying and calling out Jesus' name, making it clear who they were: fellow believers awaiting execution the next day. The Smyrnians were supposed to rescue them *tonight*!

Now came the big question: where was he? This was not Messai's mansion or any normal prison cell. A door to his right caught his attention and beckoned him to walk through. When he opened it, the area outside was light, even though the night was dark. He recoiled staring at the temple courtyard and Messai's Capital Punishment Device standing only a few feet away.

Magnus ran back through the door and slammed it. He raced across the room and threw open the door opposite this one. It led outside the temple wall and exited into the Muslim Quarter, less than one mile from Zedekiah's Cave. Jesus had shown him where Messai now held prisoners the night before their execution and how they must save them! He sprinted the escape route and arrived at the cave in ten minutes, sweating and breathing hard. The others must know! He awoke and leaped from the ground where he slept, waking Bruno, then yelling for everyone else.

"I just dreamed, and we have to rescue some believers tonight!"

"Keep your voice down! Someone outside might hear you," Bruno said. He called out more softly, "Everybody get back here! Jesus showed Magnus something we need to hear!"

They quickly gathered and surrounded Magnus who stood speaking, still trying to get his breath.

"Jesus took me where Messai holds prisoners before executing them. He will execute a group tomorrow if we don't save them! Whoever is going, follow me, and I'll lead the way."

"Hold on, Magnus, tell us where and how far," said Blake.

"The chamber by the courtyard right beside the guillotine. We can get there in ten minutes if we hurry. It may take longer coming back with ten more people."

"He plans to execute ten believers tomorrow?"

"Yes, Ollie, and they will all die if we don't save them tonight! We only need three or four of us, so who's going with me?"

Gabriel stood with two of his men. "We'll handle this first mission, and others can go next time, if they want." His determination caused everyone except Ollie to agree with him. He insisted they needed him to pick the lock and open the door, and Gabriel concurred, making Ollie happy.

"Wait, you're bringing them back here?"

"We have no choice, John. This place is big enough for a lot more people, but we can only bring those who are true followers of Jesus. We'll make sure of that before they come."

"Then go, and the rest of us will stay here and pray while you're gone."

The team left, hoping this attempted rescue would work, knowing they would die if it failed.

Seven men and three women huddled inside the Chamber of the Hearth. They had stopped praying, and now spoke in hushed tones, discussing what would happen the next day.

"I do not fear Messai or his Capital Punishment Device. We triumphed over the dragon by the blood of Jesus and the word of our testimony. Now we must not love our lives so much we shrink from death. When we die, Jesus awaits our arrival."

"I'm not afraid either, yet I dread the moment the blade strikes."

"The pastor warned us this day may come. We understood that when we followed Jesus. Don't forget what Blake and Beth Thompson said in their last video. We should do everything possible to protect ourselves, but if they capture us, we must proclaim Jesus and face death bravely, so everyone watching will witness our faith in him. Are we all ready to do that?"

"I am ready," said one large man. "I could fight and take out an AMPP man or two as they drag me, but that would not honor Jesus. So, I will walk bravely and place my head in the hole, as many others have done. My singing is awful, but I will sing his praises until they stop me!"

"We should do that now! Who cares if someone hears us?" asked a young woman in her twenties.

"I agree! Messai won't carry out the executions until 3:00 p.m., so they won't stop us. Let's sing and let our voices ring out for everyone to hear!"

They sang so loudly they didn't hear two shots killing the guards outside their door or the key turning the lock. Nor were they aware when the door opened until five people entered the room. The dim lighting allowed them to recognize that much. The group stopped singing and formed a circle again with arms stretched around each other's shoulders and fingers interlocked. Had AMPP come to torture them before their execution?

Ollie crept across the room, leaned over their circle, and spoke softly. "We came to rescue you. Follow us quickly; we have no time to wait."

One man recognized him, and his face lit up. "Oliver Barton? I have watched you on television and heard you joined the Smyrnians. Thank you for your faith in Jesus."

"You can thank me later, but right now, we have to go!"

"Come on," the man whispered to the others, and they joined him, as Magnus and a soldier led the way, and the other soldiers brought up the rear. They hurried around the northwest corner of the temple and exited the Mount into the Muslim Quarter, the cave nearly one mile away. A voice screamed as they did.

"Stop!"

"Go!" said Magnus and pushed them forward. He slid against the wall by the opening and waited.

"I'm staying with you," said a soldier, moving across from him.

"No!" Magnus insisted. "They need you. Don't worry about me; I'll catch up."

The group fled into the darkness, but stopped and turned just in time to witness the lone AMPP man felled by the big man's fist. Magnus then ran ahead, leading the way to their safe place. They arrived, locked the gate behind them, and walked deep into the cave where the others greeted them.

"Blake and Beth Thompson! Ally Fromm! Is it really you, or are we dreaming?"

"You aren't dreaming," said Blake. "We're real, and you're standing here with us free and safe from Messai. Let me introduce you to everyone else." Ally interrupted.

"My name isn't Ally Fromm now," she said, taking Anders' hand. "I'm Ally Norstrom, and this is my husband, Anders." Both smiled revealing their special love for each other.

They continued with introductions and knew they would not sleep this night. Everyone welcomed these new additions but understood they could not bring every group they rescued into the cave. Even here, overcrowding could soon become an issue. They would figure that out later.

***

"You are certain it was him?" Messai asked, questioning the guard.

"Oh, yes, sir. I saw his face right before he coldcocked me. He was once my captain, so I would recognize him anywhere."

"Did you recognize anyone other than Magnus?"

"I couldn't see the others' faces, but the last two looked like soldiers, and they were armed."

Messai turned to Rossi, his Chief Security Officer. "This proves Chen's bombs did not destroy them. It also shows survivors are hiding somewhere nearby."

"Or perhaps they drove in and rescued the prisoners, then drove away. Remember, they used an IDF Wolf to ram your vehicle. We cannot overlook that possibility, sir."

"I prefer to think they are nearby and on foot. Did your men not report all vehicles lost when the explosion occurred?"

"Yes, sir, but they obviously stole the Wolf. What would prevent them from doing so again?"

"I suppose that possibility exists, but I still want all available AMPP personnel deployed to cover the entire Old City. Leave no stone unturned and no area unsearched. I assume another group will arrive for tomorrow's executions?" Rossi nodded.

"Make sure every media outlet announces that and includes where they are held overnight. Position guards outside the room, as we have done every night, but this time, assign full patrols to hide near every Temple Mount entrance. If they return tonight, take them alive. We will torture them until they tell us where the others are hiding. However, proceed with the search immediately."

"Consider it done, sir. If we cannot locate them today, we will cover this place like a blanket to ensure no more prisoners escape and no one gets near them."

"One more thing, Mr. Rossi. Please confirm the type of weapon which killed the two guards."

"Brilliant idea, Mr. Messai. That will tell us which military fired the shots. I cannot imagine they came from an IDF weapon or any country which makes up your NWO. The nuclear war devastated other countries' forces. This discovery intrigues me. I will report back to you the minute we have that information."

"See that you do. And get our men and women out searching for *them* right now."

Rossi left immediately. Within thirty minutes, AMPP was combing the Old City searching for followers of Jesus. Would they regret staying so near Messai's Jerusalem headquarters?

***

"I hear voices outside," Gabriel said to the soldier standing guard with him near the cave's entrance. "Get out of sight quick."

From their vantage point, they watched three AMPP members approach the gate. They stood quietly, listening, and watching their every move when the men pushed the gate and peered inside.

"It's locked, and it doesn't appear anyone has been here lately. The boss closed the place and banned all visitors, so it's just an old abandoned stone quarry. Nobody's here; let's move on."

"Mr. Messai told us to check every place in this area and leave none out. An abandoned cave is an ideal hiding place for a large group of people, wouldn't you agree? I say we check it out."

"The gate is locked, and the place is abandoned; let's go." He rattled the gate and pulled the lock up, letting it drop back and clang against the bars. When it made contact, the lock popped open.

"We're going in."

They followed him, flashlights showing the way. Gabriel and his partner moved fast, sprinting into the cave, with no concern about being heard. They were several yards ahead and aware of their surroundings, so they could run freely. The men heard them, shone their lights in their direction, and pursued them, yelling for them to stop. Gunshots rang out and bullets pinged off the rock wall behind them as they rounded a corner.

Gabriel knew they must not lead them toward the others, and the lighted portion was just ahead. Both spun and dropped to one knee, waiting for their pursuers to round the same corner. When they came, the two Americans fired three rounds. They needed no more. The three men lay dead a few feet from them. Their comrades came running, ready to engage whatever enemy they faced.

"Did you get them all, or are there more? We sent everybody else down below."

"We got them, but I fear someone outside heard the shots. I'll get the gate while the rest of you take these bodies down there, too. Somebody left it unlocked. That's what made them suspicious and brought them in here. I'll lock it and clean up footprints and blood. We need to stand guard in case their friends come looking for them or someone else shows up."

"I will stay with you again," said his partner. "But we need more so we have enough firepower if they send an entire patrol."

Three others joined them while their remaining comrades carried the AMPP men's bodies. When they reached the opening leading below, only a few group members had made it through. They called them to climb back out, then lowered the deceased men into the hole. After finishing, they gathered to talk about what happened.

"It's obvious we need a better system for getting everybody below," said Blake. "We barely got started before you guys got here."

A lengthy discussion followed with plans for getting to safety, and potential evacuation, if that became necessary. Today's events left them feeling vulnerable and exposed. No plans seemed sufficient to allay their fears, but they continued sharing ideas, hoping one would stick. The greatest concern was their inability to conduct further rescues. That meant more believers would die, and they were powerless to stop it.

In Messai's office, Rossi reported back to his boss. "The patrols searched all day, sir, but found no rebels, and only arrested some Jews who have not taken the mark. However, there is one interesting development."

"What might that be, Mr. Rossi?"

"Every patrol returned and reported, except one. The men have tried contacting them, but every attempt failed. I assume something bad happened and suspect *them* again. Each team was assigned a specific area to search, so we know where the missing group went."

"Send every patrol there tonight! We cannot wait until morning and give them another opportunity to elude us again. Losing three of our men in exchange for capturing the Smyrnians would be a good trade. The men would gladly give their lives to achieve that, assuming they are dead. Get the patrols there now, Rossi, and find them!"

Within minutes, AMPP patrols raced across the Muslim Quarter, bound for a small section that included Zedekiah's Cave.

Magnus interrupted Blake's planning meeting. "I think we need to get everyone below, because I know how Messai operates. You can bet he deployed teams to search for whoever whisked away the prisoners, and knows where each team went. If only this group failed to return, he has already sent every available AMPP patrol here looking for them. They will undoubtedly search this place because he will make it clear they must not leave any location out."

"Then we probably have little time," Blake said. "Clean your areas so they can't tell anyone was here and get below fast." They all took off without waiting.

***

Michael and Hadassah sat in Petra with her Uncle Mordecai, Ben and Miriam, Alexander and Elizabeth, and others from the kibbutz. Michael called the meeting and took control right away.

"The Smyrnians face extreme danger right now. Does anyone else sense that?"

"I do," said Miriam. "I dreamed again last night and saw AMPP invading their safe place and dragging them away handcuffed. They led them before Messai and his Capital Punishment Device, and the dream ended. I awoke shaking and perspiring, but didn't tell Ben."

"Miriam, you should have told me so I could pray! I don't understand why I wasn't shown that this time. Every time before, we both felt the same thing. How about the rest of you?"

Elizabeth raised her hand and whispered, "I had the same dream."

Ben's phone vibrated in his pocket. "What's going on? No one can reach me here." He looked, and was shocked at what he saw. "It's a text from Blake, but how is that possible? I can't send or receive texts or get calls down here. I only have signal on the mountain." The others looked at him, their minds pleading with him to read Blake's words.

"Ben, if you get this, please have everyone there pray. We are all holed up in Zedekiah's Cave, close to the Temple Mount. AMPP is searching for us right now, and they know we are somewhere in this vicinity. I'll call first thing tomorrow morning, if we survive. Just pray!"

"This is serious," said Alexander. "We must spread word throughout Petra for our people to pray."

Soon, 144,000 occupants of the Rose-Red City were praying for God's protection over their fellow believers hiding from the brutal forces of Aissa Messai's Peace Patrol in Jerusalem.

***

"This has to be it because there's no other place around here where that many people could hide. Summon every patrol and get them here."

"We don't have a chance," Gabriel said. "They outnumber us ten to one. We have to reach the others and make sure they all get down this time, then join them. If AMPP finds us there, we have no choice but to fight. Jesus, please help us," he uttered as they hurried toward the hole.

"We need to cut the lights just before we go down and leave them in the dark," said another soldier. "Does anyone remember where that main switch is?"

"I've got it," Gabriel said. "When you reach the hole, I'll throw the switch, then use my phone for light, and follow you."

"Bring those bolt cutters!" a loud voice said from outside.

The snap of severed steel... a clanking padlock on the stone walkway... the metal door slamming against a concrete wall... excited voices... pounding feet. Gabriel reached the switch and jerked it down. Darkness engulfed him. They had removed lights for the first two hundred feet, so no one could see them if they looked through the gate. He hoped the AMPP men had not noticed them.

There was no time to think about whether the troops made it or if everyone else was already below. Gabriel spotted the hole ahead, turned off his light, fell to his knees, and crawled from there. A quiet voice said, "We're all here, hurry!" He felt the opening and dove in head first, trusting his friends to catch him. They did, then pulled him into the house remains where the others huddled. The group stood silent, breathing softly, listening as voices from above reached their hearing.

"There's no one here. This place is completely deserted, and we're wasting our time. The longer we stay in here, the more time we give them to escape again."

"Spread out and check every part of this cave, then we can leave if we don't find anyone."

"Over here! There's a hole which looks like it leads down to another area."

"Somebody go down and check it out."

"We don't have time to jump down there and run around. Hold my feet, so I can shine my light and look around. If it looks big enough for a bunch of people, we can go in. Otherwise, we would waste our time searching it."

The man stuck his head through the opening, and they grabbed his feet, holding him upside down. He twisted and turned, shining his light in every direction until he seemed fully satisfied and ready to come back out.

"Pull me up. This place is only big enough for a few people. There's no way a group the size we're looking for could fit."

"Are you sure? Let some others drop in and look around so we're certain no one is down there."

"Do you want to explain to Mr. Messai why we wasted enough time here to allow his most hated enemy to escape?"

"Okay, I'll take your word, but I still think someone should go in."

"I saw nothing and heard nothing. Do what you want, but I'm leaving. Who is with me?"

Hands raised, and some started walking back toward the entrance. The man reluctantly yielded to his colleague, and followed. Everyone below stayed where they were, cramped in the tiny space, refusing to take a chance on any of Messai's men staying back and watching for them to emerge.

After an hour of misery in the remains of the Crusader period house underneath the main section of Zedekiah's Cave, the group stepped out and prepared to climb back through the opening.

"They will return tomorrow morning, and search every inch of this place," said Magnus. "There is no way we can hide from them down here or up there. We have one option: leave the cave for a while and come back when it is safe. The question is, where can we go?"

"I know just the place," Ollie said. "We walked right past it on our way here and talked about it. The Garden Tomb is a short walk, which will only take a few minutes. Messai also ordered it closed, so no one should be there. It even has apartments where guests once stayed, and other places where we can live. Maybe we'll do what Jesus did and stay there three days, but it may take longer. Whenever we feel it's safe, we'll come back."

"I like that plan," said Magnus. "AMPP won't give up easily. They will search this cave more than once and keep coming until they're convinced we're not here. We can't stand around here and talk. We need to leave for the tomb *now* before they show up again."

They left nothing that would give away their presence, then turned out the lights and departed their new safe place, hoping to return soon. The soldiers would take shifts watching the entrance and AMPP's visits searching for them. That activity would determine how long they must stay away before returning.

Their temporary home would remind them daily of Jesus' resurrection and his power over their enemy. It was possible, once there, they may not want to leave until he returned. However, they understood the cave provided the best shelter and accommodations because of their number. Who knew when AMPP may discover them and force them to evacuate again? But they hoped to move back and make this place their home until Jesus returned and took them to their eternal home.

Rossi and three AMPP captains stood in Aissa Messai's office early the next morning explaining why they returned empty-handed after searching all night for the Smyrnians. His wrath had already spewed forth after hearing what he considered excuses.

"Mr. Messai, we searched the entire Muslim Quarter, but didn't find them. We even went door-to-door, questioned residents, and rummaged every house and business to ensure no one is hiding them. None of those locations were large enough to hide them all, but we searched them anyway." Messai interrupted him.

"So, gentlemen, *is* any place there large enough?"

"There is one, sir," explained another, "but we searched it thoroughly and found it completely abandoned."

"Where is this place?"

"Zedekiah's Cave, or Solomon's Quarry, sir," Rossi said, taking charge as the captain became more nervous when Messai's questions intensified. "The cavern is expansive and large enough for an immense crowd, but the men searched every part and found no sign of them."

"I know the cave well, Mr. Rossi, and understand its potential for housing their group. Are you certain they searched *every* portion? Did they examine the lower level below the main grotto?"

"Yes, sir. They discovered that during their search and checked it out. It is small and not nearly big enough for a group their size."

"Deploy patrols immediately to search *every* part, including that area."

"I will send them right away, sir." He turned to his captains. "Call your troops and go. Be sure you climb down and inspect every nook and cranny of that level. Report back the minute you finish."

The men wasted no time obeying his order, and should arrive at the Cave within fifteen minutes.

"Mr. Rossi, one more thing."

"Yes, sir?"

"Did you find which type of weapons fired the ammunition that killed our guards?"

"Yes, we did, Mr. Messai. I apologize for forgetting to give you that information. The bullets came from an M27 IAR used only by the United States Marine Corps. It seems the Smyrnians recruited elite American soldiers to help them out."

"We battle a formidable foe, Mr. Rossi, but they are no match for us. Hunt them down and bring them to me, so I may eliminate them. We will have a mass execution which clears the way for our rule. Nothing can stop us now!" He would soon regret those last words.

CHAPTER 4

Michael surprised Hadassah as she walked alone through Petra's Siq. She loved walking and praying in silence, and the three-quarter mile entrance into Petra provided the perfect opportunity. He had found her here before, but this time he swooped down from rock cliffs above.

"Are you ready?"

"Michael, stop doing that. You almost caused me to jump out of my skin. Wait, ready for what?"

"Another journey, of course. I assumed you would want to find the answer to your final question after our last trip."

"Let's go!" she said, reaching out to grab his hand.

"Not here; do you want someone to see us? Let's climb the mountain to our usual spot where we can stay out of sight. I'm just kidding; we are invisible when you travel with me. Come on!"

He took her hand and they rose, rapidly ascending two hundred and sixty feet and clearing the stone walls lining the entryway. She was prepared this time and could hardly wait to visit the temple in heaven again. *The first angel!* He held the bowl filled with Yahweh's wrath and took a step forward the last time she was there. Surely she had already missed what happened after that.

They soared higher, and she was Esther again, preventing the wicked Haman from destroying her people. Yahweh poured out his wrath, and Xerxes hung Haman and his sons on the gallows. Then her people slaughtered Persians until his wrath was complete. Aissa Messai was much like Haman. He sought to destroy Jesus' people but failed, and would now face Yahweh's horrific wrath.

Hadassah's heart pounded as they arrived and Yahweh's temple appeared again. She bowed as before, falling on her face, and joining Michael worshiping the Creator. Her excitement about seeing the angels and discovering what would happen next disappeared, and she longed to continue worshiping for all eternity. Michael's hand touched her chin and lifted her head, bringing her back into the action once again. Anticipation flooded her mind.

All seven majestic angels still stood, the first, one step in front. Nothing had changed. Time had passed on earth, but things remained the same in heaven. The realization hit her: time is different in eternity! She missed no action, even though she had been gone for days! The angel took one more step, his bowl still emitting eerie black vapor, and boiling with something not visible to her eyes. A noise startled her, breaking her concentration on the mighty angelic being. It sounded like a rumble of thunder from far below. The moment felt frozen in time that did not exist.

***

The Smyrnians talked after reaching the Garden Tomb, wide awake after their short, brisk walk. John raised his hand and halted the discussion.

"Did anyone else hear that? Shh... everybody stop talking and listen."

They all heard it now, a low rumble coming from inside the earth, foreboding and fearful. Though they realized there was nothing to fear, the sound still sent shivers down their spines. They stood looking at one another, questions on each face, until John spoke again.

"A harbinger of a massive earthquake. Remember the tremors before the first quake? This is worse, a violent convulsion signaling something far more powerful. Three earthquakes are mentioned in Revelation, two have already happened, and the third is only months away. Reports listed the first two as magnitude 9.0 and 9.5 on the

Richter scale. The world has never seen a 10.0 quake, but they will now as time winds down. If they understood what's coming, they would repent and turn to Jesus, but they can't do that now because they took Messai's mark and followed him."

They trusted John based on his seismology expertise and wanted to hear more. "What *is* coming, John? I assume your studies equipped you enough to tell us," Blake said.

"Remember the 9.0 quake when Beth was freed from Messai and the devastation it caused?" Their nods and facial expressions showed they remembered it well. "That quake was so catastrophic it ravaged the entire world. A 10.0 will be thirty times stronger than that one."

He paused, allowing that to sink in before he continued. *Thirty times stronger! Was that even possible?* Their shock rendered them so speechless they could only sit and wait to learn more.

"The second major quake only affected Jerusalem, but this one will affect the entire world again, just like the first. The earth will convulse for at least an hour, but probably much longer. Tsunamis will strike every major body of water killing millions, causing massive flooding, and destroying property for hundreds of miles. While that happens, the earth will keep shaking violently. The intensity will literally reshape the planet and make it nearly unrecognizable. It will happen soon."

"Wow..." The word escaped Ally's mouth, but they all thought the same thing.

***

The rumble stopped, and the angel strode calmly until he reached the edge of the temple court, then stood looking down on the earth. Hadassah had not noticed that! Now she peered down and stared at what she had missed: the same astounding view that amazed every astronaut who traveled into space. The globe hung beneath her like a magnificent spherical ball suspended in midair. The sight took her breath away.

"Beautiful, isn't it," asked Michael, enjoying her sense of awe and wonder. He waited patiently, allowing her time to regain composure and speak again.

"Amazing," she said, the word floating from her mouth like a gentle whisper.

"I never grow tired of it, and I have seen it since Yahweh created it six thousand years ago. I call this place my home with a view. But that isn't why we came today."

A loud voice rang out bringing Hadassah back into the moment. "Go, pour out the seven bowls of God's wrath on the earth." The mighty angel swooped down with such force the wind would have sent her tumbling had Michael not caught her before it did. They watched the heavenly messenger of judgment streaking toward the earth like a shooting star, then rapidly encircling the globe, across, up and down, diagonally, he zoomed, making Hadassah dizzy.

"Faster than the speed of light," Michael said, answering her question before she could ask it.

She saw the angel complete his last circle and shoot back toward them with such speed he was not visible until he stood before them again. He bowed toward the temple before entering with the empty bowl in his hands. The remaining six still stood stoically in line waiting their turn. Hadassah knew it would not happen immediately in earth time because bowl one must complete its work.

Another sound caught her ear and turned her attention back toward the earth. Wails, screams, and angry yells rose from below as judgment one hit human beings. No one showed her what the bowl contained, but she now understood how awful it must be. However, something else disturbed her even more than the cries from below. The earth was no longer the beautiful globe she saw before. Now the dark, foreboding vapor which emanated from bowl one became a thick inky fog turning it black. Hadassah heard the rumble again, louder now, a portent of something even worse coming.

"We must leave. Our purpose here has ended for now, and Petra awaits us. Let's go." He rose and helped her stand on shaky legs, giving her time to process what she had witnessed. His words were welcome news. She had been eager to come, but now could not wait to leave. They lifted off, with Michael flying close beside her, ensuring she made the trip safely. This day had been hard for her.

He decided to make one stop, which would show her what came from the bowl, hoping that would make her feel better. They sat unnoticed outside the entrance to Zedekiah's Cave.

"Why did we stop here? Is this where the team is hiding from AMPP?"

"It's where they have been hiding, but today they moved to Jesus' empty tomb because they knew AMPP would come looking for them again. Not a bad place to go when you need to get away, huh?" His smile showed he was trying to lift her spirits.

"Not bad," she said, forcing a smile. "Michael, I want to go home. Can we leave now?"

"If you can wait a few minutes, I will show you what was in the bowl."

"Really? How can that happen here?"

"Be quiet and listen, then tell me what you hear."

"I hear voices coming from the cave. I thought you said they aren't here?"

"*They* aren't here, but Messai's goons are, and you will see what was in the bowl when they exit."

The voices increased in both intensity and volume. It was obvious the men were under duress and walking quickly. Something, or *someone*, was forcing them out! Hadassah wondered if she and Michael were getting ready to fight another battle. The men ran out, and she gasped at what she saw.

"Michael, their faces are covered with huge sores! Their pain must be excruciating!" She quickly put her hand over her mouth, fearing they may have heard her.

"Don't worry; they can't hear or see us. Do you understand now what was in the bowl?"

"It's awful, Michael. They're bleeding, and yellow stuff is running down their faces and necks. Are those things all over their bodies?"

"They cover them from head-to-toe, Hadassah, and they hurt worse than you can imagine. When Yahweh pours out his wrath, he does it right. By the way, that yellow stuff is called *pus*."

"Stop it, smart aleck; I know that. I also realize why black vapor poured from the bowl, and why we heard screams and wails after the angel poured it out. But God's wrath is just beginning, isn't it?"

"Yes, it is, but these sores won't leave when the other judgments come. Things will get worse and worse until Jesus returns. Now we can go home. I hope you feel better after seeing this."

"I don't know about better, but thank you for showing me." The pair lifted off and headed home.

***

"Blake, you will never believe what just happened here. I think you guys are good to move back."

"Slow down, Gabriel. We left a few hours ago and figured we would need to stay here at least three days until they give up and stop searching for us there. What could have happened that makes you think we can come back now? Besides, we want to enjoy this place for a while."

"We were right, AMPP came early and brought multiple patrols. They were only inside two hours, not enough time to look everywhere, although I'm sure they searched the bottom part first. But they came out a few minutes ago and were not doing well."

"What do you mean they weren't doing well?" John asked, the others listening with Blake's phone on speaker.

"They were hurting and limping, in obvious pain. I'm not sure what happened in there, but they had large open sores completely covering their arms and faces, oozing yellow pus, and bleeding."

"What caused that?" Steve asked. "Nothing inside the cave did that to us. What you described typically comes from bacteria, but it doesn't happen that quickly. If bacteria caused it, the same thing would've happened to us."

"So, do you think it's safe to go back, Steve?"

"If we're talking about health concerns, yes, I do. Does anyone foresee security concerns?"

"I don't. After watching them leave, I'm sure they won't return." Gabriel's certainty gave them confidence. They trusted his military experience in situations like this and would follow his advice.

"I say we go back tonight," said Ollie. "Staying here where Jesus rose from the grave feels good, but we don't have electricity or lighting like we do there."

"I agree with Ollie. We need electricity and clean water, plus the cave has much more living space and hiding options. Let's sleep this afternoon, and we'll walk back at midnight."

No one disputed Blake's words. They loved the Garden Tomb, but everyone realized Zedekiah's Cave was where they needed to stay. They would make the trek back *home* tonight.

***

Messai's men were the first to contract the disease, leading to speculation that it may have come from the cave. When family members and comrades also developed symptoms within a few days, pandemonium ensued, as reminders of another worldwide pandemic fifteen years earlier engulfed the planet. But this one was different. The effects were external, extremely painful, long-lasting, untreatable, and incurable. The world needed to hear from their leader, and as usual, he obliged.

"Ladies and gentlemen, the world's most brilliant scientists and medical minds are working around the clock trying to determine what caused this plague. They have narrowed the possibilities down to two: Staphylococcus aureus, commonly known as Staph, which may have entered our AMPP patrols' bodies inside the cave where they searched for insurgents. This can be highly contagious and spread through person-to-person contact."

"A more plausible explanation revolves around radiation from the recent nuclear warfare which ravaged our planet. Radiation can remain trapped in the stratosphere, then suddenly break through and fall to earth. Lingering radiation can pose a threat for five years, however, as your risen messiah, I will end it much sooner than that. Though painful and potentially life-threatening, this hazard will eventually dissipate."

"I attempted to negotiate peace between countries which would prevent such devastation and loss of life, but did not accomplish that until significant damage was already done. The world may be paying for their atrocities today. Please do not give up hope or lose faith in our dream of worldwide peace and prosperity. I am doing everything possible to resolve this situation and continue moving us toward that goal. Together, we will attain it. Thank you for having faith in me and each other."

His words fell on unreceptive ears as people began turning against the man they viewed as their savior days earlier. The disease spread around the world at an alarming rate as more and more people found themselves covered with the ugly festering sores which characterized it. They flooded doctor's offices but got no relief. The agonizing pain was relentless and kept people home from work, causing businesses to suffer as Messai's promise of prosperity slowly crumbled.

To make matters worse, the skin disease did not affect him, as he remained healthy and abscess free. However, the sores broke out on everyone who bore his mark. The outbreak spread, affecting one person, one family, one community at a time, leaving none disease free. They battled their worsening pain and failed to notice one group the disease did not touch: followers of Jesus.

Messai continued promoting the nuclear fallout theory, yet would not allow his forces to reenter the cave. That created an opening for the Smyrnians to move back in. Executions also stopped since no one, including Caiaphas, could perform their duties. Neither could Messai nor the dragon and his army prevent the disease from spreading to his followers because it came from one far more powerful than them. They did not realize this was the beginning of their eternal end.

***

The team settled back in, discussions now taking a different turn. Word came that security forces would no longer enter the cave and executions were temporarily suspended. With safety concerns lessened, thoughts turned to what they should do next, with Anders leading the conversation.

"We must realize, even though AMPP can't perform their duties for now, Messai still commands the dragon's demonic army. Therefore, we can't relax because they can find and attack us anytime. Our greatest weapon is prayer. We can all attest to victories we've experienced because we prayed. Our focus must turn to prayers of protection for ourselves and our fellow believers."

"I agree with that, but I'm opposed to taking nothing but a passive approach," said Trey. "We still need to fight Messai, but how can we do that with his army stymied and executions stopped?"

"I feel the same, Trey," said Magnus. "But we can't kill Messai, and AMPP is incapacitated right now. Prisoners don't need rescuing, because none are being arrested. What can we do?"

"Jesus and Yahweh have taken control and the battle is no longer ours to fight; it belongs to them."

"Come on, Anders, we can't sit around here on our derrieres till the Tribulation ends. We two big men love to fight!"

"So do the *two big men* in heaven, Bruno. Think how much fun we will have watching Messai's feeble attempts to defeat them! I saw this time while eating the scroll. I mentioned these three words to Ally one day, but I haven't told you. Remember when Jesus showed me the words, *reign of terror*, and they came true right after I shared them with you? It is now time to tell you the next three words."

"Let me guess: *Wrath of God*."

"No, Blake, but good try. *Dawn of deliverance*. Let me explain. In Luke, Chapter 21, Jesus spoke about this exact time we live in now. He said, 'People will faint from terror, apprehensive of what is coming on the world, for the heavenly bodies will be shaken. At that time they will see the Son of Man coming in a cloud with power and great glory. When these things begin to take place, stand up and lift up your heads, because your redemption is drawing near.'"

"We are witnessing that beginning right now! People are fainting from terror because the sores cover their bodies and they face uncertainty about what may come next. The heavenly bodies were shaken during the first quake which John talked about and we lived through. These things are taking place, and Jesus will soon come with power and great glory!"

The group broke out in praise, but Anders lifted his hand and silenced them. They realized he wanted to finish his message, and finish he did! "Dawn comes with the first hint of daylight and signals the coming of sunrise. Jesus said these things will happen right before he comes. This is the dawn of destruction for the dragon and Messai, but the dawn of deliverance for us!"

They applauded again, but he raised his hand one more time, showing he needed to say one more thing. They stopped clapping and listened, fearing his words may turn negative, but expecting the opposite. He leaped to his feet, and the words exploded from his mouth: "We must stand and lift up our heads, because our redemption draws near!"

Everyone jumped to their feet and joined him praising Jesus. Their voices reverberated off the cave walls and echoed down every corridor and alcove, surely carrying outside, as well. The group could only hope no one else heard them. But then, who cared if they did?

Michael and Hadassah flew another mission the day after their encounter in heaven. This time they traveled back to Zedekiah's Cave.

"Why did we come back here, Michael? You brought me here and showed me what was in the angel's bowl. Did the Smyrnians come back here to live?"

"Yes, they're here, but I want to show you much more than that. It is pretty cool, even if I do say so myself. There I go using their word again," he said. "Look what Yahweh has allowed me to do?" He spread his hands and brought them around the cave's opening, creating a shield which covered the entrance's entire circumference.

"What is that? You just trapped them inside so they can't get out!"

"Do you remember me telling you about bubble-wrapping Trey and Rickie's plane when they flew to China?" She remembered that and his other exploits well, so she nodded yes. "This is similar, but they can walk in and out if they choose. It will not keep them in, but it will keep others out. You are looking at their shield of protection for which they prayed!"

"Michael, that really is awesome! Will they realize they have protection? What happens if they walk outside the cave? Where…"

"Whoa with all the questions. You must not bother yourself with such things because they belong to Yahweh alone. But since you asked… they may not know the protection is there right now, but they will figure it out. It does only apply inside, but Yahweh's wrath will render AMPP and others powerless to touch them when they come out. However, the dragon and his demons always linger."

"I hope they are careful. Perhaps they will stay inside until the Tribulation ends."

"I wish that too, Hadassah, but unfortunately, they won't, and more will die."

"Please don't say that, Michael. Surely Yahweh won't let that happen."

"Sadly, this protection will end. During the remaining time, Messai or the dragon will kill more. That's the price they pay for missing the Rapture. He reached out to everyone before taking his people home, but many refused to believe. A certain pastor warned everyone in advance with specific details, yet he was mocked. Thankfully, his message was left behind, and many watched it and turned to Jesus. For that, I am grateful."

That ended their trip on another somber note. Yet, she could not help but thank Jesus and Yahweh for giving everyone left behind another opportunity to believe. And now she also thanked him for placing a shield of protection around his people. Please come soon, Jesus, she whispered, realizing no matter how much she wanted that now, enough time remained for Messai to slaughter many more believers. They returned to Petra following another thrilling and successful journey.

***

Messai was right about one thing: the festering sores did not go away quickly; in fact, they did not go away at all. They continued to worsen and spread across the world at warp speed. Not a single person who received his mark remained unaffected. One would think they might learn only *marked* people suffered the painful, incurable disease, but that never crossed their minds. However, Jesus' followers did not miss it. They rejoiced that God poured out his wrath on Messai's followers, but protected them.

The Antichrist's promise of peace and prosperity continued crumbling, as well. The economy steamrolled toward a worldwide Great Depression. Food shortages created global hunger that saw formerly prosperous people now malnourished and starving. One blogger gained many followers with his blog titled, *Mudslide to Hell*, in which he accurately pointed out where the world was headed under current conditions. He did not know how right he was, and neither did the world.

Messai's news conferences angered people more than they encouraged them. His refrain was always the same: *don't give up hope, for peace and prosperity will come!* People realized the fallacy of such a proclamation and shouted Moshe and Eliyahu's former favorite word: *LIAR!*

The Secretary-General took advantage of the situation in another way. He instructed physicians to euthanize anyone without the mark who sought medical attention or was hospitalized with the sores, not realizing the disease affected none of them. *Population control is the answer,* he reasoned. He had discovered the perfect way to execute them without using his Capital Punishment Device. But more than any, he wanted the Smyrnians.

"Beelzebub and Belial!" he screamed. The two demons appeared and bowed before him.

"Yes, Master. We are yours to command. Tell us what you require, and we will do it!"

"Find the Smyrnians, and bring them to me. I will execute them myself, with your help."

"Master, the dragon sent all our demons searching for them, but we cannot find them anywhere. It seems they disappeared. Maybe they succumbed to starvation or contracted the sores and died."

"No, they did not; they still live!" he bellowed. "Their stench fills my nostrils, and their voices fill my ears. They are hiding, and we must discover their location and destroy them!"

The Great Red Dragon appeared before him. "Aissa, my princes are yours to command, but not yours to berate! The other princes and the entire horde are searching everywhere for them right now. Do you not think they would bring them to you if they found them?"

"Yes, Master, I do. Forgive me; I am so eager to annihilate them. It is *him*! The false messiah hides them, and we must not allow him to win that battle!"

"Silence!" roared the beast. "Do you want to experience the sores like all the others?" He glared into his man's face again. Messai's eyes glowed, and yellow and red flashed from them. The beast already consumed him, but times like this required intensifying the indwelling. The man threw back his head, and a deep-throated scream poured from his mouth. All twelve demon princes appeared, joined by the horde, packing the room. *"Find them!"* He was unaware they still lived right under his nose in the cave he abandoned after AMPP contracted the disease while inside it.

***

"We need food," John said, stating what was on everyone's mind. "We stocked up when the restaurants left us so much every night, but now they're closed, and our supply chain is gone. There's only enough left for one or two more days. Does anyone have suggestions where we can find something to eat? We need to figure that out soon."

"Why did you ask *us*, John?"

"Because *we* have to find food, Anders. I suggest we throw out ideas now!"

"Okay, John, I will *throw out an idea*. I suggest we ask Jesus and trust Him to provide our food."

"Look, Anders, I know he provided, and I remember promising to always trust him after Messai's resurrection, but perhaps he wants us to get our own food this time. He has done so much for us already, and we don't deserve it. Maybe he wants us to help ourselves for a change."

"John, do you remember the Model Prayer Jesus taught us to pray? In the middle of that prayer, he said we should ask God to *give us our daily bread*. That can also mean, *give us today the bread we need*. The scroll contained this very situation, and I just saw the answer. I read this: *tell them to ask and it will be done*. If we're going to ask, we must do what he taught us."

They bowed their heads and prayed that one line aloud together: *Jesus, give us today the bread we need*. They looked up but saw no immediate miraculous answer. John concluded their prayer with humble words, revealing his increasing faith: *We will wait for you to provide.*

"It's almost 7:00 p.m.," said Blake. "Ben will call any minute. Who wants to walk up front with me where we can get service?"

"Is that safe," asked John. "There I go again with my lack of faith. Of course it's safe, so I'm going. Anyone else?" The inner circle followed and looked forward to hearing from Ben again.

This time, Ben and Mordecai climbed the mountain without Michael and Hadassah. They did not even mention they were going. Ben placed the call, and Blake answered. The conversation quickly turned to the young couple's most recent disappearances and what happened while they were gone.

"Blake, Mordecai and I traced the times Michael vanished and realized miracles happened every time. We discussed that with you, but now Hadassah goes with him every time. I don't understand that, but it has happened more often recently. Have you noticed any miraculous events lately?"

"Have we noticed any miraculous events! You wouldn't believe everything that has happened."

He proceeded telling the two men about AMPP searching for them and how Jesus miraculously protected them. Then he shared the most recent happening. "They had us trapped and were coming back to arrest us the next morning. We moved to the Garden Tomb at midnight."

"Wow!" Ben said. "Talk about a place to hide! You couldn't do any better than that! But get back to Michael and Hadassah and what has happened."

Blake told them about the sores and Messai's news conferences they watched on their phones. They had not seen many, but enough to realize what was happening around the world.

"So you think sores have broken out on everyone who took the mark?"

"That sounds like what he's saying. But we don't have them, and I bet neither does any other believer in Jesus."

"Do you recall what day and time that happened?"

Blake gave details and heard Mordecai speak loudly. "I knew it! I don't know what they had to do with it, but it happened the same day!"

"I can't answer that for you, men. My advice is, don't worry about it. I know you have free time on your hands, but surely you can find better ways to occupy it than thinking about them."

"Let me change the subject," John said. "Our food supply has run out because restaurants closed due to people suffering from the sores. We need a way to get food!" He thought for a moment, then went on. "I trust Jesus to provide, but I wondered if you guys have any suggestions."

"He has provided here, John, in big ways. We have more food than 144,000 people can eat, and it comes fresh every day, manna from heaven. No one here has ever tasted anything like it, but it is delicious! We asked the same thing God's people asked in the desert: *what is it?* That's why they called it *manna.* The Bible says they ate the food of angels, so I think that's why it tastes so good. It comes in different flavors too; fruits and vegetables, meat, even desserts for my sweet tooth!"

"You just described the scroll!" said Anders with a big smile. "Every page tasted different like I was eating a four-course meal! Evan had obviously eaten the same thing, so God definitely feeds you with food from heaven in Petra!"

"The Bible calls it the food of angels? You mean angels eat?" Bruno asked. "Maybe that means we will eat the same thing in eternity. If it's good enough for the angels, it's good enough for me!"

"I doubt this means we will eat the same thing, Bruno. But if we do, I am okay with it too!"

"Jesus just showed me our answer," Anders said. "When we end this call, I'll explain it. I can't believe I didn't recognize it from the scroll before now!"

They finished the call, and the group went back inside where he could tell everyone how Jesus would provide their food, at least for the time being. He didn't know if that would last the entire time they needed it, or they would have to find another supply later. For now, it solved their problem and would relieve John and the others. They listened as Anders broke the news.

"The restaurants and vendors who closed left storehouses of food just sitting there going to waste. Someone needs to eat it!" He had a twinkle in his eye.

"Are you suggesting we steal food?" asked Blake, struggling to believe what his partner said.

"The Old Testament book of 2 Kings tells about the Syrians besieging Samaria, the Northern Kingdom's capital. The siege caused a severe famine, and the people were starving. Elisha the prophet said they would have abundant food the next day!"

"How could they have plenty food the next day if they had none?" Ally asked her husband.

"That shows how awesome Jesus is, Ally. At twilight, God sent the sound of chariots and horses like a mighty army, and the Syrians heard it. They fled into the hills leaving everything behind, including... all their food!"

"Shortly after, four lepers who lived outside Samaria approached the Syrian camp to surrender and found it deserted. They ate, drank, and carried off plunder. Then they realized they were wrong, so they went and told the gatekeepers, who told the king. Israel plundered the camp and had all the food they needed! Jesus showed me that story when I ate the scroll like I was watching a movie, but I didn't know what it meant until now. He has provided us food just as he did for Samaria!"

"Anders, are you absolutely sure?"

"As sure as your name is Blake Thompson! So, who will go out *at twilight* and reap the harvest?"

"We've been fetching food every day, so we know where the restaurants are," said Omar. "But we will need help to carry that much food!"

"The soldiers will go so you others can stay here and be safe. But we need Ollie the locksmith," Gabriel said, glancing at Ollie who grinned and nodded. "We will protect Omar, Ahmad, and Hala, and help carry food. This group will eat well tonight!"

The group prayed for them and sent them out. They arrived at a row of restaurants in the Muslim Quarter, five minutes from the cave. Four soldiers stood guard while the three Jordanians, eight remaining troops, and Ollie walked to the first establishment's rear door. Ollie picked the lock, and they entered a large pantry area with big freezers along the back wall, all packed with both perishable and non-perishable food. It would all keep in the cave. Some *use by* dates had expired, but they deemed everything safe to eat. They filled empty bags, which were piled in one corner with all the food they could carry. The sixteen of them returned with what appeared to be a month's food supply. The group celebrated and thanked Jesus for his abundant provision.

"That's only one restaurant," said Ollie. "There are many more. And what we brought back tonight amounts to less than half their stock. Let's make food runs every night and bring all we can store. We brought fresh meat and dairy products we can enjoy until they're gone, along with cans of meat, fruits, and vegetables that will last a long time."

"Jesus has provided indeed. Partner, I sure am glad you ate that scroll," Blake said, and smiled.

One problem solved, they settled into Zedekiah's Cave still wondering what the remaining time would bring. They would take life one day at a time as eternity drew ever closer.

CHAPTER 5

Months passed, and the sores sent from Yahweh continued growing worse. Messai's demonic army failed to locate the Smyrnians, and he could no longer deal with thoughts of their existence. So he summoned Rossi to his office. The man stood before him frail, wearing loose clothing, and covered with open festering lesions, bleeding, and seeping yellow pus.

To this point, he had demanded others stay away for fear the contagion may spread to him. Now Rossi's appearance caused him to draw back, seeing the awful disease up close for the first time, and shocking him, yet not assuaging his anger. He was determined to exert his power once again and begin searching for all who opposed him, the Smyrnians topping his list. They would face the Capital Punishment Device, if he must pull the lever himself. An evil grin covered his face mentally picturing the possibility. Rossi cringed, recognizing what was coming.

"Mr. Rossi, you do not look well, so I assume others who bear the sores look the same."

Rossi nodded his acknowledgment without saying a word, certain his boss sensed his dread. He knew Messai's boss too, so he understood something evil was coming.

"However, we must not allow this condition to stop our quest for world domination. You must realize our efforts concern more than peace and prosperity. Those things are only possible when one all-powerful individual controls the entire world, including the global economy and population. The dragon granted me that role and empowered me to fulfill it. Today, Rossi, we attack again to remove those who oppose our agenda. They have mocked us long enough, so the time has come for action."

"Inform all AMPP personnel they must return to work tomorrow. I will reward those who fight through the pain and return to battle with double their previous pay. Those who refuse will face execution. I assume that is ample motivation and will allow them to make an informed decision."

Rossi nodded again, still speechless, now wondering how his men could serve with such excruciating pain, but realized they must. He cared about his men, but they swore their allegiance to Messai and took his mark, so their only option was obedience. He would inform them at once.

"Well, Rossi, aren't you going to say anything? Speak up now, or face the device first, with me serving as your executioner!"

"Yes, sir, Mr. Messai, I was just making mental notes of your orders. I will inform all AMPP personnel immediately and report back after I finish."

"I expect you will not waste one minute. You earned this position because of your no-nonsense, businesslike approach. Continue performing it well, and you shall reign with me forever!"

Rossi cared nothing about the man's promise, but fear for his life drove his decisions. Many days he wished he could go back and refuse the mark, and wondered why he had not looked into joining the Smyrnians. He pushed the thought from his mind and left to obey his boss's command. His fate was sealed the moment he received the mark, but he understood none of that. He would serve Messai now and soon suffer eternal punishment with him. His story paralleled that of many others. He turned to leave, but stopped when the Secretary-General informed him of one more thing.

"I will leave for the Vatican later this afternoon and meet with the pope. He must assure me of their dedication to our cause or face punishment, as well. That is all, Mr. Rossi. You may go now."

***

Michael and Hadassah flew high again toward their previous destination. She knew this excursion had another important purpose, but did not understand what it was. They flew in silence, her mind longing to understand, her mouth refusing to ask, and arrived at the familiar location. The scene had not changed, and no heavenly time had passed. She joined Michael, bowing before Yahweh.

When they rose, the low rumble met her hearing again, still eerie and foreboding. If only she understood what it meant, but she did not. Would it accompany every trip? She was certain this would not be their last. The sound was louder now, and she felt trembling from below. Michael stood still, like he did not even notice it. It signified something coming and gave her chills.

Six angels now stood holding their bowls, the first having completed his task, which brought the incurable sores. The second angel took a step forward, and Hadassah shook, both from fear and anticipation. She looked at Michael, but he did not return her glance, then whispered, but he did not reply. Her gaze returned to the mighty angel who was about to initiate judgment number two.

The heavenly being zoomed away at the speed of light like a falling star shooting toward the earth. The planet remained dark, the black vapor from bowl number one still covering it. Hadassah recalled the earth's beauty from above before the first angel poured out his wrath. She now realized that would never return. Her eyes tried to turn away from the coming scene, but they could not.

The angel encircled the globe, leaving streaks of light around and across it, and forming thin beams of light inside the blackness. The white circles instantly turned red and dripped crimson liquid onto the earth. *What could that be?* The wails and moans returned, and she realized it was bad again. The beam shot upward, and the angel stood before the temple, then walked inside.

"The second judgment has begun. Are you still glad you came?"

Once again, he startled her, and she jumped when he spoke. "I still feel honored that Yahweh would let you bring me to witness such major events as time winds down. Why can't we just stay here instead of going back and watching the judgment unfold?"

"No, we must go. But after you view it, we will return to Petra again where it cannot touch us."

"It almost seems unfair that others must experience it, but we and those who follow Jesus do not."

"When they took the mark, it sealed their doom. While Yahweh's people suffered persecution, the Antichrist's followers prospered and rejoiced over their hardship. Do you recall what the world did to Moshe and Eliyahu's bodies after he murdered them?"

"Yes, I do!" she said more defiantly as things became clearer for her. "They celebrated their deaths and abused their corpses. Messai's followers also cheered each execution because they believed his lies about peace and prosperity. Now they're getting what they gave, only worse."

"I suppose that's a good way to put it," Michael said, shrugging his shoulders at her. "Payback will increase in intensity, but they will long for these days when Yahweh sends them to their eternal doom. It does not pay to reject his love sent through his son."

"That's Jesus, isn't it? How can people reject what he did for them through his death on the cross and refuse to believe in him? Wait, we all did that before the Rapture, didn't we? Well, not *you*, but you understand what I mean," she said with a sheepish look on her face.

"It makes no sense now that you understand, does it? The love of Jesus or the wrath of his father doesn't seem like a difficult choice." He rested his head on his hand and rubbed his chin.

"When you put it like that, it makes me wish I could go back in time before the Rapture and tell everyone to follow Jesus. Will his followers experience the dragon's wrath anymore before he returns, or will only Messai's followers face Yahweh's wrath?"

"I would prefer to withhold that answer from you, Hadassah, but since you asked, I won't. Messai will unleash his wrath on believers again, starting soon. He's still convinced he can win the last battle and will not go down without a fight. Unfortunately, believers in Jesus will be his targets."

"That seems less fair than what the others experience from these bowls, Michael. Why won't Yahweh protect them with such a brief time remaining?"

"Realize that part is the good news, young one. Soon Jesus will return, defeat Messai, and give them ultimate and eternal victory!"

Young one... he had never called her that before. It made sense coming from an eternal being who existed before the universe was created, she reasoned, and chuckled under her breath. She still found it hard to believe they were such close friends. Then a voice whispered, *do not forget you are Esther. Your friendship with my mighty warrior angel was no accident.* A smile covered her face like many times before. "Let's go, Michael," she said. "The time has come." They soared away toward Planet Earth to witness the continuing devastation of Yahweh's wrath.

***

Messai's private jet landed in Rome. His personal limo picked him up and drove away for the Vatican and his meeting with the banished and powerless pope. He hated the man and his inner circle now more than ever. Like his servile Jews, they would either submit fully to him or pay the price for their insolence. The limo arrived, and he stepped out and walked toward the Apostolic Palace, each step bringing more determination to subjugate the former religious leaders.

He entered the pope's former apartment, now his own, and then the papal office, which he also claimed. He smelled the pope's presence and realized the man had occupied the room during his absence. Moving into the meeting room, he sensed others had been there, as well. *The cardinals*, he growled to himself. *These insolent fools attempt to make a mockery of me when I am not here. Surely they understand I am omnipresent and know their every move.* Everyone except the *Smyrnians*, he reasoned, hatred flooding his soul again. He pushed it aside and summoned the former pope and cardinals to meet with him in an hour. They had better not be late.

What was that sound? A faint rumble coming from far below captured his attention and sent anticipation racing through his mind. *Yahweh's son.* The one his master had tried to overthrow for millennia now gave signs he would attack soon. *Let him start the battle. I will defeat him and he will fall before me.* This time his demonic army would be ready.

The pope arrived first and greeted him, bowing as required. Sores covered his body too, just like Rossi's when his head of security walked into his Jerusalem office. The disease surely affected the Smyrnians too, so when he found them, they would not escape him this time.

"Welcome, Gregory, thank you for coming early. You and I have things to discuss before the cardinals arrive."

Gregory. No one used his chosen papal name. *Supreme Pontiff* was his appropriate title, but this man relished humiliating him in private, public, and around his peers. His hatred flared now, directed toward the larger-than-life man standing before him. But he could not deny the prosperity Messai had brought to him and his remaining constituency. His mind weighed the balance between submitting to him and reclaiming his own former glory, so he tested the waters with his reply.

"Thank you, *Aissa*. I am honored to welcome you back to Rome and the Vatican."

"*Never* call me by my name! The title is *Your Majesty* for everyone, including you and your weak pawns."

And *my* title is Your Highness, he wanted to scream back, but such an angry outburst was not a good sign considering Pope Gregory's intentions during their meeting. "Please accept my apologies, Your Majesty. I will not make that mistake again." Such groveling stung him and increased his anger, but he would remain calm.

"Have you and your pawns entered my office and this room, Gregory?"

He considered lying but understood Messai was fully aware of the truth. "Well, sir, you were not using the rooms, so it seemed appropriate..."

"Silence!" The roar was so loud anyone nearby must have heard. "I smelled your aroma the minute I came in. *Never* enter my space again, do you understand?"

"Yes, sir, I..."

"Good. Now, is there something you want to tell me? Say it before they arrive."

How did Messai know his intentions to address their lowly status and demand restoration to their former glory? He must find the courage to stand up to him, regardless of the consequences.

"Sir, you have treated the cardinals and me with contempt when we deserve respect. We have many adherents who obey our directives and abide by our decrees, so it would serve your best interest to elevate us so they witness that and continue worshiping you with their whole hearts. Sir, we demand your respect and will, in turn, treat you with respect and give you our worship."

"You fool! You are in no position to *demand* anything! Bring in your pawns so they can hear how I answer your demands... *now!*"

The pope stepped out and summoned the cardinals standing outside the door. When they entered, Messai ordered them to sit around the conference table while he sat at the head where the pope once sat.

"Listen to me, you imbeciles. You now serve me rather than your former false god! When you united with my One World Religion and took my mark, you became mine."

His voice turned into a low growl the men had not heard before, leaving them terror-stricken before the world's most powerful man.

"You would have nothing without me. I returned your prominence and restored your prosperity, which also extends to your followers. They bow to me daily, pray toward my temple in Jerusalem, and worship me. They see you as mere shadows of your former selves who no longer command their allegiance or respect. One glance inside their minds will show you that."

A large crystal ball appeared before them showing the few remaining Catholics around the world. The pope and cardinals watched as homes filled with their former adherents bowed before images of Messai and worshiped him. They watched his press conferences and leaned on every word, celebrating his declarations of peace and prosperity. Why shouldn't they, since they experienced it themselves? The onetime Catholic leaders realized their former positions no longer existed.

"Now, do you understand? You serve *me* and do *my* bidding. Your insolence leaves me one step away from obliterating you and everything in this pitiful place. Submit to me or watch it happen!"

The group sat shaken by his evil voice, which they knew came from somewhere, or someone, other than him. He excused them to leave, and they moved to another room to discuss their situation. Messai moved behind the pope's desk and sat defiantly as they filed past him on their way out.

"We cannot deny the facts," said Gregory, his leaders encircling him inside a small room. "He arose from nowhere and was proclaimed the messiah. Then someone brutally murdered him, and he rose from death. Sound familiar?"

"After the disappearances destroyed our religion, he restored our glory and financial prosperity when we joined him," said another.

"But his demanding attitude does not befit the messiah," yet another said. "And these sores. Should he not protect his own who serve him from such diseases?"

"Or heal us when they came," said Gregory. "But we must weigh the facts. We realize what our eyes have seen, things which only the true Messiah could do. I recommend we closely monitor his activity and make future decisions based on our observations." They all agreed.

***

Messai's phone rang: Rossi. It must be important or his security head would not interrupt him here.

"Mr. Rossi, please tell me why you would call me at such an important time."

"Because I have important news, sir. Have you seen images from ocean cams around the world?"

"No, I have not, Rossi, nor do I have time for boring news, which only comes from remote sources since the disease rendered reporters unable to do their jobs in the studio."

"But sir, you must see these. It is urgent that you look."

Messai finally agreed and ended the call, thinking this wasted his valuable time. He pulled up one major news network and heard the reporter's voice before seeing images. No reporter appeared on screen since the sores covered their bodies, but spoke remotely from their homes while videos showed. The man spoke weakly, like others who suffered from the crippling disease.

"On the screen, you will see pictures from every major body of salt water, including aerial shots miles from land. The scenes defy description and bring back memories of Moshe and Eliyahu, the two prophets who terrorized the earth. Now I cannot help but ask if they returned to life and are sending the plagues again? Or one may wonder whether they cause them from beyond the grave, even though that sounds impossible. Whatever the case, something created this and it comes at the worst possible time with people suffering excruciating pain from an unknown, incurable disease."

Images appeared, rotating from one sea to another... no water, only blood. Hardly believing his eyes or the reporter's words, Messai called his driver immediately and met him outside the Palace.

"Take me to the closest beach... fast." The driver sped away, weaving through the streets of Rome. No traffic filled them, since people afflicted with sores could not drive. It even shocked Messai to see Rome looking like a ghost town. His chauffeur scrambled to figure out which beach was closest and opted to head south thirty miles to Anzio. He had no choice but to drive in spite of his pain.

They arrived in twenty-five minutes at a scenic vantage point, and Messai jumped from the car looking out over the beautiful Mediterranean Sea. Except this time it was no longer the stunningly gorgeous vista he remembered. Dark red depths sent blood rolling onto formerly pristine beaches, creating an apocalyptic landscape signaling the potential end of human existence. Red Tide? No, real blood. The Antichrist understood it meant the great final battle would come soon, and he welcomed it. He got back into the limo and called his chief security officer.

"Did you witness it for yourself, sir?"

"Yes, I did, Rossi, and I called to tell you what it means. The false Messiah creates havoc setting up the final battle, which we must win. I will return tomorrow so we can develop a strategy for victory. In the meantime, I will create some havoc of my own." Foreboding words, but he must counter *his* every move. He would call *check* with his next move and put the pressure back on *him*. The Antichrist had his enemy right where he wanted him, and checkmate now seemed inevitable.

***

"Anders, thank you for telling us how to get food," John said, chowing down on a plate of canned tuna and vegetables, with canned peaches for dessert. "I'm pretty sure we raided every local restaurant and market, and thank Jesus we did! None of us will go hungry!"

"Jesus *is* the one to thank, John. All that food was going to waste if we didn't take it. Everyone else is so infected with the sores they can't leave their homes, and many are too sick to eat. Jesus showed me the answer to our food problem. That's why we are eating well today!"

"We owe our cooking capability to Kathie," said John. "She suggested also getting stuff like pots and pans, silverware, and matches to start fires. Our pantry is stocked with everything we need!"

He was right. They stored all the canned foods down below where the cooler temperature would keep them safe. Kathie assured them canned meat would last indefinitely, so they stored piles of it, taking her word.

"And thank you to the soldiers for collecting all this wood for fires," Bruno said, chewing his food while he talked.

"Dear, stop talking with your mouth full," Mila said, reprimanding him. The big man's face turned red, and he dropped his head like a small child whose mother scolded him.

The others laughed at him. They could hardly believe Jesus allowed them to enjoy life so much before his return, giving them food to eat, and fire for cooking and keeping warm. This was almost too good to be true, and time would soon prove it was.

"Look at them so happy and enjoying their lives during the Tribulation," Hadassah said, as she and Michael sat unnoticed inside the cave, watching the group eating and having fun. "I hope this continues for them until Jesus comes." His expression told her it would not.

"Messai will go on a rampage soon because he knows the time is short, and more will die."

"But how is that possible while Yahweh pours out his wrath on him and his followers? The sores and whatever the second bowl contained. I thought..." Her words trailed off, and she stopped.

"Messai will rally and fight back, but Yahweh will keep the pressure on. His wrath will become more and more intense leading to the great final battle. I wanted you to see them like this before that begins. Now, you wanted me to show you this bowl, didn't you? What do you say we go check it out?" He flew before she had time to move, but she soon followed and caught up.

"Where are we going?"

"Fly with me, and you will find out."

He took the scenic route, passing familiar places, and allowing her to enjoy the journey before they reached their destination. They departed Jerusalem and flew south, then turned left and soared above the border fence until they saw the crossing point where they rescued the American soldiers. Memories of that night came flooding back, and they stopped to celebrate a miraculous victory.

Lifting off again, he took her over Galilee basking in the lush beauty of the green landscape which flourished during Israel's rainy season, then continued up the Golan Heights. He stopped again at the site where they rescued Trey, Rickie, Bruno, and Magnus. They talked about how intense that experience was, which gave him the opportunity to explain his role in what happened.

"I knew it was you!" she said. "Tell me all about it!"

"All I did was push two Jordanian military vehicles into a couple of rocks so they overturned. The hard part was deflecting those pain rays back toward the Chinese choppers. That was tough, but worth it when the pilots screamed as the rays hit them and their choppers exploded in midair."

She loved hearing his stories as much as he enjoyed telling them. Now that he had taken her with him a few times, they meant even more to her. Flying again, they passed over Camp Filon where she watched him orchestrate the connection between her uncle and Paul Johnson, then looked down at the military bunkers which housed six of their groups. She did not want the adventure to end, but realized he would soon show her the results of bowl number two.

He continued all the way to Banias where she and he, along with the Heavenly Host, helped Anders and Ally ward off the dragon's army, then celebrate their wedding. Still no revelation of the second judgment sent by Yahweh. She recognized the beautiful city of Haifa coming closer and looked forward to the gorgeous Mediterranean Sea that bordered it, a favorite view since she was a child.

The sight that greeted her eyes defied reality. The clear blue water was dark, crimson, and gloomy. "What...?" The word escaped her mouth, leaving the question unasked. She could not tell what filled the vast sea, but knew it was not water. Michael swooped down quickly, leaving her aloft, filled a vial with the red gunk, and returned to her before she could react. Taking her hand, he poured a small sample into her palm... *blood*!

"Michael, the red lines I saw when the angel poured out his bowl were *blood*! He turned the earth's water into blood!"

"Yes, but not all."

"Only the Mediterranean?"

"Every salt water body. Let's go lower so you can see what's happening." He took her hand, and slowly led her down till they flew just above the shore. Dead and rotting fish lay everywhere.

"Michael, this is awful. Have the sores healed so they only deal with one judgment at a time?"

"I'm afraid not, Hadassah. These aren't like the plagues Moshe and Eliyahu sent where the previous one ended when a new plague began. These plagues keep accumulating until they bring the full weight of God's wrath, and eventually lead to Jesus returning and fighting the great battle."

"Who can stand under the weight of such horror?"

"They will stand defiantly against Yahweh and his angelic host, including me. The plagues will weaken them, but they will rise and fight one more time. That battle belongs only to Jesus."

He had shown her enough again for one day. They soared across the Mediterranean, turned by the Red Sea, and continued south to Petra where Mordecai and Ben awaited them. The men would seek an explanation from them, as they always did, but no explanation would be given. After Jesus' return, Michael would gladly tell the entire story, but they would not care about hearing it then.

Earth's population reeled from weakened physical conditions caused by sores covering their bodies, and the infections and illnesses which naturally followed. Only believers in Jesus, the true Messiah, remained untouched by them. Every person who took the mark was now covered with the ugly, malignant lesions which refused to heal. Medical knowledge held no answers. Now the blood-filled oceans only intensified their horror.

Rossi started reassembling his army. Every member of AMPP reported for duty, not from loyalty, but because Messai gave the choice between double their previous pay for showing up or execution if they did not. The decision was easy. They were a ragtag group, ill and suffering, yet willing to do their job and collect pay, which would make them among the world's wealthiest people.

Their orders were clear: find and eliminate followers of the *false Messiah*, with enormous bonuses for every Smyrnian arrested and executed. Caiaphas returned to his position, as One World Religion leader, as did NWO leaders. Their goals remained peace and prosperity, but they believed those could only come when they ruled the world. World domination still required removing everyone who stood in their way. Messai met with Rossi and the trusted captains of his most effective patrols.

"Gentlemen, it pains me to witness your grave conditions. I cannot explain why the sores have not affected me, but I sympathize with you. When we accomplish our goals, I promise this disease will leave, and you will live in perfect health. Thus, we must unite as a mighty force which conquers the world!"

Halfhearted applause came from the sick and frail individuals sitting around his table. Even in their weakened conditions, they continued to buy into the lies flowing from his deceitful mouth. The world's populace slowly started believing them again, too.

"Citizens of our great planet, I stand before you today, not seeking your help, as I have often done, but to make you a promise. Never in history have people faced such opposition to achieving their greatest goals. Since I introduced my goal of peace and prosperity greater than you have ever seen, one catastrophic event after another has hindered our progress."

"The current physical pain and suffering, and our oceans and seas turning to blood again, are the worst yet. In light of those things, I understand your hesitancy to believe we can realize that goal, but trust me when I say we can, and we will. Today, our NWO heads and One World Religion leaders unite to redouble our efforts to achieve them. I humbly ask for your support as they do."

"AMPP just returned to work despite suffering the same condition which plagues you. I admire their commitment, and their belief in our objectives. They will give their all to change your future. Thus, we are revamping our search for rebels who seek to stop us, and reinstating use of the Capital Punishment Device to bring them to justice. A wonderful person dedicated to our cause informed Mr. Rossi, my Chief of Security, the disease does not affect those people. How he got that information, I do not know. But I now ask you to turn in anyone you see who is without sores."

"The day will come when your sores heal and the ocean's waters become beautiful and teem with life again. Join me, and let us believe together, for all things are possible for those who believe!" Remarkably, they did, and it all began... again.

***

Trey and Rickie left the cave with Omar, Ahmad, and Hala to secure some supplies. Since the latter three were Palestinian and the former two spoke Arabic well, they were natural choices for this mission. Blake instructed them to proceed with caution at every turn, and they promised to heed his warning.

This was their first time out in months, and the freedom and fresh air felt amazing. They realized they were taking a chance, but knowing the sores immobilized AMPP patrols made them feel safe, and almost indestructible. Blake's warning left their minds, and they strode confidently through the Muslim Quarter, without fear. They encountered few people, but saw some and waved from a distance.

They finally found a small market open for business. It sat on a normally busy, but now deserted street, the perfect place to purchase supplies. Trey and Rickie stood guard while the other three went inside. They heard them talking to the owner who was undoubtedly glad to have the business. His voice sounded weak and they knew he stayed open despite sores covering his body.

Omar wished him a speedy recovery and asked if he could help him. The man thanked him and told him no one could help his condition, so they walked out and rejoined their partners. Neither of them witnessed the man's body twisting about as he morphed back into Beelzebub, the dragon's demon prince when they left. The demon informed Messai who dispatched AMPP patrols at once.

"The disease is worse than I imagined," said Ahmad. "I don't know how that poor man is working."

"He's such a nice man," Hala said. "I wish we could help him, but we can't take him back with us and put the team in jeopardy. My heart breaks for everyone else who suffers like him."

"From what we have heard, that includes the entire world," said Rickie. To which Trey quickly replied, "Everyone except believers in Jesus, it seems."

"Let's take the long way back," said Omar. "The others will just think it took us longer than expected to find supplies. It should be wet because it's the rainy season, but the sun is shining, and it feels good out here."

"Perhaps we can walk out to the Garden Tomb!" said Hala, excitement in her voice. "I love that place and wish we could have stayed there longer."

"I don't think that's a good idea," Trey said. "Walking around out here is dangerous enough, but going outside the city walls is a chance we shouldn't take."

"Oh, come on, don't be, what do you Americans call it, party poopers?" Hala laughed as the three sprinted away from Trey and Rickie and darted through the Damascus Gate, bound for the tomb.

Before the two pilots could follow them, they heard a loud shout, sending shivers racing through their bodies. They knew someone directed the command toward their three comrades.

"Halt!"

The pair ran toward the sound and pulled up short, greeted by a horrifying sight. An AMPP patrol, covered in bloody lesions, and wearing short sleeves to lessen the pain in their arms, had tackled the trio and bound their hands behind their backs. They longed to charge in and save them, but counted thirty patrol members, fully armed, eyes searching for others nearby. They ducked behind a house and could only watch and listen as the men dragged their friends away.

Once the patrol was out of sight, they ran to the cave, which was only two minutes from the gate. When the group saw only the two of them sprinting toward them, they realized something was wrong and ran to meet them.

"What happened?" asked Blake. "Where are Omar, Ahmad, and Hala?"

Rickie tried to catch his breath before answering, but finally said, "AMPP got them."

"No!" Ally said, screaming for her friends. "We have to save them! Who is going with me?"

"Ally, we can't do that," Blake said in a comforting voice. "AMPP will have every available patrol guarding them and looking for us."

"He's right, Ally," Anders whispered, pulling his wife into a tight embrace.

"But you came for us when we were captured. How can we sit here and let Messai slaughter them?"

"Bruno and I will go, and we need you soldiers with us fully armed," said Magnus.

"We will go," Gabriel said, "but I need to tell you something. We exhausted our ammunition supply. When Thomas and I took down the three AMPP men, we used our last three rounds. That's why we didn't engage the patrol when they returned looking for their comrades. We continued standing guard with empty rifles, wanting to make you feel safe. I apologize for deceiving you."

The others stood there shocked, realizing their ultimate human means of protection was gone. They couldn't possibly face AMPP unarmed.

"Let's go up front and watch the news on our phones," said Blake. "You can bet Messai will hold a press conference to announce their capture. Perhaps cameras will also show the AMPP presence around the Mount and temple. That will tell us whether we stand a chance of rescuing them."

They walked toward the entrance, hearts broken for their friends and colleagues. Many of them would not be there had it not been for the three Jordanian soldiers who helped when they needed them most. Trey and Rickie, Bruno and Magnus, and the twelve American marines owed their lives to them. Anders and Ally grieved with them, as he remembered this from the scroll and could hardly bear the thought of what they would endure. He would keep that information from his wife and the group. *Please do not tarry, Jesus* he whispered as they walked.

CHAPTER 6

Hadassah met Michael at their usual place atop the mountain, excited about their next journey. She sat waiting for a few minutes before he arrived, uncharacteristically late. His look told her this was no normal meeting. Fear, dread, sadness, she could not find the right word to describe it. He sat down beside her and looked out over the mountains, lost in thought.

"Michael, what's wrong? Is it time for the third judgment? Is it worse than the first two? Are we going again to watch the third angel *do his thing?*"

He normally made fun of her for asking so many questions, but not today. She even tried to sound humorous with the last one, but he still sat unmoving, staring into space like he had not heard her. She touched his arm and whispered softly, "Michael, are you okay?" and he looked into her eyes.

"I can't hide what will happen today and tomorrow from you, Hadassah. Every part of me wants to keep you from knowing, but I must tell you."

For the first time since he revealed his true identity to her, she did not want to hear his news. If only he would keep something from her this once, but he would not. She braced herself and waited.

"Three of our close friends will die tomorrow, but what they experience before they go will be far worse than death."

Her mind ran amok with thoughts of which three he was talking about. Could he mean Ben, Miriam, and her Uncle Mordecai? No, if her uncle was included, he would have also said family. She considered others, then the truth hit her and she breathed their names.

"Omar, Ahmad, Hala..."

"Yes," was all he could say. Her eyes became misty.

"Don't tell me anymore, Michael; please, I don't want to know. Tell me after Jesus returns, when it won't matter. Please don't tell me now."

He spoke again, as though he heard nothing she said. "AMPP captured them today, and almost got Trey and Rickie, too." Anger covered his face as he said the name. "*Beelzebub* deceived them and allowed AMPP to take them. When I get my hands on him again, I will..." His voice trailed off, his mind filled with vengeful thoughts. That day would come soon, and he was ready.

"Tell me if you must. I promise to be strong."

"AMPP will torture them tonight, trying to force them into giving away the others' location, and they will begin with Hala while Omar and Ahmad watch. Then they will turn to them."

"No! Michael, we must do something! We can't sit here and let AMPP have their way with them!"

"I would if Yahweh would let me, but we cannot interfere during the second half of the Tribulation. The Bible says things will turn horrible for all who believe in Jesus after the Rapture. That's the price paid for failing to trust in him before it happened. The good news is, the moment they leave this world, they will see Jesus and live with him forever where everything is perfect. Messai will have his moment, but he and his followers will experience eternal punishment, which is far worse than anything he does to them tonight. We must pray they have enough strength not to tell him or AMPP about Zedekiah's Cave."

***

Omar, Ahmad, and Hala sat on the cement floor with their hands still bound behind them, not knowing what would happen next.

One thing they knew for sure was the next day, at 3:00 p.m. they would die in the guillotine. They discussed that among themselves.

"It's my fault. I was the one who wanted to visit the tomb. If we hadn't gone outside the city wall, they would never have spotted us and captured us."

"Hala, stop blaming yourself," said Omar. "I suggested we take the long way back, remember?"

"And I sure didn't stop you from going. In fact, I ran with you as fast as I could."

"You're right, Ahmad, we all took off together, even after Trey tried to stop us, and now here we are. What do you think it will feel like tomorrow?"

"We won't know until then, Hala, but we have to stay strong and shout the name of Jesus until…"

"Until the blade drops," said Omar. "I suppose we have all night to think about that."

They heard the key enter the lock, then the door opened, and four AMPP goons entered the room. Each looked hideous covered with boils, but all were enormous, with the appearance of pure evil. The four men walked over to them, and the largest and most evil looking, spoke, his voice gravelly.

"We need some information from you three, and we can get it the easy way or the hard way. That part is your choice. If you tell us where the Smyrnians are hiding, Messai will spare your lives and set you free. But if you refuse to yield that information, we will use all means possible to extract it from you. If that happens, you will beg for the device long before 3:00 p.m. arrives."

"We will give you no information," Omar said defiantly. "I can only tell you we were once like you, but Jesus, the true Messiah, gave us real life."

"You speak bravely now, but that may change before the night ends. However, if you give us the information, we will still allow all three of you to walk free. How about it, you two? Does either of you want to act more wisely than your friend? Talk quickly, and do not waste our time!"

Ahmad and Hala sat silently, heads down, not looking at the men. Neither said a word.

"Speak, now!" the gargantuan man said, reaching for them with a huge hand. "You have one minute to decide whether you live and go free, or suffer and die. Mr. Messai renamed the Chamber of the *Hearth* next door the Chamber of *Horrors*. Maybe that will help you decide. One minute!"

Hala spoke first. "I can only speak the name of Jesus. He gave me true freedom, and I will never deny him. Neither can I tell you anything about my fellow believers in him."

Ahmad followed her. "I only wish you were as we are, except for these chains. But the only way you can have that is by believing in Jesus, the Messiah. It is too late for that because you received the mark and are eternally doomed. Whatever happens to us, tomorrow afternoon we will be with Jesus. You will suffer far worse for all eternity. I say only his name: *Jesus, Jesus, Jesus!*"

That name sent the man into a rage as he commanded the other three, "Bring her to me!"

"It takes big men to hurt a woman! How about being real men and trying one of us!" said Omar.

"You made your choice, and it starts with her. The good news is, you get to watch. And to show you Mr. Messai's generosity, give us the information any time, and you still go free."

***

"We should at least go see how close we can get," said Trey. "Maybe Messai will get cocky and let down his guard. Magnus, what do you think? You worked for the man. Isn't there something we can do?"

"I can tell you what will happen, if that's what you want me to do. You're right, I worked for Messai, one of his top men, and I have commanded patrols on nights like this. First, security will be on high alert, what AMPP calls *Code Red*. That means no one, and trust me when I say *no one*, is getting near the temple, or the Temple Mount tonight. Hundreds of AMPP personnel will stand guard, and after our previous rescue, they will specifically look for us."

"Second, and I hate to tell you this, Messai's henchmen will do everything in their power to get information from our three friends before tomorrow morning. His torturers will do whatever they can to force them into giving up our location. If they survive tonight, they may be unrecognizable when they face the guillotine tomorrow. Those goons enjoy torturing their captives."

"Please allow us soldiers to scout out the situation. We will be careful and return quickly with information about their security and any possibility of getting close enough to attempt a rescue."

"Only if I go with you. I understand better than any of you how to deal with this situation."

"If Magnus goes, I go," said Bruno.

"May I say something?" Rickie asked. They all turned to look at him, wondering what he may know that they did not. "I heard one man say something as they took them away today: *Chamber of Horrors*. I'm sorry I waited to tell you that."

"That's what Messai called his torture chamber when I served as a patrol captain."

"We never saw that when we were there before you came and rescued us. They left us alone in the room until you showed up. I'm sure we would have stayed there until 3:00 p.m. the next day."

"No offense, but you are not Smyrnians. He wants us more than anyone and has done all he can to find us, even bombing two of our safe places. I hate to think how far he will go tonight to get that information from Omar, Ahmad, and Hala. He will begin with her. Messai always starts with the women and makes the men watch, hoping they'll break seeing her endure such brutal torture."

Crying came from some of them, anger from others. The soldiers with Bruno and Magnus left and promised to return soon if they could not get near them. All others gathered in the Freemason's Hall to pray through the night and next day for their friends.

***

Two men dragged Hala into the next room and threw her face down on the floor. Pain shot through her body as her knees hit the concrete, followed by her chin. Someone pulled her hands forward, spread them apart, and fastened them securely with a rope stretched from the wall. Next were her feet, secured the same way. It took all she had to keep from crying out from being pulled so tight.

Facing the floor, she could not see what was happening, but she felt everything. One man ripped her shirt open, exposing her back. The night air felt cold on her bare skin without the protection of her shirt. She asked Jesus for strength to face whatever was coming. Voices came from outside the room, followed by a command from inside.

"Bring them in and chain them to the wall!"

She knew it was Omar and Ahmad. They struggled against their captors but fought a losing battle as Hala heard the chains snap shut around their wrists and ankles. Omar called her name, but it sounded like he was far away. His words echoed softly in her head before the door opened again. She recognized the voice this time... Messai.

"So, we finally meet. You escaped my mansion the night your friends rammed my car, killed some of my men, and injured me, but you will not escape this time!" He spoke to Omar and Ahmad. "She gets the cane until one of you talks. You can stop us and save her anytime by telling us where we can find your other friends. Do that, and all three of you go free."

"No!" Omar said, his voice breaking into a sob.

"Soak the cane for the greatest punishment! Now again, will you tell me what I need to know?"

"Tell them nothing!" she said, her voice loud and strong. Neither man spoke.

"Okay, men, they seem to have escaped the sores, so let's inflict them ourselves. You may begin."

Hala stiffened awaiting the blow, then tried to relax so her back would not be so taut. *Wham!* The heavy, wet cane slammed down on her back, tearing her skin, and creating pain like she had never experienced. Omar and Ahmad watched her hands and legs jerk uselessly against the ropes.

"Again!" Messai said, his voice evil and diabolical.

The cane smashed into her back again, and she almost screamed from the pain, but squeezed the ropes to help choke back an agonizing cry.

"Wait," Messai said. "Tell us where your friends are, Hala, and this will stop. That is all it takes."

He knew her name! Of course, he was the Antichrist whose knowledge and power came from Satan himself. *Jesus, why are you letting them do this to us?* She quickly erased the thought. Prayers for strength raced through her mind, and she knew Jesus heard them.

"Gentlemen, how about you? Will you really allow your friend to suffer such punishment simply because you refuse to give us one small bit of information? You can stop this, if you will."

Both longed to do whatever it took to save their partner and friend from this brutal beating, but realized they were powerless to stop it. They also understood they were next, whatever that meant.

"Again! And do not stop until one of them talks."

The beating continued until her mind could take no more, and she mercifully lost consciousness. The men stopped, and left her lying on the cold concrete bruised, bleeding, and unconscious, then turned their attention to the two shirtless men chained against the wall.

"Would either of you like to talk, or shall my men start again?"

Omar spoke. "You may kill us, but the one you cannot destroy will destroy you! His name is *Jesus*, and he will return soon to..."

Messai's own hand slammed into Omar's stomach, stopping him before he could finish, and knocking the wind from his lungs. Another punch landed, and he threw up. Messai moved quickly to avoid the spew coming from Omar's mouth. "Men, I release this job to you, and I trust you will perform it well. Please inform me if they tell us what we need to know." When he left, the torture continued with Omar. The man reiterated he would stop if Ahmad revealed where the Smyrnians were hiding. If he did not, his turn came next.

"We enjoy this, but it is unnecessary," the man said. "Mr. Messai has been more than generous with his offer to release you, but you must accept his generosity. Any word for me?" Silence...

A fist landed on Omar's chin, followed by another on the opposite side. He felt blood spurt as his lip burst from the blows. Another punch directly to his nose snapped his head back into the stone wall, causing everything to go black. Cold water splashed in his face and awakened him.

"You're not getting off that easy," the man said, then spit in Omar's face and laughed. Ahmad tried not to, but looked over at his friend's face. If he didn't know who it was, he would not have recognized Omar. Blood ran down his face dripping from his chin. His nose was obviously broken and his eyes were rapidly swelling shut. Both lips looked like they would explode any minute.

Wham! Wham! A metal bar slammed into each shin shattering both tibias. Omar slumped as his legs would no longer support his weight. "Will you talk now?" Only groans came from his mouth. Messai's goon stepped forward and unleashed a knee to Omar's groin, and he blacked out again. If consciousness returned, he would beg time to pass quickly and for 3:00 p.m. to come.

The man turned to Ahmad who braced himself and prepared for what was coming. He would never give away his friends. He had hoped to remain alive until Jesus came, but that would not happen now. *Come quickly, Lord Jesus* he muttered just before the first punch landed.

***

The soldiers left with the two big men and walked toward the Temple Mount. What they saw shocked all of them, except Magnus. He tried to tell them what they would find, but none would listen to him. One hundred yards from the Mount everything was blocked. They walked the entire perimeter but found no path of entry. Beyond that they observed what appeared to be thousands of AMPP personnel covering the Mount and surrounding the Temple. The importance of this night was showcased for anyone who dared approach. They searched for a way, but finally gave up and returned to Zedekiah's Cave to tell their comrades the grim news.

"We found it exactly as I told you," said Magnus. "No one will get near the Mount tonight."

"All we can do is pray for our friends to find strength in Jesus to face death tomorrow," Blake said.

"That isn't all we can do. We must pray for them to find strength for what they suffer tonight. I have seen the punishment, and inflicted it, as well. Many men and women do not survive the torture. Whatever happens, I hope they have the courage to not divulge where we are."

"I have no question about that," said Ally. "They will never give Messai that information."

"My heart breaks for them," Beth said, then the group returned to prayer. It was their only option.

***

"We must go tomorrow," Michael said to Hadassah, low enough so no one would hear. "We will leave at 2:30 p.m."

"2:30 p.m.? That's an odd time. We usually go early in the morning."

"Shh... keep your voice down. Let's go somewhere we can talk." He led her to their favorite spot atop the highest peak surrounding Petra.

"Now tell me, Michael, why 2:30 p.m.?" Then the truth came to her in an instant.

"That's right, Hadassah," he said, reading her mind. "Yahweh's angel will pour out the third bowl the minute Omar, Ahmad, and Hala are killed. His anger when his servants are slaughtered by Messai intensifies now with each one. But I have some good news."

"How can there be good news when the Antichrist will murder our friends tomorrow?"

"Yahweh has a special surprise for you when we arrive, but He forbade me to tell you what it is."

"Michael, why is Yahweh so good to me? I don't deserve it."

"You are highly favored among women, Hadassah, and Yahweh sees your heart. You chase after his heart and have performed your duty *during such a time as this.*"

She buried her head in her hands and wept. "But Michael, I am so unworthy. I am only a woman who loves Yahweh and who longs to do his will and serve him with my whole being."

"That's why he honors you. We will leave from right here tomorrow at 2:30 p.m. Be on time, so you won't be late for your big surprise!"

She assured him she would arrive before 2:30 and shuddered with excitement, even as her heart grieved for her friends. Her mind raced wondering what tomorrow would bring. What was her special surprise? *That's enough, Hadassah. Get some sleep because tomorrow will be a big day!*

***

Hala awakened, still bound, face down on the floor in the Chamber of Horrors. Pain wracked her body, and her back felt like it was ripped to shreds. *Omar? Ahmad?* She called out softly, hoping no one would hear her. No response came until a faint groaning came from behind her.

"Hala, I am glad to hear your voice. I feared you died when you lost consciousness."

"Ahmad!" Her pain briefly gave way to joy at hearing her friend's voice. "Omar?"

"He hasn't regained consciousness yet. They beat him mercilessly. Be thankful you can't see him. I feigned passing out and endured a few more punches without flinching, so they gave up. My pain is horrible, as yours must also be, but I fear Omar did not survive. I called his name many times, yet he has not replied or moved. It was horrible Hala. They shattered his face and broke both legs. I don't understand how he endured it as long as he did. But neither of us talked!"

"There was no way we would give the others away. Jesus gave us strength!"

"Will you two keep it down so a guy can get some rest?"

They both said it at the same time. "Omar?!"

"Who did you think it was? Of course, it's me, you crazy people. Whoa, I hurt all over, can't stand, and my shoulders are out of socket holding my weight. I didn't realize I weighed so much until now. I can't see, and my face feels like it has been run over by a truck."

"I assure you all those things are true, my friend. They treated you very badly, and I thought they killed you."

"Nope, I am very much alive, and I have an idea. Let's sing praises to Jesus! Who cares if they hear us now? Does anyone know the time or whether it is daylight or dark?"

"I can't tell in here, but it's time to worship Jesus! We will see him soon. Are you guys ready for that?"

"More ready than you realize."

They began singing and praising the name of Jesus so loudly they did not realize the time was 2:45 p.m., nor did they hear the door open and several men enter. As the men removed their bonds and dragged them from the room, their singing did not stop. The device loomed before them as they went, but Jesus awaited them in minutes. This was the most exciting day of their lives!

Michael and Hadassah arrived at Yahweh's temple for the third time during this series of seven judgments. They bowed and worshiped, then looked toward the five remaining angels who stood solemnly, holding bowls filled with Yahweh's judgment, and waiting for something to happen. All five bowed their heads in silence for a brief time, then lifted them and burst into song.

Hadassah realized it was 3:00 p.m. in Jerusalem, and her friends had died, causing silence followed by celebration as they came to meet Jesus! The third angel stepped forward and beckoned her to come. *Me?* she wanted to ask. Instead, she stepped into the temple court and stood beside the mighty angel who dwarfed her in stature. Her surprise awaited, but what was it? Her heart beat so loudly she thought it may jump out of her chest. The angel stood motionless, and Michael smiled.

People came toward her laughing and rejoicing as she strained to see who they were. All three appeared in front of her at the same time: *Omar, Ahmad, and Hala!* Yahweh allowed her to be the first to welcome them home! Tears streamed from her eyes as she witnessed the amazing experience of believers slaughtered by Messai coming home! Hala stepped forward and embraced her, followed by Omar and Ahmad. Hala spoke through a smile of pure joy.

"Thank you for caring enough to tell us about Jesus. If you had not shared his good news with us, we would not be here. Now, we must go, but we look forward to seeing you again soon!"

The temple doors opened partially, and a nail-pierced hand reached through to receive them. As they entered, another angel placed sparkling white robes on them, and the hand led them inside. Hadassah realized it was Jesus but could not speak, although inside she was rejoicing. The doors closed, and she turned and looked at the third angel again. He moved quickly, leaving the temple court and zooming toward earth faster than the speed of light.

***

Immediately following the executions, Messai traveled to the airport and boarded his private jet for a flight to Vatican City. He sensed a storm brewing among his latest proselytes there. Gregory's attitude reeked of rebellion and revolution and must be squelched before it went too far. That is exactly what he intended to do in no uncertain terms upon his arrival.

The jet landed, and the driver picked him up and drove him to his headquarters, the pope's former office and conference room inside the grandiose Apostolic Palace. Changing the structure's name was a priority and must happen soon. The word *Apostolic* glorified their former religion and focused on followers of the false Messiah, who they previously worshiped. *Palace* was a good word, certainly one that fit his status as god of the One World Religion, but it may still need to go.

As he walked into the building, potential names floated through his mind. Messai's Mansion… House of God… the Royal Residence… None really connected with him, but he had plenty of time to think and could seek advice from his religious leaders if needed. Entering his office, he summoned Gregory and a select group of his *pawns* to a meeting. He despised the name *cardinals*.

They joined him and sat around the large conference table. He alone needed to speak today.

"Gentlemen, I left our last meeting with concern about your attitudes and actions. I wish to thank you for uniting with our One World Religion, which has benefitted you greatly. However, I remain uncertain about your devotion to me as your god and your commitment to our cause. You must understand no division or rebellion is acceptable and will be met with swift and severe punishment. I assume you have watched some executions of rebels in the Capital Punishment Device?" Their reaction showed they had all been subjected to those times of unspeakable horror.

"Several things will happen soon. The name of this building will change to something more current and appropriate. I have considered such titles as *Messai's Mansion*, which fits the place which serves as my headquarters outside Jerusalem. A title such as *The Royal Residence* makes sense for the palace where the world's leader resides. But in keeping with the historical purpose of this structure and our religious theme, especially as it relates to me, my favorite designation is *House of god*. After all, this will be the house where *god dwells* when I am here."

He looked for their reactions, and saw them clearly. They said nothing, but the looks on their faces betrayed their inner thoughts and feelings. Anger, disgust, shock, and his personal favorite, *hatred*. Purpose accomplished, he would now drive home his point and send them away from his presence.

"So, gentlemen, you must pledge your allegiance to me and support and worship me as your risen messiah." Only a few weak nods told him where they stood. "Please confirm that *all* of your adherents have received the mark and placed my likeness in their homes for daily worship. My people are checking records in every country worldwide, and AMPP will soon pay visits to all whose names are not listed. I assure you those visits will not be pleasant."

"Now, I would love to continue, but the leaders of former world religions who now make up our One World Religion will arrive within the hour. *Gregory*, I expect you to join us for that meeting." He relished the anger flaring inside the man when he used his name rather than his official title and loved embarrassing him before his pawns. "That will be all, gentlemen, until we meet again. You may see yourselves out." They left quickly and reconvened down the hall once again.

***

The third angel emptied his bowl of Yahweh's wrath upon the earth. Hadassah could not see the contents, but crimson streaks crisscrossed the previous ones. Dark red layers now inundated the thick black vapor covering the earth, and Hadassah heard them gurgling. That made little sense, but she kept watching. Faint screams rose as human beings experienced another escalation in Yahweh's wrath. This time, she would receive the meaning before she and Michael returned home.

The mighty angel arrived with greater force than Hadassah had witnessed before. Hurricane-force winds blew her over and sent her tumbling. This judgment had unique significance, which she realized was in direct correlation to Yahweh's anger at the deaths of Omar, Ahmad, and Hala. Now joined again by Michael, she kneeled and listened as the third angel spoke.

"Just are you, O Holy One, who is and who was, for you brought these judgments. For they have shed the blood of saints and prophets, and you have given them blood to drink. It is what they deserve!"(Revelation 16:5-6)

Hadassah looked at Michael and mouthed, *drinking water?!* He nodded affirmatively.

"The angel is right; they deserve it!" she said, thinking of her three friends murdered by Messai.

Her mind spun with pictures of people covered with bleeding, oozing sores, unable to work, wracked with pain, and blood-filled salt water and beaches littered with dead, rotting, stinking fish. Now, bubbling streams of clear water ran with pure blood instead. How much worse could Yahweh's judgment get? She would get those answers as he revealed them. The time of the end drew near! Another voice interrupted her thoughts. It sounded like the altar speaking.

"Yes, Lord God, the Almighty, true and just are your judgments!" (Revelation 16:7)

The angel turned and entered the temple, leaving angels four through seven remaining. Hadassah realized the third adventure with her mighty heavenly warrior friend had ended, but four remained. She had questions for him when they departed, but another sound came first: the low rumble from below. It raised another question for which she needed an answer: *what was that?* Then he motioned for her to follow, and they were bound again for Planet Earth. He provided one answer.

"Do you remember reading about the martyred souls under the altar in Revelation, Chapter 6?"

"I remember, but not well. What does it have to do with what we just saw and heard?"

"The souls under the altar cried out, asking Yahweh to judge the inhabitants of the earth and avenge their blood. So, they asked for his revenge to fall on earth's entire population."

"That's it, Michael! Everyone on earth faces Yahweh's vengeance for murdering those who believe in Jesus during the Tribulation. Messai isn't the only one who pays the price; they all pay!"

"And after their cry, each was given a white robe and told to wait a little longer until the full number of their fellow servants were killed, just as they had been."

"The white robes placed on Omar, Ahmad, and Hala before they entered the temple! They are among the martyrs who are now waiting to greet other believers in Jesus who will be killed. And they will only wait a little while longer because the end is near!" Understanding that excited her!

"Don't overlook the last line in verse 11: *...were killed just as they had been.*"

"Messai's Capital Punishment Device," she said, anger flaring in her voice.

"Yes, but not only the device... everyone murdered by the Antichrist from the time he took power. Doc Sanderson, who you recognized on our first trip to heaven, was the first Tribulation martyr. AMPP murdered him the night he believed in Jesus. It began with him and includes every person killed by Messai from then until now, yet a few remain."

She now understood the reasoning behind Yahweh's final judgments and why the timing was important. Three judgments down, and four judgments remaining. Six years down, and one year to go. The reality of how close they were to eternity with Jesus really hit her for the first time.

***

Messai crossed the room and pressed his glass into the refrigerator's water dispenser ready for a cold drink as he awaited his next group of attendees. Thick red liquid flowed down the side of his glass and accumulated slowly on the bottom. The glass fell from his hand and shattered on the floor, blood splattering onto his patent leather shoes. The pope and cardinals heard the commotion and raced back in. They threw open the door and found him staring at the floor.

"Your Majesty, are you okay?" asked the former pope. He despised using that title for Messai.

Messai turned with a glazed look on his face, but regained composure quickly and spoke loudly. "Of course, I am okay, fools! I told you to stay out of this room!"

The other men now stared at the glass. "Blood," said one, then walked to get water from the sink. He turned the handle, and blood oozed from the faucet.

"Sir, Moshe and Eliyahu caused this before, but how has it happened again?"

"How am I supposed to know?" he yelled.

We thought you knew everything, ran through their minds. They left and made a frantic ten-minute trip to Trevi Fountain, hoping to find the popular tourist attraction still bubbling with crystal clear water. But their hearts sank when they saw the same thick red liquid filling it and streaming down its sides. Would the madness never stop? Yes, it would end soon when Jesus came and they joined Messai in the fiery place of eternal punishment. That madness would be far worse.

CHAPTER 7

With the world's supply of drinking water now exhausted, people became desperate, as they had twice before during these seven years of tribulation. But this time blood did not go away, and the water did not return. The earth transformed into a dystopian-like society, as people covered in hideous, malignant sores stumbled through abandoned towns seeking water, but found none.

One difference involved bottled water, which remained clear, and gave Messai an idea before the situation reached a crisis stage. He confiscated every container of water and other drinks AMPP could find, and made sure he and his men got theirs before anyone else. They needed strength to fulfill their duty. Then he rationed it, giving limited free water to people whose supplies ran out.

His motivation was twofold: first, regain the world's confidence in him, and second, discover Smyrnians, who surely needed water, too. He required the mark for those who received water, and *they* did not have it. His evil ploy may have worked if their water was affected by the third judgment, but it was not. Believers in Jesus had all the fresh, clear water they wanted or needed.

One place a water shortage should have existed was Petra, but water was in abundant supply there. That desert area averaged a meager fourteen inches of rainfall per year, but most of that fell during the winter's rainy season. Now rain fell regularly, and the water system worked to perfection, collecting more than enough. Jesus gave his people everything they needed to survive.

In Zedekiah's Cave, the water flowed continuously from the area known as Zedekiah's tears, so named for Judah's king who reportedly wept as he fled Jerusalem through the cave when the Babylonians captured the city in 586 B.C. The water never stopped running, nor did it ever turn to blood. It remained clean and pure. The Smyrnians living there enjoyed the refreshingly cold liquid every day. It also reminded them of Zedekiah's grief while they grieved their friends' deaths.

This day, as they sat and talked, everyone felt it. The rumble under their feet started again and was much stronger than before. The ground shook and their feet bounced, as they heard cans of food rattling below. The sound increased until they could no longer hear one another speak for a few seconds, then stopped.

"The time is getting closer," John said. "If the pastor was right, we have nearly one year before Jesus returns, but the quake won't wait that long. Anders, did you notice anything about timing?"

"Before Anders answers that, John, how many more times are you going to say, 'If the pastor was right?' We know without a doubt he was right!"

"That's not what I meant, Blake. I'm just trying to figure out when the quake will come, and I believe it will happen in less than a year. It's hard for me to stop thinking like that when I focused on those things my entire career."

"I get it, John," said Anders, "but for now, you understand more about the earthquake than I do. I don't even remember a quake from the scroll, but Jesus never shows me those things until they happen. We depend on you and your knowledge of quakes for this one. That's one thing you bring to the team, and right now, we need it."

Everyone could tell that pleased John. "I wish I had my equipment with me, but I still have a lot of experience right up here, which we can depend on." He tapped his head and smiled. "What I know for sure is, this one will be more catastrophic than any of us can imagine. Remember what I said, thirty times stronger than the first one. And it will strike worldwide again and devastate the entire globe. No one will escape it, and the world will be a different place when it ends."

"That is unfathomable to me, honey, but I trust all that knowledge and experience *right up there*," Kathie said, then smiled at him and tapped his head, too.

"What does Revelation say about this quake, John?" asked Bruno. "It sounds like you know."

"Let me show you all how my expertise matches scripture. The Bible mentions three earthquakes during the end time, but what I described to you before was based on my studies, not on what the Bible says. I understand how destructive a 10.0 quake will be if one ever hits. The science of seismology tells us that. In the scientific community, we often talked about the possibility of a 10.0, but doubted it would ever happen."

"So, after I said that following the first rumble, I read for myself what Revelation says about the third quake. Listen, and you will understand what I mean." He picked up his Bible and read Revelation 16:20. *"Every island fled away and the mountains could not be found."*

"You mean the earth will be flat?" asked Blake. "It's a shame I won't get to report that story!" They all glanced his way, and he said, "Come on everybody, I'm just having a little fun. Although, it would be kind of cool, don't you think, Anders?"

Beth smacked his arm. "Aren't you leaving someone out here? I could report that story better than you any day! *I'm* just kidding, sweetheart," she said with a grin. *"Or* maybe I'm not."

"If the quake is that catastrophic, it begs the question, do we want to stay in here when it hits? Being underground will likely mean *buried* underground."

"You're right, Steve, we need to talk about that," said Anders. "But I promise Jesus will show us what we should do when the time comes."

***

"Welcome back... *again*, you two," Ben said as he and Miriam, Alexander and Elizabeth, and Mordecai greeted Michael and Hadassah when they walked into Petra. "I trust you enjoyed another fun adventure today."

"We had a good time, Ben, but we also learned about some current worldwide events."

"Exactly how did you learn these things if you only walked outside Petra," asked Mordecai, ever Hadassah's protective uncle and rigid military man. "You need to explain yourselves again."

"No offense, Uncle, but these things are important, and you all need to hear them. How we learned about them is *not* important. Remember your promise to never ask again?"

Michael did not give Mordecai time to reply before sharing the news. "Horrible malignant sores broke out on everybody who worships Messai and took his mark, and they won't heal. People are in such pain they can't work, businesses are closing, and the economy is collapsing."

"*And,*" Hadassah said, jumping ahead of him, "salt water turned to blood, then fresh water. It's like Moshe and Eliyahu's plague, except this time the blood won't go away, and people are more desperate for water than ever!"

"The Smyrnians will die of thirst!"

"Oh no, Miriam. The blood affected all water, except believers. Ours is all fresh and clean!"

"That doesn't even make sense," said Mordecai. "How is that possible?"

"Everything is possible with Jesus, Uncle! It didn't affect our water here in Petra, did it? Besides, how do we even *have* water here in the desert? That doesn't seem possible either."

"Okay, niece, you made your point, and I agree." He walked over and gave her a warm hug.

"These plagues are not like the Egyptian plagues Moshe and Eliyahu replicated. Did you say the waters turned to blood at different times?"

"That's right, Ben," Michael said. "If you can call these *plagues*, first came the sores, then later salt water to blood, followed by fresh water. But these seem more like *judgments* from Yahweh."

"Do you think there will be ten of these *judgments*, like the plagues?" asked Elizabeth.

"No, only seven," Michael almost replied before catching himself and saying nothing else. Hadassah noticed that and shook her head ever so slightly at him. He mouthed, *close call.*

"There isn't much time left before Jesus comes, Elizabeth, so there may be less than ten. We may get that answer if these two keep going on adventures," Alexander said, smiling at the pair.

"I'm thinking seven," said Hadassah. "That seems to be Yahweh's number." She grinned at Michael, who put his hands on his hips and shook his head at her.

***

Aissa Messai finished meetings in Rome with his religious and government leaders, their primary focus finding out how the Smyrnians avoided sores and continued eluding AMPP. They celebrated the capture and execution of three Jordanians, but they were of little consequence. He wanted their leaders and was more determined than ever to root them out. Before leaving for Jerusalem, he berated and belittled the former leaders of Catholicism so much they hated him even more. He would execute them if he did not need them to keep their people in line.

Now back in his Jerusalem mansion, he summoned the only ones capable of finding the Smyrnians. He confined Levi, Chana, and all other servants to their quarters before meeting with his two chief princes inside the soundproof basement room where no one would hear them.

"You already know why I invited you here," he said with the dragon's growling voice. "We must find them. They have made a mockery of me, and now it appears *he* protects them from the disease and their water from the blood. Beelzebub, you did well deceiving the three in the store and allowing us to capture them. Belial, you led them to the gate where we could easily capture them. *But* how could you let the other two escape?"

"Your Majesty," said Belial, "we tried to make them run with the others, but they resisted our pull and eluded the patrol. Next time, I promise we will..."

"No excuses! Anytime we lure some of them out of hiding we must make it count. Do you consider yourselves weaker than the Host?"

"No, Your Majesty," said Beelzebub. "They are a formidable foe, but we have overcome them before and will defeat them once and for all in the great last battle, which is coming soon."

"Plans are underway for that battle, and you are correct, we *will* win! But can you please stay in the present and stop constantly talking about the future? We must get them *now!*"

"Your twelve princes are ready, and we can hardly hold back the horde. They got another taste of blood as you tortured and beheaded the three. Now they want the others as much as you do."

"Who among the princes can devise a plan to trap them? Perhaps we should talk about who we can rule out. Baal cannot help because sexual temptation seems useless at this point."

"I agree, Your Majesty," Beelzebub said again. "Leviathan and Lilith cannot help either. The rebels will not travel the bloody seas for Leviathan to target them, nor is Lilith needed to attack children."

"Nor will Mammon or Orias work against them," Belial said. "No greed exists in them, and they have no interest in astrology. Such attacks would be completely ineffective."

"Paimon is out too," added Messai. "He has done amazing work for our master during the final years of history, but his help is not needed now against them or anyone else."

"That leaves four, besides Belial and myself. Shall I call them?"

"Yes, get them here now!"

Ten minutes later, Abaddon, Haborym, Legion, and Gog stood in the room, as formidable and powerful as the other two, and obviously just as pleased Messai chose them.

"Welcome to the team, princes. We have one priority: destruction of the Smyrnians. They have eluded us too long, with *his* help. Is *he* stronger than our master?"

"No!" shouted the six demonic creatures standing before him.

"Is his *host* stronger than you?"

"No!" they said again, streaks of lightning flashing from their grotesque bodies.

"So tell me, what will help us draw them out, then capture and destroy them?"

Abaddon stepped forward. "Your Majesty, destroyer is my name, so if my fellow princes can lure them out or uncover their whereabouts, I will completely annihilate them as I have many others!"

"You have already served well, Abaddon. Nothing would please me more than delivering them to you and allowing you to perform that task like no one else can. Thank you for arranging the Capital Punishment Device and bringing the perfect men to serve as executioners and torturers. Observing their work against the three was priceless. I only wish they had given up the others. But the beatings still gave me great pleasure. You even allowed me to throw a punch."

"That was a small sample of my work, Your Majesty. Give me other opportunities, and I will multiply that tenfold!"

"I want to witness that! Now, Legion, we cannot do this without you. We must have a million members of our demonic horde under your authority ready to attack when we uncover their hiding place. Your troops did their job well when they led the five at En Gedi to AMPP. Without their help, the capture would not have happened. We need that same performance this time."

"Do not worry, Majesty, the horde will not fail you." His pride showed at Messai's commendation.

"I trust they will not. Must I remind you about his Jewish followers escaping your grasp when they fled from us, or the great number of troops you lost?"

That humbled the mighty demon, remembering how a great defeat preceded his triumphant victory.

"I also recall hearing of two men your troops possessed two thousand years ago, but *he* cast them out and freed the men from your clutches. I only mention those times as reminders of *his* power. I do not believe you will allow that to happen with these Smyrnians. Once your troops take hold of them, deliver them to Abaddon. He and AMPP will take it from there. Remember, we are a team!"

"Haborym, you must stand ready at all times. The master endowed you with a special gift: his fire. One blast from you can destroy them all at one time! If we locate the entire group together, I will allow you to incinerate them like the master has often torched other rebels."

The beast unleashed a blast of flames from his mouth and hurled them around the room with his hands, leaving no doubt he was ready. Although a demon of few words, he never failed when the time came for action.

"Hold on beast of fire; save the flames for *them*! Gog, your work has been ongoing for years, and you led the Chinese Communist Party right into our trap. Now you must keep them on track and lead them into the final battle. That will remain your role while we handle the Smyrnians."

"It is my honor, Your Majesty. I enjoy controlling their weak minds, while allowing them to believe they dominate the world in their own power. They follow like pawns in my hands."

"Excellent!" said Beelzebub. "Your army is prepared, Majesty. To the battle, princes!"

They screeched and howled, Messai joining them, with millions of the horde in another place.

In Zedekiah's Cave, Anders leaped to his feet from a deep sleep, and Ally jumped up beside him.

"What was that, Anders. It hit me too, and shook me harder than anything has since I believed in Jesus in Evan's dorm room that night."

"I remember from the scroll! Messai just assembled every demon at his disposal to find and attack believers. We must tell the others."

They ran side-by-side calling them, but didn't find anyone until they reached the Freemason's Hall, where they discovered everyone already talking excitedly. Each one experienced the same thing. Something evil occurred, and it affected them. The cave was unusually cold. They all sensed it and started shivering, which had not occurred for nearly three years.

"What happened, Anders?" Beth asked. "I haven't felt this chill since that night in the box truck."

They all realized who brought the chill: Messai. Now, if they only understood what it was about.

"The scroll showed Messai coming after us with the full force of the dragon's army. That time has come. I don't understand how Jesus kept us safe here, but his protection may soon disappear."

"You're right, Anders. I had no doubt things would change after AMPP captured and killed Omar, Ahmad, and Hala. And I guarantee you they didn't just kill them; they brutally tortured them, hoping they would tell them our location. Messai is like a wolf. When he gets a taste of blood, he always wants more. And we all know whose blood he wants."

"But he has hunted us for a long time, Magnus. What makes that any different now?"

"He now knows the sores didn't affect us because he saw for himself our three comrades had none. The bloody water didn't affect us either. I don't understand it, but Messai realizes we are protected from it too. When his anger reaches the boiling point, his wrath explodes. He realizes the time is short, so he is making his move now."

"Will Jesus keep protecting us here, or will we have to move again?" Ollie asked. "If we must move, where would we go? I don't have that answer this time."

No one noticed Gabriel sitting against the wall carrying on a conversation with someone, as Michael had often done. Anders said, *we need to pray*, and they did. They needed an answer from Jesus like they had received at crucial times before, but it seemed far away on this night. The chill worsened, meaning the enemy was getting closer to discovering their location. Jesus would come soon, and they hoped he would let them survive until he did.

***

"Hadassah, the time has come for judgment number four. Are you ready for our next journey?"

"Yes! Say the word, and I will fly with you any moment!"

"Let's go. We don't want to miss this one because it will be the worst yet." They took off running toward the mountain realizing they had no time to spare.

"Hold on! Where do you two think you're going in such a hurry? If you're off on another *adventure*, I want to go with you. I need to see what you do on these trips."

"Uncle!" He caught her by surprise and left her thinking of ways they could get away from him.

Michael spoke up and saved her from lying to the man who raised her and adored her. She never wanted to tell him an untruth. He did not mince words.

"With all due respect, sir, Hadassah and I must take these journeys alone. Jesus always shows us something when we go and has commanded us to bring no one with us. So, sir, you cannot come."

Mordecai's face flushed with anger, a look both had seen before. "I am still your superior officer, Michael, so if I demand to go, you cannot stop me."

"I understand that, Aluf sir, but..."

"However, I have seen how important these adventures are to you, so why are you standing here talking to me? It appeared you were in a hurry, so go. I will be here waiting for you when you get back." He winked, turned, and walked away. They ran, now with less time than before, and reached the mountaintop exhausted and breathing hard, but they must fly. After making sure Mordecai had not followed them and no one else was looking, they headed off to observe judgment number four.

***

Blake was fast asleep when he sensed someone close by. Whether he dreamed or this was real, he could not tell. A mighty being stood before him gleaming so brightly he could make out a form, but no face. Beth slept soundly beside him, unaware of what was taking place.

"Blake Thompson, I am Gabriel. Yahweh sent me with a message for you. Jesus called you to lead his people during this crucial time before he returns. Be strong and courageous, for he will guide you and strengthen you for this task. Attacks against his followers are beginning, and they need your help. Some will die, but you must save others. Follow what Jesus tells you to do."

"The Smyrnians must also find another safe place. The dragon and his horde will find you and come against you with all the forces of hell. Jesus revealed this to his servant, Anders Norstrom, but he doesn't understand it yet. When he does, you must act quickly. Listen and obey, Blake, for the Smyrnians' lives, and the lives of other believers, depend on you."

The angel disappeared, and Blake awoke, his mind contemplating what just happened. Perhaps it was only a dream since protecting his teammates consumed his thinking, or maybe it happened because Gabriel recently told them his name. Both made sense, but what if an angel did appear with a message from Jesus? He sent word to others; why not him? He needed to speak with Anders.

***

Meanwhile, invisible evil demons buzzed through the air searching for people who followed Jesus. Legion sent them to every continent, bent on discovering and destroying the enemy who prevented their master from ruling the universe. His demons would rule alongside him. Their bloodthirsty minds screamed for satisfaction, and only one thing would bring that: *their* deaths.

Haborym awaited word, destruction on his mind, too. His master instructed him to employ his greatest asset, torching places where *they* met, incinerating them inside. He could hardly wait to receive news which would propel him into action. The dragon entrusted his fire to him alone, and he relished every opportunity to destroy the beast's enemies using that gift.

There it came! Abaddon's voice entered his mind. There was no mistaking the gravelly voice which mimicked his master's own. Haborym tried to contain his excitement when he replied.

"Give me good news my fellow prince. How many have Legion's hordes found, and where?"

"They discovered groups meeting in many areas, and we start tonight in London, England. I have those locations, along with the times they meet, and will accompany you as the master ordered."

"I enjoy traveling with you, Abaddon. Princes rarely travel with each other, but we love crushing the master's enemies together. How soon can we leave? I can hardly wait to breathe my fire and watch them burn."

"You do the crushing, my friend; I only stand back, watch, and enjoy. We may leave anytime. Three houses in London unknowingly await your flames tonight. The horde will meet us there to keep them inside after you ignite the places. This will be fun!"

They stopped by Messai's mansion, informed him of their success, and told him their first mission would occur this night. The three celebrated, along with Beelzebub and Belial, then Abaddon and Haborym left for their destination. The party was just getting started.

***

Blake rose quietly to keep from waking Beth, then ran to wake his partner.

"Anders, did you dream tonight?" Anders stood, rubbing his eyes, and led him a few steps away.

"Nope, I have slept like a baby all night. Why did you ask me that, and why did you wake me?"

"Oh, it's nothing, really. You have heard from Jesus so many times, and with all that's going on, I thought he may have shown you more stuff from the scroll. We may need to make some important decisions soon to stay safe, and I want to make sure we do exactly what he says."

"You need to lighten up, partner, or the pressure will get to you. We need your leadership, so keep it together for a little while longer until our problems go away forever. Now, let's go back to sleep."

"You're right. Just let me know the minute you learn anything from the scroll."

"Look, I believe something is coming too, Blake, and it bodes badly for us. When it comes, Jesus will show me, and I will tell you. It may also affect other believers, so we should stay alert."

"I wasn't going to tell you this, but I either dreamed something, or the Angel Gabriel appeared to me a little while ago and delivered a message from Jesus."

"Okay, I'm awake now, so what did he say? If Gabriel appeared to you, what he said is important."

"Like I said, it may have only been a dream, because I spend a lot of time thinking about protecting us. Gabriel just told us his name, too, so I may have been thinking about him before I fell asleep. But if it was an angel, you're right, his message is important. That's why I'm talking to you."

"What does this have to do with me if he appeared to *you* and spoke to *you*?"

"He told me attacks against Jesus' followers will come soon, and we must save them by following exactly what Jesus tells us to do. Then he said *we* will need to move because the dragon and his forces will find us. Finally, he told me Jesus revealed all of this to you, and it will become clear to you, but by then we will have little time to act. However, *I* am the one who must listen and obey to save us and other believers."

"There you go again, partner, taking all that responsibility, and putting pressure on yourself."

"No, *he* told me that! They're depending on me, but I'm depending on *you* telling me what Jesus showed *you*!"

"Wait! I remember, and I see it clearly! Houses on fire, believers meeting inside, trying to escape, but something is trapping them so they can't get out! Jesus always shows me things right on time, meaning it either starts now, or has already begun, and will continue until someone stops it. That someone is us, so we have to do something!"

"Where is it, Anders? Do you see a place?"

"Nothing, only houses engulfed in flames, lighting the night sky. *Night*, Blake, it's happening at night while believers meet with their groups! But I see houses burning, so I fear we're too late."

Anders seemed entranced now, speaking to Blake from somewhere else as action took place.

"Tell me what you see. Think, Anders, do you see any landmarks that give you a location?"

"None, Blake, just a city in shambles, devastated by the nuclear war."

"Okay, a *city*, one destroyed in the war; that narrows it down. Let's name a few. If it's New York or Chicago, several landmarks still stand, which you should recognize."

"It isn't them, but it's a large city with automobiles driving on broken streets."

"What type of automobiles? Can you see people's faces to tell what they look like?"

"No, but they're all going the wrong way... and busses, tall, red busses. I've got it, Blake; it's London again!" he said, snapping out of his trance. "We have to tell Ollie and Amelia! Their family and friends who survived the earlier attacks still meet with other believers every week. Let's go!"

The minute they told them, both started calling family members but got no answers. This was just like before. They realized what their loved ones may suffer this night. Less than one year, and they would have survived the Tribulation, but in their hearts, they realized some would not.

Abaddon and Haborym laughed and howled with glee as houses blazed in London and Legion's horde surrounded them, preventing windows and doors from opening. Screams from inside filled them with delight until they ceased and the night became silent again. The Smyrnians must hear about this horribly exciting night. But they needed to find them first.

***

Michael and Hadassah flew quickly, but they were not moving straight up, as at other times. They traveled west across Europe, confusing her, since she understood they would go back to the temple in heaven to watch the fourth angel pour out his bowl. The spirit of Esther surged in her again, and she found herself in fifth-century B.C. Persia. The evil Haman convinced her husband, the king, to order Yahweh's people annihilated in every province of the empire. Someone must save them! Now, she was Hadassah again 2,500 years later as Jesus' followers tried to survive the Tribulation.

"Michael, where are we going? We're late and must hurry to reach the temple in time."

"Yahweh said we must pass over London first to better understand the fourth judgment. I don't know why any more than you do, so we will find out together."

They passed over Rome and sensed the evil of Messai's headquarters rising from the Vatican. France came next, then crossing the English Channel, and London came into view. She had heard much about the famed London fog, but now dark black smoke rose from below.

"Let's go lower and see what's happening." Getting closer, a horrible scene came into view; houses blazing with screams coming from inside. The people inside screamed a name, not in fear, but anticipation: *Jesus!* Believers burning alive, yet excited about meeting *him*! Then they saw *them*.

"Go, Hadassah!" Michael yelled, just as the two demon princes noticed them and screamed for Legion and the horde to come. By the time she understand what he meant, he was already far above her. She flew fast, but they flew faster, and drew close. Her heart raced as she struggled unsuccessfully to elude them. They were experienced, but she was new at this flying thing.

Michael turned around, then zoomed back toward her, screaming her name, but was too far away to reach her in time. The air turned cold, and she realized they were right behind her. She knew Michael could not help her and saw him pull up and stop. He left her at their mercy! Hadassah readied herself for their sharp talons to dig in and rip her to shreds, but felt nothing.

She dared not look back and continued flying in a desperate attempt to reach her partner. He pointed behind her, and she turned to look. A line of mighty ones formed between her and the horde. The demons reversed course and fled from Yahweh's Heavenly Host, howling and cursing. Michael motioned for her to come, and they flew without a word. Her heart pounded, but she knew they could not be late for their appointment. They arrived at the temple and bowed before the Lord.

The fourth angel already stood out front and ready to leave. Michael and Hadassah continued kneeling and watched the mighty angelic being leave with such speed he vanished in seconds. The force sent wind crashing into them, leaving him standing strong, and her sprawling ten feet behind, flat on her back. She now understood how the Host had arrived so quickly when she needed them.

Michael came and lifted her with his powerful arms. She looked toward the earth to see the angel, but he had disappeared from her sight.

"Michael, where did the angel go? Did he fly faster than our eyes can grasp?"

"Look elsewhere, Hadassah," he said, and she turned her head in all directions, finally noticing the streaking beam of light, but it was not going toward the earth.

"Michael, he is going toward the sun! The heat will incinerate him, like those believers tonight!"

"Just watch, as you did the other times."

She stared at the angel and directly into the sun. It should have blinded her, but it did not. The sun appeared no brighter than earth or any other planet to her eyes. It seemed she wore the most powerful sunglasses ever made, which dimmed its brilliance. She now saw the angel clearly as he flew near the universe's most luminous and scorching orb. He did not circle the sun as the others circled the earth, but dumped the contents of his bowl directly onto it.

The sun shone like Hadassah had never seen. Though she could not feel it, she knew its temperature had just increased exponentially. The invisible ozone layer appeared, a layer of ozone gas encircling the earth and acting as a shield from the sun's harmful rays. Already severely weakened, nuclear radiation from the war now finished it. She witnessed the sun's heat-producing infrared rays and skin-damaging ultraviolet rays blazing straight to earth with nothing to hinder them.

"Messai sent fire to destroy Jesus' people; now Jesus sends heat to punish the people who received his mark," said Michael, now understanding this fourth judgment better. "The end is near."

Screaming and blasphemy rose from the earth. She could not imagine how awful this judgment would be. One thing she knew, Jesus was in control, and she trusted him. *Come soon, Jesus.*

CHAPTER 8

"We have to stay a step ahead of them," said Blake. The group sat in the Freemason's Hall comforting Ollie and Amelia and discussing how they could obey what Gabriel told Blake.

"How are we supposed to do that if we don't know where they will strike next," Ollie said, his voice still filled with anger.

"Anders knows," Gabriel said. "That's how you figured out they would hit London this time, wasn't it?"

"He's right, Blake. I need to be alone with Jesus while you all pray for me. It's dangerous to leave the cave, but after we talked, he showed me I must meet him where he rose, the Garden Tomb."

"That is far too dangerous, Anders. Remember what happened to Omar, Ahmad, and Hala when they left the city, and they nearly got Rickie and me, too. Can't Jesus show you those things here? Go down below; you will be safe there."

"If Anders believes that's what Jesus told him, he should go."

"But Gabriel, even you guys can't protect him now. You used all your ammo, so you're powerless against AMPP and Messai without weapons."

"That's true, Gabriel," said Magnus. "But remember, you're not just fighting AMPP. Your battle is against the rulers, authorities, and powers of this dark world, meaning Messai and his NWO leaders. And you fight against the spiritual forces of evil in the heavenly realms: the dragon and his demons. I witnessed their power and found no man can overcome them."

"You're right, Magnus, *no man*. But we don't fight with the weapons of the world. We demolish strongholds through the mighty power of *Jesus*!"

"I don't need anyone's protection. Jesus told me to meet him there, so he will protect me. I'm leaving now and trusting you to pray until I return."

"Anders, are you sure Jesus told you to do this? I'll go with you, if you'll let me."

"No Ally, I must go alone and stay until Jesus tells me what we need to know."

She hugged him. "Then go, and I will trust him to bring you back to me."

"We'll all wait here for you, partner. Go, and I pray you return soon."

They followed Anders to the entrance, then he walked out into the dangerous world outside.

***

Aissa Messai flew to London the night of the attacks and released a statement informing the public he would tour the *burn zone* early the next morning. The number of homes torched by Haborym extended far beyond those belonging to Ollie and Amelia's family. Others they helped put their faith in Jesus also perished in his flames, but unknown to Messai, they went to their real home with Jesus. Messai stood before cameras and sore-covered reporters for the first time in weeks.

"Ladies and gentlemen, seeing this carnage grieves me deeply. I promise we will do everything we can to find those responsible and bring them to justice. To family members and friends of those killed, I offer my condolences. This is why we must renew our efforts to bring peace and prosperity to our world. These kinds of things will not happen in that world when we achieve it."

"Please remain patient as medical experts work to find a cure for the sores, and scientists work to discover a way to turn our oceans and streams back into the beautiful water which previously filled them. Continue worshiping me and enjoying the benefits of the mark as we await that day."

Beelzebub, Belial, and the other chiefs sat howling with laughter as he spoke. Haborym danced in the ashes of one house blazing fire from his mouth and proclaiming more victories in the days to come. Messai could hardly stifle a chuckle watching them. Reporters asked questions, and he gave terse replies to each, eager to fly on to Rome and his Vatican office. His princes would join him there as they plotted their next burn party. Let *his* people feel the heat, he mused within himself.

The sun broke over the city bringing more light than usual and beaming down on those gathered for his announcement. Reporters dropped their microphones and ran for their lives, their skin turning red when the blazing rays scorched their bodies, and the oppressive heat seared their flesh. The pain of severe burns on their already sore-covered arms and faces was unbearable. Only one remained unaffected by the heat: Aissa Messai. With cameras still rolling, he stepped to the microphone and spoke again.

"Ladies and gentlemen, I must end this question-and-answer session to protect the men and women who are in attendance. The sun suddenly began affecting our planet in unusual ways, blazing, and scorching people. I will travel to Rome and stay in contact with meteorologists, astronomers, and those involved in space exploration trying to determine the cause of this strange phenomenon."

"But I will say this before I leave. This continues the pure evil unleashed by the self-pronounced prophets, Moshe and Eliyahu, which they claimed their false god sent upon the world. I reiterate, no loving being could act out of such hatred and anger. It almost seems they unleashed these curses before they died for us to experience later. The sores, followed by our water turning to blood, and now this *sun* plague. Let us cry out against them together as we prove our ability to overcome through our own power and knowledge. Protect yourselves during this dangerous event. I will address you again from my Rome office the minute I have an update. Until then, stay safe."

***

Anders exited the cave outside the wall of Jerusalem, a short walk from the Garden Tomb. AMPP personnel caught his eye covering the entire area on every side. He could not possibly get past them without being seen, but he must obey Jesus, so he started walking. He passed through the middle of a large patrol, unseen, and untouched.

This reminded him of their earlier travels when Jesus made them invisible to AMPP. He remembered Evan acting like a kid and poking fun at guards who could not see him. That brought a smile to his face and a whisper to his lips, *I miss you, friend.* He continued until he reached the tomb, not seeing the two powerful members of the Heavenly Host walking on each side of him.

After entering through the abandoned gift shop, he stepped out and turned left toward the tomb. The place was quiet and more peaceful than when they were there before. He stopped in his tracks when the opening came into view. Brilliant light emanated from inside drawing him in like a magnet. He could not stop if he wanted to, but nothing would cause him to miss this meeting.

He moved steadily and resolutely toward the door, his heart racing, both from excitement and trepidation, the magnetic pull too powerful to resist. The radiance should have blinded him, but he looked directly into it, even though it grew brighter with each step. He finally stopped in front, now close enough to reach out and touch the light, but he dared not. A voice spoke from inside.

"Come in, Anders."

He stepped into the resplendent glow, and a charge flew through his body like an electrical shock. The charge seemed to propel him through the door and onto the rocky floor inside. To his right lay the two carved stone slabs, one of which held the dead body of Jesus until his resurrection. The protective bars previously installed for protection from sitting and climbing tourists were no longer there. Anders stood wrapped in Jesus' glory again, sensing his Lord's presence.

"Welcome, Anders, it is good to see you again. Thank you for staying faithful. I wish we had more time to talk, but you must save my people. However, important things first." Though Anders could only see a form, he could visualize Jesus smiling before he finished that sentence. "Angie and Evan said tell you they are doing well, and they hope you and Ally are happy." Now Anders smiled.

"Sit down," Jesus said, motioning toward the slab beside him. Anders reluctantly sat but could hardly keep from falling facedown before the glorious being sitting next to him.

"The time has come to reveal what the scroll showed you about this time." Another glorious one appeared and stood before him. Who was this? He expected no one but Jesus.

"Hello Anders, my name is Gabriel, and I stand in the presence of Jesus. I have come to help you understand what you saw." The voice sounded familiar, but Anders couldn't determine who it was. Maybe an angel he heard speak while he was in heaven? He had no time to think about it.

"Jesus showed you a place where the forces of evil will destroy believers, if the Smyrnians do not save them. There is no need to write it down because he stored it in your memory bank."

An image instantly flooded Anders' mind, a place, but he could not tell where.

"You must go back and share this with Blake Thompson, then devise a plan to rescue Jesus' followers from the enemy's hand."

"But how can we rescue them? We can't leave the cave and have no way to leave the country if they live outside Israel. Please tell me what to do."

Gabriel vanished, leaving Anders stunned and still trying to figure out whose voice he heard. Before he had time to consider that further, Jesus spoke again.

"Our time here has ended, Anders. The Smyrnians are a creative group, so they will figure out how to rescue my people. But we will show you details when they are needed. Go save my people."

Anders found himself alone inside the empty tomb, with its cold, gray walls. Jesus disappeared, and with him, his brilliant glory. No resplendent glow covered the door, and only silence filled the stone room. He realized he needed to move fast, so he stood, walked through the open door, and sprinted toward the street outside. In less than five minutes, he would arrive back at the cave.

***

With the depletion of the ozone, the world's condition deteriorated rapidly as the unimpeded sun blazed down. The radiation was so intense photosynthesis became impossible. Plants had already turned brown and would die within days. Farmers could not save their crops with irrigation systems pumping no water and clogged with heavy, thick blood. Without plant life, the food chain would quickly break down for animals and humans alike.

Anyone walking outside encountered the sun's unfiltered ultraviolet radiation, too. Severe sunburn occurred instantly on any exposed skin. The heat was so oppressive covering skin with enough layers to prevent burns was nearly intolerable. Air conditioning no longer sufficiently cooled houses, and overused electricity caused blackouts in many major metropolitan areas. People believed Messai's proclamation about Moshe, Eliyahu, and their god, and angrily cursed both them and Yahweh, failing to realize they were the ones under his curse for rejecting Jesus.

The earth was quickly reaching the ultimate crisis, and Aissa Messai needed to speak again. He did so from inside his office at the Vatican.

"Ladies and gentlemen, there can be no doubt we face a catastrophic time. The bad news is, meteorologists tell me our ozone layer is depleted, leaving the earth unprotected from the sun's damaging infrared and ultraviolet rays. Thus, we bear the full brunt of the sun's heat and DNA damaging radiation."

"The good news is, the ozone layer has experienced significant critical changes throughout the history of the universe, but it has repaired itself every time. While each such incident could be viewed as critical, human beings have survived them all and continued to thrive. We will survive this one, too, and life will be better than ever. Experts are working hard to discover a way they can speed up that process. Protect yourselves, and trust the scientists to do their job. We must further ration our water supply for now, but I assure you, we will get through this together."

Somehow, people covered with malignant, bleeding sores, having limited water to drink, and now suffering significant burns and heat-induced illnesses from the fiery sun still believed his lies. Only believers in Jesus understood the truth, and he hated them for it.

***

Anders walked inconspicuously toward Zedekiah's Cave, taking care not to attract attention to himself. No AMPP personnel noticed him as he strode through their midst. He enjoyed the security provided by Jesus, even though he could not see the mighty angels walking with him. Still, when he neared the entrance, something told him to keep walking, which made no sense, but he did. Above him, Beelzebub and Belial floated along covering Jerusalem for their master.

"Look," growled the chief demon, "he is one of them! But notice who protects him; the Host."

"Yes!" said Belial. "We can take them and him!"

"Not yet, Belial. We will follow him and let him lead us to their hideout. When he reaches it, the Host will leave him, and we will inform the master."

"Why not just summon the patrols and let them charge in and take them all at once?"

"He has protection, so I am sure they have it, too. We will check things out when he arrives, then proceed from there. If no protection exists, we and the patrol will handle it immediately! But if it does, we will leave and return with the master's full army. They will not stand a chance!"

Anders entered the Damascus Gate and walked through the Muslim Quarter, while the two demons followed. He prayed Jesus still protected him, but realized he could not wander around all day. Finally, all options exhausted and hoping his intuition only came from nerves, he went back through the Gate and continued along the city wall until he reached the cave. Not knowing what else to do, he ducked inside.

Beelzebub and Belial flew to the entrance and touched the protective shield. They glanced at each other, then left quickly for Rome. The shield could stop AMPP, but it was no match for their army.

"Are you sure no one followed you?" Blake asked his partner.

"I'm not sure at all, Blake. Something didn't seem right, and when I got close, I felt compelled to keep walking. I hiked all over the Muslim Quarter and finally had no choice but to enter the cave."

"We can't worry about that now, so let's call the group together and get to work. It sounds like a group of believers out there somewhere depend on us to save their lives, and we must move fast."

"Make sure Trey, Rickie, Gabriel, and the soldiers come. They will be pivotal to the rescue."

"By the way, have you seen Gabriel? I looked for him earlier and couldn't find him. We thought he may have followed you, even though he was unarmed. He seemed concerned about you going."

"No, I haven't, Blake, but..."

"But what?"

"It doesn't matter; it's not important. What does matter is rescuing those believers before Messai reaches them. We have a lot to do, partner, so it's time we get back on the battlefield!"

Blake thought nothing more about the dropped sentence, but Anders followed him, reflecting on the mighty angel's voice in the tomb. *No, it couldn't be*, he mused, and shrugged it off... for now.

***

"Yes, Master, it was Anders Norstrom, no doubt about it. We never let him leave our sight."

"The cave! I knew that is where they have been hiding! No other place around there can hold so many people. They are ours now!"

"We would have taken him, majesty, but the Host protected him. When he ducked into the cave, we checked the entrance, and found it covered with a shield, definitely Michael's handiwork, because we have seen it before. Your men cannot penetrate it, but our princes and the horde can!"

"Excellent! Then we must plan the attack immediately! Abaddon, Haborym, and Legion can carry out assaults on houses, and you two can lead the charge against *them*."

"Excuse me, Your Majesty, capturing *them* is more important than anything else right now, so I say all the others can wait until we complete this mission. We need the princes and horde to ensure they do not elude us again. Legion commands the horde like no other, Abaddon is the ultimate destroyer, and Haborym's fire succeeds when all else fails. Imagine them burned alive inside the cave with no way to escape, sir. I recommend we lead the entire army into this battle."

"That is why you are the chief demon, Beelzebub. Belial, what is your opinion?"

"I completely agree with my fellow chief, Your Majesty. And I would add one thing: the Host may well show up for this one to protect *them*. If they do, we will need all the firepower we can bring."

"You are right, Belial! We cannot go against the Host with a small unit. We will win the war, but we need to capture or eliminate them and win this battle before we do."

"It will also surprise me if *he* does not show up to lead the Host," said Beelzebub.

"You refer to Michael."

"Yes, Your Majesty. You know how badly I want him, but you also understand his ability and power when he leads the Host. Let us plan for that probability and call the army to battle."

"Come!" Messai screamed.

The dragon roared and appeared with them, sparks flickering from his mouth. "You found them! Great job! All three of you are correct about leading the full army into battle and never allowing them to leave the cave. We can either destroy them inside or capture them and take them all straight to the Device."

"We will decide that when the time comes," said Messai. "Now, let us call the troops together in Jerusalem and prepare to annihilate our greatest enemy. I will be present to watch them die!"

The call went out, and soon Abaddon, Haborym, and Legion were on their way to Jerusalem, followed by the other princes and millions of the horde. This time the Smyrnians would not escape.

***

Michael called Hadassah to an emergency meeting, which she understood was unlike their recent times together. The tone of his voice betrayed the urgency of what was coming.

"A great attack will take place, and it may require me leading the Host into battle. The Smyrnians' lives are at stake, and the situation is dire, but we will avoid conflict if we can."

"I'm ready, Michael. Tell me what you need from me, because I'm up for the fight!"

"You can't go with me to fight against the horde, Hadassah. It's far too dangerous."

"Have I not proven myself a worthy warrior? Please, Michael, I want to help protect our friends!"

"You are worthy, but not ready for this. However, you and I will go first to prepare the way."

"I hope we go to the cave because I haven't seen our friends in a long time."

"We will see them, but they won't realize we are there. And I will introduce you to *my* favorite colleague," he said with a smile, leaving her wondering who he meant and what they would do.

***

"Where are Gabriel and his men?" Blake asked as the meeting started. "We need their military experience to help us plan this rescue. I don't have a clue how we can pull it off, but they can offer good advice and suggest ways to get wherever those believers live."

"Blake, don't forget Rickie and I have military experience, too. We were pilots, but that doesn't mean we have less expertise than they have for ground operations. And this rescue won't happen without a plane and pilots. We can't get to other countries any other way."

"I didn't mean to leave you guys out. Both you and they need to plan these exercises; you for the flight, and they on the ground. That's why we need all of you here."

"We don't have much time because the attack will come soon," said Anders. "But there's another problem we need to resolve as we plan for this one. My intuition tells me something or someone invisible followed me here and discovered our hiding place."

"Beelzebub and Belial, the dragon's two most powerful demons," Magnus said. "I heard their names several times and how mighty they are. If they followed you, I'm sure they know where we are and have informed Messai. That means they are planning an attack against us right now."

"Where is Gabriel?" Blake asked impatiently. "Will someone get him, please?"

"I saw him and the men go down below as I walked to meet Ally after I came back from the tomb."

"You knew we were meeting, Anders, so why didn't you stop them?"

"I don't know, Blake, but they looked like they were doing something important, so I let them go."

"We'll start without them and talk about travel first. Trey and Rickie, you're up. Any ideas?"

Michael and Hadassah arrived and walked through the middle of their meeting, unnoticed. Her heart filled with joy, and a wide smile broke out on her face. She walked to some and pretended to embrace them, even as they talked. But Michael waved her on toward their destination.

"Here's where we go down, Hadassah, and where you will meet my colleague." He pointed down through the hole leading below, and she refused to wait, jumping through the opening before him, and landing with a thud. He followed quickly to make sure she was okay. When they heard voices and the sound of work ahead, she started moving fast, amazed at her night vision in the cellar. Michael grabbed her and pulled her through a door into a stone structure which looked like a house.

"Hello, partner, I thought you would never get here. You must be slowing down in your old age."

Hadassah saw the man leaning against the rock wall but dared not say anything yet. He and Michael obviously knew each other well and continued their banter before he introduced him.

"Hadassah, allow me to introduce you to Gabriel, my partner among the Heavenly Host."

She stared, an astounded look on her face. "You mean, Gabriel, Yahweh's messenger angel?"

"You expected someone else?" the mighty angel asked. "What has Michael told you about me?"

"That doesn't matter. We have work to do, but it sounds like your men are already doing it. Hadassah, Yahweh sent Gabriel here much like he sent me, placing him in an American military unit and bringing him to the Smyrnians. You played an important role in that, remember?"

"I do, and I recall seeing you, but I didn't realize you were... *Gabriel*," she said, whispering, still in awe of him.

"He has delivered many messages to our comrades, and now works to uncover their escape route. The sounds you hear are his men reopening a tunnel which has been closed for hundreds of years."

"Some people call this place Zedekiah's Cave because the story goes it provided his escape route from Jerusalem when the Babylonian army destroyed the city two and a half millennia ago. Others say that is only legend and the cave is merely the place Solomon or Herod quarried stones to build Yahweh's temple. The former are correct, and Zedekiah's getaway tunnel exists, but it was blocked years ago. We must reopen it so the group can elude the attack that is coming soon."

"Show us your men's handiwork and let's see what still needs to be done."

Gabriel led them out and down a corridor, lit with flashlights, and ending at a wall which was barricaded years earlier to prevent anyone from going through. The soldiers hammered away at large stones stacked and sealed, covering the opening, but their progress was slow, much too gradual to finish in time for the people living above them to escape.

"Men, let's stop and head back upstairs. Jesus called our team to save believers around the world who will suffer the same fate as Ollie and Amelia's family if we do not act quickly. I have friends who will work while we are gone. Head on up and tell them I will be there soon."

"Okay, Michael, it's your turn. I know your power outshines ours, so I trust you will have this wall down when we get back." His men would never believe that was possible.

After they climbed back up and were out of hearing, Michael smiled and said, "Okay, you heard the angel, let's get to work."

She picked up a sledge hammer so heavy it nearly pulled her backward when she swung it.

"No, no, that is far too much work; let me show you how it's done." He pulled back his fist, and prepared to slam it into the wall, causing her to jump back. "That's also too much work." Then he placed one hand on the stones, pushed gently, and they collapsed into a pile of rocks.

"Michael, how did you do that?" she asked, staring at the pile. "I'm sorry, I forgot who you are."

He laughed at her and walked into the tunnel no one had seen for years, as light shined, allowing them to see clearly. "Come on, let's check this thing out. We need to know if it goes all the way to where Zedekiah and his officials came out. If we find more blockages, we'll remove them, too."

"*We* will remove them? Don't you mean *you*?"

"We're a team. Regardless what either of us does, we both share the credit."

They walked through the entire passageway until she saw light rays ahead. The exit! They popped out in a valley past the mountains surrounding Jerusalem. How far had they walked?

"Yep, this is it!" he said. "After Zedekiah exited here and fled, the Babylonians captured him and took him to Babylon, where they slaughtered his sons before his eyes, killed his officials, and put his eyes out. Pretty evil, huh? Messai is even more evil, and he wants the Smyrnians more than anyone else. We must lead them to safety and protect them from him. Let's go back now so Gabriel can show them their pathway to freedom!"

They made the long hike back and climbed out into the cellar. She wondered how long they had been gone and checked her watch. Ten minutes? Impossible! That walk must have taken hours. She looked at him and realized Yahweh's warrior angel did the impossible again. She loved hanging out with him and could not wait for the next part of this adventure.

***

The world continued to suffer from horrific sores, a lack of water, other than the bottles Messai rationed, which were rapidly running out, and a fiery sun with nothing stopping it from scorching the earth, and them. They turned their anger toward Yahweh, a being they did not believe existed.

Messai led the charge, even as he planned a massive assault which would destroy his most hated enemies who *did* believe in Yahweh and his son, Jesus: the Smyrnians. That all-important attack consumed his time, but a quick press conference followed by public service announcements shown every thirty minutes each day fanned the fires of hatred. His brief live statement set the stage.

"The enemy of everything we believe in bears responsibility for these assaults on humanity. Moshe and Eliyahu unleashed plagues which claimed many lives, which they attributed to their false god called Yahweh. They emerged from the wicked cult called Smyrnians. These people continue using those evil powers to perpetrate heinous attacks, while bowing to the same malevolent being."

"I urge you to keep your faith in me and our goal of peace and prosperity as we work to find and eliminate our common enemy. My assistants are close to achieving that as I speak. I denounce the Smyrnians and their so-called god and ask you to join me. Our troops should destroy them any day, and I promise to inform you when they do. When that happens, the plagues will cease."

Simple, pertinent, inflammatory, and hope-inducing, all rolled into a neat package. People worldwide believed their sores would disappear, oceans, lakes, and streams would turn clear, and the sun would return to normal when their savior removed the Smyrnians. So, they berated *them*, cursed their god, and worshiped and prayed to Aissa Messai.

***

Gabriel and his men finally joined the group discussing ways to conduct a rescue effort in another place while they were trapped in a Jerusalem cave. They heard Jesus' command through his angel *Gabriel*, but received no instructions for carrying it out. Blake led the discussion.

"Trey and Rickie, you're our remaining pilots after we lost Paul and Bradley and the Israeli pilots moved to Petra. Your experience flying missions is unmatched, but you can't fly without a plane, and we have no way to get one."

"Can the Israeli soldiers help us? We couldn't have rescued Anders and Ally without their help."

"Not a chance, Trey," Ollie said. "Their superiors were onto them. That's why they couldn't give us food and had to find another way to help."

"Maybe they can find some other way now," Beth said, shrugging her shoulders.

"We can't even reach them to ask now," said Blake.

"Jesus told us to do it, so he will provide a way," Anders said matter-of-factly.

"It's time for Ben's call, and we need their input. Trey, Rickie, and Gabriel, come with me. We can only get signal near the entrance, but only a few of us need to go so AMPP won't see us if they're hanging out up there. We'll come back soon." Blake's phone rang when they arrived.

"Ben, I'm glad you called, because we need help. Jesus sent his angel, Gabriel, to both Anders and me and told us we must rescue a group of believers before Messai kills them. They already burned Ollie and Amelia's families to death, and it appears others will be next. The scroll showed Anders their location, and he will remember it when we need it. We have to go, but we have no plane to fly. We need a miracle!"

"Blake, this is Mordecai. Perhaps I can help with your miracle. We abandoned three military bases following the nuclear attacks on Israel, including one IAF base with a couple of bombers and helicopters, *and* one 707-320B left behind."

"A 320B is available? I wasn't aware the IAF used those. Which base?"

"Tel Nof. We stored nukes there and couldn't take a chance on personnel staying with other nukes flying. So, we got everyone out and left everything there. How we got the 320 is my little secret."

"I don't care how you got it; I'm just glad it's there. It will get us anywhere we need to go if they left fuel, and it's still good. Tel Nof is about thirty miles from us, right?"

"That's correct, Trey. You and Rickie can get the thing running, and it will get you anywhere within a 5,000-mile round trip. You can also carry 150 passengers, which hopefully means you can rescue an entire group of believers. If you have contact information, call the leaders and ask them to get their people to a central location where you can land, then fly them back to Israel."

"That is literally a lifesaver, Mordecai. We'll try it and pray Messai and AMPP don't catch up to us. More believers will soon die, if we don't hurry. On behalf of every one of them, thank you."

"Don't thank me; thank Jesus. Only he could arrange something like this. Do you remember what he said to you when he showed you the Chinese valley?"

"*Get them out.* I will never forget, and you're right, he's saying that again this time. Blake, we need to get back and start on this right away."

"One more thing, Ben. Anders believes Messai knows where we are. I won't take time to tell the story, but please pray for Jesus' protection. If they reach us before we can get away from the cave, we're all goners. And we still don't know where to go, so we need lots of prayer."

"We'll get right on that, Blake. Call or text me if trouble comes up. I got your last text down below, so I hope that will happen again. We can quickly call on everyone here to pray any time."

"I will, Ben, and that may happen any minute. Magnus is certain Messai has every demon under his control, and they are planning to come after us right now. We have some major decisions to make which can't wait. We'll talk to you in three days, if not before."

CHAPTER 9

Aissa Messai sat in his Jerusalem office awaiting his demon princes. He could hardly resist charging Zedekiah's Cave leading multiple AMPP patrols to blast through Michael's shield and destroy the Smyrnians hiding inside. The Antichrist had waited a long time and experienced many disappointments, but this would be well worth the wait, and he planned to enjoy every minute.

He walked outside and looked down at the *device*, dreaming about them standing in line, each beheaded individually, he himself pulling the lever. The vision brought such pleasure Messai briefly considered rejecting any thought of killing the group inside their hideout, but he realized the demon princes were right. If that opportunity presented itself, he could not pass it up.

Walking back inside, he found Beelzebub and Belial standing behind his desk. Their evil smiles revealed wickedness which could only come from hell itself. There was no doubt they were ready.

"I assume you were daydreaming, Master, fantasizing about the device ending their lives."

"Yes, Beelzebub, the idea is nearly overwhelming. Belial, do you have a progress update?"

"Your army is ready. Abaddon and Haborym will arrive soon, followed by Legion and his troops."

"We inspected the cave, Master, and found the entrance penetrable by our strength or Haborym's flames," Beelzebub added. "Michael has power over humans, but his inventions cannot stop us."

"When we burst through, all the princes except Legion will guard the entrance so they cannot get away. He will swarm them with the horde and overwhelm them before they realize what happened. The little demons stay thirsty for blood, so they will be hard to stop. However, if you prefer we capture them and lead them to your device, they will honor your wishes."

"That thought tempts me almost beyond my ability to withstand it, Belial. We shall decide when the time comes, but annihilating them matters most, whether there or here."

The two aforementioned demonic princes joined them, clearly excited about destroying their enemy. Neither wasted any time giving their input.

"Your Majesty, I request permission to perform my specialty and destroy them myself. If you want them to die horrific deaths, I will ensure that happens and allow you to watch."

"Ah, Abaddon, I love your enthusiasm. You will certainly use your ability to destroy them, although we will need to contain the horde and allow them some fun, too."

"Imagine fire filling their underground *prison* and consuming them as they desperately try to escape the flames. Their screams will fill the air as they perish."

"Your fire is always appealing, Haborym. This event is so important, we will all obliterate them together, including the horde. They deserve their opportunity, as well. It sounds like our plan is ready, and we only await Legion and the horde. They will arrive soon."

***

The group walked back into Freemasons Hall and shared Mordecai's information with the others. Blake would contact leaders everywhere to arrange a pickup time and location. Trey and Rickie would head to Tel Nof after plans were finalized and get the plane ready to fly.

"I agree with rescuing other believers," Anders said, "but we may need to save ourselves first. Messai will come for us soon, so we must decide what to do. If we wait, he may kill us in here."

"My men and I may have found our answer," said Gabriel. "Come with me and I'll show you what I mean. We could be gone all night, but we need to know if it works because our time is short."

"Rickie and I, Magnus and Bruno, and Ollie and Amelia will stay here and make plans for rescues," said Trey. "We may work all night too. Can your men stay with us?" Gabriel nodded his approval.

"Let's go," Blake said. "Anders and Ally, John and Kathie, and anyone else who wants to come, bring your lights and follow Gabriel."

Michael and Hadassah stood by helping some climb down through the hole. Doing that while invisible was fun, and they laughed their way through it. Beth would have fallen if Hadassah had not caught her. John came down clumsily, and Michael saved him from injury. Soon they all stood wondering what Gabriel couldn't wait to show them.

"Come around the house," he said and walked ahead, leading the way. When they neared the opening, he stopped just short. "The wall which stood here was installed to block the exit tunnel, but when we removed it, guess what we discovered? Friends, welcome to our escape route," he said proudly. "The work isn't finished yet, but if we all work together, we can accomplish it quickly."

He shined his light toward the opening, then stepped inside. They heard him gasp and ran forward till they reached him. Gabriel regained his composure quickly, knowing his fellow archangel had done his miraculous work again.

"I'm just kidding," he said with a smile. "Before you enter, let me explain. Most people do not believe King Zedekiah fled from the Babylonians and Jerusalem through this tunnel. To many, the story is nothing more than legend. Follow me and decide the truth for yourselves. I must warn you again, the walk will take hours. Only go if you think you can make it."

They all followed him into a long passageway which continued far beyond what their lights showed. They walked for five hours before finally glimpsing rays of light shining ahead. Gabriel continued until they stood near the opening which led outside. Their faces revealed the shock they all felt, everyone except Anders who instantly recognized this scene from the scroll.

"Where are we?" asked Blake.

"South of Jerusalem, headed toward the desert," Gabriel said. "We angled right just before the Temple Mount, went under the southern city wall, continued below the mountain, and reached this exit near Jericho. Zedekiah and his army walked this same ground over 2,600 years ago. The Babylonians captured them in the Plains of Jericho, possibly trying to reach and cross the Jordan River after they exited the cave where we are standing right now."

"I hope that isn't bad news for us," John said. "If Messai knows about this, we're toast."

"We can't worry about that, John," said Blake. "If they attack the front entrance, we will either leave through this tunnel, or die up there. That sounds like a clear choice to me. How about you?"

John shrugged and nodded his head, as all the others agreed. After stepping out and looking things over, they entered again and began the long walk back. The time was 2:00 a.m. now, and exhaustion set in. When they returned at 7:00, the entire night would have passed.

***

"One question comes to mind," Messai said, speaking to five demon princes after Legion arrived with millions of the demonic horde. "My men entered the lower level and found only a limited space enclosed by solid walls, much too small for their group. However, we should still confirm there is no other opening. Legion, send your troops to search until they are certain no exit exists."

"You are right, Your Majesty. We should take every precaution to ensure escape is impossible."

He immediately sent ten thousand of the horde to conduct a thorough search. The tiny demons buzzed away, salivating, driven by bloodlust. Messai warned if they encountered the Smyrnians, some must stay and prevent them from leaving, while others returned to lead him and the princes to them. Seeing their thirst for blood, he finally sent Legion after them to ensure that would happen.

"We must not wait to attack. Once Legion reports on any potential getaway route, we should proceed at once. I recommend thousands of the horde stand guard around the entrance today, prepared to call us anytime should they attempt an escape. Then we attack at dark."

"I agree with Beelzebub," said Belial. "Everything is ready, so there is no reason to wait."

"Abaddon and Haborym?" asked Messai.

Both agreed, and they made plans to conduct the all-out assault that night. They would unleash the power of hell against their enemy and annihilate them once and for all.

"I would like to make one suggestion. If we capture them alive, let's bring them here for execution. Legion's horde can drag them to the device, where Abaddon will pull the lever. Other horde members can carry their bodies and throw them on the altar, and I will ignite and incinerate them instantly, as you, Beelzebub, and Belial watch."

"I love your plan and your enthusiasm, Haborym, and we will consider it should everything go as planned. But if anything goes awry, we will be forced to kill them there."

"Yes, Your Majesty, my fire will serve the same purpose inside the cave, and I will probably enjoy that even more," Haborym said, smiling and bowing his head before his master.

"Then all is decided!" said Messai. "My two chief princes, go join Legion in his search so we confirm the enemy cannot leave their *prison*."

Beelzebub and Belial soared away, eyes peeled for any additional opening which could provide a potential means of escape from their enemy's underground prison. If they located one, they would stand guard there themselves with thousands of tiny demons waiting until they emerged. An additional incentive driving that decision involved Michael. If the Smyrnians needed protection, he would undoubtedly show up. Defeating him also would bring their greatest victory yet.

***

Both groups were excited to report their news when the company returned. After trying hard to speak first, Trey ultimately yielded the floor to Gabriel.

"We discovered and opened the same escape tunnel used by King Zedekiah 2,600 years ago," said the mighty messenger angel disguised as a military leader.

"You mean that story is true?" Ollie asked, obviously bewildered and amazed.

"Apparently so, Ollie. We walked five hours before reaching the exit and found ancient military artifacts along the way. And the tunnel ended near where the Bible says Zedekiah, his sons, and the army encountered the Babylonian military and were all killed, except the king."

"Finding a way out of here is great, but it puts us twenty miles farther from Tel Nof."

"You're right, Trey, but if Messai attacks, we must pursue our only means of escape," Blake said.

"All of you continue to mention Messai will lead the assault. I remind you again, a host of demons under the direction of the dragon's most powerful princes will come against us. Messai now controls the entire demonic horde and will send them en masse. We are powerless to stop them."

"And I continue to remind you, Magnus, the dragon, Messai, and their demons are powerless against Jesus and his Heavenly Host," Anders said, trying not to embarrass the big man.

"I understand that, but I also want to prepare everyone for what's coming. The demons are more powerful than any human being has ever witnessed. The assault will be like nothing you have encountered before, and if we do not leave, our deaths will be horrific. I recommend we go now."

"We're all exhausted," said Blake. "I think we should get a couple hours sleep before we leave. It's obvious you stayed awake all night, too."

"I agree with Magnus," John said. "Waiting is too dangerous. We should take all we can carry and leave immediately."

"Two nights before Messai would force me to marry him, sleep seemed impossible," Beth said, her voice soft and assuring. "When I felt the most helpless and alone, a voice came to me, the sweetest voice I had ever heard, and whispered what I now know are the words of Psalm 4:8. *In peace I will lie down and sleep, for you alone, Lord, make me dwell in safety.* I lay down and slept all night, the most peaceful sleep I could remember. We need rest before we go."

"Beth is right," said Blake. "We've all had a long sleepless night, and if we do make it out, we'll have another one tonight. We need strength to walk, which reminds me, where are we going?"

"Can I talk now?" asked Trey. "If you'll let me, I'll tell you what I've been trying to say, but couldn't find an opening." He appeared frustrated, but grinned anyway. "Rickie and I, plus the American soldiers have to stay at Tel Nof to conduct rescue missions. Mordecai said the IDF abandoned it, meaning people could live there unnoticed. Tel Nof is one of Israel's three top airbases and has space for a lot of people. We say it should become our new safe place."

"If it's another twenty miles from the exit, Trey, that means we need to walk fifty miles to get there," Blake said. "Can't we find somewhere closer?"

"Jesus prepared Tel Nof just for us, and Mordecai told us about it. Where else would a plane be sitting and waiting for us? We also need a place to bring believers when we rescue them, and it would help if we're all together. If we average three miles an hour, we can get there in two nights."

Anders raised his hand, and Trey motioned for him to speak. The group's respect for him and willingness to hear from him had grown with each passing day.

"I planned to tell you this when we reached the exit; I saw that in the scroll." They listened closely as he continued. "A military base appeared, but I didn't see the name. Based on Trey's description, I now recognize it: Tel Nof. We need to go forward with the plans of both groups."

"Do we all agree with that?" asked Blake. Everyone raised their hands, some more slowly than others, but the decision was unanimous. "Let's get some sleep, then we can wake up, load up, and hit the tunnel by 5:00 p.m. We should be out by 10:00 p.m. and walk all night toward Tel Nof."

"Shouldn't we post a guard?"

"No, Magnus, we should not," said Beth. "I trust Jesus to guard us, don't you? Let's all sleep like I did that night. Then we'll be ready when it's time to go."

The entire group walked to their spaces, crashed, and slept nearly all day. It was the best sleep any of them ever had. *Beth was right*, Magnus would think when he awoke. *Thank you, Jesus.*

Michael and Hadassah finished a conversation with Ben and Mordecai. When they were out of sight, he led her to their usual meeting place atop the mountain.

"What's going on? I know you didn't bring me up here for a hike. Something important is going down, isn't it?"

"The Smyrnians will walk through the tunnel tonight and leave the cave. The demons will attack and find them missing."

"But your shield. They can't penetrate it, can they?"

"Beelzebub and Belial will demolish it and lead their army in tonight, but will not find our friends. However, the possibility still exists they will find the exit route. The Host and I will stand guard there while Gabriel walks with them. If the demons come, we may face a major battle."

"I want to come, Michael."

"No, you cannot come this time. It is much too dangerous, and you could be killed. I could never explain to your uncle how I failed to bring you back and what happened to you. Besides, I'm fond of you, too, and refuse to let you die at Beelzebub's or Belial's hands. I haven't told you this, but they want you almost as much as they want me."

Her face grew pale. "Why me? I'm only a normal Jewish girl and a nobody, other than the Aluf's niece. Oh... is that why they want me?" she whispered.

"No, they want you because the spirit of Esther lives in you, the same Esther who once foiled their plan to destroy Yahweh's people in Persia."

She realized the truth after hearing his explanation, but it did not deter her will to fight. "I would rather face them and show them they can't overpower me," she said defiantly.

"I know you mean that, but Yahweh won't allow it, and neither will I. If this battle takes place, it will be so fierce we may not survive."

"Don't say that! You have to survive, because if you lose, everything is lost."

"I never know when we fight the dragon's forces. They are powerful and destructive, and are determined to remove me more than any other. Let's hope they don't discover the exit so we won't have to worry about a battle. But Yahweh may intervene before a fight starts."

"What do you mean?"

"If that happens, I will take you with me, how about that?"

153

"Say the word, and I'll be ready to fly!" They left and walked back down the mountain together.

***

Beelzebub and Belial flew south of Jerusalem near Jericho, overseeing the horde, who searched the landscape above them for any hole leading underground which might open into a cave. The pesky little demons zipped in and out, up and down, often smashing into cliffs thinking they saw an opening. The two princes could hardly keep from laughing at their clumsiness, but still applauded their effort. If an exit was there to be found, they would almost certainly find it.

Legion suddenly dove toward the place where one horde member zoomed in and disappeared. The other two princes saw him and flew closer, watching their cohort vanish into the same spot. They moved in and entered right behind him. All four stood inside a wide tunnel which seemed endless.

"Good work, Legion," Belial said. "This has to be it, so let's see where it leads. Follow me."

Legion commanded his demonic horde to stand guard outside while he and his fellow princes checked out the tunnel. The three sped through the passage at warp speed, arriving in the cellar within minutes. They stood below the opening listening for sounds from above, but heard none.

"There is no one here," said Belial. "This must not be the place."

"There is one way to know," said Beelzebub. "Stay here while I go up there and check things out."

He flew through the hole before they had time to reply and popped into the main cave. Floating along, his night vision illuminating everything, he barely contained his excitement at what he saw. Smyrnians and others lying everywhere sound asleep. He wanted to kill them where they lay, then saw one standing to oppose him, not a warrior, but Yahweh's messenger angel. How could he get so lucky? He prepared to attack the most meek archangel. If nothing else, Gabriel's demise would attract the ire of his mortal enemy and fill him with rage and thoughts of avenging his death.

"Gabriel," he said, deriding his foe with his tone. "I never imagined finding you here. Your friend, Michael, cannot save you now. Prepare to die!"

He hurled himself toward the archangel who stood his ground, neither moving nor flinching. *So easy*, Beelzebub said, roaring in for the kill. Gabriel extended his arms and stood staring down the mighty demon, who suddenly came to a screeching midair halt. A multitude of the Heavenly Host brandishing gleaming swords joined the messenger angel from nowhere, hovering over him before he rose to join them. The massive beast spun and flew toward the hole.

"You cannot protect them against our army. Bring your Host and bring Michael. We will do battle this night, and we shall destroy you, and win this war now and forever!"

He reunited with Belial and Legion below, and they flew back through the passageway as quickly as they came. Their next stop was Messai's office to inform him of their good fortune.

***

Hadassah heard a familiar voice whisper her name. Rousing from sleep, she stumbled over to him.

"What are you doing? If my uncle catches you here with me this late, we will both face his wrath. Wait, and I'll come with you."

"There is no time to wait. Something important has come up and we must hurry!"

She followed him, her heart racing again, feeling the rush of excitement and trepidation which consumed her every time this happened, but waited till they were out of hearing before she spoke.

"Are you taking me to battle with you? I'm ready to fight, Michael! You know I can handle myself with the best of them and help you lead the Host to a great victory tonight!"

"We won't fight tonight."

"If we're not fighting, does that mean they didn't discover the tunnel?"

"They found it, and Beelzebub nearly slaughtered them as they slept."

"Then we have to fight! If we stand back and do nothing, the dragon's army will kill them all!"

They walked up the mountain and were unexpectedly joined by another who climbed with them. Hadassah jumped from fear when she realized she now walked between two men.

"My fellow archangel and the Host protected them today," Michael said, nodding in Gabriel's direction. "If he had not stood boldly before Beelzebub, they would all be dead right now."

"But how did you...?" she asked, her question trailing off and stopping before she finished it.

"How did the messenger angel stand before the mightiest demon of hell? Is that what you ask?"

"Gabriel, I didn't mean to..." she said, her question ending in mid-sentence again.

"Offend me? Believe it or not, the mighty warrior angel who walks beside you is not the only one brave enough to fight. I can be as capable a fighter as he, when the need arises."

She had dug a hole from which she could not escape, so she chose not to speak again. Thankfully, Michael came to her rescue.

"Don't let him fool you into thinking he stood alone, because even I wouldn't do that. The Host stood alongside him, and the *brave* chief prince fled like a frightened little baby."

"Both of you stop it," she said without thinking about who she was talking to. "Please tell me where you are taking me, and why."

"Whoa, listen to you calling us out," said Michael, giving her a curious look. "Yahweh has a surprise for us, and for Messai and his army of demons tonight. Right now, as we speak, our friends have entered the tunnel and begun their walk to freedom. At the other end, Legion and his horde lie in wait for their exit, while Beelzebub, Belial, Abaddon, and Haborym have broken through my shield and follow them."

"They're trapped! We must do something! Summon the Host, and the three of us will join them and fight to protect those amazing believers in Jesus. If we don't, they will all fall into the destroyer's hands. Stop messing around and let's go!"

"Come with us; we have another familiar journey to take."

Each archangel grabbed a hand and lifted her, flying straight up. She did not understand where they were taking her, or why, but the spirit of Esther filled her again as they rose higher. Her people in Persia sat in their homes, unaware their enemy would rise against them and destroy them. She longed to fight for them, but realized that did not include combat for her. After doing her part to influence her husband, the king, she would stand back and let Yahweh take it from there.

They landed in their familiar place before Yahweh's temple in heaven. The three remaining angels stood holding bowls in their hands. She joined the two archangels kneeling before their Lord, then rose with them and watched them greet their colleagues. The angel was about to pour out the fifth judgment! But why were they here instead of defending their friends at Zedekiah's Cave? Michael said Yahweh would fight this battle, so she stood still and focused on the mighty angel.

He stepped forward and held out the bowl toward them, then lowered it, revealing its contents. Hadassah looked closely and saw nothing inside, but realized she could not see the bottom. The bowl was filled with empty, black darkness. What could that mean? Before she could process those thoughts, the angel left them and dove toward Planet Earth. Moans and screams still filled her ears as people suffered from sores and extreme burns rendered by the fiery sun blazing on them.

This time, the entire earth was not affected. The angel did not encircle it as the first three angels had done. Instead, he honed in on specific locations, starting with Jerusalem. When he poured out Yahweh's wrath, she saw no streams of light encircling the globe. Only inky black darkness appeared. The angel continued across the ten nations whose leaders formed the NWO, spreading darkness everywhere he went. Hadassah had never seen such deep darkness.

The angel returned and entered the temple. What this judgment meant, Hadassah did not know. But she was certain the two archangels accompanying her would show her soon. They bowed and flew away. This time she knew their destination was either the entrance or exit of Zedekiah's Cave.

*****

Blake led the group through the passageway, now about halfway through, not knowing what awaited them when they reached the end. Where was Gabriel? His men said he went ahead of them to look for any enemy who hid watching for their arrival, but he wasn't sure he bought their story. Something unique existed in Gabriel too, but he fought to deny what his mind struggled to believe. The passageway suddenly flooded with light, interrupting his thoughts.

"What's going on?" John asked from behind.

"Don't ask questions, John," said Anders. "Think about it like this: if Jesus can provide light for our friends in Petra, why can't he do the same for us in this tunnel? Don't forget, he called himself the light of the world. Just trust him!"

The ground shook under their feet, throwing them into stone walls as they grabbed each other. The rumble was so loud this time they could not hear one another speak. Small rocks and other debris littered the path ahead, but the passageway remained clear for walking when the tremor stopped.

"This is *really* the worst place to be when a quake strikes!" said Steve. "I didn't think about that when we started this hike!"

Gabriel walked back toward them, holding out his hand, signaling them to stop and listen.

"Keep walking and do not fear. We will reach the outlet by 10:00, right on schedule. However, I still would not be surprised if the enemy shows up and attacks us, so stay vigilant."

Something was different about the way he talked. He spoke with authority. And Jesus said *do not fear* many times. Blake pushed the thoughts from his mind again and followed him. Refreshed by their sleep, continuing was no problem for the group. But none of them realized enemy troops both followed them and waited ahead, leaving them helplessly trapped between.

The four demons walked steadily, never letting the group leave their sight. Messai sat close enough past the exit to observe their attack. Because of the distance from the Temple Mount, taking them back as prisoners to face the device was impractical, so they would slaughter them when they left the tunnel. There was no escape this time, so victory was near.

The chief prince's thoughts turned to his most hated foe. He longed for him to show up with the Host. His army was too strong for the warrior angel, so he could not possibly defeat them now. Visions of destroying Yahweh's mighty archangel nearly caused him to laugh with glee. But Michael would not come alone this time; Gabriel would join him. Two archangels in one night! The dragon would love hearing news that ultimate victory was now assured.

Two hours ahead of them, Legion hovered outside, holding back the horde who longed for their moment of slaughter. Messai looked on from a distance, anticipating the group's arrival even more than the little demons, if that was possible. This night would fulfill his dream and catapult the dragon and him to victory, and their rightful place on thrones ruling the universe. Fantasies of watching them die entered his mind again, and he held back a scream which must wait till they lay dead before him. Unable to contain himself, he ran to Legion.

"Tell me my prince, how will you destroy them? Will the Host show up? We must leave none of them alive after tonight!"

"You will be pleased with what you witness tonight, Master. Wait for their arrival, then sit back and enjoy the show!"

"I plan to do exactly that, Legion. Seeing them trapped between our two groups, trying desperately to get away with nowhere to run has me more excited than words can express."

"It will give us great joy to bring you such pleasure, Your Majesty. The time draws closer!"

***

Michael and Hadassah looked on expecting Yahweh's wrath, though neither knew how it would look. Gabriel had left them and returned to the group. He knew, yet Yahweh still withheld it from the two of them. This time, that did not bother Michael. He looked forward to a surprise.

"The time must be close. The demons surround the exit, and you said the four most vicious princes are behind them. If we don't do something, they will die!"

"I told you this is Yahweh's night when he will pour out his fifth judgment. We can't interfere, nor can we let Legion discover our presence. So keep quiet, and we will see Yahweh's wrath in action."

She got the message and checked her watch: 9:00 p.m. Darkness should have obscured her sight, but an eerie, green glow hovered around the opening. She leaned over and whispered.

"What is that?"

"The essence of pure evil, coming from the dragon's man and his demonic army, which will allow them to see our friends when they exit the tunnel."

"Michael!"

"Shh... Stay quiet and keep watch. Yahweh will let us know if we are needed. If we are, I only hope the Host comes to join us, because we would have no chance without them."

What? He was unsure whether they must fight, or whether the Host would come if the need arose? Fear crept into her mind, and she fought against it, realizing a battle with the powerful forces of evil may be imminent. Michael appeared unafraid, so that gave her some relief, although her greatest concern was for the people walking through that tunnel.

Blake glanced at his phone. 9:45. The exit was close now, and anticipation combined with the usual trepidation caused his heart to race. Or was that just from the long walk without stopping? Ahead, a strange light caught his eye. It was dark outside so no light should shine through the opening. Drawing closer, the light appeared green and wispy, like eerie fog hovering over landscape during the early morning following a rainy night.

But this wasn't morning; it was night. The greenish color bothered him too, nothing normal about it, but something very abnormal. Dread crept into his mind, although Gabriel walked confidently ahead, showing no sign of apprehension, so Blake followed, trying to appear courageous, as well. Less than one hundred yards remained now, and the glow remained, unchanging. Fear of leading the group into an ambush gnawed at him, but he kept walking.

Gabriel reached the opening and waited for everyone else to catch up before stepping out. Standing beside her husband, Beth squeezed his arm, her hand rubbing across the same chill bumps which covered her arms. Both knew what that meant; evil lurked nearby.

"Wait," Blake said. "Something isn't right. We should stay in here for now."

"We should turn back," John said from the rear. He and Kathie turned and slammed into an invisible wall that stopped them in their tracks. Blake turned to see John lifted in the air, his feet dangling, his hands grabbing at his throat, trying to pry loose unseen hands gripped tightly around it. Kathie screamed and Blake remembered how the former United Nations Secretary-General died before the council elected Messai to replace him. He understood what was happening.

"Run!" he yelled as John dropped to the ground, gasping for breath. Two American soldiers lifted him and ran forward, pushing Kathie ahead of them. Others were thrown into the cave walls, while some tripped and fell trying to get away. The invisible force suddenly released them, and they sprang forward through the opening, running into the backs of those already standing outside.

Blake saw him first, followed by the others: Messai. The green glow made his face appear more sinister than ever. An evil laugh erupted from deep inside him as he screamed to invisible troops.

"Attack! Destroy them, my princes!"

"Let's go, Michael! We have to help them!"

Beelzebub exploded from the tunnel hearing that name. His archenemy was here! Both saw him, joined by three other mighty demons, flying toward them. The extreme chill consumed the group rendering them immobile and facing immediate slaughter. Messai's evil laughter echoed off the rocky opening behind them. The fate of Zedekiah would now be theirs. They prepared to die and meet their Savior. No rescues would happen, and more believers would likely meet the same fate.

Michael longed to fly away with Hadassah and protect her, but he could not. They watched helplessly with the others as utter chaos raged around them.

CHAPTER 10

Seconds away from destruction and death of the worst kind, thick blackness abruptly engulfed the area surrounding the cave's exit, blinding Messai and his demonic horde. The darkness fell so suddenly it left them no time to react. But their enemy responded with great speed.

Michael grabbed Hadassah and lifted her to safety, higher above the fray. The chill disappeared instantly and Gabriel yelled, "Go!" Blake and company raced away, heading northwest on a lighted pathway, their view unhindered as light beamed through an opening leading the way. They realized Jesus had once again saved them from awful deaths with a brief time remaining before he returned. When they reached Tel Nof, repairing a plane and rescuing believers would begin immediately.

Behind them, tiny horde members crashed into each other and slammed into the mountainside. Beelzebub's blind rage turned to blinded eyes as he hurtled through the place vacated by his archenemy and *her*. Cursing and screaming pierced the spirit world, but soon ended when the creatures and their leader realized they were blind to each other and everything else.

"Your Majesty, are you okay?" asked Beelzebub, understanding his responsibility for his master's well-being.

"I am fine, you brutish beast, but I cannot see. Come and help me."

"I apologize, Master, but I cannot see either. Something blinded us. Can any of you see?"

Quiet *no's* came from his entire army, without a single *yes*. Tiny demons whimpered until Legion screamed *Silence!* "Talk to us, Your Majesty, and we will find you," Belial said.

Messai talked, and they did their best, but tripped and stumbled until they finally gave up.

"Haborym, send your fire and light up the night!" They heard the demonic prince huffing and snorting, but no fire came. He said nothing.

"Come!" Messai shouted, but the dragon did not appear, as he always did. "*Him,*" the man continued. "He cast the spell of darkness and blinded us. We must dispose of him and his magic!"

"What must we do tonight, Your Majesty? How can we leave this place and return to your office?"

The night was silent, all of them realizing there was no solution for their dilemma. The darkness would force them to remain until *he* released them from their black prison.

***

"Shouldn't we take a break before we continue?" John asked. "We're all exhausted from our long walk and that experience back there and could probably use a few minutes to catch our breath."

"I'm sure you're winded after everything that just happened, but we really must keep walking," said Trey. "If we don't cover fifty miles in two nights, more believers will die. That means averaging at least three miles each hour with small breaks for rest. I understand it will be intense, but think about those believers and it will help you keep going."

"You're right, Trey. I will do my best to keep up with you so we can get there on time."

When they reached the darkness perimeter, their light faded into normal night. Much of the journey would travel through forests which kept them concealed. Their flashlights would allow them to see where they were going, but they must be careful not to run down batteries.

Before continuing, they turned and looked back. The darkness was so black it left nothing visible. They had no concern for what happened to Messai and his legion of demons. They only hoped the blinding darkness would stall them long enough to give the group time to reach the airbase and start rescuing believers before the enemy reached them first.

***

"Hadassah, we must return to Petra now. They have Gabriel to help them complete their journey."

"Please, Michael, can we stay with them a little longer? I want to be near our friends and enjoy their company, even though they don't realize we are here."

"No, we must leave them. Thank Yahweh we didn't have to fight tonight. Do you understand his fifth judgment now?"

"Yes, the darkness. It explains why the bowl was empty and black with no contents. Why did it affect only Messai and his demons, and not the Smyrnians?"

"Do you remember the angel did not empty his bowl on the entire earth, as the others did? The darkness only affected Messai's kingdom, which involves specific places. Can you guess where those are?"

"Jerusalem and Rome?"

"You understand more every day, Hadassah! Yahweh has taught and trained you well."

"*You* have trained me well, and Yahweh used you to teach me."

"I suppose I did have a lot to do with all you have learned," he said, puffing out his chest. "Now, let me ask you a second question: what other parts of Messai's kingdom plunged into darkness?"

"The ten nations whose leaders serve him in the NWO," she said smiling.

"You really have gotten it, haven't you? Let's head to Petra and let these people get to Tel Nof."

"Okay, I'm ready. Michael, thank you for bringing me with you tonight. I will never forget the experiences we shared and all I have learned because of them."

"Yes, you will, very soon, because they will no longer matter in eternity. Oh, and you're welcome."

She smiled in agreement as they soared away, now anticipating eternity with Jesus, Michael, and many others even more than she had before.

***

At the Vatican, the pope and cardinals met to discuss their options, when the place was suddenly plunged into deep darkness. The pontiff sought to abate their fears as their worlds turned black.

"Brothers, do not be concerned. We have encountered other hardships since joining Aissa Messai's One World Religion. Whatever our feelings, we cannot reverse course after taking his mark, *but* we should stand our ground on certain matters, and we all agree some things must change."

They did not realize this was only the beginning, and something would indeed change soon, which would end their existence.

"I say we reach out and tell our people to follow your papal decrees, rather than Messai's orders."

"I second that," said another cardinal. "We must keep our longstanding traditions, and I believe we can do that, even as we serve Messai."

"If Messai is God, how can he act like he loves others but treat us with such contempt?"

"He has also treated us well. Don't forget he allowed us to continue living here."

"He took away the pontiff's position! I am not convinced the man is who he claims to be."

The debate raged for several minutes until the pope spoke again. "Now brothers, you must remember the one thing that matters most: we watched Aissa Messai die, then return to life. That makes him the true messiah, which is why we worship him and serve him."

"Are you sure it isn't because he restored our prosperity and position? Our religion was finished, as were we, until he saved it, and us. If we had not started worshiping him, we would have lost everything. *That* is why we followed him."

The debate started again, but when it reached its peak, the darkness evolved into more than blackness. It turned to despondency, depression, and despair, overwhelming the men with intense gloom and doom. They stopped talking and the cardinals crawled to their rooms, feeling their way in total blindness. When they arrived, each slid their hands across altars they created and grasped Aissa Messai's statue. They kneeled, asking him to bring back light and hope, but nothing changed.

In the coming days, desperation overpowered them. Israel and other nations which surrendered to the New World Order experienced the same phenomena. Crippling sores, bloody water, and searing burns from the scorching sun handicapped their bodies, while stifling darkness claimed their minds. None understood that each new judgment brought them closer to their end.

***

"My phone says 2:00 a.m. Surely it's time for a break now."

"Okay, John, we'll stop for a brief break, but I warned you to get in shape. My pedometer says we have walked eleven miles. We should double that by daylight, putting us close to our schedule. We'll need a hideout during the day, but we have to reach our destination tomorrow night. That may mean pounding it extra hard so we get two or three more miles than tonight."

"If you keep pushing us at this rate, Messai may not need to kill us."

"You'll make it, dear," Kathie said. "Don't worry, Trey. I'll carry my husband if I must."

"I'll give John his break, but then we'll pick up the pace and make up an extra mile tonight."

"Ooh...," John moaned, "get ready to carry me, honey. Sounds like I'm going to need it."

They picked up the pace and gained the extra mile but would still need to walk twenty-seven miles the next night to arrive on time. Four American soldiers would stand watch in shifts while they slept in a grove of spruce trees. They would sleep while it was daylight and leave when dark came, giving them the most time possible to complete their trip. That meant setting out at 8:00 p.m., planning to reach their destination before sunrise at 6:30 a.m., an ambitious goal.

They settled into the grove, large enough to fit them all, but small enough they must huddle together to sleep. The trees provided protection and shade, and dimmed the light enough to make sleeping easier. They lay down, hoping for rest, which would give them strength for tonight.

A soldier walked back in, eased over to them, and said, "Come here, guys; you have to see this."

Trey and several others followed him outside the grove. What they saw blew their minds, yet they should have known.

"Wow," Trey said. "Nothing changed after we left the cave. How long will it stay like that?"

"It's like an impenetrable wall of darkness," said Blake, "That's the craziest thing I've ever seen."

"But we have light in here," John said with a hint of consternation in his voice. "From a scientific perspective, that's impossible." He stuck out his hand, and it vanished into the blackness.

"Don't step in, John," Anders warned. "Jesus sent the darkness to torment Messai's followers and clear the way for us to reach Tel Nof. But it may end when we get there. He will give us time to make the trip, and no one will realize we're here. We are completely protected!"

"Then we need to get going! We can rest after we get there."

"We can rest for a few hours now, Trey, and still leave earlier than we planned. It is 7:30 now, so if we sleep until early afternoon, then leave, we should arrive by midnight."

"I agree, Blake," said John. "My body may not make it without some rest. We don't need to post a guard because no one can break through the darkness to get in here. I will set my phone alarm for 1:00 p.m., and we can leave by 2:00. That gives us ten hours to get there by midnight, but we can take more breaks and still make it well before daylight. Does everyone agree?"

"Good idea, John. Even I could use more rest along the way. Let's get some sleep."

"I'm glad you came around to my way of thinking, Trey. My alarm is set, and I'll be up and ready to go at 1:00!"

John turned, walked over to Kathie, and lay down. Within two minutes, they heard his gentle snoring. A few minutes later, their bodies exhausted, they all did the same. 1:00 would come more quickly than they wanted, but excitement about their journey would drive them on.

***

Messai and the demons became much more subdued. The thick blackness absorbed their voices, preventing them from hearing one another, and rendering them silent. Though no one heard them, they screamed and cursed Yahweh's name, and the name of Jesus, not knowing people throughout his kingdom did the same. No one thought darkness could be worse than that brought by Moshe and Eliyahu, but theirs did not compare to this.

Messai quieted himself and listened for his master to speak. The dragon could not come, but they could communicate telepathically since the beast lived in him. His mind heard the voice clearly.

"Aissa, we must not allow *him* to defeat us with the last battle so near."

"We will not, Master. Fill me with all your power, and I will overcome this plague and lead your army to victory. Some who secretly oppose us will go first. They cannot stop us!"

People throughout Messai's kingdom languished in oppressive darkness, but suffered even greater agony. The malignant sores metastasized to every part of their bodies, while the scorching sun seared their skin, leaving them in excruciating pain which would not go away. Now mental anguish, combined with physical torment nearly drove them insane. Yet, they continued cursing the living God and refused to turn from their wicked lifestyles to worship him. The world reached an ominous state as its end drew near.

***

"Hadassah, do you understand the darkness?" Michael asked as they sat alone in Petra.

"What more is there to understand? Yahweh sent it on Messai's kingdom as the fifth judgment."

"True, but the meaning goes much deeper."

"Tell me, Michael. I want to understand everything Yahweh is doing during these final days."

"Yahweh spoke light into existence the first day of creation, and Jesus called himself the light of the world. He is light, and when people reject the light, only darkness remains. Messai's people refused the light of his love and chose the dragon's darkness, so Yahweh gave them darkness."

She sat listening, amazed by what she heard, and hungry for more. *Ooh* escaped from her mouth.

"Yahweh has a purpose in everything he does. Nothing from him is coincidental. Jesus said the wicked will dwell eternally in *hell*, a place of tormenting fire and utter darkness. Sound familiar?"

"Bowls four and five: the sun scorching people with fire, and total darkness, final warnings of coming judgment. But they cannot heed them because they took the mark."

"Right again. Now, these last things are important. Are you ready?"

"You know I'm ready!"

"Do you remember what happened the last three hours Jesus hung on the cross before he died?"

"Yes, Michael! Darkness covered the whole land from noon to 3:00 p.m.!"

"Yes, those hours brought the darkest time in history when Jews and Gentiles joined forces to crucify the Lord of glory, the true light. When they sought to extinguish the light, darkness reigned until he finished Yahweh's redemptive work by giving *his* life so people can experience *real* life."

"Numbers always have meaning when Yahweh includes them in his work. Like the number seven, the number three signifies completion. That darkness disappeared in three hours, meaning the current darkness will leave in three days, giving the Smyrnians time to complete their journey with no one detecting them. When it goes away, the light's return will embolden Messai and give his followers false courage to unite and attack Israel."

"Wow, I see the full picture now. Yahweh is carrying out his plan with precision accuracy."

"Don't miss this last thing. The three days before Jesus rose from the grave represent the three remaining months before he returns. He will come soon, Hadassah!"

"You're right! With so much happening, I failed to realize his coming was so close! Do you think the Smyrnians have thought about that?"

"Gabriel will make sure they do. That's his specialty. But me, on the other hand...!"

"Stop it, Michael. I am well aware of your *specialty*, and you are awesome. But Gabriel proved he can be tough, too, when the situation calls for it. And he is very sweet."

"Sweet! That's the best word I've heard to describe my partner. Wait till I tell him you said that!"

"Don't you dare! Yahweh made both of you amazing in different ways, and I am thankful he allowed me to know you both. I sure hope Gabriel reminds them about the three months."

***

1:00 arrived and John's alarm sounded, waking him from a sound sleep. He looked around and realized he was the first to rise. This provided him with the perfect opportunity to have some fun.

"Rise and shine, everybody!" he said, running around the grove of trees, shaking each one.

"Keep it down, John," Blake said. "Do you want someone out there to hear you?"

"They can't hear me, Blake. They're *in the dark* about what's happening in here," he said grinning.

"I can't believe I slept in," said Trey, rubbing his eyes. "I was sure I would be the first one up. What time is it, anyway?"

"1:00 p.m., the time you said we need to get up. Why are we waiting?"

Everybody was awake now, so they opened some food and ate before starting their journey. They went out to check the darkness and found it the same, meaning they could walk again unseen and unheard. Anders stopped them before they left and announced he had something important to say.

"Have any of you thought about today's date?"

"Who's had time to check the date, Anders?" asked John. "Is this your birthday, or something?"

"No, today is June 11th, 2036. Does that ring a bell to anyone?"

"Three months," Ally breathed. "Jesus will return in three months!"

"How many rescues can we conduct in three months?"

"We're not talking about *rescues*, Blake. We only have to conduct *one* rescue mission."

"One? Jesus gave us what we need to rescue believers all over the world, not just one group."

"He showed me the scroll while I slept, Trey, and I saw it clearly: one group. But I couldn't tell where they were."

"What do you mean you couldn't tell where? Didn't you say Jesus showed you?"

"Gabriel showed me one big section of the scroll with more action than I could process. I'm talking about the *angel* Gabriel, not *our* Gabriel," he said, smiling at the soldier. "Some huge things are coming during these three months, so much I couldn't figure it all out. The one clear thing is, we must rescue one group of believers from the same city, and the time is short."

"How soon will you know when and where? The *how* is sitting at Tel Nof waiting for us."

"I can't answer that, Rickie. Perhaps Jesus will show me while we walk or after we get there, but he will show me soon because there isn't much time left."

"I trust you, Anders, but I was so sure we would rescue people from lots of places. If we're only going to one place, it must be a huge deal. We'd better get that plane ready, in case we have to go tomorrow."

They walked twelve hours, took regular breaks, and arrived safely at Tel Nof Airbase at 2:00 a.m. Everyone was exhausted, but with such little time remaining, there was no time to worry about being tired. They didn't know when the outside darkness would end, but wanted to locate the plane and get it ready for flight before it did. After a little sleep, they would start working.

Ben spread the word calling everyone in Petra together for a special announcement. It was quite a sight to see 144,000 people packed all over the main city, with others sitting above or hanging off cliffs. He could not help but admire the sight of so many Jews who worshiped their true Messiah. Finally, he emerged from his trance and spoke, his voice thundering throughout the Rose-Red City.

"Today is June 11, 2036. Does anyone understand what that means?"

"Three months until Jesus comes!" someone shouted from high above, their voice heard by all.

"Yes!" Ben said, his excitement pouring out with his loud proclamation and leading to a cheer erupting from every part of Petra. "We have enjoyed our time here, but we will soon trade this city for a better location!" Another excited roar filled the place. "We should relish these last three months, but also pray daily for our fellow believers out there. Who knows what they may face as time winds down and the enemy lashes out against everyone who follows Jesus."

"They will fly rescue missions and put themselves in great danger saving the lives of others. The dragon's demonic army has joined Aissa Messai preparing for the final battle. But nothing will stop his pursuit of Jesus' followers. Our prayers may mean the difference between life and death for them, and I want them to survive and join us when we all meet our Messiah at his coming!"

Applause echoed off the rock cliffs that would surely frighten any demon away if they were near. "Let's pray now!" another voice called out. The man immediately cried out, asking Jesus to protect their comrades who believed in him and rejected Messai. It was a powerful moment.

"More may happen in these three months than has happened in almost seven years," Michael said.

Ben's eyes searched everywhere until he spotted the young soldier. He did it again, speaking boldly about what the future held, seeming to know everything in advance. He dared not interfere, but allowed him the opportunity to continue.

"A winner take all war will happen soon, pitting the Heavenly Host against the dragon's evil army. We realize the beast cannot win, but he still thinks he can. Our role is praying without ceasing until September 11th. Will you do that?"

"Yes!" said the previous voice, others chiming in this time. There was no doubt they meant it, and Jesus would hear the cries of his people in Petra for the next ninety days.

***

One and a half days had passed since Messai's kingdom plunged into debilitating darkness. The blackness was now so dense each individual felt trapped inside their own private cocoon, with no escape. They could neither see nor hear beyond the enclosed, silent space in which they existed. That left millions entombed in a sightless, silent world from which escape seemed impossible.

Outside the cave, Aissa Messai sought to push his way through the solid black wall imprisoning him, but found it impenetrable. Terror fought against his mind as rage tried furiously to escape his mouth, yet he stayed mute. The dragon's voice no longer entered his mind, nor did he hear words from the demons he knew surrounded him. He realized who perpetrated this attack and would spend this time until light returned, doing one thing: planning his coming assault on *him*.

Beelzebub and Belial chose the same course of action, even though neither could communicate with the other. Both had one thing on their minds: *Destroy Michael*. They could hardly wait.

The ten NWO kings shared their angst, yet each believed Messai would end the darkness and guide them toward world domination. He promised they would reign with him forever, and none doubted he would fulfill his promise. That hope helped them survive inside their blind and deaf cocoons.

At the Vatican, Gregory prayed to his new messiah, hoping the man could hear his silent cries. Fear consumed him as he considered the power Messai wielded and his unrestrained rage against him the last time they met. How could he cross the man? He thought about Roman Catholicism, and its longstanding tradition. Could he have missed the truth? The Smyrnians proclaimed what happened on September 11, 2029 was the Rapture when Jesus took his true followers home to live with him. Was that possible? No, Aissa Messai must be the messiah, and he would worship him. If he did not... he erased the thought quickly, yet his fear returned.

All hoped the darkness would leave soon, but each passing hour made that seem less probable. None considered what it meant for their future, but they would not understand if they did. Yet that future drew nearer every day, and nothing could prevent it.

***

Tel Nof looked every bit the part of a deserted military base when the team rose from sleep at 8:00 a.m. and saw it. It sat unoccupied for over three years and was now overgrown with weeds, and its buildings were in bad disrepair. They had bunked down wherever they could six hours earlier when they arrived; now they realized the amount of work required to make the place habitable again. But it needed to look like no one lived there anyway, so locals would not suspect their presence. Although, that big plane taking off and landing would arouse suspicion. That was inevitable.

Thankfully, plenty of canned food remained, allowing them to eat a good breakfast. It wasn't ham and eggs, but it tasted just as good to hungry people. Trey and Rickie went searching for the 320B the minute they finished and found it right away in an otherwise abandoned hangar.

"There she sits, Rickie, a beauty, just waiting to get in the air again! Let's see what it takes to make that happen. She needs to fly, and we need her to rescue believers, so it's time to get to work!"

Initial inspections showed this would be no easy task, especially if necessary materials were not available. They made a list of everything they needed and started searching for parts. Mechanisms needed lubrication; batteries were completely dead, and they hoped they would charge; tires needed inflating; fuel tanks and any remaining fuel must be checked, along with cylinders, hydraulic systems, and landing gear.

The task appeared daunting and would require much effort. They called for help, most of the group showed up, and the work began. By day's end, they completed every job the best they could, and Trey deemed the aircraft flight worthy. He could not guarantee safety, but it would have to do. To stay inconspicuous, he and Rickie would not fire up the engines until time to leave. Hopefully, that would come soon. Several of the group sat in the large meeting room discussing plans after dinner.

"The 320B is as ready as we can get it," Trey said. "Rickie and I just need to know when we're leaving and where we're going. Anders, are you sure we're only flying one mission? That plane will make several flights, and we can go as many times as needed for the next three months."

"The scroll never lies, Trey, and I clearly saw one mission. But I remember a good-sized group and much danger when you go. If space is available after we hear how many they have, some others need to go with you for backup."

"The darkness is still there, so maybe we can get this done before it goes away."

"Not likely, Rickie, or the scroll wouldn't have shown such danger. I didn't see *this* darkness, so that must mean it will disappear prior to flying, although I wish it would stay until we get back."

"Anders is right," Magnus said. "And you can bet the dragon will know you are going and have his demons ready to stop you, if he can. Their power outmatches any earthly force or ability."

"We encountered them when we flew to China to rescue you and Bruno, and I would rather not go through that again. But I will for believers who are in danger. That was the most harrowing time I ever lived through in all my piloting experience. If Rickie hadn't fought in prayer, and someone else hadn't fought for us, we would never have made it, and you guys wouldn't be here today."

"It will be worse this time, because he will pull out all the stops. I have witnessed it before and understand how destructive his forces are when he sends all twelve *princes*. They are brutal and have proven unstoppable from my experience. Many powerful people and armies have become their victims. This mission concerns me, so I want to go with you."

"We wouldn't dream of going without you, Magnus, and Bruno too," said Rickie. "We need big men who love to fight on our side. Others need to come for prayer support and help on the ground. I just hope Jesus shows us soon where we have to go, because time is getting short."

"He will, Rickie, I'm sure of that. I wish I could remember details from the scroll which would show us, but nothing is clear. All I can see are people who need rescuing."

"Well, it is 10:00 p.m. now, and we all need to get some good sleep. Whenever the day comes, everyone must be rested and ready, especially the pilots," Blake said, looking at Trey and Rickie.

"10:00 means the darkness has been around for two days," said John. "It is unnatural, like the worldwide earthquake and other phenomena we have seen during the Tribulation, so it could change anytime. I sure wish I could figure it out, but science is useless when it comes to things only Jesus can do."

"You're right, John, so the best thing we can do is not think about it, and go to bed. Alertness requires ample rest, so as this group's physician, I order everyone to bed!" Steve said.

They crashed, slept all night, got up the next morning, and spent the day double-checking everything on the plane and ensuring all was well. It was, so now they waited for more instructions.

***

The day flew by, and before they knew it, nightfall returned, and they all fell asleep at 9:00, unaware of anything happening outside their haven. 10:00 arrived without their knowledge, and a cool breeze wafted through Messai's kingdom. He still lay imprisoned inside his cocoon of thick darkness when things suddenly changed. Moonlight illuminated the night sky, appearing bright as daylight after three days of blindness.

Then Messai heard his demonic army screeching and howling and saw them coming together before him. He joined the horde, howling with delight, and celebrating their victory. *He* had lost!

"Come!" he said with a scream which should awaken the dead, although it did not. But it aroused the one he desired. The Great Red Dragon appeared from nowhere and joined their party, his howls overpowering theirs and throwing them to their knees paying homage to their ruler.

"We have overcome!" he shouted. "And this is only the beginning! Aissa, we must destroy the traitors now, then assemble the armies and prepare to march against our mortal enemy and annihilate them! Where is Gog?"

The huge demon prince came and stood before him. "The time has come, hasn't it Master?"

"Yes, my prince. The day draws near for you to entice them to march. They will do your bidding, and we will lead them to battle, and be victorious! Choose those who will assist you and get ready to leave. This is our hour, and the power of *true* darkness will prevail!"

The sound of over one million demons poured through the heavens. Human beings could not hear them, but two sitting on thrones in heaven did, as did one standing in Petra, and another lying down at Tel Nof. Each realized this awakening meant the last battle would happen soon. One other felt it too. Anders rolled over gently so he would not awaken his wife and prayed silently to Jesus. *Please show us who we must rescue.* He went back to sleep, trusting his Savior to handle the details.

Messai returned to his mansion and would meet with Rossi in his temple office at 10:00 the next morning to plan the attack. It would happen swiftly and catastrophically, leaving nothing, and no one remaining. He would inform his NWO leaders and contact General Chen to execute the strike. The general needed one more chance to prove himself before leading his army into the final battle.

***

Michael and Hadassah sat atop the mountain in their favorite spot. "I must go on another journey alone," he said. "This one will be too dangerous to take you with me, but if I return alive, we will take our sixth journey to discover Yahweh's next judgment. I hope you look forward to that."

"Michael, please don't say that again. This journey sounds like it may be your most dangerous yet. I remind you, if you get yourself killed, all will be lost."

"I have no choice. Serving Yahweh is not always easy, Hadassah, and he never promised it would be. He said the opposite, telling us we must put on his armor because our fight is not against human beings. We wrestle against *spiritual forces of evil in the heavenly realms.* That refers to the dragon and his demons who are unseen by people, but fought by the Heavenly Host."

"I know that, but it seems the battles get harder as time goes by. I realize the great last battle will come soon, but if you die before then, Yahweh cannot replace you. You must stay alive to fight that one!"

"I plan to do just that, but there is never any guarantee. I promise you the Host and I will fight with all of our might to defeat Beelzebub, Belial, and their army again. They are easy, remember?"

"No, they are difficult. I witnessed that for myself. I know you must go, Michael, but please come back so we can take that next journey, then you can fight and win the last battle."

They walked back down the mountain together, neither speaking, feeling the weight of this moment. He understood its importance and was ready to summon the Host to fight.

CHAPTER 11

Blake missed ten calls from a number he did not recognize as he and Beth slept and noticed them when he awoke. His calls came only from Ben or other Smyrnians. Who could this be? Voicemails were left after each call, so this was urgent. Beth interrupted him as he pulled up the first.

"Wait, Blake. What if Messai somehow found your secure number? This could be a trap, so you need to be careful and not take any chances."

"The transcriptions make no sense. All I know is they tried to leave messages but got cut off every time after just a few words. There are ten calls and ten messages, so it must be urgent."

"It seems like someone was desperate to speak to you, assuming the calls are legit. Maybe if we listen to every message we can figure out what they were trying to say."

He opened each message and listened to them in order. The first contained two words and stopped.

"Mr. Thompson..."

Message Two: "Mr. Thompson, we..."

"Beth, this will never work. The person didn't have time to record anything."

"I'm not so sure. Let's listen to the next two, because I may hear a pattern developing."

Message Three: "believe in..."

The two of them looked at each other shocked at what they heard.

Message Four: "Jesus..."

Blake did not slow down now, but opened the next one.

Message Five: "We live..."

Message Six: "Vatican City..."

"Blake! Roman Catholics joined the One World Religion, and Messai just moved his headquarters to Vatican City and took over the Papal Palace! These people may be in trouble!"

Message Seven: "fear..."

Message Eight: "lives..."

Message Nine: "Please help..."

Message Ten: "They know..."

"How smart was that to keep calling and leaving a few words at a time to get his message across? Either his battery died or AMPP men got him. I realize it's dangerous, but I'm calling back."

"I feel strongly about this, too, but I don't want you to give us away. How can we be sure it isn't a trap? AMPP may listen when you call or even track our location."

"That's all possible, but we have to call because they may really need us. Get the others, and when they get here, I'll call and let them hear the conversation."

Beth ran and returned shortly, followed by several others. Blake played the messages for them.

"I dreamed again last night, but I thought nothing about it because it wasn't like other times. This seemed like a regular dream, not like I traveled anywhere, just things I saw and heard."

"Tell us your dream, Magnus. If it aligns with the messages, I want to hear it before I call."

"It does more than align with them; it may tell the whole story. I saw three men wearing red robes sitting in a dimly lit house and two men wearing helmets. There were also several women, two wearing habits, and some children. They held open Bibles and prayed softly to Jesus. When they finished, the robed men ran to a huge palace and sneaked inside, making sure no one saw them. The women wearing habits walked to another building, and the other two men with kids ran somewhere else. I thought, man, what a weird dream, but perhaps it wasn't weird after all."

"Your dream was no accident. It came the same night the man called and asked for help. I'll call him right now and take it from there. If he doesn't answer, I'll leave a message and ask him to call at 6:00 this evening. All Vatican employees should be off work by then."

He touched the call symbol. It rang once and went to voicemail, stating the caller was unavailable. Blake left a message telling the man to call at 6:00 p.m. and he would answer his call. He would wait with his phone in hand, and others would be with him, eager to learn what the call was about.

***

Messai noticed his Chief Security Director's appearance when the man walked into his office. "Rossi, you look much better! Have your sores healed?"

"Yes, sir. They disappeared last night at 10:00 while I sat thinking about this morning's meeting."

"10:00 p.m.! That was the exact time I dispelled the darkness and caused the moon to light up the night! Have you spoken with AMPP personnel to verify they experienced the same thing?"

"I called every captain and confirmed that!" This one miracle restored his faith in and allegiance to his boss, and brought back his animosity toward the Smyrnians. Messai must be the messiah.

"We overcame, Mr. Rossi, and that means our hour *has* come! Do you understand that?"

"I do, Mr. Messai, and I am honored to serve you and help you assume your rightful place as ruler of the world. After you delivered us from darkness and healed the sores, nothing can stop you!"

"You have served me faithfully and will be rewarded accordingly when our master and I set up our eternal kingdom. Now I must check with the NWO leaders and ask if they also experienced healing at 10:00 last night. If all are cured, we must begin preparations for the attack!"

He called every nation's leader and received affirmative responses from each, then brought General Chen into the meeting via speaker phone.

"General, Mr. Rossi and our NWO leaders informed me they experienced healing from the sores at 10:00 p.m. I assume the same is true worldwide. How about you and the fine men who lead the People's Republic of China? Have your sores disappeared too?"

"The president planned to contact you soon and tell you our sores are gone and the sun has returned to normal. Plus, our waters are crystal clear again! Have you also experienced those things there?"

"Mr. Rossi, check the basin outside, and contact our people who live near the Dead Sea, Sea of Galilee, and the Mediterranean to ask if their waters are clear. General Chen, you made my day!"

The director placed the calls as Messai walked across the room to get a drink from the tap. Pure water flowed into the glass! Rossi returned reporting clear water outside, while getting identical reports from around Israel. There was no need to contact others. The five plagues had ended!

"General, you are responsible for destroying the traitors. Have you stationed units capable of such demolition along the BRI, and can they provide the firepower to carry out the assault? Now, for you, Mr. Rossi. You will work with our NWO friends to make plans for the great battle."

"I will start right away, sir. Are you attending the meeting, or shall I speak on your behalf?"

"You can handle that. When we finish here, Caiaphas and I are leaving for the Vatican to meet with the pope and his pawns. They must get on board with our plans or face the consequences of their rebellion. I also want to witness their cure for myself."

"Mr. Messai," General Chen said, interrupting their conversation, "I will prepare my men and wait to hear from you. Is that acceptable?"

"Yes, General. I trust you can handle this better than the debacle at Lifta?"

"You can count on me, sir. I will never let you down again."

The call ended, Rossi left to set up an NWO meeting, and Messai prepared to board his private jet for Rome. He should arrive by 4:00 p.m. and host his meeting the next morning. Things were falling into place. *The dragon must be pleased*, he thought with an evil grin as he climbed on board.

***

Blake's phone rang at precisely 6:00 p.m. and he answered without giving his name, to be safe.

"Hello, may I help you?"

"Mr. Thompson, my name is Lukas, and I am calling you again from Vatican City. Please listen, as I must talk quickly and speak softly."

"Go ahead." Just as he said that, the phone cut off and the call dropped. Blake did not hesitate. He touched the number immediately and called back. No answer. He tried again; same result. Then his phone rang, and he saw the man's number on the screen.

"This is Blake Thompson, I'm listening. If the call drops again, we'll keep calling each other until we finish our conversation."

"I have to hurry because the cardinals must return to the Palace before 8:00 p.m."

Blake's mind raced with questions. The cardinals? They followed Messai and received his mark, so why would they meet with this group? Wait, Magnus saw men wearing red robes!

"I never believed Aissa Messai was the messiah, but neither did I truly follow Jesus before the Rapture. Instead, I followed the false traditions of Catholicism, unlike many of my friends who had accepted Jesus as their Savior and lived for him alone. Even after the Rapture, I failed to repent and turn to him. I later discovered some others, including leaders, who were just like me. We understood what we needed to do, but could not find the courage to obey."

"However, when Messai enforced the mark, we decided we would not take it, regardless of any consequences we may face. We met and watched a video one of our nuns recorded when you and Beth shared your stories on National TV before you went into hiding. All of us prayed together and asked Jesus to come into our lives, and he did. Everything changed for us that night."

Blake pulled Beth close and kissed her, while the group celebrated as the man continued.

"Three cardinals and two nuns avoided taking the mark and haven't been checked, even though their names aren't in the database. My partner and I are members of the Swiss Guard, who protect the pope and the palace. We didn't take the mark either and have also escaped capture. Our group fell in love with Jesus and meet regularly to study his Word. There are other groups in Rome, too."

"Messai returned here a short while ago, and something is about to go down. The cardinals have been in meetings with him before and witnessed his growing ire toward them, and this place. You may think he supports us, but he doesn't. He hates us. Jesus appeared to all of us in a dream three nights ago and stood before us saying, *come out of her, my people.* We prayed and asked him what to do, and he gave us your number! Can you help us?"

"Jesus told us we would rescue a group of people, and he would show us where. Now we know! Give us a time and place, and we'll fly there and get you. Please don't wait, because it sounds like you have very little time. Call me when you know details. We have a plane ready and can fly anytime. It seats one hundred and fifty, so bring everyone who needs to come."

"I'll call you when we figure all that out. Pray for our safety, especially for the cardinals, nuns, and us guards and our families. If they catch up with us... *I have to go!*"

The man ended the call so quickly and with such an anxious voice, it gave the group reason to fear for his life and the lives of his fellow believers.

"Blake, if they could leave at night, we'd have better cover for flying in and out. It would be much better than flying into Rome in broad daylight. We may even get out before they notice us after dark. If the other darkness had stuck around, it would've helped a lot. But we'll work with what we have and trust Jesus to protect us like he always has."

"You're right, Trey. When Lukas calls, I'll suggest that. I'd call back now, but someone may have come in, and I don't want to give them away. But I'll be nervous until I hear from him."

"Let's get our plans together so when he calls, we can take off immediately," Rickie said. "The flight to Rome should take around three and a half hours, so if we can leave before midnight, the entire trip could take place under cover of darkness. I hope they take your suggestion, Blake. Now, who wants to go with us?"

They could not take all twelve American soldiers, so Gabriel and five more opted in. The other six would stay and protect their friends and family at Tel Nof. Ollie and Amelia were a must, with their previous experience, as were their two big men, Bruno and Magnus. Anders, Ally, and Blake would go. Beth talked her husband into letting her make the trip, too. And they needed Steve in case medical issues arose. Pilots Trey and Rickie completed the group. The trip was dangerous for so many original Smyrnians to go, but with only three months left in the Tribulation, who cared?

***

Michael pulled Hadassah aside and spoke quietly. "The battle takes place tonight. It happened last minute, so I have to go mobilize the Host. This one may be tough, and I fear the dragon will pull out all the stops, meaning he has most likely chosen Beelzebub and Belial to lead his army."

"The dragon? I thought he turned everything over to Messai."

"Messai will handle the next one. It will be catastrophic. The dragon will use tonight to set it up."

"I don't understand any of that, Michael. What I do understand is, you will be in grave danger, and possibly lose a battle, or even worse, get killed, which would ruin everything."

"Don't worry, Hadassah. This war is racing toward its conclusion and we can't back off or walk away from a fight. I'll make you a deal. You stay here and pray, and I'll go fight with everything I have. Wait for me atop our favorite mountain and trust I will meet you there."

With a smile and a wave, he was gone, leaving her alone, fearing for his life, and the future of Jesus' people. The hour was late enough that others would think she was asleep, so she headed straight to the mountain and climbed. She reached the top and fell to her knees, crying out to Jesus and Yahweh for the Host and the battle they would fight. Michael did not say, but it undoubtedly involved believers too, so she also prayed for their safety. This would be a sleepless night.

***

Messai and Caiaphas arrived in Rome and visited a famed restaurant before traveling to the Vatican. The place was packed, but *he* needed no reservation. He had taken little time to enjoy the Eternal City since assuming control of Roman Catholicism's former headquarters and moving into the Palace, so he was overdue a good time. Whenever he dropped by popular spots, his adoring public either heaped praise on him or shied away because they feared him. He relished both.

When he walked in, the crowded restaurant's patrons stood and applauded as the owner led his entourage to a prominent corner table. He could not let this opportunity pass.

"Friends," he said before taking his seat, "it thrills me to see you healthy again and out enjoying yourself in this wonderful city, which

I now call my second home." More applause, whistles, and shouts of praise. "It gave me great pleasure to rid our world of the disease and bloody waters. The darkness provided the perfect opportunity to accomplish that. So, here we sit today healthy and ready to achieve the peace and prosperity I have worked so hard to bring. And we *will* achieve it! Please also welcome our One World Religion leader, Caiaphas."

The upscale establishment's atmosphere was about to turn raucous when Messai held up his hand. "Friends, please, we must not turn this fine restaurant into nothing more than a nightclub. Get back to your meals, and I will also enjoy mine. My people will send a press release and contact some of your most trusted news sources, then I will host a spontaneous news conference following dinner, something I did not intend to do, but I want to share it with you. After that, I will retire to my office at the Palace, which is now called the 'house of god.'" He sat, joined by his security patrol.

Within thirty minutes, reporters and cameramen began pouring into the restaurant, forcing patrons to rise and stand around the walls. None cared, because they had lucked out and would be part of a worldwide news story. Messai continued his meal, paying no attention to the crazy scene developing before him. When he finished dessert, he wiped his mouth, put down the napkin, and stood facing the cameras and crowd, who eagerly awaited his words.

"First, I would like to thank Marco and his wonderful staff for a spectacular meal and great service. Join me in showing them our appreciation." He led the cheer, clapping in Marco's direction, as the owner's staff stood alongside him. "I also thank you for supporting the New World Order. Your commitment and perseverance will now be rewarded." He again acknowledged their ovation.

"We continue our pursuit of rebels who seek to prevent that goal and have made great progress in that endeavor. Now allow me to share some private information which may surprise you. A source informed me yesterday some former cardinals and nuns of Roman

Catholicism failed to take the mark. How that escaped our attention, I do not know."

"However, while I am here, we will find them and present them with an opportunity to follow your example of obedience. I hope they do so, showing their support for our agenda. If they refuse the mark, they shall be the first since the sores began to face the Capital Punishment Device." Silence filled the place as people recalled images of that horrific experience. "Ladies and gentlemen, do not fear such news, but celebrate a new beginning toward peace and prosperity!"

Now they nodded their approval, turning and smiling at one another while clapping and whooping again. Messai obviously enjoyed the moment and waved as he walked toward the door, shaking hands and signing a few autographs along the way. He left the restaurant feeling good about the acclamation he received, but also wondered if he made a mistake by making his announcement. He got caught up in the moment and it came out. His men must now ensure the rebels were caught.

**

Blake's phone vibrated at 9:00 p.m. He stood holding it, half hoping for a call, but not really expecting to receive one. He answered, listening for the guard's voice.

"Mr. Thompson, Aissa Messai came here and just held a news conference. He's on to us and is sending AMPP to search for the cardinals and nuns. Can you come tonight and get us out of here?"

"We can leave in thirty minutes. Tell me when and where and we'll meet you there!"

"Are you familiar with Pratica di Mare Airbase near here? The Italian Military operates it, but the cardinals have close contacts there who will grant you permission to land and allow us to leave with you. We will arrange everything, then meet you outside. We must board quickly and fly out immediately. Can you get there before 2:00 a.m.?"

"Our pilots said the flight will take three hours and thirty minutes, so that should be about right if we leave now. Both are familiar with the airbase. I'll call you shortly before we land."

"We'll get everyone together and prepare to depart. We're leaving our homes, possessions, and jobs, but it's necessary. There are fifty of us, if everybody comes. I look forward to meeting you, and those who come with you, before 2:00 a.m."

"Jesus is coming back in three months anyway, so none of that matters. We'll see you in a few hours, Lukas, and welcome to the Smyrnians." He ran to get everyone ready. Danger may lurk ahead, but this trip would happen quickly, so they wouldn't have time to consider that. It was go time, and they had no choice.

***

Messai entered his office and summoned Gregory to meet with him in thirty minutes. The big meeting with the former pontiff and cardinals would happen at 8:00 a.m. the next day. But he wanted to slam the man tonight for allowing some of his leaders to slip through without taking the mark, even though Messai understood his own people also bore responsibility for that oversight.

An AMPP patrol would conduct a surprise raid tonight and arrest the traitors. He would parade them into the meeting tomorrow and give them an opportunity to take the mark. If they refused, the others would watch him sentence them to the device, describing what would happen to them. *That will shock them, but if they only realized what was coming next,* he mused.

"Come in, Gregory," Messai said in a voice that caused the pontiff to shudder and wish he could turn and leave, but he could not.

"Sit," he said, more a command than an invitation. Gregory obeyed and remained silent as pure evil stared at him for a full minute. The pope sensed hellish eyes burning a hole right through him.

"Gregory…" Messai drew the name out with his patent low growl. "Have you hidden something from me? You should realize by now you cannot conceal anything from the messiah."

Gregory's mind screamed, *run*, but he felt glued to his chair. He realized what the man referred to. Three of his own cardinals and two nuns refused the mark, and he protected them, pulling strings to get their names included in AMPP's database along with his and the others. He knew if Messai ever discovered it, trouble would follow. Now that day had arrived, so his only recourse was to lie.

"I don't understand what you mean, sir. Why would I hide anything from you? I'm a man with an honorable reputation, just as you are, so I would like to think we have been honest with each other."

"Gregory, you choose your words carefully, but you cannot fool me. Will all your cardinals attend our meeting tomorrow morning?"

"Yes, sir, they received your summons and will all be here."

"Good! I am so excited about seeing three of them that I asked AMPP to come and greet them. Do you understand now what I am talking about?"

The man searched his mind for an answer, but none would suffice. He just wanted away from Aissa Messai. "They are always glad to see you, Your Majesty. I look forward to our meeting."

That was it. The meeting ended and Gregory went away filled with dread about what would happen the next morning. Perhaps he could get to their rooms and warn the men tonight. Or maybe they should all flee. No, he would wait and learn what the morning brought.

***

Seventeen Smyrnians boarded the 320B at 9:30 p.m. and prayed the engines would start. If they did not, the mission would fail and the believers in Vatican City would die. Rickie and Trey set all the switches, and the big moment came. Trey flipped the start switch and the right engine roared to life. The left engine was next and followed suit. Fourteen passengers cheered their success!

Trey backed the large aircraft out of the hangar and proceeded to the runway. At 9:45, they climbed into the air bound for Rome. The flight should be smooth and simple, and flying the shortest route directly over the Mediterranean Sea, should take less than three and a half hours.

They all settled in and met to plan for any emergencies which may require intervention. If Lukas was right, everything would be prearranged at Pratica di Mare, so they should be down and up without even shutting off the engines. The fuel was good for 5,000 miles, and their entire flight would be around 4,000. If all went as planned, they hoped to be back at Tel Nof before daylight.

"We shouldn't have to deplane," Blake said. "I'll call Lukas before we land, and they can meet us and board quickly. Hopefully, Trey can turn around and get right back in the air."

"I remember we were flying somewhere," said Anders, "but I don't recall anything else about our trip. So, I assume that means a safe and successful flight."

"It will surprise me if things go that smoothly, because I'm sure the dragon knows where we are."

"That's why we brought you and Bruno along, Magnus," Anders said with a mischievous grin.

"I hope you're right, Anders. I just know too much about his power and how he operates. But I'll go with your inclination and enjoy the flight." He put his seat back and closed his eyes. All was well as they flew across the beautiful Mediterranean below. It would have been nice if it was daylight so they could enjoy the view. Everyone joined Magnus getting some sleep as Trey flew on with his trusted co-pilot sitting beside him.

Michael soared from heaven with the Host flying in endless waves behind him. He left nothing to chance, but brought a huge

number of mighty angelic Host, in case their mortal enemy showed
up to stop the rescue mission. Their leader missed few opportunities
as important as this one. They dove and headed for the plane
carrying seventeen of Jesus' closest followers.

In Petra, Hadassah sat atop the mountain, still praying for the
believers, whom she understood may be in danger, and for Michael
and the Host. She would pray all night and hope Mordecai and Ben
did not miss her. A voice interrupted her prayers.

"Uncle! What are you doing here?"

"Hadassah, I know you come here often with Michael, so when I
couldn't find you, I knew where to come. What brings you up here
all alone during the night? You wouldn't come unless you have an
important reason."

"It is my favorite place to be alone, so why would it surprise you
to find me here?"

"Hadassah... don't try to fool me. I heard you praying long before
I reached you. What is going on? Michael isn't in his place either, nor
is he with you. This concerns him, doesn't it?"

"It concerns our friends, Uncle. I have this feeling they need our
prayers tonight, and Michael sensed that too. So, I came where I
sense Jesus' presence most, here atop the mountain."

"Then why isn't Michael here praying with you if he believes our
friends are in such danger?"

"Uncle, please! You may either pray with me or leave. I need to
talk to Jesus and can do that with or without you. That is your
choice. Now, if you will excuse me, I must keep praying."

Her directness hurt him briefly, but he realized she was right. "I
know this is important to you, Hadassah, so I will go back and join
you, praying from below. You need to pray alone. I will honor that
and not ask any more questions. Good night, my dear. Talk to Jesus;
he seems to always hear you."

Eight hundred miles flying over water after leaving Tel Nof, the
big military aircraft suddenly shook violently, then smoothed again

in two minutes. The passengers awoke with a start, but most turned over and fell back asleep. Blake and Beth did not, but sat talking.

"Bad turbulence," he said. "That happens crossing the Mediterranean. I'll walk to the cabin and ask Trey if we hit bad weather."

"Please do that. Something about that brought back memories of our first flight to the farm when you and John were in Kansas meeting with Doc Sanderson."

"But that was a bad storm, wasn't it?"

"Yes, so perhaps that's what happened to us now. Please go ask Trey and Rickie."

"That was pretty bad turbulence, guys. Did we run into a storm or a bad crosswind?"

"The air seems smooth," Rickie said, "and it's a perfect night for flying. I'm not sure where that came from, but it was rough."

The plane shook again, even worse than before, and sent Blake crashing to the floor. Trey fought to keep from losing control of the aircraft, but the shaking continued, causing the other fourteen passengers to join them, while hanging onto seats trying to remain standing.

"What's going on, Trey?" Ollie asked. "After our experience flying across the Atlantic with Bradley, we get a little nervous in situations like this."

"I hope it's turbulence, Ollie, but this is unlike any turbulence I've flown in before. It's strange. If I didn't know better..." he stopped right there.

"The horde," Magnus said. "I was sure the dragon wouldn't let us make this trip. He wants those believers dead, which also tells me he has something even greater in mind."

The 320B convulsed so badly it turned on its side and threw them all to their left, into seats and walls. Trey hung on for dear life, trying desperately to level the aircraft out, with no success. It sounded like it would break in half any minute.

Michael saw the 320B ahead, then he saw *them*. Beelzebub and Belial screamed instructions, as the demon horde attacked the aircraft more viciously with each yell. Who led them? Legion! Of course, he commanded the tiny, destructive demons, who always thirsted for blood. Abaddon was there too! The destroyer! He was right, Beelzebub brought them all for this one. Even Haborym! His fire would send the plane flaming into the water below.

"Let's go, Host! *Hadassah, pray!*" his voice thundered, also drawing the attention of his hated foe.

Michael! She heard his voice clearly and spun to see him, but he wasn't there. *Michael, where are you?* Now the word echoed in her ears coming from far away. *Pray!* The battle was happening right then, and Michael needed her! Hadassah wished the entire 144,000 below were praying with her at this moment, but they slept, unaware of what was happening a thousand miles away. She collapsed face down and cried out to Jesus, not caring who heard her.

"*Beelzebub!*" Michael yelled and saw the mighty demon spin toward the incoming Host, eyes glowing red and yellow. He saw them from this distance, glowing more the closer they got. The Host charged forward with swords drawn. This battle would be greater than any previous ones.

Inside the 320B, everyone except Trey lay on the floor holding on to seat legs or anything else they could grab. The aircraft convulsed and suddenly nosedived toward the sea. Outside, the demon horde covered the plane completely, making it appear like a gigantic swarm of killer bees flying and attacking together, now diving toward the water.

Michael had no time to think or wait. He had not planned for this and was unprepared for the massive demonic army they were about to face. While thousands of tiny demons controlled the plane, millions more now flew toward them, with the demon princes leading the charge. Beelzebub and Belial flew directly at him and he realized he was powerless to stand against them.

"Why didn't I prepare? How could I let my guard down and put everything in jeopardy? Yahweh, forgive me! Hadassah, PRAY!" He tried to retreat, but it was too late. Beelzebub slammed into him with such force it sent him reeling, dazed and unable to respond. He tried to regain composure, but something rammed him from the other side. *Belial.* Michael felt himself losing consciousness and saw the two princes attacking with Abaddon and Haborym. His eyes blurred and he lost sight.

Anders stood and prayed louder than they had heard him before. How did he stand so firmly as the plane shook so violently? None of them could even get to their knees, much less stand. But he stood strong and erect, unmoving, his voice so loud they heard it above the noise. *Scripture!* He quoted Bible verses, then started calling out names.

"Away from us, demons! The one with us is greater than the one who leads you. We proclaim *his* name, *Jesus*! He disarmed your power and authority and made a public spectacle of you. He triumphed over you by *his cross.* We are more than conquerors through him! You are already defeated, Beelzebub! You cannot win, Belial! You will be destroyed, Abaddon! Your horde must release us, Legion! Your fire is extinguished, Haborym! Victory is already ours through Jesus!"

The shaking increased until the aircraft could not possibly continue flying. The group had no time to check on each other. They struggled to protect themselves, not realizing Michael was about to lose his life as he fought to save theirs. Neither did the group at Tel Nof know the plane carrying their friends was about to plunge into the Mediterranean Sea, killing them all. Far away, the Great Red Dragon, called the devil, or Satan, who leads the whole world astray, celebrated his greatest victory. He was unstoppable now.

CHAPTER 12

Hadassah lay stretched on a sandstone boulder atop Petra's highest peak, praying loudly, her tears forming a tiny river flowing across the rock, her voice reverberating off nearby mountains. She fought alongside Michael and the Host from afar, but realized in her spirit, the enemy was winning the battle. Her prayers increased with such intensity and volume that she was completely unaware of her surroundings. Distant voices joined hers, their prayers also piercing the night.

Neither Ben nor Mordecai understood why they were praying, but that did not stop them. Both men's voices echoed throughout Petra, and one-by-one, others began praying, too. The same thing happened at Tel Nof, sparked by John and Kathie. It spread to four vans filled with believers driving from Vatican City to an Italian Airbase. None were there fighting the battle, but they fought just as hard in prayer.

Gabriel tore through the sky, reaching his fellow archangel simultaneously with the demonic princes. Darting from underneath, he grabbed Michael, and with all the strength he could muster, hurled him upward, as the four converged from all sides. He grunted as they rammed him, then fluttered straight up, disoriented, intense pain shooting through his body. But he had to reach his partner.

Rendered helpless and barely conscious, Michael heard Beelzebub scream his name and knew the beast was coming to finish him. Thoughts of eternity with Yahweh before he created the universe, Lucifer's fall, his own battles with the fallen angel, the

Smyrnians, Hadassah, and many more flashed through his mind as one vast scene. Massive hands grabbed him and he resigned himself to his fate. Gabriel saw it, made an abrupt right turn, and flew rapidly back toward the plane.

A robust member of the Heavenly Host swept Michael into his arms as four others surrounded him. A hundred Host were on the mighty princes before they realized what had happened. Legion and the horde focused only on taking down the plane and failed to notice them. They smashed into the enormous demons, sending them reeling. When they saw the overwhelming odds, Beelzebub, Belial, Abaddon, and Haborym fled past the battle line, leaving Legion and his horde of demons at the Host's mercy. The entire heavenly army flew at them, swords flashing, tore their grips from the aircraft, and sent them tumbling through the air. They joined the princes, fleeing for their lives.

The Host grabbed the big aircraft, slowly stabilized it, and sent it once again toward its destination. Fourteen passengers stood shakily, faces pale, and nauseated, then sat quickly, as two pilots breathed a sigh of relief. Blake looked to make sure everyone was okay, but found one was missing.

"Where's Gabriel?" he asked.

The five soldiers ran toward the back and met Gabriel staggering down the aisle. They reached him as he collapsed into a seat halfway toward the front.

"Gabriel! What happened?" Steve asked, racing toward them and kneeling in front of him. The man did not reply. "Somebody bring my bag, quick!"

While Steve tended to Gabriel's injuries, Blake watched, wondering again who this man might be. Thoughts of Michael came too. Were the names coincidental, or was there more to them than met the eye. He would receive answers someday, but for now, none of that mattered.

Hadassah now sat staring out over the barren wasteland surrounding Petra, prayers still silently escaping her lips. Michael's voice had gone silent. She no longer heard his cries for prayer ringing in her mind. Her whole body felt numb, and tears rolled down her cheeks. She kept whispering his name, *Michael*, as one question continued pounding her brain: *Is everything lost?* A sound startled her. Two massive beings soared toward her. She jumped to her feet, but her legs refused to move.

They came closer, and she recognized the Host carrying someone in their arms. Michael! The mighty angels lay their wounded leader at her feet and flew away without saying a word. She wanted to yell and ask them what happened and what she needed to do, but nothing would come except one word: *Michael*. She wept and continued softly crying his name. The warrior was dead.

She lay her head on his chest and felt it slowly rising and falling. He was breathing! In the quietness of the moment, he whispered a name: *Gabriel*. He said it over and over. *Gabriel... Gabriel*. "What happened, Michael? Is Gabriel okay?" Hadassah realized their teasing was all in fun. The two archangels were partners in Yahweh's work and cared deeply for each other. She hoped Gabriel was safe, but her most pressing concern was taking care of her dear friend.

Her inclination was to run and bring Ben and her Uncle Mordecai, but Michael did not look like the soldier they knew. He was his true self, the mighty warrior angel who led Yahweh's army. She must handle this herself. The Host surely trusted her or they would not have brought him. She could not take him below, but he needed help. A voice came from above as Hadassah stood, mouth wide open, entranced by what she saw.

"Arise, my warrior."

The archangel floated off the boulder, levitating five feet above the ledge. A halo of brilliant light encircled his head, and continued across his entire body, healing him inside and out. His eyes opened, he gasped for breath, sat up in midair, and looked at her, his face covered with concern.

"The battle was hard. I wouldn't be here if Gabriel hadn't rescued me from the demon princes. He saved my life, Hadassah. We have to go check on him and find out if he's okay. The princes closed in and were ready to finish me, but he came out of nowhere, grabbed me, and threw me upward to safety. I heard him grunt as they narrowly missed me. All four must have smashed him. Please help me get to him. I'm weak, Hadassah, but we must get to Gabriel."

She did not hesitate or ask him the questions burning in her mind. He needed to find Gabriel, and she needed to take him. Questions could come as they flew, but they would make no difference now. They lifted off and he led the way, with her by his side supporting his weight, as they sailed away toward Rome, over the Mediterranean Sea.

Steve cared for Gabriel's wounds. Bruises covered his upper torso and face, showing he had fallen onto something while the plane rocked back and forth. But one thing baffled the surgeon: a large burn on Gabriel's left side. It looked like no other burn he had treated in all his years practicing medicine. Whatever did this burned through his flesh and exposed his ribs. The burn required immediate treatment. Steve realized he had not brought sufficient medication to prevent infection, so he cleaned and dressed the wound, then turned to checking his unconscious patient further.

"What caused that?" asked a soldier after Steve finished dressing Gabriel's burn. "There's nothing back here to burn him."

"Nothing we've ever seen caused this. I can't explain it, but he needs more treatment than I can give here, and that doesn't need to wait another four to five hours."

The others left to pray for their fallen comrade while Steve sat with him. They realized the extreme turbulence came from no natural source and understood who caused it: Messai's demonic army.

Michael and Hadassah arrived and saw the plane. He celebrated the Host's victory as the huge aircraft sailed smoothly toward Rome. Hadassah suddenly found herself standing inside, looking at her friends. *How did that happen?* This new journey with her friend never got old and brought fresh experiences every time they traveled. The incorporeality and ability to pass through plane walls was amazing! Yet, here she stood with Michael looking down at Gabriel lying before them.

"Haborym," Michael said, anger in his voice. *Can archangels feel anger,* she wondered. He lifted both hands and gazed toward heaven, his lips moving, but no audible words coming from them. Steve watched the bandage peel away, exposing the open wound. He wanted to do something, but his hands would not move. Flesh covered Gabriel's ribs, then continued growing upward until the entire burn disappeared and skin covered it, looking like nothing had happened.

"Michael, did you see that?" Hadassah asked. "Of course, you did. What was I thinking?"

He only smiled as his fellow archangel returned his smile, then opened his eyes and spoke to Steve.

"Hey, Steve, I'm okay now, but I appreciate you helping me out. That turbulence must have really thrown me for a loop and caused me to hit my head on something."

"It looked worse than that, Gabriel. There was a bad burn I couldn't do anything about. It was... Oh, forget it. Let's go tell the others." He had witnessed a miracle, but would keep that to himself.

When Steve started walking, Michael helped his colleague up and hugged him before he followed. Gabriel winked at Hadassah, too, as he left. She waved with a wide grin as Michael took hold of her arm. They disappeared through the plane wall and flew toward Petra. Questions entered her mind, then left, and she realized her previous thought was right: none were worth asking.

***

While the flight continued, a night raid took place in Vatican City. AMPP patrols acting on anonymous tips knocked on doors and searched homes looking for cardinals, nuns, and any others who rejected the mark and worshiped Jesus, instead of Aissa Messai. They burst through Lukas' front and back doors and shattered windows, dashing into the house, ready to apprehend the rebels.

The story remained the same at each house. No one was home, but ample evidence pointed to their recent presence. They would apprehend any cardinals missed during the raids at the upcoming meeting. Messai would crush the movement before returning to Jerusalem.

Unknown to AMPP, the believers sat at Pratica di Mare Airbase awaiting rescue. "Are you certain they can get us out by 2:00?" a Cardinal asked Lukas. "We felt compelled to pray for them earlier, so I hope nothing happened that will make them arrive late. If Messai finds us, we won't survive."

"Blake Thompson promised me they will arrive before 2:00, and I believe him. We prayed like Jesus told us to, so if we have faith, we must believe he will answer our prayers."

"You're right, Lukas. My faith has stayed strong since I believed, and that can't stop now."

"Cardinal Giordano," a man said, and waved for them to come. "Your plane will land shortly."

Lukas' phone rang as the man spoke, and he saw Blake's name. "Mr. Thompson, they just told us you're getting close."

"We should land within fifteen minutes, Lukas, no later than 1:45. I'm sorry for being late, but someone, or something, attacked us and nearly crashed us into the Mediterranean. I'm sure the demons did it, but Jesus saved us. If he hadn't, we wouldn't have made it, or rescued you. That tells me Jesus wants you out of there, so get ready to fly!"

They ended the call, and the group hurried to meet them. When the plane broke through the clouds and descended toward the runway, they quietly rejoiced. It touched down and taxied to where they stood. Trey and Rickie switched places for the return flight. The minute all were on board and the door closed, Rickie took off, and they climbed into the sky, bound for Israel. The Smyrnians got acquainted with their new teammates during a smooth flight until they landed safely in Tel Nof.

***

A few hours later, Messai sat in his Vatican office, joined by Caiaphas, watching Gregory and the cardinals enter. They had undermined him long enough. Gregory would either turn the cardinals and nuns who refused his mark over to him or pay the ultimate price. Surely, the man realized by now, he could hide nothing from the risen messiah. After giving him an opportunity to release the rebel's names, AMPP men would enter and scan every person, revealing which men remained unmarked. The former pope and cardinals took their seats.

"Did you forget something?" Messai bellowed, pointing to an image of himself standing by the door. The men had overlooked both the statue and Caiaphas standing beside it.

What? Gregory thought. *Messai demanded he, the pope, bow to his statue?* Then he saw AMPP men standing around the room fully armed. How could he bring himself to bow before the man's image? He had taken his mark and allowed him to remove him and his leaders from office and take over the palace. But this was asking too much.

"Now!" Armed guards stepped forward, clearly showing their intention to use force if they refused. Caiaphas lifted his hands, and the statue came to life, ordering them to bow.

Gregory rose and led the way, the others following. He bowed low before the statue and almost crossed himself, stopping just before he did. Messai recognized his slip-up but did not mention it.

"Take your seats, gentlemen. There is one urgent matter we must cover before we continue. Gregory, have all individuals serving under you received my mark?"

"We received your mark publicly, and the media covered it."

"Men," Messai said, motioning to his AMPP patrol, who produced scanners and prepared to check each person there. Every man willingly submitted, and results proved they all had the mark.

"Sir, I cannot believe you would question our integrity or our allegiance to you," said Gregory.

"Silence! I learned some of your cardinals refused the mark. Are they all present now?"

No one spoke, including the former pope, yet faces revealed they knew some were absent.

"Cardinal Giordano, where are you?" Messai asked. No one raised their hand. He called the names of two others, with no response again. "Gregory, where are they? Bring them now!"

"Perhaps they are ill this morning, Your Majesty, because I have not seen them."

"Check their rooms!"

A half-dozen men hurried out to check three apartments where the missing cardinals lived. They returned ten minutes later.

"Sir, neither of them is home. Clothing and personal items are missing, so they may have escaped."

"What about the nuns?"

"Last night's search failed to locate them, and every situation seems the same."

"Gregory, I am disappointed in you. You are responsible for maintaining the integrity of this institution and ensuring your adherents follow me. It seems you lost control of your people."

"Mr. Messai, I had no idea..."

"That is enough! Search every square inch of this city until you find them, then bring them here! My men will sequester the rest of you in your rooms until further notice and make sure you do not leave. This meeting is adjourned."

The AMPP patrol accompanied each man to his apartment and left to join the search for escapees they would not find. Those they sought joined their fellow believers in Tel Nof three hours earlier.

Blake's phone rang at 7:00 p.m. and he answered, eager to tell Ben and Mordecai about the successful rescue and the battle they faced pulling it off. The other two were equally eager to hear.

"Ben, I'm glad you called, because I have good news for you! We rescued fifty believers from Vatican City and Rome last night and returned here to Tel Nof before daylight."

"Did the plane work for you?" Mordecai asked before Ben could say a word.

"It worked great!" Trey answered before Blake could reply.

"Would you two slow down so we can all talk?" Ben asked. "Blake, tell us the story from start to finish. We haven't talked to you since you left Zedekiah's Cave."

Blake shared the entire adventure from leaving the cave until the present moment, with Trey and others interrupting and interjecting often. Hearing about the darkness stunned Ben and Mordecai, but the demonic attack during the flight told them why they felt the urge to pray. Blake allowed Lukas, Cardinal Giordano, and the others to speak with them. It was a glorious conversation between believers in Jesus who would soon meet and live together forever.

"Mordecai, do we need to know anything else about this place?" Ollie asked.

"These come to mind. First, we stored gravity nukes south of the base. Stay near the main base and you will avoid them. Second, the mess hall may still have food remaining, so enjoy it! Finally, you should find a cache of weapons in an underground bunker. I will text directions after we finish this call. You will need them if they discover you are there."

"That helps!" Blake said before saying goodbye. "We won't go anywhere near the nukes, but we will enjoy the food and protect ourselves with the weapons. Thank you, Mordecai!"

His text came soon, and the treasure hunt was on for food and weapons. More food remained than they could have dreamed, and the weapons cache would protect them far longer than three months. They were all set to survive until September 11th.

"Come!" Messai shouted, his voice full of rage. Beelzebub and Belial appeared and approached him slowly, heads bowed.

"Did you allow Smyrnians to infiltrate this place and help *his* followers escape?" The two beasts stood silently, both looking toward the other, but neither speaking. "Speak!" he screamed again.

"We discovered their plot just in time and unleashed an all-out assault on their plane, Your Majesty. We had them and were about to take them down when Gabriel appeared from nowhere and saved Michael, then..."

"Michael again? You allow one of *his* troops to control your thinking and let down your guard. How can you, the leader of my powerful army, continually lose to *his* pathetic excuse for an army?"

The mighty evil demon recoiled at that attack on his power and military capacity. "Sir, I have heard you say we kill the snake by cutting off its head. Michael leads them, so if we destroy him, they are powerless against us forever. Therefore, we seek him first every time."

"Fool! In seeking one, you allow others to win. So, while you went after Michael, Gabriel came to rescue him. That allowed others to attack, and you were unprepared for them."

How did he know that? both demons wondered. "Let me explain, Your Majesty," Belial said, trying to help his partner and appease their commander-in-chief.

"You have no explanation or excuse! Because of your incompetence, who knows how many of *his* followers escaped our grasp again? I want them! Send the entire army to find them, so AMPP can bring them to me. They will all face the device before the great battle comes!"

They left at once to carry out his orders, yet realized their chances of success were low if *he* protected them. However, if they could only get Michael, their efforts would be rewarded. They would give their all and leave nothing to chance. Let the search begin!

Messai now sat alone, preparing for his return flight to Jerusalem in two days. He must stay long enough to ensure everything was ready for the onslaught. Chen would handle that, while he focused on other matters. Caiaphas must ramp up pressure on his worshipers. The NWO leaders would plan the final battle, which was coming soon. His mind raced with thoughts.

A jolt suddenly threw him from his chair onto the floor. The room rattled as things fell and crashed with loud sounds. *Earthquake!* He stood and raised his hands as Caiaphas often did, then screamed louder than he ever had. The shaking stopped, and things returned to normal. He smiled and said aloud to no one but himself, "I have all power! No one can defeat me!"

***

"Earthquake!" said one new Tel Nof resident, diving under a table as they all ate lunch together.

"Not yet," John said, still joining him, as did the others. When the shaking stopped, he continued. "Each tremor gets more powerful leading to the massive quake described in Revelation 16. It hasn't happened yet, but will come soon. It will reshape the entire planet, making it unrecognizable compared to before. We must decide how to protect ourselves."

"Won't it coincide with Jesus' coming, John? If they occur simultaneously, we won't have to worry about it."

"I don't understand how it will happen, Blake. But it will be absolutely devastating when it does, so I'd rather not be here to witness it."

"We can't prepare for that kind of devastation," Ollie said. "All we can do is wait and see what happens, then watch for Jesus to come. That is one thing about which we are absolutely certain!"

"Do we sit here for three months and do nothing?" asked Bruno. "I planned to fight Messai as long as I could! If we're not going on any more rescue missions, I want to do something which slows him down or stops him from slaughtering any more believers."

"He may not be finished with us yet, Bruno," said Anders.

They all knew he saw everything in the scroll, so they became quiet, wondering what he meant by that. He did not elaborate further, so they could only wait and hope to survive.

***

Michael and Hadassah walked down the mountain and entered Petra. They met Ben and Mordecai returning from another peak after calling Blake. The day and night without sleep, combined with long flights and rigorous activity, caught up with her, and she looked exhausted.

"Hadassah, did you pray all night up there?" her uncle asked.

"I did, Uncle, because I couldn't stop. No one told me why I was praying, but I heard a voice begging me to pray. Did you hear it too?"

"We didn't hear a voice, but knew we needed to pray. Others joined us, praying all over Petra. It was such an amazing experience that I feel absolutely certain our prayers were answered. Were you praying all day too, Hadassah? You didn't return till evening, so I wondered..."

Michael interrupted his question. "Someone needed your prayers and Jesus answered them, Aluf."

"I wish you could explain that to us in more detail Michael, but I won't pry any further. If you want to tell us more, I assume you will. If you don't, that's okay."

"Thank you, sir. I am just speaking from experience. Jesus has done many miracles because we prayed. But he doesn't always tell us why we need to pray right then, only that we must pray. Praying is one of the most important things we do because prayer changes things."

"You are wise beyond your years, Michael. I thank Jesus for bringing you to us."

"That means a lot coming from you, Rabbi."

"Michael, how many times have I told you to call me Ben?"

"More times than I can count, and you must admit, I have done well. But it hasn't always been easy because I have such great respect for you. Thank you for loving me and mentoring me in my walk with Jesus."

Tears rolled from Ben's eyes, and he embraced the young soldier. "Sometimes I have felt it was you who mentored me. You have taught me many things. Thank *you*."

"Aluf, you have also made a difference in my life. I'm still amazed that I know the IDF Major General and he calls me his friend. Thank you for accepting me and allowing your niece to travel with me on my adventures."

Mordecai extended his hand. "A Major General does not hug, Michael, but I will shake your hand and thank you for serving the Israeli Defense Force and our Savior, and for protecting my niece."

Michael feigned jumping toward him, arms open, then laughed and firmly squeezed his hand. It was a powerful moment between the three men. Hadassah stood back and enjoyed it.

"It's after 8:00, and we all need a good night's sleep," she said. "I'll see you tomorrow morning."

They parted ways, crashed, and slept all night, except for one. His night was just beginning.

***

Legion's horde flew over Italy and Israel, the two most likely destinations for the traitors. Legion called off the Italy search and summoned his troops to Israel. He knew the Smyrnians rescued them because they saw them through the plane's windows, and Israel was their last known location. He must tell Beelzebub and Belial. They would not want to miss this party.

The tiny demons checked all former Smyrnian hideouts, starting with Zedekiah's Cave, where they flew from entrance to exit, hoping to find them holed up there again. But the cave was deserted. Ein Gedi, abandoned bunkers across the Golan Heights, and two vacated Bedouin camps came next, with the same results. Beelzebub and Belial called in every prince and the entire horde. If Israel's residents could see them, the sky would turn dark because they covered it.

At Tel Nof, Beth awoke at 1:00 a.m. and pulled up an army-issued blanket they found. The night air felt chilly, even though it should be warm, based on forecast temperatures. She thought about waking Blake, but waited, and let him sleep. The temperature continued dropping as minutes dragged by. By 2:00 a.m., she lay under two blankets and still shivered. At 3:00, she woke Blake.

"What's wrong, Beth? Whoa, it's frigid in here. It got a lot colder than the weather people said it would. Stop hogging those blankets."

"Something's not right because there's no way it turned this cold in mid-June. You don't suppose Messai knows where we are?"

"That's not impossible. Perhaps we should get up, check it out, and wake everyone else."

They found several already up, some eating an early breakfast or just having coffee, most wrapped in blankets or wearing heavy coats. Summer suddenly felt like January in central Israel.

"What's up with this freezing weather?" John asked as he and Kathie walked into the mess hall yawning and rubbing their eyes.

"I don't think it's coming from the weather," Beth said. "I believe Messai or his demons are searching for us and getting close. It always turns cold when they show up."

"Beth is right," said Magnus. "Anders told us he may not be finished with us yet."

"And this proves it," Anders said, walking in with Ally. "When we woke to these freezing temperatures, I realized what was happening right away. Messai is angry after you guys escaped," he said, pointing at the Vatican City group, "and knows by now we helped you."

"We didn't mean to cause you trouble," Lukas said. "We just wanted away from Vatican City."

"There was no way we were leaving you there," said Trey. "We're glad you're here and safe. Now it's time we all fight together and overcome Messai. We need to survive for three more months."

"I'm ready!" Bruno said. "Remember, we big men love a good fight! Right, Magnus?"

"Right on, Bruno! But I warn you, this won't be a normal fight with an ordinary enemy. We are squaring off against an invisible and powerful foe who longs to destroy us."

"We are well aware of that, Magnus," Blake said. "This enemy comes to steal, kill, and destroy, but we have defeated him before, and we can do it again with Jesus' help. Let's talk about our next moves before they find us, so we'll be ready. Any ideas?"

"Does that mean we have to leave this place?" Beth asked.

"I wish I could answer that for you, Beth," said Anders. "The scroll showed us in Tel Nof, but I can't say for sure it's where we're going to stay until Jesus comes. But that doesn't mean we shouldn't come up with a battle plan to defend our territory if we do."

"Well, why are we waiting? Let's put a plan together and get ready for war!" Magnus said.

Inside a nearby hangar, Gabriel sat talking with Michael.

"Ask Yahweh to show me what we should do, and I'll tell them. We'll win this war, but I believe his people will continue fighting battles until that time comes."

"I'll go now, Gabriel, and ask Yahweh for his help. He told me we cannot help them during these last three and a half years, but maybe he'll let us intervene now. All I can do is ask, right?"

"Go while I speak with them, but let me know when you return, and I'll meet you back here."

"I'm not sure how I will elude those demons getting to Yahweh, but I'll do my best. I wish the Host was flying with me today."

"Be careful, Michael, because you're going alone. If Beelzebub removes you, he may win the war. That has been his goal from day one, and you can't let him do it now with less than one hundred days left. Come back safely and bring word from Yahweh."

Michael flew away bound for Yahweh's throne with no guarantee he would arrive safely, or that the Creator would listen to him when he did. But Yahweh loved people who followed his son very much, so perhaps this time called for a different response. That answer would come soon.

***

Beelzebub left Belial in charge of all the other demons and flew quickly to Vatican City. He must tell Messai they were closing in. His boss wanted to be there when they found the rebels so AMPP could capture them and he could watch the device end their lives. If only Michael showed up...

"Come in, my prince." Needless words because Beelzebub had already landed in his office.

"I come bringing news, Your Majesty. The troops have narrowed their location down within a forty-mile radius west of Jerusalem. They checked every place the Smyrnians hid before and found no one. The horde now covers the focus zone."

"I have asked that you refrain from using their name when speaking with me. Is that understood?"

"Yes, Your Majesty. Please accept my apologies and rest assured it will not happen again. I assumed you would want to return to Jerusalem for their capture and beheading."

"Yes, my prince, yes! I will make plans to leave right away so I do not miss this moment! Will you focus on apprehending *them* rather than defeating *him* until we accomplish this task? After that, you may pursue and annihilate *him*. That will make the great battle much easier for us."

"I will do that, sir. He remains my primary target, but we must also remove *them*. We will handle that first. However, if Michael shows up..."

"Beelzebub!"

"I understand, Your Majesty, and will ensure AMPP apprehends them first. I will see you in Jerusalem." He left without another word.

Michael soared low through wooded areas, dodging trees, trying to conceal himself from the horde above. Their keen sense of hearing would detect even the slightest sound. After passing the dark demonic cloud overhead, he sailed outward, then straight up before seeing a gigantic figure coming toward him. *Beelzebub!* He could not avoid him, so he prepared himself to fight. The beast passed by without acknowledging his presence, his eyes staring straight ahead.

Should he attack his archenemy? Beelzebub's failure to charge him could only mean one thing. He focused on something else more important: destroying the Smyrnians. He must attack and stop him! No, he must speak with Yahweh and receive his permission to help them. Disobeying orders during these final years was not an option after his eternal loyalty to his Creator. He continued his flight, soaring faster now. Soon Yahweh's throne came into view, and he bowed before it.

"Welcome back, warrior. For a few moments last night, I thought we lost you, but I am thankful Gabriel saved you when you needed him. I heard your prayer, and I forgive you for your mistakes."

"Your love amazes me, Lord. I put everything in jeopardy with my lack of preparation and deserve your criticism and punishment."

"I have loved you from the beginning, Michael, and I will never forsake you or condemn you."

"Thank you, Lord, even though I don't deserve it. I am always yours to command, but I come with a request today."

"I know, you want to protect my people. Do you remember my decree for this time?"

"I do, but Messai will destroy them before your son returns, if we don't stop him. The demons will soon discover their location, and AMPP will attack. Please give me permission to protect them."

"I authorize you to stand against the evil forces on their behalf, but you may not interfere with human foes. They must protect themselves during the remaining days. The great battle draws near, my warrior. While Beelzebub and his horde focus on *them*, you must prepare for *it*. But remember, that battle is mine, and I have everything under control. Now go, but you must return with Hadassah soon. Only two judgments remain."

Yahweh and Jesus smiled as their warrior angel stood and flew back toward earth. He had served them faithfully, and they trusted him to continue.

CHAPTER 13

Back in Jerusalem, Aissa Messai met with his Chief Security Officer. He could leave nothing to chance. His forces must keep the populace under control, while he prepared for the coming great battle. But their primary assignment remained pursuing and capturing *them*.

"Good morning, Mr. Rossi. I received word that we may soon discover *their* location. When we do, I assume we will also find those they stole away from us that night before we could execute them the next day, along with the rebels they snatched from Vatican City. That offers the opportunity to eliminate a significant number of insurgents. Mobilize all patrols and search a forty-mile radius extending west from Jerusalem. Remember, a group that large requires spacious accommodations, and we have ruled out all previous hideouts."

"We will explore that area right away, sir. Mobilizing every patrol will allow us to form a circle around the entire perimeter, moving in as we go. If they are there, we will find them."

"I trust you will. General Chen and his troops will carry out another important mission, while the NWO leaders plan for the great battle, which means this task belongs to you and your troops. You understand its importance, don't you, Mr. Rossi?"

"I do, sir, and seek their demise as well. Nothing would give me more pleasure than extinguishing them from the earth. You can count on your men from AMPP."

"Rossi, I have heard that before, yet it has never happened. We have taken out very few of them, which makes me unhappy.

However, their destruction would bring me unspeakable joy. You would like to make me happy, wouldn't you?"

"When we capture them, we will throw an execution party, sir, hosting our greatest celebration yet. Perhaps you should include the world, as you did after the deaths of Moshe and Eliyahu. If we encircle them, they cannot escape us this time."

"I shall eagerly await further word from you. Do not disappoint me again, Mr. Rossi. I desire to see this happen more than anything else as the big day approaches. Another coming event will also shock the world. These are exciting days!"

His head of security left to marshal every AMPP patrol at his disposal to root out and capture Messai's most hated and dangerous enemy. After many failures, that would finally happen.

***

Gabriel received Michael's summons and eased outside to meet him in the hangar. He wasted no time asking the pertinent question: "Michael, will Yahweh allow us to protect his people?"

"Let's just say you and I have different roles in this, Gabe, my friend. I'm sorry; you realize I'm only having fun when I do that. I will never stop thanking you for saving my life during that fight. Here's the thing: Yahweh gave me permission to fight the demons, but the believers must battle their human foes without my help. But *you can* help them because you are one of them!"

"Right you are, Mikey," Gabriel said laughing. "People would assume we're crazy if they heard us having fun like this. They might think we're human. I suppose one could say we *are* right now."

"People assume Yahweh is always serious, but I love his sense of humor. He created everyone with the same thing, but most seldom take time to laugh, and forget that Solomon said, 'a cheerful heart is good medicine.' Think how much fun they will have with us in eternity!"

"They certainly will, but this is a serious time, Michael. Little time remains, and Jesus' followers will face death and destruction every day. I would love for them to all survive, but we both realize that is unlikely with AMPP and Beelzebub's crew searching for them. They will surely find them soon. You fight above, and I will fight below, and we will protect them the best we can."

"I agree. Get back to their meeting, and let's talk often. I'm glad Yahweh sent you, too."

They parted ways, with Michael figuring out how to avoid Beelzebub and return to Petra, while Gabriel eased back into the meeting unnoticed, to everyone except Blake.

***

"Your Majesty, we narrowed the hot zone down to thirty-five miles west from Jerusalem by twenty miles north to south. We are getting closer."

"Good work, Beelzebub, and the same to our other princes and the horde. If they all stay together, we will wipe out the entire group at once. I plan to enjoy this even more than the coming assault!"

"We will continue closing in until we locate them, then hand things over to your men and let them take it from there. Prepare to celebrate, Your Majesty!"

The mighty prince left thinking about another and planning his own celebration. Michael would come, and this time he would be ready. His evil grin revealed his insatiable appetite for that victory.

Michael flew toward the Sea, avoiding the demons, but noticed something: Beelzebub was conspicuously missing. Why would his nemesis allow him to leave alone without attacking him? It was unlike the beast to let the warrior angel pass peacefully without trying to destroy him. He must figure out what Beelzebub was planning before something bad happened. But now, he must get to Hadassah. Another journey awaited them tomorrow.

***

"Welcome back, Gabriel," Blake said. "I saw you slip out a little while ago. Is everything okay?" His thoughts still centered on the man's identity, but those questions could wait.

"I'm fine, Blake, but my mind is running wild with questions about what we should do. My military experience says we should take all measures to protect ourselves because Messai and AMPP will keep searching until they find us."

"Trust me, they *will* find us," Magnus said, interrupting Gabriel, who was clearly not finished. "My AMPP captain's experience agrees with him and says we need to heed his advice right now."

"We have all the firepower we need from that weapons cache," Trey said, "so we can defend ourselves from ground attacks. But what about aerial attacks?"

"We also have fighter jets with ammunition and bombs that will allow us to engage in air-to-air and air-to-ground combat, so we can shoot them down up there or bomb them down here. It has been awhile since you and I experienced a good dogfight, Trey."

"That sounds good to me, Rickie. Bring it on!"

"Hold on, guys, we don't want unnecessary killing," Blake said, trying to calm the two pilots down and change course to include other important factors.

"It's not unnecessary if it's kill or be killed," Bruno said. "And they definitely want to kill us."

"Jesus said we may protect ourselves," Gabriel said, then stopped, realizing he was about to give himself away. Blake was getting ready to ask when Jesus told him that, but Anders spoke first.

"Gabriel is right, and I agree with Blake and Bruno. We shouldn't kill unnecessarily, but if it becomes unavoidable, we must protect ourselves."

Once again, they listened to him because he spent time in heaven and returned to them. His words carried more weight than any other.

"Okay, I'll leave those plans to you military people," Blake said. "If you need anything from us, say the word. We will think about other issues that could arise and how to handle them."

The groups separated, with the action-minded group excited about planning for potential battles, while the rest set about other things, hoping these three months would pass quickly.

**

Messai was leaving nothing to chance this time. He called his Chief Security Officer to report Beelzebub's updated information. They must trap *his* people like caged animals, leaving them no route by which they could escape to freedom again. This was his hour when the power of darkness would prevail, and he would rule the world. He could not allow them to interfere with his plans.

"Mr. Rossi, please give me a progress update."

"I mobilized every available patrol, sir, and have formed an invincible circle from Jerusalem to the Mediterranean, extending forty miles in each direction. They cannot get past our men at any point."

"Excellent! I received new surveillance information which allows you to narrow your search zone from thirty-five miles west of Jerusalem to only twenty miles north to south. That should squeeze the enemy even more."

"I will do that right away, Mr. Messai. When we find them, shall we surround their location and hold them inside until bombers can annihilate them?"

"Absolutely not, Rossi! *I* will annihilate them individually in the device. That may take hours, but each time I pull the lever releasing that blade will be wonderful use of my time."

"We will take the entire group into custody and bring them to you. I remain honored to serve you, sir, and trust you will remember me when you come into your kingdom."

"Mr. Rossi, you should never question that. You will reign with me soon because victory is within our grasp!"

The man departed the office now grateful he saw the truth and followed Aissa Messai. He would wear his mark proudly after this and reign with him forever. And he would not allow the Smyrnians or any other followers of *him* to stand in his way.

***

Michael led Hadassah back to the mountaintop early the next morning. The sun broke over the horizon, signaling the beginning of another beautiful day in Petra. Their journey today would reveal the next phase of Yahweh's final judgment. He could tell she was excited about seeing it.

"Today will look different from the other times and will confuse you until it happens in real life."

"What's different about that? I haven't understood any bowl until it actually happened."

"But this one will look weird to you, I promise. Wait till you see it, and you will understand what I mean. Are you ready to fly?"

She lifted off before him, forcing him to catch up with her, which he did quickly, and passed her. Now it was her turn to fly faster, so he would not leave her behind. Then it happened, and time slowed. She realized it would come, but nothing ever prepared her for it. The spirit of Esther rose in her again, and this time a sense of impending judgment accompanied it.

Visions of Xerxes' wickedness and Persia's decline under his leadership filled her mind. Her heart raced recalling his violent murder by those who made Artaxerxes, his son by Vashti, king in his place. After his death, she and Mordecai also paid for his atrocities.

Her heart broke now knowing Persia declined until Greece conquered it over one hundred years later, a shell of its former glory.

She suddenly realized how that foreshadowed what was happening now. Wickedness covered the earth and it collapsed into decline before the Rapture, then continued spiraling downward under Aissa Messai's evil leadership. Yahweh's judgment would soon fall on the dragon's kingdom, destroy it forever, and usher in Jesus' kingdom of peace and happiness. Hadassah realized she was about to witness that wrath and destruction, but experience the latter for herself. That excited her!

"You were remembering Persia, weren't you?"

"Yes, and how Yahweh's judgment fell on both Xerxes and the Kingdom of Persia itself because of his wicked lifestyle. This time the dragon and his followers will face Yahweh's judgment. And the nation which rose to prominence through the dragon's power will lead them."

"And I thought you would struggle to figure this out. I hope more will become clear after you watch the sixth angel pour out his bowl, but you still may not grasp it all. We shall see."

"Well, I can't wait any longer. Come on, this girl is ready to fly!"

They soared even faster, both eager to reach their destination and see what Yahweh would show them. Everything happening on earth left their minds as they sped toward the temple in heaven.

***

"Come, *Gog*! Come, *Beelzebub*! Come, *Belial*!" Messai shouted, and the three demonic princes appeared before him within seconds.

"Yes, Master," said Gog. "This must mean the time has come!"

"It has indeed, my prince. What you have worked so hard to achieve will now become reality. They are ready to come, and the others will follow, with a little persuasion. I reserved this task for the three of you because I would never entrust it to anyone else."

"But we are close to locating the enemy, Your Majesty," Beelzebub said. "Both Belial and I wanted keep an eye on your men and make sure they deliver them to you." Belial nodded in agreement.

"Ah, my princes, Legion can handle that, and the others can assist him. He commands the horde, and Abaddon is my destroyer, thus we assigned them this task. You will help the dragon and I unite a formidable army and lead them into the great battle. We would trust no one else with that!"

"I stand ready, Master, and welcome the help of my fellow princes," Gog said again. "The three of us working together cannot fail!"

"Your Majesty, when will you give us details of this mission?" asked Belial. "I assure you we will obey your command and give everything we have to bring about your reign with the dragon."

"Gog will share the details with you today as your search continues. Caiaphas and I will fly to join the dragon and you tomorrow at a carefully selected location. Today, you may rejoin the others. When you arrive, send Legion and Abaddon back to me so I may explain their roles during the time you are away. And my princes, do not be late for tomorrow's appointment!"

The three departed, with two unsure why their master would pull them from the role they most wanted to perform. Michael would show up eventually, and both planned to seize that opportunity to eliminate him, too. Obedience was non-negotiable, so they would begrudgingly do as they were told.

But then, this new task must be urgent for Messai to include them. Gog would fill them in soon. They arrived back at the search zone and sent Legion and Abaddon to meet their master and receive orders for capturing and destroying the Smyrnians. Their fellow princes were trustworthy and would fulfill that mission with excellence. Things were moving now. Their time really had come!

***

"Where do you suppose they are today?" Mordecai asked Ben.

"I don't know, but they leave nearly every day now that the end draws near. I believe something important is coming soon."

"Yes, and we may never hear about it. The only drawback to living *in here* is not knowing what happens *out there*. Don't misunderstand me, Ben. I would not trade this home for any other place."

"Neither would I, Mordecai, yet I also miss hearing and seeing current events. That is enough to drive a longtime newsman crazy. But it also makes me want to live here forever, even realizing what's coming will be far better."

"That's hard to imagine, although I know it's true. A lot will happen during the next three months before that time comes. I can feel it coming, though, can't you?"

"Sometimes my heart nearly beats out of my chest thinking about it. I have spent almost seven years preparing for what I will soon experience, and I can't describe how that makes me feel."

"Ben, thank you for welcoming me into the Smyrnians and teaching me more about Jesus as we walked this journey together. My faith has grown so much since Michael and Hadassah helped me put my faith in him. I climbed the IDF ranks and reached the top, but knowing Jesus is the best thing that ever happened to me. I wouldn't trade this life for anything."

"I achieved success in the news industry, Mordecai, but I'll never regret leaving it to follow Jesus. He changed my life and gave me a purpose much greater than telling the news. He allowed me to tell my people the good news and see 144,000 of them turn to him. I am, of all men, most blessed."

"My only regret is that I didn't recognize the truth earlier. I wish I could tell everyone, please put your faith in Jesus before he returns, for then it will be too late. But many would refuse to listen and reject him like we did before the Rapture. Everyone must make that choice for themselves."

"I feel the same. But I am forever grateful he gave us another chance."

Both men stopped to thank Jesus for his love and grace, even after they rejected him for so many years. They prayed for others to believe in him, but both understood that would not happen now. The time for people to put their faith in Jesus had passed. That tempered their joy with a hint of sadness as they realized what unbelievers were about to face.

***

Gabriel stood alone outside the barracks where he stayed with his fellow American troops, listening carefully for sounds from above. He hoped *they* would not recognize his human form. The air was still, with no hint of a breeze that might interfere with his hearing. Nothing. He breathed a sigh of relief and walked farther. Still nothing. *Perhaps he stopped trying to locate us and is now focusing on other things before the great battle*, he thought. No, he knew the dragon, Beelzebub, Belial, and the other demons better than that, not to mention Messai.

He walked until he reached the razor-wire fence surrounding the compound. Wait, what was that? His supernatural hearing detected a faint sound overhead. A vibration? No, it sounded more like a swarm of bees, their tiny wings whirring as they moved. Out of nowhere, the truth hit him. He had heard this sound before, but it was not the wings of bees. *The dragon's army!* A million demons hovering just out of view searching for them. The others could not hear them, but he did.

Now, voices rang out above the din, not soft voices, but loud and boisterous. He recognized two immediately: Beelzebub and Belial. The two chief princes led this charge, meaning Messai was serious about finding the Smyrnians and those with them. He listened more closely.

"Lead the humans searching thirty-five miles west from Jerusalem, and spread out twenty miles on each side. Keep closing in until you find them. Belial, Gog, and I must leave on another mission, so Legion will take charge here while we are gone. I expect you to locate them before we return!"

Gabriel covered his ears until the demonic screeching subsided. They were not far away and would keep getting closer before they finally discovered their location. Michael said Yahweh forbade him to help the group fight their earthly foes, but granted the mighty warrior angel permission to battle the demons. They were the primary enemies. Gabriel would yield that responsibility to Michael, but he must tell him what he just heard. The messenger angel turned and hurried back to the barracks. He must contact his fellow archangel.

***

Michael and Hadassah arrived and found themselves on their knees before the temple again. The scene appeared surreal, with only two angels remaining. She glanced toward the earth and found it normal again, minus the darkness, combined with mournful wailing from the sores and scorching sun. The planet's beautiful blue color revealed the oceans no longer contained blood. That is how she remembered the globe when she first saw it from this vantage point. She smiled.

"Tell me what you see, Hadassah."

"The earth is normal again, but that makes no sense. If Yahweh's judgments lead to the final battle and Jesus' coming, why did they end and things become normal again?"

"Do you want me to explain that, or would you rather think about it for a while?"

"Just tell me. Everything fell into place for me while his judgments kept getting worse with each bowl. It was easy to view things declining until his ultimate punishment fell, just as it did for Persia because of Xerxes' wickedness. But how can things suddenly get better?"

"What is the *eye of the storm?*"

"The hurricane's most calm part located in the center."

"Correct. Before and after a hurricane makes landfall, wind and storm surge can bring catastrophic damage. Things can become eerily calm and deceptive when the eye comes ashore, making it easy to believe the storm has passed and calm has returned. But once the eye passes, what happens?"

"The winds explode within seconds from the opposite direction and can cause more damage than before. I get it! The first five judgments caused catastrophic damage on the earth. The sores, followed by both saltwater and fresh water turning to blood, the sun burning people, then Messai's kingdom plunging into darkness left people in utter despair. Now the world believes he removed the plagues and returned life to normal. I'm guessing that paves the way for Yahweh to lure them into his final trap. Am I right?"

"Well done! You answered correctly, and I award you an A+! Now, shall we watch what the sixth angel does to set that in motion?"

She nodded and started to speak, but the angel's movement caught their eyes and silenced her. He held out his bowl and walked toward them, then lifted off just before reaching them causing her to duck. Michael chuckled at her as both focused their attention on the angel soaring toward earth.

"Are you ready to leave?"

"What do you mean? The angel hasn't poured out his bowl yet. Please don't make me leave now."

"Wouldn't you like to see that happen in person?"

"You mean..."

"Let's go!" he said, grabbing her hand and pulling her up, then soaring faster than she imagined possible toward the descending angel of wrath.

Hadassah wondered how she was even breathing as wind rushed into her face, but it affected her no more than a fan blowing on its lowest speed. She stared at the angel, eagerly anticipating where they may be going. Barren landscape now appeared below with a slight slither of green meandering through it. None of this looked familiar.

Getting closer, the green line became a trickling river surrounded by arid desert. Though never having seen it before, she recognized the dwindling Euphrates. Seeing what remained of the once mighty river shocked her. Yet it still flowed in places until the angel emptied the contents of his bowl over it. When he did, the water dried up instantly, and the angel flew away.

Hadassah waited for Michael to rise and follow, but he still sat on air, apparently waiting for something else to occur. She did not interrupt him, but the suspense was driving her insane. After what felt like an hour, he turned and smiled.

"Do you understand what this means?"

"No," she said, barely louder than a whisper.

"Tomorrow you will, but we must watch from a safe distance. We could stay here and wait until it happens, but we will return to Petra so your uncle doesn't worry about you."

"Wait until what happens? You can't make me wait until tomorrow, please!"

"Not so impatient, young one. Tomorrow will come before you know it."

"Michael!"

"Let's go," he said matter-of-factly. Then he smiled and flew away.

She flew after him, continuing to call his name, but knowing he would not answer. Tomorrow felt like weeks away.

***

Messai recognized the sound of his princes coming near as their huge wings beat the air. Abaddon and Legion stood before him awaiting his words.

"Welcome, my princes. Thank you for leaving the search to spend a few minutes with me. Your leadership plays the most important role in the success of our mission. Legion, you lead the horde, and they always await your orders before taking action. They bear the greatest responsibility for finding the enemy. Keep squeezing in until you surround them and they cannot escape."

"I plan to do exactly that, Your Majesty. The little demons understand their specialty is search and find, and they almost never fail. Their most recent success occurred at Zedekiah's Cave. We will not let you down."

"The 144,000 escaped as they fled to Petra because *he* interfered. You bear no responsibility for that, and I have no doubt your horde will succeed this time. Now for you, Abaddon. The master named you destroyer, defining your purpose. I offer you the greatest opportunity yet to fulfill that role. Enemy groups now reside at one location, thinking they can hide from us and save their lives. When Legion's troops discover them, you will lead my men from AMPP to where they live so they may capture them. Then ensure they deliver them to me, and we will destroy them all."

The massive beast salivated, fantasizing about such an evil accomplishment. His master delighted in his enthusiasm. Abaddon spoke with the dragon's voice, one Messai often used himself.

"I will not fail, Your Majesty. Your men will be my pawns, and I will control their minds when we return, leaving them no choice but to obey my orders. I understand they serve you, but I will also flood their minds with thoughts of death and destruction."

"You have my complete trust, my prince. Now, both of you may go back and perform your duties. I will watch with joy. Remind Beelzebub, Belial, and Gog they must meet me tomorrow morning."

***

Gabriel asked for a private meeting with Anders, who still recognized the voice, but could not figure out where he heard it. The time had come for that to change.

"Anders, I am Gabriel who stands in Yahweh's presence. I spoke to you when you walked with Jesus in heaven, and you heard my voice as you ate the scroll. Then I met with you in the empty tomb. Yahweh sent me to protect the Smyrnians, but also to reveal the scroll's contents to you during these last days."

Anders sat there stunned for a moment, then fell to his knees before the archangel.

"Don't do that, Anders. I am also a servant of Yahweh along with you and others who follow the true Messiah. Worship Yahweh, and bow only to him."

Anders stood and embraced him. "You're right, Gabriel, we all serve God and follow Jesus. I will never understand why he gave me a second chance and chose me for such a special purpose."

"Yahweh loves you, Anders, but no more than the others. All who believe in Jesus are special to him. Now, tell me the next thing you remember from the scroll."

Anders' senses came alive with great clarity. "I hear loud buzzing. Hey, it's the same sound our group heard when we fled from AMPP at Ein Gedi!"

"That is the dragon's demonic army hovering overhead searching for us. If our group saw them, fear would consume them and they would flee, with no chance of survival. What else do you hear?"

"Voices and marching feet."

"Those come from AMPP patrols who search below while the demons look down from above. Messai commanded every patrol to search for us and not stop until they find us. They obey the demonic princes, even though they are unaware of their presence, just as they did at Ein Gedi."

"So, that's why AMPP was ready for us when we finally reached the Wolf. What can we do? It sounds like they surround us above and below, so how can we possibly escape?"

"Yahweh permitted Michael to battle the demons, but only we can fight the earthly foe."

"We certainly have enough ammunition and air power to do that, so... Wait, you don't mean *our* Michael, do you...?"

"He is Yahweh's warrior angel, also sent to protect his people. You remember many times some of you would not have survived without him. And only he and the Heavenly Host made sure the 144,000 Jewish believers arrived safely in Petra. Mordecai was right. Those planes could not fly with such great weight, but Michael and the Host held them aloft until they landed safely."

"I know nothing is impossible with Jesus, because he has proven that many times. Wait till the others hear who you are. It will strengthen their faith and give them greater courage than ever!"

"They must not know until after Jesus returns, Anders. That knowledge is reserved for you alone."

"Not even Ally?"

"Not even her. No one may know, but I will continue to open your senses to the things you heard and saw as you digested the scroll. Time is short. We must fight the good fight while we can."

Anders now understood how his friends and loved ones in heaven felt when they knew a secret about him they could not tell. They knew Jesus would send him back to earth. Now he realized who Michael and Gabriel were, yet could tell no one. But Yahweh revealed it to him.

***

After the longest night of her life, morning arrived, and Hadassah met Michael to fly back to the Euphrates River. The warrior angel wasted no time, but flew instantly when they reached the mountaintop. He seemed more anxious than normal, which created the same in her. Had she known six others would also be present, her anxiety level would have increased even more.

When they arrived, he stopped a long distance north of yesterday's location. She squinted, trying to view the site well enough to tell what would happen.

"Why did we stop here? I can barely see the place where the angel poured out his bowl."

"Safety first. We must allow no one to know we are here."

"What are you talking about? No one can see us, except..." She stopped mid-sentence and looked at him. "Michael, are the demons coming?"

He said nothing, but motioned for her to keep quiet, as he sat looking in all directions and listening for sounds only he could hear. She soon realized why he stopped northward. Three gigantic beasts flew from the west toward their previous location. Despite the distance, their large stature made them clearly visible and revealed their identity. Though she had never seen Gog, she recognized him alongside Beelzebub and Belial. What were they doing?

Another sight captured her attention. The great red dragon stood by the river awaiting them. Before they arrived, she heard a sound and saw a limo drive up. Two men stepped out and walked toward the dragon, dismissing the driver when they did. Both increased in stature and mass with each step, and she recognized them instantly: Aissa Messai and his One World Religion leader, Caiaphas. They no longer resembled their human form, but appeared huge and grotesque like the others.

All five joined the dragon at the same time. They walked into the dry river bed and stood facing east. Michael motioned to Hadassah and waved for her to follow. Her heart beat furiously, and she briefly wished she had stayed in Petra today. They drew close enough that fear crept into her mind and she longed to flee back to safety. Why take chances? Michael pointed toward the six gargantuan beings gathered below. She watched them, no less fearful than before.

Suddenly, the three demons merged with their masters, leaving the dragon, Messai, and Caiaphas standing alone, but enlarging beyond human comprehension. Hadassah had viewed scenes like this in movies; now she witnessed one in real life. She struggled to grasp what had happened, but had little time to consider it further before the action picked up.

The three colossal beings threw back their heads, then hurled them forward, expelling three strange looking creatures onto the dry land. From her vantage point, they looked like frogs, but she knew they were the same gigantic demons who entered the others only seconds before, having now taken on different forms. She even recognized their individual identities. How was that possible?

Gog hopped toward the east, Beelzebub went west, and Belial traveled south. After only a few feet, their former appearance returned, and they rose, soared away, and disappeared from sight in a flash. None saw Michael and her hovering nearby. For that, Hadassah was grateful and felt relief wash over her. The dragon vanished, then Messai and Caiaphas returned to their normal size and appearance. Their limo returned, picked them up, and drove away.

"I hope you will explain what we just witnessed, because I don't understand any of it."

"You will understand soon. Let's head back to Petra. The sixth judgment will begin quickly and facilitate the final battle and Jesus' ultimate victory. *His* time has come!"

CHAPTER 14

The Chinese and Russian presidents met discussing plans to attack a common enemy, unaware of the invisible guest who brought them together on this important day. Neither did they realize their plans were not their own. Gog sat between them, guiding their discussion, ensuring they reached conclusions predetermined by his master. His powers enforced the dragon's will on human beings.

"We must move soon while they suspect nothing, and make this the most devastating assault in history," China's leader said. "Messai halted our nuclear barrage, allowing us to wait until now to mobilize history's most powerful army. Our countries will lead the charge."

"Our Russian military has prepared for this moment ever since we joined forces and crippled all those other nations. We realized this day would come and cannot wait to join this unified fighting force. How soon can we move forward?"

"When every country comes on board and our armies mobilize, we will march. We must make this a massive military machine no one can defeat. Israel has survived against impossible odds many times through the years, so we must leave nothing to chance. They attribute each victory to their god, but no god is powerful enough to defeat our army."

You are right. When you defeat them, he loses, and my master reigns forever. And I will reign with him! You think you are in control, but you only do his bidding. He is lord!

As Gog performed his diabolical task, Beelzebub and Belial made their rounds, visiting every individual NWO leader first, then those of surrounding nations. Each obeyed without thinking, summoned by one greater than they.

Aissa Messai followed his princes' efforts by convening all NWO leaders in Jerusalem two weeks later. They showed up ready for action and excited about what would happen soon. But he had another decision they must make first.

"Gentlemen, our day has come, and victory will soon be ours!" That elicited a cheer from those seated in his office. "We continue pursuing the enemy who follows *him*, but another has remained defiant and challenged our every decision. They are a thorn in our side and must face punishment for their arrogance and disregard for our leadership. I speak of Pope Gregory and his cardinals."

"They took my mark and joined our One World Religion, but their hearts are not with us. Gregory cannot turn loose of his former beliefs. He demanded equality, and asks that we grant him and his leadership their *rights*. They have no *rights* except to worship me and support our joint religious effort, which unites the world under one belief. We saved them from complete collapse and restored their prosperity, yet they continue their insolence. It is time for them to pay."

"I agree," said the man from Iran, before anyone else could speak. "We must remove all infidels, including those who proclaim allegiance outwardly, but reject our ideals inwardly. They pose a serious threat to our plans."

"Our top military commander, General Chen, has prepared the People's Liberation Army Air Force to annihilate them and only awaits authorization from this group to proceed with that attack," said the Chinese president. "When his forces finish that mission, nothing will remain of Vatican City."

Messai seized the moment. "All who favor granting the general authority to proceed, say, *aye*!" They approved the mission with gusto. The PLAAF would carry out the assault within the next week, giving AMPP time to evacuate any non-residents.

"AMPP personnel continue standing guard over each room occupied by Gregory and his cardinals, keeping them detained inside. They will allow none to leave my palace. I will post guards around the entire city so no one can leave. If residents return, they will allow them in, while also attempting to locate all non-residents and ensure they exit the city. I can hardly wait to hear the reaction of their former adherents worldwide when their precious capital is annihilated!"

The men celebrated, and Messai contacted General Chen and informed him of their decision. They sensed his exhilaration over the phone and encouraged him to act speedily. Soon Vatican City, the Roman Catholic Church headquarters, would cease to exist. Many would mourn the tiny nation's loss as Messai and his NWO leadership rejoiced.

***

"Only two months remain, Blake," Anders said after another meeting with Gabriel opened more of the scroll in his mind. "Things will move fast now. I see a massive army being assembled and mobilizing for a monumental assault against an unsuspecting country. I can't tell which nation they will attack, but we all know, anyway."

"Israel," Ollie said under his breath, but loud enough they all heard him.

"And China will lead the way," said Bruno. "Magnus and I learned about them from everything that happened to us while we were there."

"Yes, we did, and we also discovered who controls them."

"The dragon," said John. "And we realize who else he controls."

"Messai," Blake said. "He calls the shots. We understand how he feels about Israel, right Magnus?"

"That's right, Blake. He hates them more than anyone, well, except us, I suppose. I heard him spew that hatred more times than

I care to remember when I worked for him. Isn't there something we can do to stop him?"

"No, Magnus," said Gabriel, "because everything written in the Bible must happen before Jesus comes. All we can do is watch and wait for his arrival, which will happen soon."

Trey agreed, but his military survival skills also kicked in. "I'm excited about Jesus coming too, but I also believe we should protect ourselves for the next two months. AMPP is out there looking for us right now. Are we going to sit here and let them capture us and deliver us to Messai with only eight weeks left?"

"I agree with my partner," Rickie said. "We need something to do, anyway, so why not keep them occupied trying to catch us? Let's make them work for it!"

"The fence is all intact, and with the arsenal we have, they can't get in here, regardless what they do. We have military personnel and other shooters, so we can defend this place. If they attack by air, Rickie and I have bombers which are ready to fly."

"Hold on, Trey. We should only use military force if absolutely necessary."

"I can't believe you said that after your troops have already killed a ton of AMPP personnel, Gabriel. Don't you think Jesus wants us to defend ourselves? We have women and children here."

"The scroll showed us under attack, but I don't remember anyone dying. Although, I saw injured people."

"Ours, or AMPP, Anders?" asked Ollie.

"I couldn't tell, but I saw it, so I think you should defend our home."

Everyone agreed, so they gathered supplies and developed protective measures which would make it hard for anyone to enter Tel Nof. Dozens of IEDs buried around the outside perimeter and wired to detonators inside. Guard posts set up inside to defend against anyone who may get past the explosives and come near the fence. Fighter jets fueled, loaded, and ready to go. They prepared well in case AMPP found them. And they surely would.

***

Messai called the three chief princes back into his office. Their task was well underway, but time was short, and they had much left to do.

"You have done well. All NWO nations are on board and ready for battle. Now, you must convince nations from every continent who can marshal an army to join us. Little time remains for you to accomplish that task. Control their minds. Perform signs. Whatever you must do, convince those who can, and we will amass the greatest fighting force ever assembled to guarantee this victory."

"We are ready, Your Majesty. Give us our assignments, and we will leave immediately. The NWO leaders agreed without hesitation, but others may require further persuading. We can handle that, since we specialize in convincing humans to follow the dragon," Beelzebub said with a sneer.

"I know you can, and I am counting on that. Gog, finish your work in Asia, then go down to Australia and New Zealand. If they reject us, leave them alone, and we will deal with them later."

"Beelzebub, Africa and Europe are yours. Africa's northern countries will join easily, following Egypt's lead, because they worship Allah and despise Israel. Don't worry about the European nations who were devastated by the nuclear bombs. None of them are strong enough to fight."

"Belial, the Americas belong to you, although they suffered more damage than Europe during the nuclear war. They also lost many citizens in the Invasion. But I believe you can convince some to join us, if you understand what I mean."

"I understand completely, Your Majesty, and will use all my persuasive abilities," Belial said.

"May we go now, sir?" asked Gog. "The time is short, and we have much to do. Everything hinges on mobilizing nations and armies to create the most powerful army the world has ever seen."

"You are right, my prince. Victory is within our grasp, but we cannot take any chances. The dragon and I depend on our three most powerful demons to create that fighting machine."

"One thing before we go, Your Majesty. Have you received any further word about *their* location?"

"No, Beelzebub, but I promise to tell you when that happens, because I understand your vested interest in that situation." No sooner had those words left his mouth, his phone rang.

"Mr. Rossi, I hope you call to share good news."

"Yes, sir. We narrowed the hot zone down, focusing on a small area, and may have a sighting."

"Tell me more, Director! Others standing here also want to hear some news."

"Narrowing the zone continued ruling out places which will not sustain their number. We searched every town and location as we moved. One site became a focal point more than any others, then a short while ago, one of our men spotted movement outside the area."

"Rossi, please omit the details and just tell me where it is!"

"Tel Nof Airbase, sir. The Israeli Military closed it following the nuclear war and never reopened it. Thousands could stay there, and I suspect when the IDF abandoned it, they left all their equipment. That may explain how they rescued the rebels. We are now concerned about remaining weapons and ammunition, and their ability to protect themselves."

"Mr. Rossi, are you telling me you fear a minor group of mostly non-military people when you pursue them with huge patrols of fully armed, highly trained personnel?"

"We do not fear them, sir. But their firepower may make capturing them more difficult. We considered an air assault, but that would mean killing them instead of delivering them to you."

"Take them alive! Surround Tel Nof and move in! Incapacitate them any way you can, then invade the place and apprehend them! I will expect them here within days, not weeks. The great battle will happen soon, and I want to execute them before it does. Do you understand?"

"Yes, sir. We will proceed as you command."

Beelzebub was ecstatic hearing Rossi's report, as were his two fellow princes. He longed to be there, but understood he must travel to Africa and Europe first. At least, he would be nearby.

***

Pope Gregory sat in his room, still unable to leave with armed guards standing outside. He realized they had angered Messai and Caiaphas, but also understood their religion would not have survived without joining the One World Religion. They had no choice, or did they? *If I had it to do over*, he said to himself, but he could not reverse his actions, regardless how much he wanted to. He and the cardinals were now at Messai's mercy. All he could do was sit, wonder, and wait.

A knock at his door. He knew what it meant: dinner was served. At least they fed them. The guard opened the door just enough for the server to shove a tray inside, then slammed it shut again. He enjoyed the food and was thankful his cardinals ate well too. What would happen now? Would Messai release them after they served a *sentence* long enough to satisfy his wrath? Or he may imprison them. Worse, he could make them examples by executing them using his *device*. Gregory shuddered at that thought. He could do nothing about it, so fretting was useless.

Cardinal Giordano kneeled beside his bed at Tel Nof praying for his former fellow Roman Catholic leaders. He realized when they received Messai's mark and joined his One World Religion, they sealed their fate. He tried to voice his opinion, but the others silenced him. Now he prayed to Jesus, his true Messiah, who would return soon. He felt sad for the pope and cardinals, feeling helpless, but also knowing when Jesus came, he would go with him. Nothing could dampen his spirit, not even his friends soon eternal demise. A knock interrupted him and he stood. Lukas.

"We think they found us."

"AMPP?" Giordano asked, already knowing the answer. *Stupid question. Why would I ask that?*

"A group is gathered in the mess hall praying while we who have military experience are standing guard all around the inside. It is almost dark, and they may choose to attack at night."

"I will go pray with the others right now. Lukas, we may not make it until Jesus returns."

"You may be right, Cardinal, but we will do everything we can to survive. AMPP has Messai on their side, but we have Jesus. I trust him." The Cardinal agreed and hurried from the room.

***

"I have to go on another mission alone," Michael said to Hadassah as they walked along the Siq.

"Don't do that to me, Michael. Last time you barely survived and had me worried sick. I'm not sure I can go through that again, and we can't lose you with the end so near."

"This time Beelzebub and Belial aren't there, and Gog is with them. They are out preparing for the battle. Legion is leading the horde, and the other princes are with him. But the Host will come and fight alongside me, so that weak bunch should be easy to stop."

"They are *never* easy to stop! Why is Yahweh sending you there?"

"They found our friends at Tel Nof and pointed them out to AMPP, who will attack soon. But they have Gabriel with them. Yahweh gave me permission to fight the demons and allows him to help our friends and their new comrades fight the human army. Mordecai told them where weapons and ammunition are stockpiled. They even have access to fighter jets and nuclear weapons, which they won't use, but the bombers may come in handy. I'm eager to hear what he came up with."

"Please be careful. That's all I ask. I will be here praying for you, the Host, and our friends."

"I will leave soon, and the Host will meet me there. We should drive them away quickly. I'm not bragging when I say that, but without Beelzebub and Belial, they don't pose a real threat. However, you still realize how important your prayers are when we fight. I know you won't let us down."

They continued on, neither saying another word until they parted and went their separate ways. She would not see him again before he returned. *Jesus, please give them victory,* she whispered.

***

Aissa Messai worked on multiple things as time wound down toward the end. He was the ultimate multitasker. Before he could reign alongside his master, he must deal with the traitors, mobilize the world's armies, capture the Smyrnians and those with them, and execute their entire group. Speaking with his Chief Security Director would give him two progress reports.

"Mr. Rossi, have your men cleared Vatican City so General Chen may carry out his mission?"

"Yes, sir. No one remains except Gregory, the cardinals, and other full-time residents. We posted guards at each entrance ensuring no one gets in or out, so the place is ready for annihilation. My men cleared an additional two-mile area outside, reporting a serious bomb threat, and telling people we need a few days to confirm or deny its credibility. That should give Chen ample time."

"Excellent work, Rossi! I could not have developed a better plan myself! I will inform the general he may proceed whenever his men are ready. Now, tell me about *them.*"

"With pleasure, sir. We confirmed they are there, and my men have the base surrounded. They are currently searching for a way inside. If they cannot gain entrance, we may need to shoot our way in, which could kill some of them. I understand you want them taken alive."

"It is okay if you kill some they rescued, but save *them* for me. Wound them if you must. That will only make things more fun if they suffer before facing the device. Do not fail me, Rossi."

"We will do exactly as you say, Mr. Messai, so you can handle other necessary details. Your men from AMPP will get the job done."

"See that they do, Mr. Rossi, or it may be your head instead of *theirs*."

Rossi did not understand why his boss made such threats, but he would obey his orders as he always did. Messai wasted no time calling General Chen the minute he finished with his director.

"General, they cleared the way, so you may proceed! I suggest tomorrow or the following day, based on what they told other nearby residents."

"We will strike tomorrow night at midnight when they least expect it. My pilots are ready."

"Perfect! Midnight is my favorite time to make things happen. Please inform me when they fly. We installed live cams inside the city and outside a few hundred yards away. I will watch both to get the full impact. Thank you, General. I trust you this time and look forward to your *handiwork*."

***

"We know they're out there, but what should we do?" Blake asked. "Do we sit tight, trusting the defense mechanisms we put in place, or be preemptive and strike first?"

"We do not attack, Blake, because some of our own could get killed," said Anders. "We continue praying and stay protected in here. Our people are standing guard around the inside protecting us, so there is no reason to take action yet. Using force should be our last option."

"Did the scroll show you that, or is it just your opinion?"

"That's a fair question, John. Jesus showed me the scroll clearly last night, and I saw the base under siege, with many wounded people lying both inside and outside. But my spirit says *we* should not attack first."

"I struggle with that," John answered. "We have often said when it's kill or be killed, we will protect ourselves. They clearly intend to kill us, so I say we kill them before they can do that."

"Magnus and Bruno are out there standing guard, but they would agree with John," said Mila. "Magnus knows Messai well. He told Bruno the man will want us taken alive so we face his Capital Punishment Device."

"I believe him," Beth said. "We all realize Messai is an evil man who loves watching people die, and we are number one on his most wanted list. He will do anything to capture us."

A loud explosion rocked the base, causing things to come crashing down everywhere inside the compound, as Beth sprinted to Blake and others dove under tables. Their decision was made for them. Apparently, AMPP just fired the first shot.

Soaring closer, Michael recognized a black cloud of the horde ahead and stopped where the Host would meet him soon. Something else caught his eye: a cloud of smoke rising from Tel Nof. He came too late! AMPP had bombed the place before he arrived! He thought first about his Smyrnian friends, then Gabriel. How many had the blast killed? Could an explosion kill his fellow archangel?

Yahweh forbade him to fight against humans, but he could battle the demons. Rage filled his mind, and he charged them alone, with no concern for his own well-being. A multitude of the Heavenly Host surrounded him and joined him rushing Legion and his unsuspecting horde, swords flashing through the night sky. They were on them before the demons realized what happened. Princes and horde alike were all focused on the events below.

The tiny beasts screeched as their bodies hurtled through the air, slammed by unnoticed assailants. Legion heard their screams and turned just in time to see Michael bearing down on him. Before he could call the others, the warrior angel crashed into him with such force it dazed him. He grunted and tried to right himself and mount a counterattack. Before he recovered, Michael sent him violently tumbling through the atmosphere, stunned, and desperately trying to escape.

Now he spun to face the remaining eight princes, minus Beelzebub, Belial, and Gog. He wished they were also here to experience his fury. The Host had already reached them. He watched the wounded and defeated brutes fleeing, as his mighty angelic army pursued them until they disappeared. His holy anger subsided, replaced by concern for the believers below inside Tel Nof. Smoke still drifted skyward, slowly dissipating. Michael longed to dive and discover its cause, but Yahweh forbade it. He must speak with Gabriel soon.

While the brief unseen battle raged overhead, Rossi heard the blast and was called to an area near the fence. He sped there and met one of his patrol captains who started talking when he saw him.

"They buried an IED, sir, then detonated it before my men reached it. However, two troops were wounded by shrapnel."

"Perhaps they are not as highly trained as we assumed. A well-timed explosion would have killed every man approaching the boundary, but they detonated too soon."

"I don't think so, sir. It appears they purposely discharged the device early. Instead of killing our men, it seems they only intended to send a warning. But I still have two men down."

"If they buried those things everywhere out here, you'd better be careful. Because they detonated early that time doesn't mean it will happen again. This one may have been a mistake."

"Say the word, sir, and we will destroy them and this whole place in one massive assault. We're wasting time and man power sitting here. Why can't we just annihilate them?"

"Because the boss wants them taken alive and brought to him. If you value your life, you will do what he says, or face the device yourself. No one crosses him and lives to tell about it."

"We will look for another way to get in or smoke them out, but it won't be easy. Any suggestions?"

"Only a reminder. The boss okayed killing anybody else there, but save the Smyrnians for him."

"We will keep that in mind. Sir, you had better hope Mr. Messai doesn't find out you spoke *their* name."

Rossi quickly wondered if he had ever done anything to the captain which would cause him to rat him out to his boss. He knew the man was safe. Now to help him take down Tel Nof and capture those inside alive.

Messai summoned Legion, but got no response, even after several tries. He screamed louder, *"Come!"* but still nothing. The princes never failed to obey his command, so he knew something was wrong. Rossi was next, and he answered right away, but his voice sounded shakier than usual.

"Hello, sir. Is everything okay?"

"How am I supposed to know if things are okay? You are the one out there leading my men trying to capture the rebels, but I suspect something isn't right. So tell me, Rossi, is everything okay?"

"Yes, sir, things are fine here. We have surrounded the base and are planning the best way to get inside and capture *them*. I informed the men you said they may kill others but must take the Smyr... I mean *them*, alive." Rossi sensed his boss's ire through the phone and wondered how he could make that mistake, but also realized he could not change it.

"Just get them, Rossi, and do not return here until you do!" The call ended, leaving the Chief Security Director trembling and alone. The man would turn up the heat on his men until they accomplished this mission.

***

Gabriel raced into the mess hall and saw his fellow believers in Jesus taking cover following the explosion. They crawled out when they saw him, eager to find out what happened.

"They got too close, so we detonated an IED. I'm pretty sure it killed no one, but I can't guarantee some weren't injured. It was a strong warning for them to keep their distance, but we don't know what they may try next. Magnus remains certain Messai ordered them to take all Smyrnians alive, so I doubt they bomb us. You can all sleep tonight while we stand guard."

"I'm not sure about sleeping. The threat of attack is not conducive to getting a good night's sleep."

"Trust me, you can take the word of this career military man. We have everything under control outside. If anything comes up, we will warn you immediately so you can take shelter. Now, I need to get back out and make the rounds to ensure everyone is in position to keep this place secure."

He exited quickly, and the others prayed together one more time, then went to their quarters and fell into bed. Fatigue combined with faith brought such sound sleep only a bomb could wake them. They would make more decisions tomorrow, but tonight, they would sleep.

Gabriel walked outside and entered a dark area between two buildings, then became invisible, rose, and soared over the fence. He flew high over the entire area around Tel Nof, his night vision illuminating the ground below, revealing the massive number of AMPP personnel surrounding their safe place. The sight shocked him until he remembered they fought, not them, but the dragon and his demons. He singled out Rossi meeting with AMPP captains and moved in to listen.

Magnus was right! Messai forbade killing Smyrnians, but commanded his forces to take them alive. That should mean no bombs or air raids; good news for them. But it meant a ground invasion was coming soon, for which they must prepare. If only Yahweh would allow him to put an invisible and impenetrable shield around the place, he could guarantee their safety. Maybe he should ask. He rose and soared toward the throne room to pose that all-important question to the Creator.

***

General Chen sat with his team securing the final details for the next night's mission. In less than twenty-four hours, they would demolish both the place and people. He shuddered with excitement.

PLAAF bombers would take off from an undisclosed location and arrive precisely at midnight. They would drop their bombs and destroy everything within the borders but nothing outside the boundary. This was their most thrilling mission yet.

"Have we overlooked anything, men?"

"No, sir. The planes are loaded and ready and the pilots have all specs on what they will do. You planned well, and Mr. Messai will be pleased."

"He will watch, so make sure everything goes as planned and he enjoys the show. We will gather here, pull up his live cams, watch the bombing, too, and celebrate our greatest achievement yet!"

Yahweh and Jesus greeted Gabriel when he arrived and fell before them in reverence and awe. He stood waiting for the Creator to speak.

"Welcome back, beloved one," Jesus said. "We missed you while you were gone, but also know you will quickly leave again. You always carry out your missions well, and this time is no different. We love watching you defend our followers with such diligence."

His smile always warmed Gabriel's heart and filled him with peace, which could only come from the one called Prince of Peace. "Thank you, my Lord, for allowing me to serve your people."

"Ah, my glorious messenger angel," said Yahweh, "you did not come here just to hang out with us. Did I detect a request coming after your last statement?" The Creator's eyes sparkled with joy.

"Lord, please allow me to protect your servants now, because the enemy seeks to destroy them."

"What do you have in mind?"

Gabriel realized Yahweh already knew his every thought, even before he spoke, but continued, anyway. "Let me bubble-wrap the base, like Michael wrapped the plane flying to China, or place an invisible shield around it like the one he put around the cave. They have served you faithfully, Lord, and spread your message all over the world. Because of their efforts, millions have believed and are now your children. Less than two months remain. Please, let me protect them during that time. Their lives are worth saving until you return, Jesus," he said, glancing to his left.

"You have a soft heart, unlike your fellow archangel who loves to fight. I realize you would also spare the lives of those who seek to take theirs, and I love that about you. Answer a few questions for me." The mighty messenger angel stood silently awaiting the first.

"Tell me why it was so important for people to accept my son before the Rapture?" Yahweh awaited his answer, and Gabriel understood he must respond correctly.

"Because those who did not would live through this wicked seven-year Tribulation."

"What did my pastors say when they warned people about that time?"

Gabriel said nothing. He knew well what the Bible said and pastors preached about the horrors these seven years would bring and how those who missed the Rapture would suffer, and many die, during them. He realized one more question was coming.

"Do you think I should disavow my word simply because they face danger now?"

"No, Lord. Your Word is true, and you cannot lie. I will help them however I can until you come, Jesus, without using supernatural power. Perhaps their own resilience will bring self-preservation."

"Remember, you must return here before I send my son. Encourage believers daily before you come, and my precious messenger angel, never forget how much we love you and our people."

"I could never forget that, Lord. Now, I must go because they need me." He bowed before both thrones again and lowered his head, then flew back to Tel Nof.

While Gabriel flew, Hadassah welcomed Michael back to Petra, noticing two positive signs: he looked okay, and he returned promptly. Both must bring good news.

"I was right, Hadassah, the battle was easy. Legion and the others were no match for us. Let me tell you, we kicked some serious demon tail quickly, and they ran away."

"Michael, you shouldn't talk like that!"

"How would you prefer I say it? *Hadassah, we defeated the demons and won a great victory.* Do you like that better?"

"Yes, I do, thank you," she said. "But it sounds like you really kicked some serious..." She stopped and laughed. "Now that you are back safe, I'm concerned about our friends. Did you see them?"

"I didn't see them, but I saw smoke coming from Tel Nof. Yahweh told me I can't help them, so I didn't go check it out. But it made me so angry, I flew into a rage and attacked the demons. The Host reached the little ones first and smashed them, then I went after Legion and slammed him so hard he may never recover. I wanted the other princes too, but my warriors also beat me to them. They delivered a knockout blow before I got the chance. Beelzebub, Belial, and Gog had better be glad they weren't there, because I would have demolished them!"

"I hope the Smyrnians and the others with them are okay. I don't want AMPP to murder them this close to Jesus' coming or Messai killing them in his device. Thank Yahweh Gabriel is with them."

They both stood solemnly considering those possibilities, neither uttering another word.

CHAPTER 15

Vatican City: 11:30 p.m. Pope Gregory lay in bed thinking about their situation. He heard guards speaking in hushed tones outside his door. They made sleeping difficult every night with their incessant chatter, making him wonder if they did it intentionally to annoy him and his cardinals. But they sounded different tonight, less boisterous and obnoxious. Maybe he could sleep, with less noise than normal. He closed his eyes, trying to block out their low voices.

Jerusalem, Israel: 12:30 a.m. The live cams showed on a gigantic movie screen in Aissa Messai's mansion. He locked the door when he entered, munched on snacks, and sipped an adult beverage while he waited for the action to begin. The place appeared so serene, with complete silence meeting his ears, even with such sensitive camera microphones. He settled in and relaxed.

Beijing, China: 5:30 a.m. General Chen's top military commanders joined him watching the same live cams Messai enjoyed. Anticipation increased as minutes passed. Breakfast items adorned their conference table, and the group feasted as they awaited the action. A call confirmed the bombers' departure from a base along China's Belt and Road Initiative. Brief applause interrupted the meal.

Vatican City: 11:50. The lack of chatter caught Gregory's attention. The guards finally stopped talking. Now he could sleep. The stillness sounded wonderful after endless nights of voices and footsteps. When he closed his eyes, sudden thoughts of Roman Catholicism's previous prominence flooded his mind. The church's history was replete with bloodshed and sinful practices. The

252

Crusades and Inquisitions stained her past. He himself had overlooked sins within the priesthood, sweeping them under the proverbial rug. Surely the church had paid enough for her sins.

11:59 p.m. Gregory opened his eyes, startled by something he neither saw nor heard. An abrupt rush of fear overwhelmed him. He leaped from his bed and started walking across the room, panic clawing at his brain. Was this a nightmare? His heart beat rapidly, and his breathing intensified. Something inside told him danger approached, but he was powerless to do anything about it.

Midnight. A brief blinding flash, combined with an ear-piercing sound erupted around him. His world turned dark, and within a millisecond, he was gone. Everyone in Vatican City experienced the same thing at the same time. The AMPP guards looked on from a safe distance, having left the city fifteen minutes before the bombs made impact. The beautiful, glorious former home of the Roman Catholic Church lay in ruins. Smoke arose, and raging fires were visible for miles.

Ships bringing cargo stalled as those on board heard the explosions, then witnessed fires blazing ahead. They recognized the area, not Rome, but specifically, Vatican City. They could only watch in shock and horror as flames covered the horizon and angst crippled them. There was no doubt the once powerful city was no more. The sailors wept. *Oh, great city*, they cried, realizing what effect this would have on their businesses.

Citizens of Rome awakened to the horrifying scene, grieving with everyone else as the horrific images filled television screens worldwide. Daylight would show nothing remained. The city which sat as a queen was now reduced to ash and rubble. *How could Aissa Messai let this happen?* many asked. He moved his office there. But they did not realize he ordered the devastation and destruction that met their eyes this awful night.

Beijing. Only *raucous* could describe the celebration occurring in the general's meeting. The men jumped to their feet and let loose, slapping backs, giving high fives, and embracing. None would ever forget this night. This time, no doubt remained that Chen's pilots had accomplished their mission. They awaited the call each knew would soon come from their leader. The table remained cluttered with empty plates, and many bowls still held ample fare for continued feasting. But they no longer craved food. What they just witnessed replaced hunger with irrepressible joy.

Jerusalem. Messai howled with glee as sparks danced around the room. A recognized visitor entered the room and joined him. The gargantuan creature breathed fire accompanied by screams so loud they would deafen any normal people. This was a prelude to their upcoming final victory.

"Congratulations, Aissa," the beast said in his patented low growl. "You succeeded at task number one, and the princes are drawing the nations to Israel to complete task number two. That one brings our reign! But one task remains unfinished, despite six years spent trying to achieve it. Your men continue to fail, so Beelzebub, Belial, and Gog will take over when they return from their mission."

"My men have them surrounded now, Master, so they cannot escape. Their capture should happen soon. Then they will bring them to me where the device will destroy them forever. That will be our most victorious moment since you raised me to power! Others may die when we attack the compound, but my men will apprehend the leaders alive."

"Summon me when they arrive, Aissa. I will come and take part in that ceremony. They will see my face and feel my fire before you take off their heads. By the time I finish with them, their skin will drip from their bodies, and they will beg for the device. But first, they will bow before me."

"I love your plan, Master, and will enjoy seeing you torture them before they die. We will discover how bold they really are when they face you. I will turn up the pressure on my patrols, but welcome the princes' help to ensure we accomplish our goal." That may happen any day.

The news about Vatican City's demise spread around the globe like wildfire, dominating every news network and causing worldwide grief and anxiety. The tiny country contributed much to the world's economy. Businesses in every nation would feel the financial crunch from declining sales and lost manufacturing jobs. Since joining Aissa Messai's One World Religion, Catholicism had returned to prominence and prosperity, rewarding those who did business with them.

Though renovated, with paintings and images of Messai replacing former religious art, people had still flocked to the tiny nation to enjoy the visual aesthetics of centuries-old architecture. It brought back memories of former lives to some. Many people would miss the place for various reasons. But the world would go on as people continued following the Antichrist, believing his promise of peace and prosperity. He appeared long enough to make a brief statement to secure their trust.

"Ladies and gentlemen, I grieve with you after losing my new headquarters and a place dear to so many. We will seek those responsible for this reprehensible act of terror and allow no one to impede our progress toward worldwide peace and prosperity. I suspect the rebel Smyrnians may have carried out this attack. They have not reared their ugly heads for a while, so this may prove they are still trying to stop us. We will continue hunting them to put an end to their heinous activity. Please keep believing, as we unite around our common goal."

Everyone at Tel Nof gathered, watching and listening to his blatant lies. They knew in their hearts he destroyed Vatican City but had no way to prove their suspicions. Anger poured from former citizens of the place, including Cardinal Giordano.

"We realized something was coming and knew we needed to leave. I warned the others, but they refused to listen and followed him for prosperity's sake. Jesus will make him pay for this atrocity!"

"Cardinal," said Lukas, "we did what we knew was right and followed Jesus. I will never regret that decision and will continue fighting for him until he comes. That will happen very soon. I will direct my anger toward trying to survive the next two months. How about you?"

"Lukas is right, Cardinal Giordano," Anders said, "and so are you. Jesus *will* make him pay, and that sentence will last forever."

"I agree with you both and understand you are right. But I am also ready to fight his men, so show me where I am needed, and I will get out there right now!"

"You are needed right here on your knees praying for us who are out there fighting, Cardinal. We all have roles. Some are physical warriors, but others are spiritual warriors. I put you in that last category. Everyone out there needs you in here doing what you do best."

"You are also correct, Gabriel. I will continue praying, knowing others will pray with me. Together, we can win this battle and survive until Jesus returns." The group now understood their roles and would defend their turf against the Antichrist's fighting machine, battling to win.

***

"Another battle will come any day, and it will get ugly," Michael told Hadassah. "The three princes will return soon, and Messai will send them to help AMPP capture our friends. Yahweh gave me permission to fight the demons, so I can't turn my head and let them win. I must fight, but also be careful while doing that. The Host will come. Hopefully, the other princes won't show up with the horde after we just kicked... I mean, after we defeated them so badly."

"But Gabriel is with them. Can't he protect them and help them defeat AMPP?"

"He will do his best, but remember, the end is near, and Yahweh promised what they're facing would happen to those who missed the Rapture and followed Jesus afterwards. Fully protecting them now would mean Yahweh went back on his Word. The pastor's video warned everyone, and it has happened just like he said. I fully protected them before, but I can't do that now."

"It doesn't seem right that he protects us in Petra but won't protect other believers."

"The Bible says he will protect Jewish believers during the last half of the Tribulation, but foretells persecution for Jesus' other followers. That's why it was so important for people to believe before the Rapture. But many didn't heed Yahweh's warning. The Tribulation gets worse until Jesus comes back, so believers must live in danger every day."

"Michael, I just want these next two months to pass, but I have a feeling they will drag by. I also wish we could help them more, but I understand why we can't."

"I would crush AMPP if Yahweh would let me, but I promise to fight the dragon's bunch every day. Jesus will defeat them soon. That's what we look forward to, and I cannot wait!"

"When are you going back?"

"Soon. When those three arrive, I will get there fast. Gabriel and I will do everything we can to prevent them from killing or capturing our friends, although I fear I will arrive too late for some."

***

Beelzebub arrived first, having finished his work in Africa and Europe. The smile on his face told Messai his mission succeeded even before he spoke. But he could also tell he wanted more.

"Master, you were right. North Africa belongs to you and will fight with us. Western Europe cannot join, as you said, but Russia is with us from east to west. The world's kings and their nations are coming together for the great battle, forming a formidable and unstoppable force. We will soon rule the world!"

"You did well, my prince, and you are correct. We will be victorious and reign alongside the dragon forever! Have you seen the other two?" Belial and Gog arrived right after he asked that.

"Welcome back, my princes! I can tell you also had success, so tell me about it."

Both reported that many countries' armies eagerly joined and would come when summoned. That would happen soon. Even though they just returned, he must immediately send them on another mission, one for which they longed, anyway. He got right down to business.

"I cannot contact Legion or the other princes, so I feel sure the Host attacked and defeated them. I should not have sent them without you. The little demons are powerless, and Legion specializes in possession, not warfare. Haborym's fire is useless against *his* forces, plus none of them are warriors like you. So, I must send you to protect my forces and allow them to capture those inside Tel Nof. But remember, you will fight alone since the others fled and will not return."

"You know I am ready, Master, because I want *them* like you do," said Beelzebub. "But I hope Michael also shows up so he can experience our power and taste our wrath."

"You must fight carefully, Beelzebub. I realize you want Michael, but you three will fight against the entire Heavenly Host. Do not allow your hated for Michael to defeat you."

"Do not worry about us, Master," said Belial. "They cannot overpower us when we fight as one."

"You did well setting up the final battle. The world's armies will gather and form an unstoppable fighting force which will win a great victory! They will not need your help. You will stay with my men and protect them until they capture our enemies and bring them to me."

"Command us, Master, and we will go!"

"*Go!*" Messai screamed, and his three mighty demons flew away faster than he had ever seen them go. Their power amazed him, and his mind told him victory was certain.

***

Messai met with NWO leaders in Tehran, Iran to finalize plans for each stage of their march to Israel. Excitement and anticipation filled the room. Leaders from four other continents joined them, hungry for action, which would give them more standing with the powerful world leader and his One World Government. He promised prosperity and prestigious positions following the coming victory. They could not refuse such a proposal since they already followed him.

"Welcome to Iran, ladies and gentlemen," said the country's enthusiastic leader. "We stand on the precipice of human history. Our nations will soon achieve the greatest triumph humanity has ever witnessed, when we join forces and follow our leader into battle. The Iranians share your excitement and cannot wait to fight alongside you! Join me in welcoming Mr. Aissa Messai who will greet you before I come back to share some specific details." Applause rocked the room as Messai strode forward, soaking up their generous accolades.

"Ladies and gentlemen, thank you for joining us in mobilizing the most powerful fighting force ever assembled! Throughout history, great empires ruled the world. But none can compare with the prolific, insurmountable army we now bring together. No nation can overpower us, especially the tiny country we will soon attack. History records their past unusual victories over individual nations, but they have never faced a force like ours. We will conquer them, then rule together from their long-standing, much sought after capital. I have made it my headquarters; now I shall place my throne there, and you shall reign with me!"

An evil smile pursed his lips as their standing ovation echoed through the meeting hall. "Now, welcome back our friend from Iran." The Iranian rose again to raucous cheers.

"Victory begins today!" He threw his right arm upward and boisterous clapping drowned out his words, forcing him to stop until it subsided, so he could continue. "China, Russia, and other eastern countries, are moving toward our Iranian military bases as we meet. Once gathered here, their united forces will march westward, moving through Iraq and across the Euphrates toward our unsuspecting foe. NWO nations will join them as they reach each border and march with them."

"Other countries who remain capable of joining will unite with their closest NWO neighbors and come, as well. African nations will mobilize in Cairo and move up from the south. Southern and Southeastern European countries will meet in Damascus. That paints a beautiful picture of our mighty military machine closing in on our enemy from all sides!" He paused again for applause, which readily came. "Now General Chen from China will tell us about the actual battle."

"Thank you, Mr. President. I am honored to lead our unified militaries into battle as we annihilate the rebel country and achieve world domination. Mr. Messai will soon inform the IDF that a united military force is marching toward Israel and convince the small nation they can defeat us as they have defeated their enemies in the past. They claim their *god* gave them those victories."

The others looked at one another and laughed. Chen joined them. It took nearly a minute for the laughter to die down, but when it did, he continued.

"No such *miracle* will save them this time!" More applause. "When we all arrive in the valley, we will set up camp and make our presence known, daring them to attack. If they come out against us with full military force, believing their *god* will deliver them again, we will be ready and waiting for them. Our air forces will take down their bombers, and our ground forces will demolish their troops, not stopping until we kill every soldier, leaving none alive."

Cheers and victorious shouts started again leading Chen to go a step further. "Then our forces will cover the land from north to south and east to west, slaughtering everyone we find as we go. When we reach Jerusalem, we will capture the city, rename it for our leader, then place him on his throne as god forever!" They started to applaud, but he held up his hand. "One more thing. Mr. Messai and Caiaphas will not stay tucked away in Jerusalem while our armies go to war. They will go into battle with us! Then we can all celebrate our great victory together!" Now he signaled for them to applaud, which they did, continuing until Messai himself stood and stopped them.

"Ladies and gentlemen, it gives me great joy to witness your enthusiasm. Victory is ours. We cannot lose! You may continue with planning, and Caiaphas and I will meet you in the valley."

He left, with Caiaphas following, to fly back to Jerusalem. This part of his plan seemed under control, but the Smyrnians remained alive. He must return and make certain his men captured them and brought them to him because he could take no chances on them eluding him again. The device would fulfill its purpose one more time when every one of them died by its blade. The great battle was now less than one month away, and this must happen before it arrived.

***

Gabriel met with everyone at Tel Nof who was not outside standing guard, trying to protect the base from an enemy bent on capturing or killing them.

"Something just changed, and the patrols are gaining ground. We seem powerless to stop them."

"The dragon's army," said John, and everyone realized he knew what he was talking about.

"John is right," Gabriel said. "I sense their presence, but we can't see them."

"We need to take cover!" said Anders anxiously. "I saw wounded people in here and out there. We must protect ourselves!"

A massive explosion shook the base, sending shards of broken glass flying through the mess hall as it caved in on one side. The fragments ripped into the group they rescued the night before. Three fell from their seats, sliced and bleeding profusely. Steve rushed toward them, but found others in similar shape. Kathie screamed and sprinted toward her son-in-law seeing him impaled by a steel beam which became a deadly missile when the blast raged through the wall.

Julie already kneeled beside him screaming his name: "Jeffrey!" They all realized it was too late. Julian grabbed his sister and held her as she wept. Kathie joined them.

"Why?" Julie asked. "He survived AMPP once. Why did he have to die less than a month before Jesus returns?"

"He's with Johnathan," John said, wrapping his arms around all three. "We will see him soon."

Steve called for Linda to help him, as he cared for the others. Pools of blood already surrounded them. He rolled one over and checked for a pulse, then motioned she was already dead. The other two were alive, but gravely wounded. He started treatment at once with little hope of success.

Blake sat up, trying to shake off the blast's impact, which hurled him several feet backwards. He saw Beth a few feet away, not moving, and unconscious. He crawled to her and lifted her head into his arms, sobbing and whispering her name, his tears wetting her hair. Anders and Ally ran and kneeled beside them. Chaos consumed the mess hall. Those who remained unharmed hurried to those who were injured, doing whatever they could to help. Julie's question filled their minds. Why did this happen with less than a month remaining until Jesus would return?

Michael dashed through Petra, found Hadassah walking near the Siq, and pulled her inside.

"The time has come, Hadassah," Michael said. "I must go now!"

She started to speak, but he left her standing alone, flying before she could say anything. That could only mean one thing. The demons arrived at Tel Nof, and her friends were under attack. Hadassah collapsed and started praying. She knew nothing else to do. If only she could go with him, helping fight Beelzebub, Belial, and Gog, but she knew that was not possible. *Jesus, please prevent other demons from joining them*, she whispered.

Michael soared like the angels who poured out their bowls on earth and arrived at the base within seconds. Smoke rose again from inside the base. Outside AMPP personnel lay near the fence, while other wounded men lay farther away. He looked for the ones who controlled Messai's patrols and created the chaotic scene of death and destruction below. He saw them! Did he dare attack without the Host? Waiting was not an option, so with no time to think, he made his move.

Those standing guard inside the fence fought back against their attackers as explosives sailed through the air into the compound. Some picked up grenades and hurled them back over the wall. Gabriel sprinted toward them from the mess hall yelling as he ran.

"Detonate the IEDs! Return their fire! We must hold them off because we have dead and critically wounded people inside!"

Those words sent Trey and Rickie into a rage. They flew into action immediately, with no time to ask who was wounded and who was dead. Realizing AMPP personnel approached the fence and were close to breaking through, they detonated the buried explosive devices and yelled for others to do the same. Screams of invaders told them the bombs hit their mark. Armed guards fired at retreating patrols, aiming to wound, not kill. However, even if some died, they were determined to protect themselves.

Michael wanted to charge Beelzebub and take out the leader first, but realized the foolishness of such a decision. He soared stealthily, approaching Gog from behind. The lesser demon specialized in mind control and was too focused on the coming battle to care about this one, or to think about an attack from the rear. Michael subdued him before he could make a sound, or the others noticed.

The battle below claimed the full attention of Beelzebub and Belial, thus neither noticed Michael approaching from overhead. He crashed into Belial with such force, the massive demon fluttered, then collapsed, incapacitated, floating in midair. Only his eternal enemy remained. Beelzebub spun upon hearing the impact and found himself facing the one he hated most. He had awaited this moment for millennia. The chief prince of hell and the mighty warrior angel of heaven would now fight each other one-on-one, with no interference. Both charged at full speed.

Blake pleaded with Beth to say something, but she neither moved, nor spoke. Beside her lay a concrete chunk, and a large knot protruded from her forehead. Her chest rose and fell with shallow breaths, separated by several seconds, the time decreasing each time she inhaled. Steve left Linda with the other wounded and ran to them.

"Do something, Steve, please," Blake said, his words barely audible.

"I don't know if I can, Blake. She's badly hurt, but I will try."

"Twenty-five days, Steve. She has to survive for twenty-five more days until Jesus comes to take us home."

Steve barked out orders for others to care for their wounded comrades. Cardinal Giordano and the nuns cared for their group members who were injured, some critically, praying aloud for everyone else as they did. The mess hall quickly turned into a hospital. Anders and Ally brought cold water, ice, and towels, while John and Kathie left Julie with Jeffrey and fetched hot water and clean linens. Steve moved from one to another, as Beth's condition worsened.

Gabriel sensed a lull as explosions and gunfire ceased, the night growing quiet once again. A sharp pain suddenly shot through his head, and his body lunged backwards as if someone punched him. He staggered and fell, a heavy thud, followed by loud grunts, filling his ears. He shook his head, trying to make sense of what he heard. Had some of their own turned on each other, or had AMPP broken through the safe barrier and surprised them? The fight sounded distant. *What is happening?*

Michael! His friend fought for his life somewhere right now. But where! This was no time to worry about someone seeing him. He lifted off and soared straight up, his eyes searching for his partner.

Trey stood, staring upward, struggling to believe his eyes. It betrayed rational logic. Rickie walked up, shook him, and called his name until Trey turned and looked at him, his face white.

"What's wrong, partner? You look like you just saw a ghost."

"No ghost. Something stranger than that. Gabriel flew." His voice trailed off.

"What are you talking about? You've been out here too long, so I need to get you back inside. Come on, let's go."

"I'm serious, Rickie. He was standing right over there one minute, and the next minute he took off and soared away. I realize it sounds crazy, but I'm telling you that's what happened."

"Okay, man, I believe you, but I still think we need to go inside and see how things are in there."

"No, you don't believe me, but that's okay. I know what I saw," Trey said, then joined his partner and walked into the mess hall. Once inside, he forgot about Gabriel and jumped into action helping wounded friends. He saw Blake with Beth, raced through the others, and slid down beside them.

Gabriel looked down and noticed Trey looking at him when he flew, but he could not change that now. Maybe he would address it with him later. In the distance, he spotted two spiritual beings engaged in a life and death battle. He recognized both and realized what had happened a few minutes earlier. Michael and Beelzebub had charged one another and collided with enough force to stun both and send him reeling. Where were the other demons? What about the Host?

He watched Michael land a mighty blow which staggered the demonic prince. But Beelzebub gathered himself and flew toward him at full speed. Gabriel was close enough now to see the demon's glowing eyes and hear his deafening scream. Michael could not withstand the blow he would receive within seconds. Gabriel covered his ears and acted without thinking again. He zoomed at warp speed, reaching the beast a split second before he slammed into Michael.

The messenger angel was less powerful than the warriors, but he hit Beelzebub with enough force to knock him off course and daze him, giving Michael time to recover. Gabriel's body ached, while his mind fought to escape the fog caused by the impact. He could only watch as his partner blasted the demon with a blow that would kill any normal person. But Beelzebub was no normal creature. He floated aimlessly for a few seconds, then returned with a vengeance to destroy his archenemy.

Gabriel believed his fellow archangel could take care of himself, but he left nothing to chance, acting quickly again, though he could barely think. His movement distracted the demon, allowing Michael to attack and deliver a decisive blow. Gabriel followed with a knockout shot, leaving Beelzebub immobilized and at their mercy. Before they could strike again, Belial and Gog swept down and carried their leader away, though neither looked coherent nor strong enough. It seemed certain they would not fight again until they healed from wounds they suffered this day.

When the demons left, the patrols pulled back, and the battle subsided. The two archangels watched the guards rush back inside to help. The believers were safe for now.

"You came to my rescue again, Gabriel. I had no choice but to go against the odds and attack those three, because they empowered AMPP against the Smyrnians. If they remained, everybody in Tel Nof would have died. The Host never came to help me, so I fought alone."

"It was a simple decision for me, partner. You needed me, so I had no time to stop and think. You had him right where you wanted him, but I thought you might still welcome some help."

"I appreciate it more than you know. Let's go make sure everything is ready for the final battle. We must finish here and return to Yahweh before Jesus comes. It is almost time."

"Yes, it is, and I am ready! We have waited many millennia for this moment. One question, before I go. Do you think the believers are safe now, or will Messai keep trying to capture them?"

"I can't answer that, but I do know their chances are much better because of all you have done."

They embraced, smiled, and flew away, both wounded and sore, but realizing one battle remained. Thankfully, that one belonged to Jesus. They would watch as he defeated his enemies.

Messai summoned his princes for three days, but they never came. After three days alone, another beast appeared the third night and ambled across the room. Messai now welcomed his presence. The gigantic red dragon spoke, the usual sparks floating from his long, pointy nose.

"*Aissssa...,*" he hissed, "we must not allow *them* to distract us from our goal. Our plans are coming together as armies gather for the great battle. You may deal with *them* after we crush and conquer. Then you can transport the device to their location and allow our military force to attack from land and air, trapping them inside. You may broadcast their executions onsite. Pull your men away so *they* will feel a false sense of security, not realizing their demise will come soon."

"*As you sssay, massster,*" Messai said, his voice mimicking the creature who possessed him. "*They* cannot escape such an assault. My men will leave and join us until we achieve victory, then we will return to Tel Nof, remove the *Smyrnians*, and rule the universe!"

"Three weeks remain, *Aissssa*. Bring the armies to the valley where you, Caiaphas, and I will join them. Then you will lead them into battle, and we will emerge victorious!"

"*Yesss, massster.* I am ready!"

At Tel Nof, guards remained posted, though things grew quiet. They could take no chances. Three died when AMPP attacked, and Beth still suffered severe headaches from the blow to her head, but she survived. Blake never left her side, continually reminding her Jesus would come any day. Trey often stared at Gabriel but asked him nothing about his flight. Answers would come soon enough. They agreed to read the Bible and pray daily, waiting for Jesus and watching for AMPP.

Two weeks later, Michael and Hadassah took one more trip. He had recovered from his encounter with the princes and was prepared for history's final days. They arrived, then watched the seventh angel pour out his bowl, return, and enter the temple. Her mind wrestled with what happened.

"The bowl's contents didn't fall to earth. They're hovering over one place. Is that…"

"Yes, *Esther*, Israel, your homeland, where the final battle will take place and you will live forever. Mordecai will join you, along with all of Yahweh's people. Gabriel and I will be there too."

I am Esther! She did not want to leave. "This dark bowl frightens me. Can I stay here?"

"No, you must go back. Don't be afraid. Yahweh has everything under control, and I will see you soon." He left her and walked into the temple, where Gabriel joined him.

"Wait, Michael, come with me! I can't go alone!" Hadassah knew she must leave, but also realized she would return soon. Fear tempered her excitement as she rose and flew away without Michael.

CHAPTER 16

"The eastern coalition crossed from Iraq into Jordan, sir," General Chen said as he met with Aissa Messai. "Their armies are now poised to enter the country. Our northern allies arrived in Syria and will complete their journey today. The African alliance gathered in Egypt, crossed the Sinai Peninsula, and reached the Jordanian border yesterday. All groups will soon enter the valley, uniting into one powerful, unstoppable military machine!"

"Good work, General! People will remember September 11th, 2036 as the day *united nations* finally took over the planet and formed a worldwide unified society. Tell me more!"

"Gladly, sir. They will rendezvous in the valley on Monday, then spend Tuesday and Wednesday organizing their units to strike. Then we both understand what happens one week from today!"

"Yes, we do," Messai said, his voice again transforming into a deep-throated growl. "We destroy them once and for all." Chen paid no attention to his tone, but continued his excitement.

"Sir, I have never experienced more excitement and less apprehension before a battle. But neither have I led such a mighty army before. Thank you again for this privilege."

"You may lead the army, but *I* will lead the battle," Messai growled. His eyes turned deep red, with yellow glowing centers. General Chen was briefly taken aback, but finally answered.

"But, sir, I am fully capable..."

"Of leading the army? Yes, you are, General, but the battle belongs to me." Chen asked nothing more. The Antichrist had assumed the role prepared for him from time immemorial.

"Has anyone seen Gabriel?" Blake asked.

"I searched for him, but can't find him anywhere," said Trey. He wanted to say more, to tell them about Gabriel taking flight during the battle, but he did not. Instead, he glanced toward the soldiers. "We thought he was with you guys. You haven't seen him either?"

One spoke for the platoon. "No, but I'm not worried. He disappeared a few times at Muwaffaq, but he always came back within a few days. The strange thing is, Gabriel wasn't part of our original unit. One day he showed up and joined us, then Robert soon named him his second-in-command. We didn't resent that, but it deviated from standard protocol. It turned out to be the right decision."

"Maybe AMPP killed him," Rickie said. "Shouldn't we go search for him instead of sitting around here talking?"

"No, just wait. He always has a reason for taking off without telling anyone, and something good happens every time he does. I promise he'll return soon and bring good news, like he always does."

That's exactly what I was thinking, Trey said to himself. *But I'm not sure we will see him here.*

***

Hadassah arrived at Petra alone, trying to decide how she could explain Michael's absence to her uncle and Ben. She was so deep in reflection she nearly bumped into them walking her way.

"What's wrong, Hadassah?" asked Mordecai. "I don't enjoy seeing my niece looking like she just lost her best friend. Speaking of best friends, where is Michael?"

"He had to go somewhere without me, Uncle, so I came back alone." She didn't lie. He did go somewhere, but they would never believe her if she told them where.

"Hadassah, I wish Michael would stay here since Jesus' return is so close. Mordecai and I hoped we would all be together when he comes. Can you find him and bring him back?"

"I can't, Ben, but I'm sure he'll walk back in here before long and tell us about his trip. I miss him more than anyone because he *is* my best friend. But I know very soon we'll all be together forever!"

That did little to satisfy Ben's curiosity, but she was right, and he realized his questions would no longer matter after one more week. He would spend that time preparing his people in Petra for Jesus' return. His excitement returned as his questions disappeared.

***

6:00 p.m. September 8, 2036.
Israeli news abounded with reports of a sudden massive military presence near Megiddo. The expansive valley where Ben Abramson led rallies amassing over one hundred thousand Jews now teemed with fighting forces from all over the world, joining with every nation surrounding Israel. Residents scurried to bomb shelters, yet realized the futility of such a move. Neither the nation, nor they could survive the catastrophic assault that was coming.

An IDF general informed the nation their military was aware of the approaching danger and had mobilized current personnel, calling in all reserves worldwide who could arrive before the attack occurred. However, military and government leaders understood they were no match for the colossal fighting machine marching toward them. The nation of Israel would soon cease to exist, and they were powerless to stop it. But they would not go down without a fight.

Even worse, Aissa Messai remained silent, many now fearing he supported their opposition. "If only Major General Mordecai Chaim was still in charge," was often heard. The nation cried out to Yahweh for deliverance, as it had done many times before, but prayers seemed to fall on deaf ears. Reality hit home. Messai slaughtered many Israeli Jews who refused his mark. Had he been their enemy all along? Events of the past seven years started adding up in their minds.

***

9:00 a.m. September 9.

An unseen force tugged every heart at Tel Nof, drawing them from the base. Each understood where they must go, yet realized the potential danger involved. Blake called them together Tuesday morning and made an announcement.

"We're going to Jerusalem. Has anyone checked those trucks the IDF left when they deserted this place? We got the planes running. Surely we can do the same with the trucks."

"What do you think we've been doing the past three months?" Trey asked, a smile betraying his light-hearted banter. "Other than rescuing people and fighting AMPP, you know, stuff like that."

"I sure hope it involves those trucks. Jesus has met our every need, and right now we need them."

"They sat for a long time, so they needed some work. Dead batteries, deflated tires, mechanical issues. But we fixed them all up, and they're ready to roll!" Rickie said with obvious pride.

"Then let's go. We shouldn't need the supplies. But what about AMPP?"

"We haven't seen them since they pulled back, but we'll check the entire perimeter to make sure they're gone," a soldier said. "The IDF is moving around everywhere, so no one will suspect military trucks driving down the road. We should get there in forty-five minutes, but we also need to prepare for the possibility of AMPP covering the place."

"We'll worry about that when we get there," Blake said. "We all know that's where we're supposed to go, so we'll trust Jesus to protect us one more time. But we can't leave Gabriel."

"Gabriel can take care of himself," Anders said. "We called and searched but couldn't find him. After he and I talked one day, I trust whatever he does. It wouldn't surprise me if he beats us there."

"I hate to go without him, but we can't wait. Let's make sure we have everyone, then take off so we can get there before Jesus comes."

Within an hour, they were driving to Jerusalem, not knowing what to expect, but certain they were supposed to go.

***

3:00 p.m.

Jerusalem was quiet as people stayed out of sight, most tucked away in bomb shelters, fearing an imminent attack. Messai was conspicuously absent, and there was no sign of AMPP. The Smyrnians and their fellow believers walked around the Old City basking in its glory. Ascending the abandoned Temple Mount, they sang praise songs from old recordings they had discovered since believing in Jesus, not caring who heard them. But no one was around, anyway. It seemed they had the entire city to themselves.

Worthy is the Lamb who was slain, holy, holy is He
Sing a new song to Him who sits on heaven's mercy seat
Holy, holy, holy is the Lord, God Almighty
Who was and is and is to come
With all creation I sing praise to the King of Kings
You are my everything and I will adore you, I will adore you
–Phillips, Craig, and Dean, Integrity Music, 2009

What a beautiful name it is
What a beautiful name it is
The name of Jesus Christ my King
What a beautiful name it is
Nothing compares to this
What a beautiful name it is

The name of Jesus
—Hillsong Worship, Hillsong Publishing, 2016

***

Blake's phone rang, startling him. Ben! 7:00 p.m., already? He stepped aside and answered, putting his phone on speaker so everyone could hear Ben's voice. The entire group joined him.

"Ben, we were enjoying ourselves so much, I forgot it was time for your call. You will never guess where we are!"

"Oh, yes, I will. You're in Jerusalem!"

"How did you know that?"

"Everyone here wants to be there too, but we can't leave Petra. I know we will all stand in the Holy City soon. I'm not sure how that will happen, but I know these people are ready!"

"I can't wait! Let me tell you what's going on here. First, everyone wants to say hello."

Ben thrilled at the sound of so many voices ringing out over the phone, many he had not yet met. He reminded Blake that was only a warm-up to what they would hear soon. Blake filled him in on all that had happened, both good and bad, causing momentary sadness. Then he told him about the armies gathered at Armageddon. Ben recalled his victory there, and the thousands of Jews who accepted their true Messiah that day. But he feared for his friends in Jerusalem.

"Blake, do you think the armies will attack the city before Jesus comes? If they do, you guys stand no chance out in the open. Can you go back to Zedekiah's cave? What about AMPP and Messai? Aren't they there?"

"There's no sign of either. This place is like a ghost town. People are hunkered down fearing an invasion. If they get here before Jesus, no one stands a chance. But we're not afraid. We trust him."

"I have told you this before, Blake. Be careful. It would be a shame to survive seven years, then die right before his coming, like the others you mentioned."

"Don't worry about us, Ben; we're okay. But I do hope he doesn't wait long."

The conversation ended with all parties excited about what the next few days would bring. None understood the exact timing of events, but they all expected their Savior's return any day.

***

September 10. Armies prepared to advance on Jerusalem with a full-blown air and ground assault. Nothing would remain after they finished. Aissa Messai spent the day in strategic meetings with his leaders and generals. Each session combined intricate planning with pre-victory celebrations.

Ground forces would depart at midnight, taking every available route to Jerusalem. Early arrivals would encircle the city's perimeter, cutting off every escape route, while succeeding groups covered the surrounding mountains and valleys. Aircraft would leave before sunrise, arriving at first light. The assault would occur swiftly and seamlessly, ending before the inhabitants of Jerusalem realized what hit them.

Messai sat alone at 10:00 p.m., after one last meeting to confirm their readiness. Details poured through his mind. Consumed by his thoughts, he did not see the cloaked figure approaching from his left. The voice startled him. He leaped to his feet and spun to face his Chief Security Director.

"Mr. Rossi, I hope this is important. The events of tonight and tomorrow require my full attention until we win this battle. Do I make myself clear?"

"Abundantly clear, sir. But I must show you something you will not want to miss." He opened his laptop computer and tapped on an application.

"Mr. Rossi, I have no time for...!"

Rossi interrupted him without acknowledging his angry outburst. What he must show his boss would overshadow everything else. He practically shoved the computer into his boss's face.

"Sir, we have kept careful watch on our security cameras deployed around Jerusalem, especially those on the Mount. Look at this footage from yesterday afternoon."

Messai glared at him, finally moving his eyes to the screen. Rossi hit play just as the man started berating him again until the images filling the screen stopped him cold. His face shone with delight.

"They are there! We do not have to chase them to their hiding place and flush them out. They came to us!" Smyrnian voices then flowed from the speakers praising the lamb who was slain.

"Silence them! *They* will be the lambs who are slain when we take off their heads tomorrow! Capture them when the armies move in and detain them until we conquer the city. Their beheadings will culminate a victorious day!"

"I knew this would make you happy, sir. We will do as you say and prepare them for your arrival."

When Rossi left, the twelve demon princes joined Messai. He sent them to ensure all went well, and they darted around the mass of humanity covering the valley floor, leaving nothing to chance.

11:00 p.m. One final guest arrived for the party. The colossal red dragon, now visible to all, stood observing his mighty military, sparks flickering from his nostrils. He threw back his head, and the sparks turned to flames rising hundreds of feet into the air, drawing the attention of every mega-army member. Suddenly, the gargantuan beast shot up higher than the flames. His massive body hovered above them and his stubby limbs now extended to the farthest reaches of Armageddon.

Two hundred million troops simultaneously bowed in worship. He unleashed a deafening roar, bringing them to their feet, responding with shouts of affirmation. Their voices reverberated off surrounding mountains, demonstrating a thirst for slaughter and an eagerness for battle. Ground troops prepared to march toward the Holy City. The revelry continued until 11:55 p.m. when the beast motioned for quiet, then raised one scaly leg to signal their imminent departure.

Midnight. The sky exploded with brilliant light. Two hundred million pairs of eyes shot upward, and history's mightiest military force prepared for an immediate encounter with an unseen enemy.

***

In Jerusalem, the believers waited expectantly atop the Temple Mount. A sudden blinding flash of light pierced the night sky, igniting the atmosphere with an intense burst of radiant energy which emitted shock waves around the globe. The Smyrnians felt it; a brief burning sensation all over their bodies, no pain, only warmth. They realized what was happening and gazed heavenward, arms raised, as if reaching for something, or someone, they could not yet see.

A furious swirling motion opened a gaping hole, revealing the light's source, none other than the source of light himself. A solitary figure emerged through the opening. They knew who he was, though his appearance startled them. Instead of the loving Savior they longed to meet, a mighty warrior appeared riding a magnificent white horse, ready to wage war with his enemies. A large sword protruded from his mouth, shiny and razor sharp, displaying a readiness for battle.

Each saw him clearly, as if standing directly before him. They were not alone. Every person on earth beheld him, too. A name covered his forehead, which no one could interpret or understand. His eyes blazed with fire of impending judgment, but his attire did not befit one riding into battle. Instead of armor, he wore a king's robe, and crowns covered his head. Even more startling, blood covered his robe from shoulders to ankles. What could that mean?

Had he already fought a battle? Would he now fight alone? His next move answered the last question.

The rider motioned to someone behind him, and an army exponentially outnumbering Messai's military machine rode out to join him. Billions, if not trillions, farther away, faces obscured, also wearing shocking attire for soldiers going to war: gleaming white, unstained linen robes. The brightness nearly blinded them. His army sat silently awaiting their king's next move.

The magnificent stallion charged from heaven, leaving the massive mounted army behind. He raced downward, descended toward the Mount of Olives just east of Jerusalem, and stopped overlooking the Old City. The rider dismounted. When his feet touched the mountain, it split from top to bottom, with the two sides moving north and south, forming a wide rift. The rider mounted the white stallion and rejoined his army within seconds.

Blake, Beth, and their teammates watched, surprised and amazed as the 2,700-foot high mountain divided. From their vantage point, they saw multitudes of people fleeing the city and disappearing through the gap. Why were they leaving? Where were they going? Better yet, from *what* were they escaping? The Smyrnians would not depart with them, but would stay, awaiting Jesus' next move.

***

In the valley, pilots sprinted toward choppers and jets. The entire military force watched for their enemy to emerge, but others came first. The sky turned black, blinding light obscured by swarms of vultures creating an eerie, dark ceiling above them. Such a massive, menacing presence sent shivers down the spines of typically courageous soldiers.

They fired into the gigantic swarm. The rhythmic intensity of machine gun chatter combined with a nonstop barrage of gunfire silenced all other sounds. Ammo appeared to vanish in midair, not reaching its intended target, while the myriad of vultures remained untouched. Artillery shells with proximity fuses detonated when nearing the soaring scavengers. The large projectiles also fell short, sending shrapnel showering back toward the earth.

The birds suddenly retreated leaving a large opening above Armageddon's perimeter allowing light to shine through and two hundred million military personnel to see *him*. A majestic white steed carrying a rider wearing crowns and a blood-stained robe stood looking down at them, eager to charge into battle. Words on the rider's robe boldly stated, *King of kings* and *Lord of lords*. His hand held no sword. The weapon extended from his mouth, ready to slay all who stood in his way.

"Attack!" screamed the dragon. "Our real enemy shows himself. Defeat him, and victory is ours!"

A triumphant shout arose from two hundred million lips as they readied themselves to destroy the solitary enemy who dared confront such an enormous army. Then they saw *them*. An army whose numbers dwarfed their own rode out to join the warrior. Light glinting off shiny white robes nearly blinded the military below, yet they stood strong, gazing up, ready for their enemy's attack.

The white horse did not move. His rider stared down at them as they waited. The ground trembled under their feet. It shook lightly at first, then harder and more violently, until it quaked with such force none could stand. Soldiers, officers, and NWO leaders lay on the convulsing earth, as nearby mountains cracked, crumbled, and collapsed, large boulders crushing those camping beside them.

Three remained standing as the quake raged. The enormous red dragon still loomed over the valley, his armies lying before him. This was his day, and darkness must prevail over the light. Messai and Caiaphas stood on his left and right, now matching his size. The beast threw his limbs skyward and released a blood-curdling scream aimed at the robed warrior whom he recognized instantly.

Lightning crashed, and thunder boomed, shaking the sky. Huge hailstones poured from above, pounding those lying on the convulsing earth. Many crawled to any cover they could find while hailstones pummeled others where they lay. The shaking continued, as the entire world experienced catastrophic demolition. Complete cities lay in ruins. It utterly transformed the earth's landscape as islands sank into the sea and mountains disappeared. The quaking did not let up.

***

The earthquake hammered Jerusalem at the same time. It caught the believers there by surprise. Most had not heard it would come. Those who knew were so captivated by Jesus' appearance, they did not remember the cataclysmic event which would accompany it. But the seismology expert among them recognized it immediately.

"It's the last quake, just like the Bible says!" John exclaimed. "This one changes everything!"

"I thought Jesus would take us home before it came!" said Ally. "What should we do, Anders?"

They all turned their attention to their spiritual guide, looking for answers. Each felt the trembling beneath their feet and grabbed one another just before losing their footing and crashing onto the stone pavement. Blake held Beth close, listening as the quake ripped mountains apart, while massive hailstones splintered trees. Anders' voice rose above the clamor, powerful and strong.

"We're experiencing this because we rejected Jesus before the Rapture. But he won't destroy us with those who rejected him during the Tribulation. Stay where you are and trust him!"

They lay flat, feeling the ground would open any minute and swallow them. Sounds of fracturing pavement and smashing hailstones mingled with the violent noise of convulsing earth and collapsing structures rendered communication impossible, but the shocking brightness of midnight radiance enabled their vision.

Before their eyes, the majestic Dome of the Rock swayed from side-to-side, then exploded into a million pieces, its large golden dome careening across the pavement.

Next the Al-Aqsa Mosque crashed down, parts flying in all directions, with some sailing over the Old City's southern wall. Their attention turned toward the glorious Jewish temple. Would Jesus destroy it, too? The answer came when gigantic hailstones crushed it, leaving only a mangled pile of debris. Their position near the Golden Gate allowed them to witness the destruction away from danger, except for some rubble hurled toward them, falling just short.

"Messai built that house and defiled it," Anders yelled above the noise, "so Jesus destroyed it!"

They all understood that, but two pressing questions filled every mind. When would this end, and when would Jesus come on and get them? He still sat confidently on his white steed, as if waiting for the right time to attack. Meanwhile, the mountains around Jerusalem disappeared. The quaking flattened them, or gigantic holes opened and devoured them. It changed the surrounding landscape forever. Though they could not see it, the Smyrnians knew the entire world looked the same. They clung to each other, dazed, nauseated, and shaken as the quake raged, reshaping the earth.

After more than an hour, the convulsing finally ceased. Two million military personnel lay dead, scattered throughout Armageddon's two hundred and eighty square miles. The remaining one hundred and ninety-eight million now stared at unending flat terrain stretching out before them. No mountains survived the catastrophic quake. Large craters dotted the landscape where massive hailstones left their mark. Vehicles and weapons were completely smashed and utterly destroyed.

The air cleared, light returned, and the warrior above them reappeared. Terror overwhelmed them as they faced an insurmountable foe unarmed, while a foreboding flock of vultures surrounded the valley, awaiting a meal which would satisfy their insatiable appetite. The warrior held out his hand, and eerie silence followed the extreme turbulence. Then, in rapid motion, he swept his arm upward.

Blake lay on the stones, still holding Beth. A floating sensation consumed his body. *Natural,* he thought, *after such violent convulsing.* He glanced toward the pavement and saw it ten feet below. A brief sense of fear shook him, and he held Beth tightly, to ensure he did not drop her. Then he realized, *we're floating; no, flying!* He looked upward and saw Jesus smiling as they rose. A broad smile covered Blake's face, and he stretched open arms toward his Savior.

This was the moment they had waited seven years to experience. Since the day he first believed, through all the turmoil of the Tribulation, watching fellow believers die in Messai's device, they were finally going home! The others surrounded them, the same rapturous look on their faces.

The one hundred and forty-four thousand Messianic Jews in Petra did not experience the quake. They remained protected as they had for the past three and a half years. However, they watched the mountains that formed the city's impenetrable fortress explode outward, clearing the way for viewing the destruction of other ranges beyond them. Through it all, they stood on smooth ground.

Ben Abramson's feet left the earth, along with Miriam and their seven children, joined by Alexander and Elizabeth Ben-Ezra, Hadassah, and Mordecai Chaim. One hundred and forty-three thousand, nine hundred and eighty-six others followed. Only Michael was missing, but he would join them soon. They merged with the Jerusalem group, both ascending together, shouting praises to Jesus as they flew. He sat astride his white horse, waiting to greet them. But there would be no time for conversation yet, as they would soon learn.

The atmosphere quickly filled with soaring, celebrating believers who had turned to Jesus after the Rapture, survived the Tribulation's horror, and now rose to meet their Lord. Upon arrival, they discovered noble steeds awaiting them, too. White robes instantly covered them, and they were mounted and ready to ride, awaiting Jesus' signal.

"They cannot defeat us!" the dragon howled trying to rally his troops. "He is less powerful than me. I will destroy him... *and* them!"

His words did little to ease his army's fear, as they prepared for inevitable demise apart from a miracle by their *god*, and the one who empowered him. They waited, somehow believing Messai would deliver them. Then the warrior charged.

The saints and angels followed. Blake looked to his left and saw Beth's long, blonde hair flowing behind her. He loved her so much. A thought entered his mind: would their relationship change in eternity? They enjoyed less than seven years of marriage after the Rapture. His musings ended as Jesus descended from heaven with a deafening shout, his magnificent steed galloping on air toward the helpless victims below. Soldiers broke rank and ran for their lives as he drew closer.

The sword coming from his mouth disappeared, replaced by a steady stream of God's word spewing from his lips. Messai's forces grabbed their heads and covered their ears trying to block out the sound, but could not. Words continued pouring forth, Bible verses gushing like a rushing torrent. Then Jesus shouted words which were sure to infuriate the three massive beings below and strike even greater terror into the hearts of their followers.

"Yahweh is God!"

His army rode close behind him, calling out responsively.

"Jesus is Lord!"

Their mounts halted as Jesus continued. They watched him sweep over the valley, God's powerful word slicing through the air like a sharp double-edged sword, striking down the once mighty military machine until none remained alive. The dragon, Messai, and Caiaphas gazed upon all two hundred million members of their army lying dead before them. The cries of Jesus' army increased.

"Jesus is Lord! Jesus is Lord!"

Hearing that name, the dragon screamed, thrashing about, flailing his arms, the title hitting home like a hammer, each strike driving him farther down, along with the two standing beside him. All three soon shrank to normal size, now miniscule compared to the sovereign king riding the mighty stallion. A powerful angel swooped down with a message signaling their doom.

"The kingdoms of this world have become the kingdoms of our Lord and of his Christ, and he shall reign forever and ever!"

"It's *Gabriel.* I knew it!" Trey said loudly, as Anders beamed a knowing smile.

"How did you know...?" Blake asked, then smiled, the truth about their friend now revealed.

The earth opened, revealing a fiery lake of burning sulfur. Molten lava bubbled, rising and falling into the blazing inferno. The Heavenly Host quickly chased down every member of the dragon's demonic horde, casting them into the fire, shrieking as the flames torched their tiny bodies. They grabbed the demon princes next. Beelzebub and Belial struggled uselessly against their captors. The mighty demons screamed as the fire seared them, realizing they could never escape its torment.

The Host now raced toward the final three left standing. Aissa Messai, the Antichrist who had slaughtered so many believers, fled, with Caiaphas, his false prophet, following. Yahweh's powerful angels soon reached them, grabbed both, lifted them from the ground, then flew over the fire, and held them out over the flames. Both pleaded for their lives, proclaiming the name they had been unwilling to speak.

"Jesus is Lord," Messai said, bowing his head, his voice low and quivering.

"You rejected the Lord of glory, sold your soul to the dragon, slaughtered Yahweh's people, and proclaimed yourself god," Gabriel said. "You shall now suffer eternally in the lake of fire!"

When those words left his mouth, the angels hurled both alive into the fire, bringing applause from believers who endured their brutality and fear-mongering during the Tribulation. The former tyrant and his accomplice howled in pain and desperation as they plunged into the scorching flames.

Jesus waved his hand, and the vultures returned. More joined them, ripping and eating the flesh of those scattered across the valley floor. Their feast would continue for days.

The dragon now stood alone to face the wrath of Yahweh. An angel more powerful and majestic than the believers could comprehend flew toward the beast standing helplessly before the king of glory. They recognized him right away, despite his massive stature. *Michael!* They stood in awe of their friend and comrade who they now realized was the mighty warrior angel of heaven. He carried something in his hand. *A chain!* Michael seized the beast and bound him tightly.

The dragon's body twisted and contorted as he morphed into his former self. The Smyrnians briefly saw him for who he once was. His scaly armor fell away revealing a glorious, magnificent being. Lucifer, day star, light bearer. How could one so highly favored fall so far? They knew the answer. He rebelled against Yahweh and tried to claim the throne for himself, then spent millennia trying to prevent the reign of Yahweh's son. Now, he must face the consequences of his actions.

Michael dragged him before Jesus, where he remained defiant. The believers could not tell if the two exchanged words, but watched the one time beautiful archangel of Yahweh return to his fallen form, the grotesque beast of hell. Michael led him to the opening above the blazing fiery lake and cast him over the edge, tightly bound. His descent stopped before reaching the flames.

He would remain chained in the abyss for one thousand years, unable to move, viewing the horror which awaited him after that time ended. One thousand years to think about what he had done and contemplate his eternal punishment to come. The Smyrnians cheered victoriously and turned back toward their Lord, then followed as his white stallion galloped toward Jerusalem. Nearing the city, the aerial view rendered them speechless.

The quake destroyed every mountain surrounding Jerusalem and divided the city into three sections, two of which lay demolished. Three valleys, the Kidron, Tyropoeon, and Hinnom formed natural boundaries separating the Temple Mount, Old City, and West Jerusalem. After the convulsing earth completed its destructive work, only one section remained intact.

The ancient City of David and Temple Mount stood alone, elevated high above the surrounding valleys where mountains and buildings stood only a day earlier. Despite its height, gentle slopes descended to the plains below. Jerusalem returned to her original glory after King David conquered the city, and his son, Solomon, built Yahweh's temple after his father's death. Mount Zion now gleamed with God's glory, as endless flat terrain stretched out beneath it. The Dead Sea sparkled in the distance, clearly visible from Yahweh's holy mountain. The sight was awe-inspiring.

The Smyrnians prepared for arrival in their favorite place, but their mounts landed in the expansive plain below. Jesus continued, descending onto Yahweh's holy mountain, David's city. An elevated throne awaited him. Twelve smaller thrones sat on each side, occupied by twenty-four elders dressed in white with crowns of gold on their heads.

Smyrnians and other believers stared at them with questioning looks, failing to understand their identity. Anders recognized them immediately. He saw them in Yahweh's throne room when he visited heaven three and a half years earlier. Twelve represented the tribes of Israel and all Old Testament saints, while the other twelve represented Jesus' apostles and everyone who had received him as their Savior. Anders realized judgment was imminent.

Each elder rose and kneeled before Jesus, worshiping him. Then they simultaneously removed their crowns, lay them at his feet, and returned to their thrones. The heavenly choir still hovering above burst into a new song of praise the believers had not heard. Unable to sing, they fell down in worship, with hands raised, until the song ended, then stood again looking on in wonder.

Something big would happen next. Everyone felt that and watched expectantly, unable to fathom what it might be. Eager to meet their Savior and see friends who had died during the last seven years, they prayed it would come fast. It did, catching them by surprise. People suddenly covered the plains farther than their eyes could see. Jesus raised his hand and silence covered the land.

CHAPTER 17

Blake stood beside Ben, surrounded by Smyrnians. They stuck together through the Tribulation and would not leave each other during this important moment. Blake noticed a separation between the smaller group surrounding him and the endless mass of humanity standing to his right. A wide chasm prevented either side from crossing. Every person's destiny was now sealed permanently.

Jesus turned his attention to those standing on his right. They had placed their faith in him during the past seven years, beginning with the Smyrnians, then spreading worldwide. He spoke gently and lovingly, affirming their faithfulness, and inviting them into his presence.

"Come, you who are blessed by my Father; take your inheritance, the kingdom prepared for you since the creation of the world. For I was hungry and you gave me something to eat, I was thirsty and you gave me something to drink, I was a stranger and you invited me in, I needed clothes and you clothed me, I was sick and you looked after me, I was in prison and you came to visit me."

His words confused them. Since believing in him, they had longed to gaze upon his face and speak with him, but he remained hidden from their sight, until now. The group questioned in unison.

"Lord, when did we see you hungry and feed you, or thirsty and give you something to drink? When did we see you a stranger and invite you in, or needing clothes and clothe you? When did we see you sick or in prison and go to visit you?"

They understood when he answered. "Truly I tell you, whatever you did for one of the least of these brothers and sisters of mine, you did for me."

The group surged forward, but stopped when Jesus addressed those across the chasm. His voice now thundered, his tone no longer gentle and loving, but powerful, commanding, and authoritative.

"Depart from me, you who are cursed, into the eternal fire prepared for the devil and his angels. For I was hungry and you gave me nothing to eat, I was thirsty and you gave me nothing to drink, I was a stranger and you did not invite me in, I needed clothes and you did not clothe me, I was sick and in prison and you did not look after me."

Wailing filled the air, as those on Jesus' left fearfully pleaded with him. "Lord, when did we see you hungry or thirsty or a stranger or needing clothes or sick or in prison, and did not help you?"

His words exploded, proclaiming a final and fearful pronouncement of judgment. "Truly I tell you, whatever you did not do for one of the least of these, you did not do for me." (Matthew 25:34-45)

A deafening *crack* split the air. The earth opened and swallowed them alive, sweeping them to their eternal doom in the lake of fire. Their screams continued briefly until the earth closed again, bringing silence. The believers briefly felt sadness, but unspeakable joy soon replaced it after the ground slammed shut and the last cries ended. All thoughts now centered on meeting their Savior.

Before they moved farther, the sound of excited voices filled their ears. Those Messai had slaughtered and others taken in the Rapture ran toward them, each approaching friends and family members who survived. Shouts and tears of joy came from both sides, as glorious reunions occurred one after another. Jesus' smile revealed his own elation as he looked down from his throne. The Smyrnians recognized their loved ones and greeted them with open arms. They raced toward each other, making collisions inevitable, but no one cared.

Evan Ryles led the way. He jumped into Blake and Beth's waiting arms, then quickly moved to Ally and her family. They grabbed each other, hugging, laughing, and crying joyful tears. This experience far exceeded anything they could have expected. Blake's emotion overflowed.

"Evan, I can never thank you enough for telling me about Jesus. I wouldn't be here without you."

"Thank you for coming to my dorm room, hearing me out, and watching the video that day. The world may never have heard about Jesus without you and Beth."

"I'm pretty sure he would have found a way without us. But I'm also sure before the Rapture ever happened, he planned to use us. We couldn't have done any of this without him. Evan, I have to say something. I'm so sorry I let you go back for the hard drive. It should have been me..."

"Are you kidding, Blake?! You didn't *let* me go back. I left you behind because I'm faster than you. That also means I beat you to heaven! Best of all, Jesus met me when I got there and fed me before we did anything else, which was a good thing because I was hungry!"

They laughed at him through tears of pure delight. He told Ally's brothers, "You're going to love the pizza!" They grinned and hugged him, showing their tight bond and shared love of pizza.

Their hug fest was interrupted by another couple sprinting toward them, arms flung open wide. Mila cried out and ran to meet them, her voice choking with emotion, Bruno by her side.

"Hans! Heidi!"

She and Bruno helped Hans and Heidi Meier put their faith in Jesus, and they all served him until Messai beheaded the Meiers in his Capital Punishment Device. That event would have devastated the Smyrnians, had not Jesus revealed himself to them.

"My heart broke when they led you before Messai. But hearing you answer him with such strong faith blessed us all. Then Jesus..." she said, stopping when Heidi interrupted her.

"Yes, Mila! Jesus! It was amazing when he escorted us home! We felt nothing when the blade dropped and experienced no lapse in time. Jesus led us to the device, and the next thing we knew, we were running through a grassy meadow with him, more alive than ever!"

"I can't wait for you to meet him," Hans said, turning and waving at Jesus. The Savior looked directly at them and waved, a big smile covering his face. They wanted to make a mad dash for him, but with other reunions taking place, they stayed and rejoiced with them, too.

Anders held Angie and their three children, laughing with glee. They came to him when he visited heaven, but Jesus prevented him from touching them then. They made up for that now.

"Baby, I don't understand how I missed it. You tried to tell me. You begged me to attend church with you, but I tuned you out. Please forgive me for missing the Rapture. Kids, you told me about Jesus and showed me what knowing him is like, but I didn't listen to you either. I missed you all so much. Now, we won't ever be apart again!"

"Dad, when Jesus told us you believed, the angels threw a private party for us as we watched him write your name in the Book of Life," A.J. said, more excited than Anders had ever seen him.

"You were a good person who just needed to trust Jesus, honey," Angie said. "But goodness doesn't get a person to heaven. Only Jesus does that. All that matters now is what you did after the Rapture. Because of that, we are all together forever. You already know what that feels like!"

"I do, and I can't wait to experience it again, baby! Let's go!"

"Hold on, Jesus has something even better planned for us!"

"How can anything be better than heaven?"

"You'll find out, daddy," said Jenny. "It's another secret we can't tell you yet."

"If I'm with you four, I'll be happy, wherever we are."

Ally walked up, not knowing how she fit into their family. She married Anders not that long ago, and now she met his wife and kids for the first time. How would they receive her? Angie pulled her in and spoke before she got the chance to say anything.

"Ally, I'm thrilled to meet you! Thank you for taking such good care of Anders the past three and a half years. I told him to marry you," she said with a twinkle in her eyes. "Things will look different in eternity. We'll be one big happy family forever!"

"Angie, thank you so much for welcoming me like this, and for telling Anders to marry me. The Smyrnians took care of each other during the Tribulation, but Anders needed me, and I needed him. Jesus gave us a spiritual connection that was better than any physical relationship. We fought Messai side-by-side and strengthened one another. Now, I give him back to you. Besides, I still have Evan. He's my best friend. We will *all* be one big happy family forever!"

They talked non-stop while other Smyrnians reunited with family members who Messai or AMPP killed during the last seven years. This was good stuff!

***

Brita, John, and Kathie scoured the rejoicing throng searching for one person. Others celebrated all around them, but there was still no sign of him.

"Where is he?" Brita asked. "Anders saw him in heaven, so he must be here somewhere."

They heard a familiar voice and spun around, weeping for joy. Brita ran to her husband and collapsed into his arms as John wrapped both in a strong embrace. Jeffrey came with him, and Julie clung to her husband who had died only weeks earlier. Johnathan captured their attention.

"We tried to save you, Johnathan, but Messai fooled everybody and took you to Brussels instead of Israel. I saw the chair..." Brita said, her voice trailing off as memories of that day flooded back into her mind.

"That was brutal, I confess, but none of it matters now. I have already told Jeffery the story, but you must all hear what meeting Jesus was like immediately after those bullets hit my body. It was the most awesome experience ever! But that was minor compared to what happened next."

"What happened, Jonathan?" Kathie asked.

"Jesus and I ran through beautiful fields, laughing and rolling through green grass. It was incredible! But that still wasn't the best part."

"What could be better than meeting Jesus in heaven and running and playing with him?"

"The captain prayed to Jesus after they shot me. I talked to him during the flight, then tried to show him what it's like to trust Jesus. I told him to watch how I died, and he did. After he saw my peace as I faced that firing squad, he fell to his knees and asked Jesus to give him what I had, and he did. That one man's decision made everything I suffered worth it!"

"Johnathan Baldwin?"

He whirled around recognizing the voice instantly. *Captain!* Johnathan grabbed his former captor and squeezed him tightly. *His smile has not changed,* the captain thought, as he embraced him too.

"Thank you for caring enough to tell me about Jesus after all we did to you, Johnathan. I am sorry."

"Oh, Captain, if you and your men had not beaten me, you would never have turned to him. He was beaten and hung on a cross so we could know him and be forgiven of our sin. I consider it an honor to be counted worthy of suffering for Jesus so you can stand here with us now, one of his true followers. I would change nothing that happened. I forgive you, Captain, as he forgave me."

The man's face erupted into the brightest smile they had ever seen. Looking over Johnathan's shoulder, he said, "Introduce me to your family."

They greeted the captain with open arms. No one had shown him such love before. Most would consider it strange from the family of a man he had brutalized and led to his execution, but he understood it. This was normal among Jesus' followers. They forgave others as they were forgiven. Because of Johnathan Baldwin's faith, he now knew pure love, which he would experience forever. An entire family, with their former enemy, celebrated this moment. Times like these were only the beginning, and they would relish them, but meeting Jesus would top them all.

***

Another voice interrupted their celebration. It claimed their attention and brought a squeal from Kathie who spun to see Doc coming from the other direction. He spoke first in typical Doc fashion.

"John, you old rascal, thank you for coming when my wife called you, and for taking care of her these last six years. Kathie, I hated to leave you, but Jesus called me to come to him. I knew I was going, but I didn't realize it would happen that fast. Those AMPP guys thought they killed me, but all they did was send me to meet my Savior. He used them to take me home."

"I'm so sorry for telling Messai about you, John. Something changed in me after I did that. A deep darkness engulfed me and took control of my mind. If you hadn't come like Kathie asked you to, I would've been doomed. When I believed in Jesus, he called me home right then, and my mind was completely focused on going. I want to hear the story of how you escaped from AMPP. If I didn't know Jesus so well, I'd assume that was impossible."

"We have lots of time to tell you about that, sweetheart, but for now I want to hold you, then introduce you to all the other Smyrnians. You're right, John took good care of me. I love you both so much. He and I married like you asked, but you are my husband forever."

"I'm not worried about that. You'll discover it doesn't work that way with Jesus. He also has a surprise for you, so get ready to hear some amazing news!"

The Tribulation martyrs knew something the people who survived those seven years did not. They would all hear it soon enough, but Jesus would reveal the secret himself when the time came. John told Doc one thing before they did anything else.

"Doc, you were the first Tribulation martyr," he said, speaking barely above a whisper.

"Oh, I know that, John. Jesus told me and explained everything that meant. I was the first fruit of many others who would follow. And..." he said, a grin creeping across his face, "he let me greet them when they came! Imagine that; me a greeter in heaven! Well, he met them first, then brought them to me and we shared our stories before I introduced them to others. It amazed me every time!"

"I'm not surprised the way you like to talk," Kathie said. "I want to hear all about it, but let us introduce you to everyone else first. How long will we have to wait for this secret to be revealed?"

***

Magnus stood alone watching all the reunions take place, wishing for one of his own. He looked for one person, finally spotted him, and ran toward him at breakneck speed. Malachi sprinted toward him calling his name with every step until they crashed into each other. Magnus lifted him and embraced him, both laughing and crying hysterically, then carried him to Blake and Bruno.

"Look at this guy," he said proudly. "A perfect face without one burn mark!"

"I don't want to talk about that," Malachi said. "Let's talk about Jesus. You guys will meet him soon and learn some exciting news you haven't heard yet." He left them wondering, along with everyone else, what that news could be. They just wanted to meet the Savior and get to heaven.

"Malachi, you did so much for Jesus, and us, after you put your faith in him. What would've happened to Ally if you hadn't gotten information that helped Ollie and Amelia rescue her? You got Trey out of a dangerous predicament with AMPP when he flew you to Missouri from New York. I could name many more. The Smyrnians owe you a debt of gratitude."

"We owe Jesus a debt of gratitude we can never repay. All I care about is living with him forever."

Johnathan walked up and called out, "Magnus, I have someone here who wants to speak to you." The surprised look on Magnus' face revealed his shock at seeing his former colleague.

"Lars? How...? What...? I heard Messai assigned my patrol to you and sent you to America after Johnathan escaped and I disappeared. But how did you get *here*? You served Messai. Aren't you the one who accompanied Johnathan to Belgium for his execution? You must tell me how you met Jesus. Only miracles could cause guys like us to believe in him. I'm all ears!"

"Okay, my friend, here goes. But after I finish, you must tell me your story, too."

***

While they exchanged miraculous experiences which caused them to turn to Jesus, another reunion occurred not far away. Hadassah cried out with delight when three figures approached her, as she stood talking to Mordecai, Ben and Miriam, and Alexander and Elizabeth. They all recognized them instantly: Omar, Ahmad, and Hala. Hadassah nearly tackled them, and they went down together, rolling around and giggling like little kids.

"You four call yourselves soldiers?" Mordecai asked. "You're not acting like soldiers."

They stopped and looked at him wondering how he could scold them now. Then he broke out laughing. "Get over here!" The entire group hugged, exchanging *Shaloms* and *Salams* as they greeted one another. The others did not realize Hadassah had seen her friends enter heaven, and they kept that information to themselves.

"We heard they captured you," said Mordecai. "I can't imagine what they did to you."

"It was more brutal than you can imagine," Ahmad said. "They caned Hala until they ripped her back to shreds, then nearly beat Omar to death. They beat me pretty badly too, but my partners had it worse. The device was a relief and seeing Jesus was far more wonderful than the suffering was painful. When the angels hurled Messai and Caiaphas into the fire, we knew the victory was ours!"

"Let's go talk to everybody else," Ben said. "They will want to see you, too!"

That led to further jubilation, which only increased as more people came. Beth's parents found her. It filled them with great joy to see her there with the believers after the Tribulation. She recounted walking through their house after the Rapture and grieving, thinking aliens abducted them. They all chuckled at people falling for such a ridiculous notion.

She introduced them to Blake and explained how he told her the truth about the Rapture, helping her trust Jesus, and shared what that experience was like for her. Blake told about them falling in love and getting married. Both hugged him. Beth's mom was ecstatic about gaining a son-in-law.

Next, they met Ollie and Amelia and listened to him tell about Messai appearing to him on his flight to America, then Beth telling him about Jesus before they left the airport parking lot. He followed that by describing how he told Amelia, and both of them spread the word to their families. Steve and Linda stepped out and shared their story. John and Mary joined the party, telling how Anders led them to faith in Jesus. Rickie said Trey did the same for him, and Paul Johnson agreed. Even Trey's deputy friend, Justin, who was killed the night he believed, came to thank him. It seemed the stories would never end, and they didn't want them to stop.

That's how it works, Beth's mom noted. More people turn to Jesus when his followers tell others what he did for them. The good news spreads like wildfire, and no one can stop it. They all wondered aloud how anyone could keep something so amazing to themselves.

***

Trey and Rickie suddenly ran toward a group of men walking in their direction. "Robert...! Bradley...!" they called out excitedly. The American Sergeant Major and their English pilot friend reached them quickly, followed by Robert's platoon members who died when Chen bombed Lifta. His remaining troops who survived came running and saluted Robert.

"No more saluting required, men," he said. "We're all members of Jesus' family here, and no one is greater than any other. No more war and fighting. You'll learn about that soon." They knew he was protecting the secret, too.

By now, they all united as one group celebrating together and trying to comprehend this was only the beginning. Then Evan spoke up and changed the focus of their conversation.

"Everyone here trusted in Jesus because another believer told them about him. But none of us would have believed without *him*."

He pointed to an approaching man walking toward them with some others they did not recognize. When they got closer, Blake collapsed to his knees, seeing the face he had watched on video many times and shared with individuals and the world. Beth fell beside him, her tears streaming too.

"It's good to meet both of you, Blake and Beth," said the pastor who left his message behind for others to watch. He grabbed their hands and lifted them to their feet. "Thank you for faithfully spreading my message. No one else could have told the entire world like you did. All these people are here because of Evan and you."

"No, they are here because of you, pastor," Blake said, embracing the man he respected more than any person he had ever known.

"We're all here because of Jesus. I could never have imagined my simple message turning so many people to him. And who could ever have imagined him using Evan Ryles to spread his truth?" His eyes twinkled with mischief as he glanced at Evan.

"Not us," said the man standing beside Evan. There was no mistaking his identity. Evan was the spitting image of his dad. "His atheism prevented him from having faith. We prayed every day for that boy to believe in Jesus, and our prayers were answered, but not until *after* the Rapture."

"Mr. Ryles," Blake said, "you have no idea how thankful I am your son contacted me that day in Chicago. What are the odds of that happening? Only Jesus could orchestrate such a meeting. It led to Ally and her family, Anders, Beth, and Professor John Baldwin, plus many others, believing in him. Speaking of them, look what's happening all around us."

***

The entire group suddenly quieted and turned their attention to Jesus' throne where the two mighty angels they witnessed earlier rose into the air and flew to them. Most realized who they were, but their humility kept them from speaking. Michael and Gabriel hovered above them, then Michael spoke boldly and powerfully, but with the human tone he used when he lived among them.

"Friends, Yahweh sent us to earth in human form to protect and guide you through the Tribulation. Gabriel joined the American military unit in Jordan and led them safely to the Smyrnians. I entered the world that day Ben Abramson spoke to thousands of Yahweh's chosen people on the Mount of Beatitudes. Another also joined me that day, although Yahweh actually sent her years earlier."

Mordecai turned and stared at his niece as her appearance changed and glorious light engulfed her. Hadassah's feet left the ground and she rose to join her two comrades.

"Mordecai Chaim raised his niece, Hadassah, and taught her about Yahweh, but she didn't realize her identity and purpose until *such a time as this*. Esther and I went on many adventures together. Ben and Mordecai, I'm sorry we couldn't tell you about our trips, but Yahweh wouldn't allow it."

"Some of you wouldn't have survived if he hadn't sent us and the Heavenly Host, although you didn't realize it then." Millions of angels appeared high above them flashing flaming swords. Some Smyrnians began calling out specific times they knew miracles occurred.

"Our flight from the farm back to New York!" Trey yelled.

"My escape from Messai!" Ally said.

"My escape from Messai, too!" Beth said, following Ally's lead.

"Our landing in Tel Aviv!" said Paul Johnson.

"You saved us at the border!" Mordecai Chaim yelled.

"Getting us out of China!" Bruno and Magnus said in unison.

"We wouldn't have landed safely in Petra without you, would we?" asked Ben softly, his voice still clearly heard. Mordecai looked shocked as that realization hit him.

The group kept on until Michael held up his hand, asking for silence so he could speak again.

"You're right about all those and many more. Each represented crucial points for continuing and fulfilling Yahweh's mission during those seven years."

The three suddenly morphed back into their earthly forms and descended to stand with them. "Now, enough with the serious stuff. It's time to meet Jesus and hear his plans for you!"

Jesus stood, brilliant light shining down from above. The Smyrnians longed to spend time with Michael, Gabriel, and Hadassah but Jesus commanded their full attention. Although the massive throng of believers stretched for miles, each felt as though they stood directly in front of him.

"Welcome, my faithful followers! You fought a good fight, finished your race, and stayed faithful. Now you receive the crown of righteousness my Apostle Paul promised I would give you this day. Well done, good and faithful servants!"

The throng remained silent briefly, humbled by their Lord's commendation, but soon broke out in shouts of joy and songs of praise, combined with deafening applause.

"By now you understand with my father a day is like a thousand years, and a thousand years are like a day. Thus, the six days of creation represented six thousand years of world history. My father divided history into two-thousand year increments to reveal his timing. Two thousand years passed from creation to Abraham and two thousand years from Abraham to my first coming, meaning two thousand years remained."

"Those years ended when I took my people home in the Rapture September 11, 2029, two thousand years after my death and resurrection in 29 A.D. The Rapture occurred on the day I foretold, the Feast of Trumpets. Many of you came home that day! Others were left to endure seven years of tribulation, but believed in me during that time. Welcome, all of you!" Raucous celebration followed those words, but they quieted when Jesus held up his hand, signaling he had more to say.

"Now, for that secret you have been waiting to hear." He winked and everyone leaned in to hear.

"On the seventh day, after creating the universe, my father and I rested and consecrated that day as a time for people to rest and refresh from their weekly labor. But the seventh day also awaited fulfillment during the final thousand years of my father's plan. It looked forward to a thousand-year rest for our people on the earth. Hebrews Chapter Four, verse 9 says, 'There remains a *Sabbath-rest* for the people of God.'"

"Revelation Chapter 5, verse 10 says, 'You have made them to be a kingdom and priests to serve our God, and *they will reign on the earth*.' That was written about *you*!"

"Revelation Chapter 20, Verses 1-3 say, 'And I saw an angel coming down out of heaven, having the key to the Abyss and holding in his hand a great chain. He seized the dragon, that ancient serpent, who is the devil, or Satan, and bound him for a *thousand years*. He threw him into the Abyss, and locked and sealed it over him, to keep him from deceiving the nations anymore until the *thousand years* were ended.'"

"You watched the dragon bound and cast into the Abyss a short while ago. He will remain there for a thousand years, unable to tempt or deceive people during that time, which means no presence of evil and no sin will exist on earth! Revelation Chapter 20, Verse 4, continues..."

"I saw the souls of those who had been beheaded because of their testimony about Jesus and because of the Word of God. They had not worshiped the beast or its image and had not received its mark on their foreheads or their hands. They came to life and *reigned with Christ a thousand years*."

"Who was beheaded in Messai's Capital Punishment Device because you refused his mark?"

Thousands of hands went up.

"Who was slaughtered by his *peace patrol* or others for following me?"

Thousands more raised their hands. Doc Sanderson waved both hands back and forth wildly.

"How many others rejected his mark but survived the Tribulation?"

Innumerable hands shot skyward throughout the multitude.

"Today you join all my father's people who make up my kingdom and reign with me for a thousand years on a renewed earth! *Your Sabbath rest has come!*"

Believers celebrated his proclamation with cheers, tears, and hugs, trying to wrap their minds around what he just told them. A thousand years to live on a renewed earth, reigning with Jesus? How would the earth look? Would it appear different from what they knew before? What would they do? So many questions... Jesus spoke again, discerning their thoughts, yet leaving their questions partially open-ended.

"The seven-year Tribulation followed the Rapture. My return occurred exactly seven years after it began. My thousand-year reign on earth starts *now*, following my second coming. Eternity begins when the thousand years end. That, my beloved, is the day for which you long!"

No applause came this time. The massive throng quietly awaited their Lord's next answers, leaning on every word like eager students soaking up their master's teaching. Jesus continued, not surprised by his listeners' silent anticipation, but unwilling to yield all the information they desired. He smiled, leaned in, stretched out his hands toward the multitude gathered before him, and spoke.

"You must *believe* some things before you can *see* them. That describes faith. You believed in me, though you could not see me. Many of you walked by faith throughout your lives before the Rapture, rejecting an unbelieving world's claims. Some of you believed in me during the Tribulation and endured unspeakable things from a wicked world and its evil dictator. You now receive the reward for that relentless strength and determination, as your faith becomes sight."

"You must *see* other things before you *believe* them, because they go beyond the human mind's ability to comprehend. In Romans, Chapter 8, my Apostle Paul wrote about what you will soon experience. To you who endured persecution or death during the Tribulation, he reminds you that *your sufferings were not even worth comparing with the glory that will now be revealed in you.*"

"He described the world you will live in for the next thousand years! His words made little sense to people before. But you are blessed to see that promise become reality!"

"*For the creation waits in eager expectation for the children of God to be revealed.* Today, you, my father's children are revealed and you alone dwell on the earth! All creation has awaited this moment! It was subjected to frustration, but now the creation itself will be liberated from bondage to decay and brought into the freedom and glory of the children of God! The earth and everything in it, now returns to my father's original purpose for it... *perfection*!"

Jesus sat down on King David's throne. His outstretched arms invited every person who had not met him to come. Millions of Tribulation saints rushed en masse toward the throne. A remarkable thing happened. Each person kneeled before him, rose and embraced him, then talked with him, yet the entire experience took only minutes. Though he sat alone, his omnipresence caused each to feel like they spent hours with him. It was a magical moment none would ever forget.

The Smyrnians came last, held up by Michael, Gabriel, and Hadassah, laughing and reminiscing as those among their number who returned with Jesus waited to introduce them to him. They shared stories of heaven and listened as the others told their experiences during the Tribulation's final years. They could have talked forever but Michael interrupted to inform them their time had come to meet the Lord. He pointed toward the one who would lead them there. The pastor whose video helped them believe motioned for them to follow and led the way to their Savior. Tears flowed as they ascended the mountain and approached his throne, hearts overflowing with gratitude and joy.

CHAPTER 18

"Welcome, friends. After walking with you through so many hard times over the past seven years, I have awaited this moment. You fought so well. Come, and let me shake your hands."

One-by-one they stepped up to meet Jesus, as he stood to greet them. Such peace none of them had ever felt. His love enveloped them, overwhelmed their senses, removed all inhibition and fear, and slowly renewed their minds. They sat around Jesus, listening as he spoke about the past seven years and taught about the next thousand years.

"Pastor, you obeyed my call to leave the video explaining what happened and what would come. All these people believed because of you. Evan, out of all people on earth, you turned to me first, then told Ally, and the two of you told Blake. Blake, I brought you to Chicago that day. Yes, you reported a story, but the reason you came was to hear the truth of what happened and face the choice of whether to believe what you heard. Your choice set in motion a chain of events that led to millions of people following me. Beth, your role was also essential. You filled it well."

"Ally, you brought your family to faith, causing others in Germany to believe. Your bravery when you became Messai's assistant yielded vital information, though that role was short-lived. Bruno, you were hesitant to accept me, even after your family trusted in me, but that made your decision more powerful and your commitment unyielding. Oliver and Amelia, your boldness amazed me. I witnessed your daring escapes, often risking your lives to save your teammates."

"Anders, once you realized the truth about what happened to Angie and your children, you became a missionary who unashamedly told everyone you could about me. Many people are here because of your testimony. Trey and Rickie, you took many risks to transport and rescue my people. Your bravery saved many lives. John, your knowledge of earthquakes and natural disasters allowed you to assist others during traumatic times. Reconnecting with your children helped Johnathan choose to share my truth with the world, even though it cost him his life. Kathie, following Doc's death, you did not rest until your children put their faith in me. Your contribution to this team was vital."

"None of this would have happened without *all* of you. Thank you."

Those last two words brought tears again, but they quickly turned to smiles. They would change nothing they did for Jesus. But now they had lots to celebrate, and the party was just getting started! The Tribulation's hardships no longer mattered. Today began a new day of wonder and adventure. Jesus then turned to another man with a glorious look they recognized was unique among them.

"Benjamin, my father and I will always remember the night you believed, and I assure you, so will Blake. Our glory covered you that night. I called you to lead our chosen people, Israel, to follow me. You carried out that task, then led 144,000 of them to Petra, the place I chose in advance for them to live for three and a half years. This Millennium holds a special purpose for them. I will reign from here, and they shall inherit the land."

"Lord, I am so sorry I missed it my entire life and failed to accept you as the true Messiah. Thank you for giving me and my family a second chance to believe, then calling me to go tell your people. I did what you told me to do, and here are your people who followed you as I did."

"I am renewing the earth, Benjamin, but I am also restoring something taken from my people."

"The borders, Lord?"

"Yes, the borders. You learned that from my word, although it is happening a bit differently than you expected throughout your life."

Alexander spoke up. "Your promise to your servant, Abraham, Jesus. You are restoring the original borders of Israel which you promised to give him!"

"You are right, Alexander. From south to north, the borders will be from the Nile River in Egypt to Lebanon. From east to west, the land extends from the Euphrates River to the Mediterranean Sea. No unbelievers remain. That land belongs to my people who discovered me, their Messiah!"

The Smyrnians had never heard that. But they saw the look of pure elation on Ben's face and were happy he would witness that promise fulfilled. They did not ask questions; they listened. Ben stepped away and told the Jewish believers what Jesus said. They erupted with a joyful shout, knowing they would now get to experience the things they had been taught their entire lives!

"You others may live anywhere you want and travel wherever your hearts desire. The earthquake reshaped the earth, brought mountains down, raised valleys up, and created a smooth, level planet, easily traversed by everyone. Some mountains still stand. You will soon understand why."

"I will now return the earth to its original glory. All of creation will function as my father and I intended. The four seasons and all nature will exist in perfect harmony, and my father's glory will fill the earth. All people who believed in me will experience that for a thousand years!"

"Lord, one thing escapes me," said Anders. "Since only believers remain, who will the dragon deceive when you release him from the abyss after the thousand years end? Surely none of your followers can turn away from you and follow him." His question pleaded for an answer.

"Ah, Anders, the scroll did not reveal the events of this time. It ended with my return. Everyone who believed in me and worshiped my father now inhabits the earth. Most of those already live in their glorified bodies. They will neither marry nor bear children. But millions who followed me during the Tribulation and survived keep their physical bodies. Those will give birth and raise families. Their children and grandchildren will do the same. They will populate the earth."

"But, Lord, we will all worship you. How can he deceive people who have learned about you and lived on a perfect earth their entire lives?"

"Those who are born must make their own decision about me. No one who entered the Millennium will ever forsake me. But many people born during these thousand years will choose to follow the dragon at the end, even though they know the truth. I realize that is difficult to understand, but do not worry about it now. Enjoy your lives on this perfect planet I made new just for you!"

When Jesus ended his explanation, his words left their minds, and their thoughts returned to a thousand years of perfect existence on Yahweh's renewed earth. Nothing else mattered now. They would live normal lives, but without temptation or imperfection, for a thousand years. After that, eternity with Jesus! Let the Millennium begin!

Immediately, water gushed from Mount Zion and Jerusalem, forming two rushing rivers, one flowing east toward the Dead Sea, and the other flowing west toward the Mediterranean Sea. The believers realized the pure, clear liquid was not just any water. It was living water, healing the land as it went! They watched the desert below them come to life, bursting forth in magnificent color, and realized this changed everything. One of their top priorities was exploring this perfect planet. A wink from Jesus told them he understood.

"We have a thousand years to talk. My Host and I have work to do, and you have exploring to do. I suggest we all get started! Now get out of here!" Jesus said, then laughed and waved them away.

Work, they all wondered, glancing at one another. What work could Jesus and his angels possibly need to do? Whatever that was, it seemed obvious he did not want them around while it was happening. They also had things to do, which had nothing to do with work. The Smyrnians walked away toward the massive throng gathered around Jerusalem and far beyond. This was day one of a thousand years, the start of a more wonderful life than they had ever considered.

**

Ben walked alone wondering how 144,000 Jewish believers could inhabit the enormous piece of land God promised to their father, Abraham. He learned about the original promise as a child and heard its dimensions years later. 356,000 square miles! Being a lifelong New Yorker, he knew nearly nine million people lived in three hundred square miles in New York City. What would 144,000 people do with 356,000 square miles of land?

He reached his people who awaited his return, then noticed an approaching crowd which dwarfed his 144,000 in number. Suddenly, the gentle voice of Jesus whispered into his ear. *ALL my faithful people, Ben.* He started recognizing folks. *Abraham!* The one to whom Yahweh gave the promise led the way, with a multitude following. How he so clearly identified them, Ben did not understand. All thoughts stopped, and he raced toward his ancestors who now saw their promise fulfilled.

"Benjamin!" Abraham said, wrapping him in a firm embrace. The group walking with him stretched for miles. "Let me introduce you to my family. This is my wife, Sarah, through whom the promise came, and our son, Isaac, with his wife, Rebekah. Here are my daughter, Dinah, and my grandson, Jacob, followed by his wives and twelve sons, from whom came the twelve tribes of Israel." Each son stepped forward and greeted Ben. He spoke briefly to the first three, but stood looking into the eyes of the fourth.

"The Lion of the Tribe of Judah," he said softly. "Messiah Jesus came through your family line. It is good to meet you." Judah gripped his hand strongly, and Ben winced from the pain. He understood why Yahweh chose Judah as the one through whom his son would come into the world. Each son came until the youngest finally stood before him. He laughed and gave Ben a big hug.

"Benjamin, my namesake!"

"It's an honor to meet you, Benjamin Abramson. I may be the youngest of my family, but I'm no less important than any of them. My tribe was often weak, but many great warriors also came from us. I consider you one of them, Ben. You led Yahweh's people after Jesus brought his people home and accomplished his purpose, doing what John foretold. I'm sure you remember another famous warrior for Jesus who also came from my tribe."

"Paul! I heard very little of his history until I met Jesus that night in my home. After that, I studied the great apostle's life and ministry and determined I would be like him when I told Yahweh's chosen people about Jesus."

"Well, let me introduce him to you!" Benjamin said with gusto as a man walked out from behind him. Ben was shocked by the man's appearance and stature. He expected a large, imposing figure who commanded the attention and respect of those to whom he spoke. Instead, he looked at a short, unimpressive man, whose appearance was even more ordinary than his own. Surely this was not Paul. The man stuck out his hand and spoke. His voice sounded even less impressive.

"Saul of Tarsus, alias Paul, Apostle of Jesus. He made me his apostle to the gentiles, but he called you to be his evangelist to our people during the Tribulation. The result of your work stands all around us. Thank you for being faithful. I saw you looking at my eyes. They gave me problems after that Damascus Road encounter, but Jesus gave me brand new eyes when I got home!"

"I'm sorry," Ben said, knowing he struggled for words. "I didn't mean to, but I'm so in awe of you all." He motioned toward the huge crowd.

"Don't worry about it. You'll get used to this as you meet more people. A thousand years should give you enough time to talk to everyone here. Welcome home, Ben."

He felt comfortable enough now to walk through the front lines meeting more people. The time for conversations would come later. For now, simple meet and greet was enough. He met King David and his son, Solomon, Samuel, and Ruth. Working his way farther back, he found Moses and Joshua, then Noah, and his grandfather, Methuselah, the oldest man who ever lived. He assured Ben a thousand years can pass quickly.

He longed to talk more with Noah, Moses, and Joshua, but that would have to wait. Then there were Seth and Abel, and their parents, Adam and Eve, the first two people Yahweh created. This was only the beginning! He marveled at these moments, but knew many more lay ahead. For now, his people needed to claim their Promised Land.

**

The Smyrnians took off to explore the restored land of Israel. Their ability to travel astounded them. Within minutes, they stood by the Dead Sea, formerly called the Salt Sea, the lowest place on Planet Earth. Its dark blue water captivated them, as it had millions of tourists through the years. But now the rushing current from Jerusalem tumbled into the sea at its northern end, bringing fresh water into liquid so saline it had long failed to sustain life. The sea sprang alive as living water penetrated its surface, plunged to its depths, and passed to the southern shore.

Fish jumped playfully from the water, and plant life emerged near the shore. On their right, where tall, never-ending sandstone mountains once stood, lay fields of lush, green grass. Streams flowed through the Negev, bringing the barren desert alive. Beautiful flowers blossomed and groves of date palm trees produced their sweet fruit. An abundance of other flora and fauna flourished.

They sprinted through the former wasteland, splashing through shallow creeks, stopping to pick dates, laughing, and eating them as they ran. The temperature stayed a perfect 72 degrees. They moved without growing tired, neither knowing nor caring about the time. Finally, standing beside the Red Sea at the Gulf of Aqaba, they realized they should head back to Jerusalem. Jesus said he and the Host had work to do. Curiosity set in wondering what he meant by that.

They took the same route back, this time stopping for a Dead Sea swim, realizing the name should change, since its waters now teemed with life. The group discussed names like Living Sea and Sea of Life, but decided they should leave those decisions to Jesus. Soon reaching their destination, they suddenly stopped near Mount Zion, staring toward the city, mouths wide open.

***

Ben's comfort level grew with each passing day. It had been weeks since he last saw his Smyrnian friends, but he hardly noticed because he stayed focused on current events in Jerusalem. Today he stood with his family, friends, and two Old Testament heroes checking out Jesus' handiwork.

"It's perfect. Exactly as I designed it."

"Exactly as I built it, father."

"Yes, but I provided materials and financed the project. However, I admit you led our people far better than I thought you could, and yes, even better than me. I didn't have the faith in you I should have had, and I ask you to forgive me. You were a great leader, son, and I'm proud of you."

"I feel honored standing with both of you," Ben said.

"You were a strong leader too, Benjamin. You led our people to accept their Messiah, no easy task. I see someone motioning for us to come, so our conversation is over, for now."

"David and Solomon, bring your new friends and come. We are ready for my announcement!"

Benjamin Abramson proudly accompanied Israel's two greatest kings as they ascended the Temple Mount, accompanied by his family, along with Alexander, Elizabeth, Mordecai, and others from the kibbutz. The magnificent new temple stood triumphantly atop the Mount, a symbol of Jesus' victory over the dragon and his forces. It would also serve an even greater purpose during the Millennium. Jesus stood atop the steps, where Messai, the false messiah often placed himself during the seven-year Tribulation. Two men walked out to join him.

***

The Smyrnians now realized what work Jesus spoke about. The rebuilt temple glistened like no other. While David's pattern remained, something was different about this edifice. They raced up the Mount at Jesus' bidding to join their friends, sensing Yahweh's presence warming their entire bodies, intensifying with every step. But they did not slow down until they stood with the others.

Before Jesus spoke, they saw and recognized the two men immediately. *Moshe and Eliyahu!* Amid all the excitement, they had completely forgotten about them. Of course they would join Jesus for this moment. Moses constructed the Tabernacle according to the plan Yahweh showed him on Mount Sinai. Both men fought Messai multiple times from this exact spot. Now they stood victoriously with their Lord. They raised their hands, calling for quiet as Jesus prepared to speak.

"My friends and followers, Yahweh's children, today we dedicate this temple and initiate its purpose for these thousand years."

Applause rang out from miles away. Each person heard Jesus as though they stood atop the Mount with the others gathered there. His voice sounded commanding and strong, yet loving and kind. But he stopped now and stood facing east, clearly expecting something to happen. Silence covered the land as everyone turned their attention eastward.

Something appeared on the eastern horizon. Silence turned to deafening noise more powerful than thundering rapids, overwhelming every other sound. The moment would have frightened them, but Jesus' calm presence filled them with hope and expectation. Brilliant light emerged, joining the noise, speeding toward the temple, illuminating the landscape with its radiance. It raced through the Eastern Gate, across the courtyard, over Jesus' head, and entered the temple, sending glorious rays beaming through it walls. The sound and light ceased.

"Yahweh's glory has returned to his temple!" Jesus said in a thundering voice. "His glory departed when Messai defiled the former house, but he now dwells among us again!"

The crowd fell to their knees in worship. Moshe and Eliyahu prayed with mighty voices, then rose and led the throng in shouts of praise. Finally, they called for silence so Jesus could speak again.

"Today is the Jewish Feast of Tabernacles. This will remain an important day every year until the Millennium ends. My father's seven appointed annual feasts looked ahead to *appointed times* on his calendar. This feast looked forward to this time and these one thousand years."

"It also commemorated my father guiding and protecting his people during their wilderness wanderings as they journeyed to the promised land. He has brought you to this day of my promised reign with you. But beyond that, the feast points to eternity when my father will tabernacle, or dwell with you forever! Every year we will assemble here in Jerusalem and celebrate the festival together. This will serve as an annual reminder that the ultimate promised land lies ahead!"

"Each annual celebration will last seven days, but you may stay however long you wish. You won't need to build booths because everything before was fulfilled in me. If you who are Israelites by birth choose to do so, you may. But on this day, we will unite as one worshiping the father. Do not worry about forgetting. I will remind you when the time comes, and every year will be glorious!"

"This temple also plays an important role during these years. No priests will offer sacrifices because I offered one sacrifice for all time and for everyone when I died on the cross. The blood of animals is no longer necessary to forgive sin. The temple is essential because it represents my father's presence on earth until this millennial kingdom ends. His glory fills his house. But this is not the only place where you will encounter his splendor. His glory will cover the entire earth as water covers the seas, and you will walk in his glory!"

"Now the time has come to send you out. If you choose to live within the borders of Israel, join the descendants of Jacob here. But you may live wherever you desire, or move from place to place. The world is yours to see and explore. Enjoy it! My father planned this for you. Those of you who lived through the Tribulation and still have physical bodies may have children and raise families. Those who already lived with me in heaven will celebrate with you. You are my beloved, and I anticipated this time with you before eternity begins. Now go, take pleasure in all the good things I prepared for you!" When he finished, the rush was on as people left to do exactly what he said.

***

Had it not been for the perfect millennial world, it would have been a sad day when the Smyrnians parted. But sad days ended with the Tribulation. They would see each other often, but planned to live all over the earth. Some would not put down roots, but would accept Jesus' offer to travel and see the world. They announced their intentions before each departed.

Blake, Beth, Anders, and Angie would return to New York City, while John, Kathie, and Doc, along with her family, would head to Chicago. They all realized the cities surely no longer existed but were eager to learn how those places looked on the renewed earth. Bruno,

Mila, their sons, and Ally would go back to Germany with Hans and Heidi. Evan opted to go with them instead of his family, as did Magnus. He would not leave the fighting partner who had battled Messai with him.

Ollie and Amelia chose London, but had many other plans in mind. They could only imagine how beautiful it must be now minus the buildings and noise. Trey and Rickie opted for back home in Missouri. So did Beth's parents. The soldiers would return to their homes. Johnathan and all of John's family decided they would return to the Rocky Mountains, which Jesus assured them still stood.

Ben and all Jewish believers would live in their homeland, with its extended borders. Omar, Ahmad, and Hala joined them. Michael, Gabriel, and Hadassah promised to visit often. They would all meet each year in Jerusalem, but committed to seeing one another more often than that.

The original Smyrnians decided before traveling to separate destinations, they would make one more stop: a farm in Missouri where they once buried three underground bunkers and made them their home. Bad memories no longer haunted them. Jesus told them to celebrate good memories in special places. None understood how travel worked. Going from one place to another happened almost instantaneously, if they wanted it to. Or they could travel more slowly. Michael told them it would be *cool*. After a few more special moments with Jesus, they headed to Missouri.

***

Ben and Miriam would have loved to visit the farm again, but their true homeland awaited them. It was far more than the tiny 8,500 square mile-country they previously called home. They now possessed 356,000 square miles, which Yahweh returned as he promised Abraham. They planned to enjoy it all, while visiting Jerusalem often. His people had awaited this day for four thousand years!

So began the fascinating adventure called the Millennium, one thousand years of Jesus reigning on earth with his followers. The 144,000 and others were thrilled to have Old Testament characters taking them to places they had never visited, plus others they knew well. Each tour included fifty people. It would take 300 years for every group to get through all areas of Old and New Testament history. There was no rush. Guides took ample time at each site, detailing their own experiences and describing the miracles Yahweh performed while they were there. Each location was amazing!

The tours started at the beginning and ended with the Bible's final book. Adam and Eve took groups to where it all began, modern-day Iraq, part of Mesopotamia, where Yahweh planted the Garden of Eden and placed Adam after creating him. The renewed earth still did not contain the garden. That would come later. But the location resembled it now, with green vegetation and flowing springs covering an area which was nothing but desert only a few weeks earlier.

Adam and Eve walked them through, pointing out specific areas. They showed them where the river flowed from the garden, then separated into four other rivers. While two no longer remained, the Tigris and Euphrates flowed beautifully again as they did when Adam and Eve tended the garden. The latter formed the eastern border of their new Israel. Each group felt the garden's presence and perfection and longed for its eternal return, which Adam promised would come.

Hadassah met them there and added a visit to her ancient home in Iran, the city of Susa. Her tour and description of events captivated them every time. She took them to the location of her childhood home where she told about losing her parents and being adopted by her cousin, Mordecai. Then came a vivid depiction of officers taking her from Mordecai's home to the king's harem at his palace. They knew her story well, so their excitement built until she finally told how Yahweh used her to bring a glorious victory, preventing Haman from destroying their ancestors.

Abraham took over in Iraq and told about his family moving from there to Haran where Yahweh called him to leave for a place he would not reveal until he arrived. Even knowing the events well, hearing him tell the story gave them chills every time, reminding them of their journey to faith in Jesus. Then Abraham led them up the fertile crescent between the Tigris and Euphrates to spend time in his former home.

Before leaving Haran, Noah took them farther north to Mount Ararat where the ark came to rest. He shared the story of God's call, building the ark, warning people about the flood, and his family's 370 days afloat. Then Abraham led them south through Syria to Jerusalem where they enjoyed Jesus' presence before continuing. That was always a welcome break from touring.

Isaac joined them in Jerusalem and traveled with them to Shechem, where Yahweh appeared to Abraham, telling him he would give this land to his descendants. Isaac and Abraham left them at Bethel, handing leadership off to Jacob. He and his sons took them into the land of Goshen in Egypt and walked them through the wonder of their new lives under Joseph's leadership. Joseph's story presented a powerful example of forgiveness, a touching moment with his brothers.

From there, Moses described the horror of slavery under Pharoah and what his life was like prior to God's call at the burning bush. The vivid details of their flight from the country captivated every group. Before leaving Egypt, they observed Passover with the new understanding of Jesus' sacrifice for forgiveness of sin. It was a highlight for every group. Moses then led them through each location of the forty years in the desert en route to the promised land. His depictions were intensely personal, especially at Mount Nebo where Yahweh showed him the land before his death.

Joshua led them from there to the Jordan River where they crossed over to Jericho. Caleb joined him as they shared their experiences of dividing and conquering the land. Tours continued with the judges of Israel, ending with Samuel, whose powerful retelling of events drew them in and made them feel part of the story. David took charge after Samuel. From his victory over the Philistine giant, Goliath, to becoming king of Israel, he mesmerized every group. He allowed them to gather stones from the brook in the Valley of Elah. Solomon's explanation of events during his rule, the expansion of the nation to near the present borders, and building the temple was priceless.

Kings and prophets followed him. Elijah, Isaiah, Daniel, and Hezekiah emerged as favorites, but each was necessary to hear the full story. Powerful women in Israel's history were also popular. Sarah, Rebekah, and Rachel filled in gaps left by their husbands. Listeners loved Rahab's story of hiding the spies and becoming part of Yahweh's people. Deborah and Jael, Naomi and Ruth, Hannah, and many others shared their experiences. They even heard from select people who stayed faithful to Yahweh during the so-called *silent years* between the Old and New Testaments.

They had walked step-by-step through four thousand years of history from creation to Jesus' birth. But for these Jewish followers of Jesus, both current and past, the story got exciting at this point. The truth of their real Messiah hit home as they heard from New Testament saints, beginning with Zechariah and Elizabeth, parents of John the Baptist, and Joseph and Mary, Jesus' earthly parents.

They leaned on every word from John the Baptist, the twelve disciples, Mary Magdalene and other women who followed Jesus. Lazarus' story of Jesus raising him from death nearly overwhelmed them. Mary and Martha added personal details to make it even more amazing. The description of Jesus' crucifixion was hard, but things got exciting when his followers told about his resurrection!

Meetings continued with Paul, Barnabas, Timothy, Titus, Phoebe, Priscilla and Aquila, and many more sold out followers of Jesus. They had missed so much. The ending left them speechless. John took them to Patmos and described how Jesus led him to write The Revelation. Every detail hit home with the 144,000 who survived the Tribulation because they lived them and now understood.

Their tour ended back in Jerusalem celebrating the Feast of Tabernacles, as they did every year, regardless where they were on their journey. They discovered Methuselah was right. A thousand years *can* pass quickly and be filled with unspeakable joy. Young couples had many children who grew up and had children of their own. Their population increased exponentially and filled the land. Though many followed their parents' teaching, others followed their own paths instead. The earth was already preparing for the Millennium's conclusion.

***

Meanwhile, something exciting was taking place in New York City. The Smyrnians spent longer than intended enjoying their former home base in Missouri before relocating to their previous homes. Blake, Beth, Anders, and Angie arrived and settled in New York City. An unfulfilled desire led the first two to choose a path they never dreamed possible during Jesus' thousand-year reign.

"One thing Jesus said excited me, Beth!" Blake said. His enthusiasm was unmistakable.

She crinkled her brow, tapped her head, giggled, and said, "I know what you're talking about. Jesus said we can have children! Blake, you know that was my heart's desire! I want to have children and raise them to worship Jesus. Can we start a family soon? Please, Blake, can we?"

"Beth, I am more than ready for that. I didn't realize we would have this opportunity. I want a family, too, the family I missed out on after my parents died. I can hardly wait to see those little Blakes and Beths running around. This is even more wonderful than I dreamed!"

"Blake, do you really mean it?"

"I have never been more ready for anything. We talked about having a baby during the Tribulation but feared bringing a child into the world with Messai in power. Our kids would have constantly been in danger. But now that Jesus reigns, the world is a perfect place for raising a family!"

"I understand we won't age during the Millennium. That means we can have as many children as we want! Since I was a little girl, I dreamed of having a large family, but I was too wrapped up in my job to get married and have kids. Now that can happen with the man I love!"

"Don't get too carried away, Beth. A thousand years could yield a lot of babies!"

"You know what I mean, silly. But we need to start soon, then we'll figure out when to stop."

"After I believed in Jesus, I regretted not believing before the Rapture so I could have gone with Jesus when he took his people home. But now I realize he had plans for us during those seven years and these thousand years. He blessed me with you, and now we will show our love for each other by having children. We must commit to one thing before we do."

"I know, Blake. We have to do everything possible to teach them about Jesus and raise them to believe in him and live for him."

"I can't imagine our kids falling for the dragon's lies. We will teach them and take them to see Jesus often. They will learn to love and worship him. Beth, I love you so much, and I love our kids even though they haven't yet been born!"

Their decision made, they embarked on a journey which would help fulfill one part of Yahweh's plan for Jesus' thousand-year reign on earth. Many others would do the same, paving the way for the dragon's release when the Millennium ended. But nothing could deter the elation experienced by Blake and Beth Thompson. *Their* time had come.

CHAPTER 19

Evan and Ally enjoyed the winter in Germany. She took him sightseeing throughout the country, introducing him to people and places he had never seen. They hit the slopes at some great ski resorts. Ally knew where to find all the equipment they needed. Jesus told them some mountains remained, and they would understand why later. Now they realized what he meant: *SNOW!*

Hans and Heidi also showed him around, allowing him to meet some Tribulation heroes who spread the gospel in Germany. Then he and Ally traveled to surrounding European countries. In Belgium, they visited the site where Messai's mansion stood before the earthquake. No evidence remained that the majestic structure ever existed. A manicured lawn adorned with beautiful flowers now covered the lot. Beyond it, a wooded grove still stood. Evan led Ally into the trees.

"This is where we hid before the earthquake hit. We hoped for any kind of opening which would allow us to rescue Beth. When the quake struck, we watched the mansion shaking and crumbling. Blake screamed Beth's name and started to charge in, but before he went, a bright light illuminated a path leading from the mansion to here. Beth sprinted out the door, raced across the path straight to us, and leaped into his arms. It was amazing! There was no doubt Jesus did it!"

"Beth told us the story after you returned, but standing here makes it come alive! Jesus showed me Beth was free, and how it happened. Now I can see her running through the door and across that pathway. I feel like I was here!"

"You should understand because you lived through something a lot like that in Jerusalem. Jesus allowing us to remember his miracles from the last seven years is pretty cool, don't you think?"

"Evan, it's so good to have you back saying things like *pretty cool.* I missed you so much. If it hadn't been for Anders, I would have gone crazy."

They continued their travels and fun, he with his glorified body, and she living in her earthly physical body. No one could have understood that possibility before the Millennium began. Now it came naturally, like learning to drive. Both looked and acted exactly like themselves, with no differences. They picked up where they left off before Evan was killed, two friends with a thousand years to navigate the world before eternity began.

Other Smyrnians did the same, while some stayed put and enjoyed peaceful lives, which felt good after the Tribulation's chaos. Travel never ceased to amaze them. No automobiles or modes of mass transit existed, but none were needed. People moved about at their own pace. One could take a leisurely stroll that lasted hours or travel thousands of miles within minutes. Evan especially enjoyed that. He would grab Ally's hand and say, *let's go to...*, state a specific destination, and they found themselves there. Most other people enjoyed it too once they figured out how it worked.

***

In London, Ollie and Amelia had the same conversation Blake and Beth had in New York. They were equally excited about raising a family. Neither dreamed it could happen now after history ended, but Jesus not only approved it, he seemed to recommend it. Ollie and Amelia gladly accepted his endorsement and wasted no time. Blake and Beth followed suit. Only days apart, Joshua Oliver Barton and Caleb Blake Thompson entered the world.

Neither realized what name the others had chosen, but they named their sons after the two men who led the Israelites into the

Promised Land. Both couples were here because of their faith in Jesus and wanted their children to have that same faith. So the next step was a trip to Jerusalem to present their sons to him. Blake and Beth arrived first. Jesus was expecting them.

"Blake and Beth! You brought someone I am eager to meet! May I call him Caleb?"

How did Jesus do it? He always knew everything about them. They gladly responded *yes* and ascended the steps to his throne.

"Lord, we present our little boy to you. We can never thank you enough for allowing us to have children during the Millennium. It fulfilled a longing in both our hearts."

"I knew that," Jesus said, the same twinkle in his eyes. "The earth must be repopulated with enough people to equal those who did not survive the judgment. It excites me when couples like yourselves who married during the Tribulation take advantage of the opportunity to have children, something most refused to do after learning it only lasted seven years."

"Lord, we..."

"Yes, I am the Lord reigning on earth, but I am also your savior and friend. Please call me Jesus from now on."

"But, Lord..."

Jesus rolled his eyes, so Blake gave up and started again.

"Okay, *Jesus*, we would never have brought a child into the world during Messai's reign. He wanted to kill us. When we talked about having a baby, we always considered what Messai would do if he captured us and our child."

"You chose wisely. However, I give you one word of caution. Teach your children well, because when *he* is released from the abyss, his deceptive power will be stronger than ever. He will have a short time but will make the most of it. His favorite target will be descendants of people who serve me. Please hand little Caleb to me."

Beth stepped forward and placed her baby in Jesus' arms. He held Caleb, looking down and smiling at him, then prayed to his father.

"Father, I thank you for our servants, Blake and Beth Thompson. They believed in me after we brought our people home, and served me, risking their lives every day for seven years. Now they have entered the thousand years with me, and I hold their offspring in my arms. Give this child the faith of his namesake who entered the Promised Land and claimed his inheritance because he trusted you. I anticipate the day this Caleb will do the same!"

He handed the baby back to Beth, then placed both hands on his head and blessed him. Blake and Beth stood weeping as they witnessed the special moment. Jesus smiled and pointed behind them. They turned around, and Beth shouted with glee seeing her friend and his wife.

"Ollie and Amelia! You too?"

"This is Joshua. He looks just like me, don't you think?"

"No, Ollie, he looks exactly like his mother!"

"Don't patronize him, Blake. Anyone can see Joshua is his dad made over, and I like it that way!"

"Joshua and Caleb, the two who had faith to lead Israel into the Promised Land. We chose those names without even discussing it," Beth said.

"I may have had something to do with that. You gave him my Hebrew name, Yeshua. And his partner, Caleb, is here too. Lay Joshua in my arms."

Ollie handed his mini-me to Jesus who also prayed for him and blessed him, then gave him back. The two couples enjoyed their reunion, and Jesus danced around celebrating with them. They liked this fun Jesus. Amelia asked, "You aren't stopping, are you?" To which Beth replied, "No way!"

They agreed to talk more and celebrate every birth. There would be many. Both stayed in Jerusalem for weeks, talking about the future until Blake and Ollie visited Jesus with a request.

"The four of us assumed living in our former homes would be like it was before. But after spending several weeks back here with you, we all realize Israel is our real home and where we want to live and raise our families. Will you allow us to do that?"

"Absolutely! I welcome your presence in the Promised Land for the entire Millennium! I told you that decision belongs to you. You may all live here or any other place you choose."

Ollie said, "We need to visit the other Smyrnians first and ask if they'll move here with us. It only seems right that we stay together now and enjoy living in a community with each other during good times after going through seven years of bad times together."

"Go ask them, and assure them I would love for them to come! Team Smyrnians were my warriors for seven years, and nothing would make me happier than them living here with me now. You need to choose a place where you can create your own community. You have lots of options!" Jesus pointed in every direction.

"I may have just the place in mind, but we need to discuss it with the others," Blake said.

Ollie nodded, certain they were considering the same location. Their discussion walking back to Beth and Amelia confirmed that. The next day they left, traveling to visit their teammates, asking each to join them, creating a Smyrnian community in a place they all loved. Their first priority was finding Ben Abramson, then on to New York City to speak with Anders and Angie Norstrom.

***

Ben and Miriam, Alexander and Elizabeth, Mordecai, and several members of the kibbutz rested and talked about their day touring Haran. Special guests, Michael, Hadassah, and Gabriel, joined them. Those three popped in unannounced at places along the tours and surprised them. Today more special guests showed up. Moshe and Eliyahu came, something the group always enjoyed, and stories flowed as they sat around a campfire on a cool, but perfect evening.

Neither Blake nor Ollie understood how they found the group so easily, but now adjusted to this perfect world, nothing surprised them anymore. They walked into the middle of their conversation.

"Look who's here!" said Michael.

He jumped to his feet, ever the playful one, and once again one of them, even though he was still the mighty warrior angel of heaven.

"Wait till you see who we brought with us!" Ollie said.

Beth and Amelia walked in carrying Caleb and Joshua, wide smiles covering their faces. Miriam jumped up and ran to them. Tears of joy streamed down her face as she ran.

"You both have babies!"

"I present to you Caleb Blake Thompson, and..."

Beth nodded at Amelia who said, "Joshua Oliver Barton."

"Caleb and Joshua! Perfect Biblical names for two sons born during the Millennium!" said Ben.

"Let me hold them both," said Miriam.

She took a baby in each arm and began singing lullabies and whispering Bible verses over them. They passed them around until everyone there had held them, or at least seen them. All four parents stood in awe when two mighty angels held Caleb and Joshua in their arms. Such a wondrous thing could only happen during these thousand years.

"Israel is our homeland too, Ben, so we four have decided we want to live here with all of you. We're on our way to invite every Smyrnian to join us. What do you think?"

"You're right, Blake! This place has been like a magnet pulling our team here since we came together. It is time for us to fulfill that calling. I hope every Smyrnian and their family will come and live in Yahweh's land. Have you considered where you might live?"

Blake and Ollie pulled Ben aside and whispered with him for a few minutes. The others could tell from his nodding and smiling he agreed with their plan, and was excited about it, but they returned and told none of them what was said. Instead, Blake asked another question, and Ben answered.

"By the way, what are you doing in Turkey? If I heard right, this is outside the borders."

"We're touring the Bible's history from beginning to end. This is Haran where Abraham heard Yahweh's call to leave for the Promised Land. A different guide leads us through each location and takes time to explain what happened there. Then we travel to our next stop, learning as we go. It will take three hundred years to get all 144,000 of us through, but Blake, this is the most amazing thing I've ever done."

"Who are the tour guides? They must be pretty incredible to handle all that."

"You may not believe us if we tell you, Ollie, but I am one!" said Hadassah.

"Let me guess, Iran, where ancient Persia and its capital city, Susa, were located," Beth said.

Hadassah smiled and nodded, affirming she was right. Their experiences piqued Blake's interest.

"Can we take the tours, or are they only for the 144,000?" he asked.

"Of course you can! But you will have to wait your turn until they have all finished. Like Ben said, that should take about three hundred years," said Michael.

Ben brought things back to the present. "What if I introduce our guide for this leg of the journey?"

Abraham appeared around the corner and sat down with them as the four Smyrnians looked at him, clearly shocked and surprised. They were even more stunned when he asked another to join them, calling for Noah. Blake and Ollie were speechless, something their wives had never seen. Abraham got down to business. He understood their desire and wanted to make sure it happened.

"I heard you say you want to join one of our tours. The schedule is packed, and we have to get all 144,000 of Yahweh's chosen people through. That means the first opening is three hundred years away. I also heard you mention bringing the other Smyrnians to live with us in Israel."

Abraham recognized them! All four wept, and the two men started to kneel at his feet.

"Don't even think about it! We are all men and women who surrendered our lives to serve Yahweh and his son, Jesus. None is better or greater than any other. You may have faced more danger during the last seven years than we did in our entire lifetimes," Abraham said.

"But both of you left so much and lived with so much faith," Ollie said.

"So did you. Blake, Beth, and Ollie, you were big time reporters, but you walked away from your careers to follow Jesus. Amelia, you left your prominent position as a member of Parliament to do the same. What? You didn't think we knew about such things or how to speak your language? The Smyrnians are heroes in heaven! We should bow down to you," Noah said.

"He's right. We celebrated your work every time someone believed and welcomed home those killed by Messai. Now we are all together, and that will never change. Let's make the most of these years, then we will discover what Jesus has planned for us after this," said Abraham.

"We'll bring the others and be ready for the first available tour. Three hundred years gives us time to watch our families grow. Call ours *The Smyrnians* tour!" Blake said.

Three hundred years seemed like forever before, but in the Millennium, years, decades, and centuries passed quickly. Blake and Beth, and Ollie and Amelia would leave to gather their friends and teammates, then come back to live where they belonged: the Promised Land.

***

"Gabriel, it sounds like you have work to do. You need to get there before they do!"

"On my way, Michael!"

"Michael, where is he going, and what is he doing?" asked Hadassah.

"How am I supposed to know?"

He grinned at his answer, and she punched his arm, folded hers, and awaited his answer. Only she could get by with punching an archangel.

"Okay, okay. He's headed to make sure none of our friends turn down the opportunity to move here and join us. Gabriel can be convincing."

"I can't wait to give them all a big hug!"

Gabriel reached Germany first. He easily swayed Bruno and Mila, but where were Evan and Ally? *Those two are out running around*, he thought. *They will come without convincing, if we can find them.* Magnus would not allow the other big man to go without him. The next stop? Chicago, on his way to New York. John, Kathie, and Doc were already packing when he left.

Interestingly, Angie and Anders were the hardest to persuade. Brooklyn was no longer the busy city with crazy drivers, honking horns, slums, and crumbling buildings. Now all of New York City and its boroughs looked more like Central Park. Anders felt like he was making up for seven lost years with his family back in their former home. Gabriel got through to her before him.

"Anders, I haven't been to Israel, other than our time after Jesus returned. You got to live there. I want to go travel the country and see what it looks like now."

"But baby, I enjoy living here with you and the kids. It helps me remember our good times together before the Rapture."

"Anders, we will live together for eternity! But before then, we have a thousand years, and I want to spend them in Israel. Please, honey, can we at least go for a while?"

"I told you *no* too many times during our lives, especially when you begged me to attend church with you and the kids. I refuse to make that mistake again. If you want to see Israel, we'll go, and I'll show you the entire country from north to south and east to west."

Gabriel left, another task successfully completed. Two more stops in Missouri would fulfill his mission. Trey and Rickie should decide without hesitation, but he wasn't so sure about Steve and Linda. Michael whispered that he must not leave them out. All four were locked in by the time he flew back to Israel. He would leave the Baldwins and Sandersons to John, Kathie, and Doc. They were not original Smyrnians, but their parents may still want them living in Israel.

Blake and Beth, and Ollie and Amelia found every member of their team already packed and ready for their move to Israel to join the Smyrnian community. Millennial travel would help them arrive quickly. The Thompsons and Bartons would lead the way and guide them to Haran where they could spend time with Ben and Miriam and share the good news about their decision. Upon arrival, they would discuss location options for their new home.

First, they introduced them to the two newest Smyrnians: Joshua Oliver Barton and Caleb Blake Thompson. A celebration ensued which would have turned into a full-blown party had they not been eager for Israel. They could get acquainted with their youngest members there. They still did not understand couples having babies during the Millennium, but those answers could come later.

"We start in Haran," said Blake as they prepared to leave.

That made no sense to John. "I thought our destination was Israel. I understand enough about geography to know Haran was in Turkey and is now just some ancient ruins."

"We're going to Haran because Ben and Miriam are there, plus some other people you definitely want to meet. Trust me, they'll give you all the information you need before we leave there. It's actually an important biblical site. You'll find out when we arrive."

"Okay, I'm with this group, wherever that takes us, because I want us to all be together forever! Lead the way. I'm ready to go!"

"Does anyone know where Evan and Ally are? I hate to leave them," said Beth.

"You can never tell with those two. They run around all over the place and only come home for a little while, then are gone again. We'll send out search parties after we get there," Bruno said.

Soon they were on their way to Haran, a group of Jesus followers with a new place to call home: Israel, Yahweh's Promised Land. They would all be together again, but not in buried bunkers hiding from a brutal enemy. This time they would live in a place where peace and perfection ruled.

***

Evan and Ally sat laughing and talking with Ben and the group at Haran. He introduced her to Abraham and Noah, whom he had already met and spent time with in heaven. They learned about the tours and watched for their friends, who would come soon. *Some little birds told us*, Evan told the others, glancing at Michael and Hadassah.

"We wondered where you two and Gabriel went. I looked at Ben and said, 'they did it to us again.' But I have no reason to worry about my niece when she takes off with Michael now."

"You never needed to worry about her when she was with me, Mordecai. I couldn't convince you then, so I'll show you now."

He stood and morphed into the warrior archangel, then became a man again. The others laughed because now they realized who he was. A large group arrived and interrupted their fun.

"Evan? Ally? How did you get here? We couldn't find you to tell you we were coming."

"How we got here and why doesn't matter, Blake. All that matters is I beat you again!"

"I knew you were out enjoying yourselves, but I missed you, and I'm glad to see you."

Mila hugged her daughter, then gave Evan a big squeeze, too. Abraham and Noah surprised them when they walked up and introduced themselves. Ben explained the tours, revealing why they were in Haran answering John's question and satisfying his curiosity. Then Blake told them about their upcoming tour, still three hundred years away. Everyone assumed that was the most exciting news until Beth and Amelia walked in carrying their babies. Ally squealed and ran toward them.

"You have babies? This is the most exciting thing that's happened since the Millennium started!"

"Yes we do, and we're not finished!"

They played with Caleb and Joshua until Blake got serious about their important decision. He saved the announcement for that moment and hoped they all agreed.

"Drum roll, please. Ollie and I think we should take over the dragon's lair!"

"Banias! I bet we got a glimpse of how it looks *now* when we left that day!" said Anders.

"Remember how scared I was when we went there? Well, I'm not afraid anymore because Michael bound the dragon, and things have changed. So, I'm ready for Banias!" Ollie said.

"But we aren't talking about living there, because we have a better suggestion," said Blake.

"How can anything be better than Banias where Mount Hermon's melting snows send the Jordan River's headwaters flowing right through the middle of the place? The natural beauty is amazing!"

"Very poetic, Ally, but have you seen Tel Dan?"

"I remember driving past that on our way to Banias, but we didn't stop there."

"If you thought Banias was beautiful, wait till you see Tel Dan!"

Ollie and Blake continued, telling about Tel Dan's ruins and the construction potential, and how Mount Hermon still stands and those same Jordan River headwaters pick up steam and cascade through the tel. And it was only three and a half miles from Banias, so they could visit anytime they wanted. Everyone agreed, leaving only one decision remaining. Blake started that discussion.

"Before we go, we should choose another name for our new home. Any suggestions?"

"Do you remember which verse *Smyrnians* came from?" Evan asked.

"Revelation 2:10. I will never forget that verse. It says, *Do not be afraid of what you are about to suffer. I tell you, the devil will put some of you in prison to test you, and you will suffer persecution for ten days. Be faithful, even to the point of death, and I will give you the crown of life.*"

"That's right, Ally. We had faith in Jesus and weren't afraid of Messai during the Tribulation. He put some believers in prison, persecuted us all, and many even died. But they were faithful till their last breath. Now we have all received the crown of life and are reigning with Jesus. I say we name our new home *Smyrna* to remind us from where Jesus brought us to where we are today. But instead of Turkey, our Smyrna will be in the Promised Land of Israel."

"Evan is right. Don't give up the name you chose when you started. *Smyrna*, home of the *Smyrnians*. It's perfect. When you get there, you'll understand," said Abraham.

They stayed in Haran one more day until Ben's group left to continue their tour. The Smyrnians left for their new home, excited about what lay ahead for them.

***

The Millennium moved along, and the group flourished. Smyrna became a vibrant community as the Smyrnians took pleasure in

Yahweh's beautiful creation and built homes from the abundant stone and stately cedars of Lebanon. Fertile northern soil yielded plentiful grain and vegetables. Grape vines, combined with fruit, olive, and nut trees dotted the landscape. No animals died, as creatures and people were at peace with each other. Food came from the land.

Blake and Beth loved watching Caleb grow through the years. His favorite pastime as a young boy was riding lions which roamed the forests around Smyrna. He whooped and laughed, clinging to their manes as they ran like the wind. Bears became his wrestling partners. They rolled and frolicked, neither ever winning, both simply having fun. He chased wolves through the trees. They often followed him home waiting outside for him to reemerge and pursue them again.

Once Blake found their son playing with a poisonous viper, and Beth screamed, then laughed, remembering snakes were harmless during the Millennium. Caleb could not resist any wildlife. Everything that walked, crawled, or flew seemed drawn to him, and he to them. His parents could only shake their heads at his playful nature and thank Jesus for their safe and peaceful environment.

Caleb's love for animals created his productive activity during these thousand years. Along with fruits and vegetables, milk, butter, and cheese were also staples of the Millennium diet. He loved milking goats and cows, churning butter, and making cheese. He considered none of that work because he enjoyed anything involving the creatures Yahweh created to provide for human beings.

Joshua's interests differed from Caleb's, but the two remained close friends. Joshua was less playful and more serious. His quiet nature made him one who needed time alone. Caleb often found him leaning against a tree reflecting on life or quietly talking to Jesus. He sometimes charged him from surrounding trees riding a lion and scared him so badly he scurried up the tree. He did not always understand his playful friend.

Joshua worked the fields and groves that provided fruits and vegetables and grains for bread. He often joked calling himself and Caleb bread and butter. As they grew older, both became powerful leaders. Their parents taught them about the dragon's release when the thousand years ended, and they united, ensuring their peers stayed focused on Jesus.

Beth and Amelia each gave birth to six more children, giving both seven sons and daughters, symbolizing perfection. Watching them grow and play with children of other Tribulation survivors gave them great joy. The Smyrnians increased exponentially as many among their number married and had large families.

Grandchildren and great-grandchildren married and had children. Smyrna expanded from Tel Dan to Banias and beyond, a shining beacon of hope glowing with Yahweh's glory. Visitors came from everywhere to meet their Tribulation heroes. Some called the city Jerusalem of the north. The name was appropriate because Jesus' presence dwelled there uniquely to all other places on earth.

When three hundred years passed, the time came for their biblical history tour. The entire population of Smyrna took the tour, dividing into groups of fifty. Michael guided them to Iraq where Adam and Eve met them, and their tour began. The community did not reunite for a hundred years, only meeting in Jerusalem once a year to observe the Feast of Tabernacles. But the years flew by, and before they knew it, they all returned home after their most amazing experience ever.

Israel's population exploded as the same thing happened among the 144,000. It also occurred worldwide. But though the number of people increased dramatically, attendance at the Feast of Tabernacles in Jerusalem did not. Those who survived the Tribulation, and most first generation believers, never missed. But future generations grew less interested in their family's faith. They enjoyed the bliss of the restored world order, but chose their own way, instead of following Jesus.

Human nature remained for those with unglorified bodies. They retained their ability to choose their master and would soon become the dragon's unsuspecting targets as he made one last attempt to prevent Jesus' reign. Only two groups among their descendants avoided apostasy: families of Jewish believers living throughout Israel, and all Smyrnian offspring living in Smyrna and Banias.

***

Blake awoke to Beth shivering and shaking the bed. He rolled over and held her close, his body now shaking with hers, frigid temperature consuming him too. Panic briefly set in.

"Blake, what's wrong? I haven't felt this since... since *he*..."

Her words ended, her voice quivering so much Blake hardly understood what she said. But he knew who she meant by *he*: Aissa Messai. But Yahweh's angels threw him into the lake of fire, along with Caiaphas, so he couldn't be causing this. His wife's teeth chattered as he clung to her hoping his body heat would warm her. But his faded fast, and he realized he fought a losing battle.

He instinctively checked the time: midnight. Why did things always happen at midnight? The Rapture and Jesus' second coming both occurred at 12:00 a.m. Time never mattered during the Millennium, so he had not thought about the date for a while. It hit him. September 11, 3036!

"Beth! I know what's happening!"

"What is it? For a thousand years, we've had peace, and now this happens. What does it mean, Blake? Tell me," Beth pleaded, her body quivering, and her voice trembling.

"The date, Beth! Do you realize what day this is? September 11, 3036!"

She regained her composure, and the tremors lessened, though the freezing temperature continued, and goosebumps covered her body. It all came together in her mind, and she jumped out of bed.

"It's him, Blake. One thousand years ago the Millennium started, and the Bible said the dragon would be released from his prison when the thousand years ended! It ended today at midnight!"

They dashed from their house toward other homes. Yelling to awaken their fellow Smyrnians was unnecessary because they sprinted toward them, all experiencing the same symptoms. Smyrna turned into a chilling place where an evil presence attempted to trap them inside the city. They gathered quickly, leaders arriving first. Blake realized they must break free and get to Jerusalem.

"The Millennium has ended!" shouted Anders, his wife and children by his side. "Michael released the dragon, and the beast is already deceiving people all over the world! Do you realize how many Tribulation survivors' descendants have not followed Jesus like we did? Right now, he is convincing them to follow him and overthrow Jesus! What should we do?"

"Let's get everyone here and make sure no one gets left out. Where are Caleb and Joshua?"

"We're both here, dad," said Caleb, his friend and partner standing beside him.

"Mobilize your families to spread the word, telling everyone we're leaving Smyrna and going to Jerusalem. Tell them all to confirm their entire family is with them, then meet us here."

"Let us all bring our own families. We can do that much faster and be ready to leave sooner."

"You're right Trey. What was I thinking? Everybody go tell your clans, and anyone else you come across, then come back and let us know when they're all present. We need to get out of here fast, but we won't leave until we know everyone is accounted for."

Everybody dispersed and moved out immediately to gather the thousands of people who now made up the Smyrnians. The process required twelve hours. At noon the next day, they deserted everything and left for Jerusalem. Blake reminded them no one should look back because what lay ahead was even better than what they left behind in Smyrna. With no time to waste, they used Millennial travel and covered the 150-mile distance in one hour. The evil chill accompanied them all the way, but everything changed, and warmth returned, when they reached their destination.

CHAPTER 20

Around the world, people who followed Jesus sensed the chill and witnessed others acting strangely. The peaceful world turned violent as gangs gathered chanting, cursing, and calling for war against the world's unsuspecting capital city where peace reigned. Their voices clamored for the death and destruction of everyone living in Israel, yet no one realized what caused such anger.

The dragon now operated alone. His demons and the man who represented his presence on earth were cast into the lake of fire a thousand years earlier. He had spent that thousand years chained in an abyss suspended above the flaming, bubbling molten lava. The flames occasionally touched him, intended to remind him their torment was his future, but that would not happen now.

Michael made a crucial mistake releasing him. He had lain low for a thousand excruciating years and convinced the mighty archangel he intended no further harm or insurrection. Michael took the bait and fell into his trap. Now he would assemble an army even mightier than his previous fighting force, then attack and eliminate the one who claimed the throne and a kingship which did not belong to him. *I will still rule the universe*, he growled to himself.

He had entrusted his efforts to others before, and they failed him, even his powerful demon princes. *This time I will handle it myself.* The Great Red Dragon morphed into his true self, the beautiful fallen angel whose only goal was to overthrow the one who expelled him from heaven, and destroy his prize creation: human beings. He was Lucifer, Light Bearer, Day Star, Anointed Cherub, who became of necessity, Satan, the adversary who plotted and devised evil, and the devil who accused and slandered believers. Since his expulsion, hatred fueled the motivation to carry out his evil plan.

The last two names became real as he rapidly traversed the world sowing seeds of discord and planting lies in gullible minds. His falsehoods turned people against the one enthroned in Jerusalem and organized them into an evil army bent on destruction. His global journey completed, he led his troops marching toward Jerusalem. They came together, a military force with whom *Jesus* and his followers must reckon. The satanic mob surrounded Israel's borders and prepared to move in.

***

Jesus stood atop the temple mount beckoning the Smyrnians to come. His warmth and glory filled them, dispelling the chill. He pointed outward, moving his finger in a circular motion, drawing their attention to the innumerable, menacing throng approaching Jerusalem from all sides. The army spanned many miles in every direction. Defeat was surely inevitable.

Their leader came into view, his appearance so radically different from before it shocked them. Instead of the hideous red dragon, the glorious being they briefly glimpsed when the Millennium began appeared. They recalled how he morphed back into the beast that day when Michael chained him and threw him into the abyss. Today, his magnificent countenance did not change.

No one could miss his strikingly handsome features. The breeze blew his long dark hair, and his tall, toned body strode confidently toward his target, attracting his followers like a magnet. Blake battled his senses fighting to convince himself this was the enemy behind Aissa Messai's brutal regime. He snapped to reality, thankful to hear a familiar voice. *Ben!*

"Do you recognize him, Blake?"

"Yes, I do, even though he doesn't look like himself."

"Oh, but he does, Blake. You now see him for who he truly is: Satan, the devil, adversary, deceiver, Yahweh's former angel of light. This is his final attempt to overthrow Jesus and claim the throne."

"Why are we standing here? We have to fight! If we don't win this battle, all is lost!"

Blake turned to rally his Smyrnian forces, but Ben stepped in front and stopped him.

"No, this battle isn't ours; it belongs to Jesus. We must yield to him like we did before. This time not even Michael, Gabriel, or the Heavenly Host will fight beside him. The Prince of Darkness challenges the Light of the World. I have faith Jesus will defeat him and light will prevail."

Every fiber of Blake's being wanted to stand beside his Savior showing strength and determination to fight, as did Trey and Rickie, Bruno, Magnus, the troops, and every Smyrnian. Jesus motioned for them to stand down, as he stood tall, staring down the army's leader. The battle was imminent.

The powerful, yet angelic voice rang out loudly and clearly. *Attack!* The Smyrnian and Jewish believers found themselves surrounded with no escape as the enemy charged at Millennial speed. Their leader did not stop until he stood facing the King of kings. Raising his sword high above his head, he screamed for his forces to annihilate the defenseless crowd standing helplessly nearby as he destroyed the enthroned Lord.

Is this the way it ends? Blake thought to himself. Could Jesus be victorious before, only to be defeated now? He steeled himself for the attack, along with everyone else. Ben smiled confidently, leaving Blake longing for the same faith his friend exhibited. The army moved forward, and a thunderous crash shook the atmosphere. Heaven opened, and fire blazed down before they could come any closer. Within seconds, the inferno reduced them to ashes, then disappeared.

The glorious being standing before Jesus turned to flee, but Michael met him, confronting the traitorous former archangel face-to-face. Without a word, Michael seized him, and the ground opened, revealing the fiery lake below. Screams and wails emanated from its depths. Messai and Caiaphas still howled in pain as flames continually torched their bodies. Satan joined them when Michael hurled him into the everlasting fire, screams also escaping his mouth as the hellish blaze engulfed him. The ground closed, sealing his eternal doom and signaling Jesus' final victory.

***

All believers stood in shock, not knowing what they should do. Everything that just happened contradicted the peaceful thousand years they had enjoyed. None could imagine what would come next. Jesus gave them no time to consider that as he instantly lifted from the ground and ascended to heaven, taking them with him.

Tribulation survivors who lived through the Millennium with unglorified bodies sensed something the moment they arrived. It hit them like a lightning strike, sending an electrical current racing through their bodies. Each one experienced the transition. Their physical appearance remained the same, but they were instantly transformed from human beings into spiritual beings. Mortality became immortality, imperfection became perfection, and temporary became eternal. The Smyrnians gazed at each other, one look revealing the glorious truth.

"Now I understand what some of you tried to tell us. This feels amazing!"

Blake grabbed Beth and lifted her into his arms. They all hugged one another, laughing, and dancing.

"Don't worry, Blake, you'll get used to it," Evan said. Then he laughed at his friend.

Those who had been there before excitedly ran toward the throne room, but Gabriel instructed them to wait. The others only stared, amazed at what they now viewed for the first time. Gabriel told them they had time for a quick tour, *but don't take long*. He instructed the experienced ones to show *newbies* around, chuckling when he used that term.

Every tour began in the magnificent room where Yahweh's throne sat surrounded by twenty-four other thrones. Every Smyrnian bowed before the throne, even though Yahweh was not on it. Tribulation martyrs and raptured family members who had waited to show friends and family members what they had experienced were disappointed by his absence. The group returned, overcome with emotion following an incredible encounter. Jesus spoke and calmed their minds.

"The things you witnessed are indeed awe-inspiring, but my father and I have far greater things planned for you! What you are about to see clears the way for those things to come."

"What can be better than this?" Blake asked Beth in a soft whisper.

Jesus instructed them to look out over the expanse at the earth. Dots of light popped up everywhere below them, countless bodies rising toward heaven, moving past them into a large judgment hall with an elevated great white throne. They came and came. When the last entered, Michael closed the door. The Smyrnians knew that meant bad news for the people inside.

The Heavenly Host spread throughout the believers who realized something huge was about to happen. The entire Smyrnian clan stood interspersed with angels who would watch the marvelous event with them. Intrigue filled humans and angels alike as they anxiously awaited the coming event. They did not wait long. Jesus waved his hand, and the fireworks started.

Giant asteroids hurtled from space toward the earth, some hundreds of miles wide. They broke through earth's atmosphere traveling thirty to forty thousand miles per hour, each smashing into the uninhabited planet with fifty million megatons of force, creating two hundred billion trillion watts of energy per asteroid. Every continent fell victim to the massive falling fireballs. Brilliant flashes of light caused those watching to shield their eyes. The earth erupted into a colossal firestorm, burning everything worldwide and destroying the planet itself. Believers looked on horror-stricken from heaven as their former home went up in flames, then ceased to exist.

Before they regained their composure, the sun exploded, sending a gigantic fireball accelerating through space at warp speed. One-by-one, the moon, stars, and planets blew apart, galaxies imploded, and the sky collapsed like an enormous folding curtain. One final massive explosion rocked the great expanse. Its elements dissolved in blazing fury and gradually disappeared, leaving nothing in existence but heaven itself. Stunned believers silently witnessed the grand finale.

The judgment hall doors flung open, claiming their attention once again. People who had rejected Jesus during their lives on earth now faced his father to pay the price for their rejection. Michael, Gabriel, and other angelic beings opened books containing the deeds of each person. But the tomes highlighted their most crucial moments, every time they rejected Yahweh's offer to accept his son as their Savior and Lord. Their cries filled the judgment hall in unison.

"Please, Lord, give us one more opportunity. We believe! Jesus is Lord!"

Believers heard Yahweh's voice ring out from inside. "I sent my son to die for you. I gave you opportunities to believe in him and receive him as your Savior, but you rejected him. You heard the truth, but refused to believe it. Now you have waited too late. The day of salvation has passed!"

Michael handed another huge book to Yahweh who sat on the throne. The cover read, *Book of Life.*

"The names of every person who believed in my son's death and resurrection and surrendered their lives to him are written in this book. All whose names are not found will suffer eternal punishment in the lake of fire. I prepared it for the devil and his angels, but you will join them because you refused this precious gift: my son." Those outside strained to see Yahweh's face, but could not.

Weeping continued from people who knew he spoke about them. They realized their names were not written in the book, and continued pleading for one more chance, which they understood would not come. Yahweh pronounced their sentence, and his mighty Heavenly Host dragged them away and cast them into the fiery lake of burning sulfur where they joined Satan in blazing flames which would never end. They would not cease to exist, but would suffer forever, yet never die. Last, the abode of the dead, and finally death itself, were cast into the fire. The opening closed for the final time, and memories of them vanished forever. A new existence would now begin for true believers.

***

Yahweh walked from his heavenly throne room, shrouded in glory, still invisible to his people. They looked on, realizing this moment's importance to their future, and eager to know what would happen. While they watched, massive hands shot from the cloud, sending a steady stream of matter rushing below. Reaching its destination point, the matter began swirling rapidly, light flashing from inside the swirl. An orb began taking shape.

The matter spun wildly, then slowed to reveal a perfect globe within the swirl. When the spinning stopped, a brand new earth appeared. The planet looked spectacular from their vantage point. Those watching saw the same stunning view Hadassah witnessed earlier, with one major change which did not escape her attention.

"Michael, the earth is not the beautiful blue globe we once saw. Where did the oceans go?"

"Yahweh removed them from his new earth, Hadassah. They are no longer needed. The air we breathe and the oxygen we need come from Yahweh and Jesus. Oceans covered seventy percent of the earth's surface, leaving only thirty percent for habitation. Old

Testament saints who lived by faith in Yahweh, and New Testament Christians who believed in Jesus and lived for him, will populate the new earth. I'm sure you realize there are a *lot* of them! Notice the ocean's blue hue has been replaced by the light of his glory. See how the earth gleams?"

He was right! Her curiosity satisfied, the pair turned their attention back to Yahweh, still enshrouded in the glory cloud, and ready to act again. His large hands moved in rapid succession, matter flying from each with such speed, no one recognized it. Elements zoomed through space, finally becoming visible to gazing eyes. Countless celestial bodies settled into place in Yahweh's new universe. His eternal creation completed, Almighty God moved away, and yielded to Jesus.

"Do you approve of my father's handiwork?"

Excited applause and shouts of praise made it clear every believer did. The great throng longed to see Yahweh, but listened for what they would hear next. Jesus spoke, and they soon knew.

"Forty days after I rose from the grave, I came back here to fulfill my promise that I would prepare a place for you. My work has continued from then until now, and the time has come for you to see my masterpiece. But instead of viewing it from here, you will watch it come down from above!"

Not that long ago, all the believers ascended to heaven. Now they descended back to a newly created earth where they would live forever. A colossal sight appeared from above, causing them to stare in awe and wonder. This was new to everyone. Jesus built it with the angels help and spent two thousand years prior to his Millennial Reign getting it just right. Now the unveiling finally came. Everyone sensed the unparalleled excitement and anticipation of this moment.

Blake pulled Beth close and held her. Anders did the same with Angie, eager to learn what Jesus would reveal, which neither of them saw in heaven. Silence became an exciting buzz as billions of eyes looked heavenward. Brilliant light beamed from high above. A massive glistening object emerged and hovered overhead, then descended slowly, approaching the earth. They recognized buildings. Skyscrapers? No, enormous houses with rooms extending into infinity.

"It's a city!"

"No city can be that big, Anders," John said.

"Jesus built it, and Yahweh provided the material, so what do you expect?"

Their discussions quieted as they stood silently, awestruck, the city drawing closer. They suddenly realized all their fellow believers formed a massive circle around the city's earthly destination. The Smyrnians did not know where they were, but as the place came into full view, it became apparent they would stand right outside it. Their hearts raced, and their minds exploded with expectancy.

Each shielded their eyes as radiant glory flooded the earth. The city rested, giving them a close-up view, even though the entrance was elevated, and getting to it required a steep climb. Its high wall stretched upward far beyond their sight. Twelve prodigious foundations supported its enormous weight, each embossed with the name of an apostle of Jesus. The foundations were made of precious gemstones, with dazzling clarity, each a different color. Their brilliance overwhelmed the onlookers, including those who had already been in heaven and had never seen the city either.

Everyone recognized this place. It was Jerusalem, but a colossal *new* Jerusalem! With their eyes adjusted, viewing its splendor seemed normal, though still mind-blowing. Light gleaming from inside enticed them to enter through the gate directly above them. Were their eyes playing tricks on them? No, the gate was not only made of pearl; it was one gigantic pearl with *Judah* etched in bold letters. A mighty angel stood guard outside.

Since the foundations bore the names of Jesus' twelve apostles, and the name Judah identified this gate, they felt certain eleven more gates existed, each engraved with another tribe of Israel. They wanted to see them all, but with miles and miles of wall to their left and right, who knew how long that would take? They longed to race up the incline and sprint inside, but the gate remained closed. Jesus, ever omnipresent, appeared and spoke, visible to everyone surrounding the wall.

"Who wants to enter the city?" he asked.

A roar left no doubt about the multitudes desire. Then they grew silent awaiting his next words.

"I realize you are eager to go inside, but you will enjoy this city forever, so you have plenty of time. Michael will come and give you information which will prepare you for what you are about to experience. Then you may enter and check it out for yourselves!"

Another roar greeted Michael, the loudest cheers coming from his friends, the Smyrnians. He too miraculously appeared to everyone when he spoke.

"Welcome to eternity! This is New Jerusalem, the city *Jesus* built for you!"

His shout fired up the multitude even more, as did his next words. He shocked them when his booming voice drowned out their latest eruption. The entire throng instantly stopped celebrating and listened.

"I will answer your most pressing question first. The city's design is a perfect cube, and its dimensions are 1,500 miles long, 1,500 miles wide, *and* 1,500 miles high! The wall is 216 feet thick! You will understand that when you walk through the gates!"

1,500 miles long, wide, and high? They struggled to believe him, but soon started shouting again, eager to walk inside. Michael raised his hand and quieted them once more, then paused.

"He loves making us wait. Look at that mischievous grin covering his face," Ben said.

Michael glanced his way and smiled even wider. The mighty angel was such a kid at heart.

"You will find no temple where four former temples once stood. The temple symbolized Yahweh's presence among his people, but neither is needed now because he dwells with you! His presence will fill the earth, and never leave you, wherever you go. You will meet him soon!"

"Neither will you see the sun and moon because they serve no purpose in eternity. The glory of Yahweh and Jesus illuminate both the city and the earth. Their radiance shines far brighter than the sun, and not only supplies energy, which produces miraculous plant life, but also eliminates darkness! There will no longer be any reason to fear, so once the gates open, they will never close again! You will live in peace and security forever!"

With that enthusiastic declaration, Michael stepped aside, bowed before Jesus, and allowed his Lord to take things from there. The great multitude grew silent, yearning for his words, realizing they would soon enter the *true* eternal city.

"I told my followers something that resonated with believers for 2,000 years before I returned. *My father's house contains many dwelling places.* Behold my father's house! New Jerusalem contains space for any who choose to live inside, or for those who opt to spend time here as they come and go. This is the new earth's capital city. Many will visit; some will stay. The world has more than enough space for everyone to live anywhere you desire. You will never be overcrowded!"

"No impurity will ever enter this city. All of you, because you were cleansed by my blood, and your names are written in the Book of Life, may go in. So, if you are ready, follow me inside!"

The mass of humanity began climbing up toward the elevated city of God. Their voices erupted in glorious harmony singing a new praise song to Jesus as they ascended. No one had heard it before, but it flowed from the lips of these who were redeemed by him. Ben led the Jewish believers in songs of ascents which now glorified their risen Lord. They moved methodically, none rushing or pushing, reaching the gates in waves, and walking through. When they stepped from the gates into the city, they moved to one side and gazed in all directions, words failing them for several minutes.

Beth finally said, *"Wow..."* One word; no more, it trailing off as though the glittering, shimmering scene before them took her breath away before she could utter another.

That word expressed how they all felt. No words sufficed for the resplendent glory their eyes beheld in this breathtaking moment. Not just a *golden* city, but a city *made* of gold, *pure* gold, like clear glass... *heavenly* gold, they thought. And not just *part* of the city; the *entire* city! Yahweh's glory reflected off everything in sight, emitting an intoxicating luster, leaving them spellbound. None moved until they could withstand the dazzling display of brilliant luminance.

Slowly both their eyesight and minds adjusted to their never-ending celestial existence. They wandered along, soaking up the magnificence of New Jerusalem. Nothing like this ever existed on the former earth, but this was not *that* earth. If the city was this amazing, what must the outside earth look like? They yearned for it but also longed to stay in this place. Roaming on, they feared even touching the pure golden objects stretching endlessly before them.

They walked and walked, losing all track of time. How far had they traveled? None of them could answer that question. How long since they started? Days? Weeks? Months? They did not know, but it was irrelevant because though time still existed, it no longer mattered. Schedules, deadlines, commitments, appointments were all elements of the previous world. *Freedom* defined this world.

Only one meeting held significance for them: viewing their Creator's face and hearing his voice. Unsure when that would occur, they continued touring this magnificent metropolis, sharing the experience with others as they went. Finally able to speak, they began conversing about their new lives, and the awesome things they had already witnessed.

"I didn't see any of this when I went to heaven."

"Neither did we, sweetheart, and we were there seven years," Angie said, answering her husband's contemplation. "Jesus spent 2,000 years getting this city ready, but allowed no one else to see it."

"Do you remember the verse we read, and wondered what it meant? *No eye has seen, no ear has heard, no mind has imagined what God has prepared for those who love him.* I understand it now."

"You're right, Anders, because our minds could never have conceived anything like this."

"Beth is right," John said. "We talked about it many times, but our thoughts were centered on earthly things, not heavenly things. Nothing on the former earth ever compared to this."

"I wasted my life chasing earthly things. If I had only realized then what I understand now."

"Doc, those things mean nothing now. I chased them like you did, but it was like chasing the wind. We never caught them. But when we found Jesus, we discovered what life was all about."

"Kathie is right, Doc," John said. "We all chased earthly things and bought into Satan's lies. Now we're here together witnessing the real truth for ourselves. We need to release those old things and set our minds on new things."

"Yes, like this street we're walking on," Blake said. "Have you noticed it?"

The group had been so focused on other things, they had not looked down. Now they did. The street was the same pure gold that made up the entire city, transparent, like glass, with no impurity, clear, and perfect. After recognizing that, they walked gingerly, not wanting to mar its perfection, then realized that was not possible, so they ran and jumped, enjoying Jesus' handiwork.

***

Ben and the 144,000 shared the same experience as their fellow believers who had each lived life far apart from Jesus until they discovered truth and followed him. Their journey had been glorious, beyond anything they could have dreamed possible. But they would soon have an encounter which only Yahweh himself could orchestrate. It came suddenly, and without notice.

They entered a vast open area which appeared to be the city center. Walking through, they were careful not to make a sound. Wispy fog floated through the air, concealing something of great significance. They considered going around or leaving the place altogether, but an irresistible force kept them there. Another large group of people approached them from the right.

"Blake!"

Ben ran toward his dear friend and former employee who helped him believe in Jesus. They shared an embrace only true believers could understand. Then everyone joined them, tears flowing as they wept for rejecting Jesus before the Rapture, but also celebrated all he had done in their lives. The moment brought a mixture of joy and sorrow.

A large hand extended from the fog, touching each face. Their Creator and God wiped away their tears forever. Every group experienced it when they stopped here. They understood this final revelation of Yahweh's greatest work. Metamorphosis fully reversed the six-thousand year curse and restored his original intent for human beings. Pain, death, sickness, and weeping no longer existed. Past heartbreaks and struggles were removed, and everything was made new.

The former things were not important. From this point forward, they would live this new life with no thoughts of their previous existence. That temporary experience was not really life at all. This new reality was true life, and it would never end.

They gasped as the fog began lifting, and a huge throne appeared. The fog raised slowly, revealing massive feet and muscular legs, a powerful chest and mighty arms, then a thick neck and chin. Before the final unveiling, they all fell on their faces, hands raised in worship and praise.

"My dwelling is now with you. You will be my people, and I will be with you, and be your God. You will come here to worship, but we will also share a personal relationship. Now you can look at me and commune with me. Welcome, beloved children. I look forward to eternity with you!"

They all lifted their heads at once and looked into the face of Yahweh. Whatever they expected, his appearance was exponentially greater. No fear consumed them, only love more pure than the city's gold. Their omnipresent God extended his arms, and embraced them all simultaneously. Warmth flooded their glorified bodies, sealing the change inside them. They were finally *home*.

None wanted to leave his presence, but much more awaited them in the New Jerusalem and outside its walls. They wrestled with thoughts of leaving or staying until he made the choice for them.

"You will see my face here often, but I will also be with you everywhere you travel on the earth. I created it for you to enjoy. Your first stop holds the most amazing experience of all!"

Questions flooded their minds. How could anything top what they had already done and seen? They looked into his eyes, eagerly waiting for him to explain those words. He did, and their hearts raced with anticipation.

"I concealed the Garden of Eden for seven thousand years. But I have reopened it exactly like it was when Adam and Eve lived there so you can experience it just as they did! Follow the river. It leads to the garden, then runs outside the city. Enjoy yourselves, and I will see you again soon!"

They now heard the rushing water and saw the river cascading from under the throne. The street separated into two sides with the river flowing between them, its water pure and clear, like everything else in New Jerusalem! Beautiful trees lined the river on both sides, loaded with enticing fruit. *The tree of life*, they heard Yahweh say, obviously taking great pleasure in his revelation. They must sample both!

Each picked fruit from the trees and bit into it, juice flooding their mouths with sweetness like they had never tasted. Healing power circulated through every part of their being, empowering them and preparing them for all things yet to come. They kneeled beside the river and drank deeply of its cool, clear water. Life surged inside them as the water flowed into their new bodies. *The water of life!* They felt renewed as the refreshing liquid revitalized them and exuberant energy replaced fatigue forever. Weariness and exhaustion would never return!

They kept going, enjoying New Jerusalem, the living water, and delectable tree of life fruit. Suddenly and unexpectedly, they found themselves in the garden! Once again, the sensation they felt when they entered was unlike anything previously known to them. Perfection everywhere! Lush green grass, flowing streams, animals, trees, and flowers covered the place. Pure, uncontaminated air filled their lungs. All of their senses heightened to perfection.

They ran, laughed, rolled in the grass, and never grew tired. Their bodies experienced no weakness or pain, and never would again. They picked more fruit and drank from the garden's streams. What was next? They could stay in Eden, but a desire to enjoy all the earth now offered drove them on. They followed the river to where it exited the garden and flowed under the city wall, then parted ways with Ben's group, who chose to stay. The Smyrnians walked out the gate, stepped into the earth, and discovered Yahweh's promise was true. He had removed the curse.

Once outside the wall, the single river separated into four flowing east, west, north, and south. Life emanating from the water refreshed the earth as it flowed. Ahead, flora and fauna existed in abundance. Trees grew by the riverbanks. Tributaries branched off, creating more rivers, creeks, and lakes. Animals grazed green grass that stretched for miles and lapped up the life-giving water, while a stunning azure sky spread out overhead. Such tranquility the previous world never offered.

The group traveled a path leading toward mountains with snow-capped peaks which caused them to stand and stare again, mouths open, eyes fixated on the astounding landscape surrounding them.

"Snow!" said Evan and Ally. The snow excited some, but others said they would rather stay below and enjoy the snow from a distance. The new earth held something for everyone.

After hiking between mountains, they entered an expansive valley and halted their journey, taken aback once more by what they saw. Among the animals feasting on sumptuous greenery, large and small dinosaurs wandered about, more soaring overhead, flying with various species of birds, while others swam or waded in the cool water. Land, air, and sea creatures intermingled peacefully, none harming the other, returning to their pre-curse state. Caleb, the animal lover, led the way.

"Come on, they won't hurt us. No one is harmed or dies on the new earth!"

He ran through the valley, caressing every animal he passed, regardless of size. A Tyrannosaurus rex approached, but he did not shy away. Walking under the creature, he stroked its large stomach, which stood six feet off the ground. A Brachiosaurus stopped feasting on leaves from a tall tree long enough to lower its head, allowing Caleb to climb aboard and slide down its long neck. The others joined him, enjoying an earth where former carnivores now ate grass with herbivores in Yahweh's new creation. They spent hours delighting in experiences that would last forever.

Following the winding path, weaving through valleys, hills, fields, and plains, the Smyrnians were clueless about how much time had passed since they left New Jerusalem. Time no longer mattered to them, only what their eyes had seen and the ecstasy that filled their hearts. The city would always be there, and they would visit often, but Yahweh's new world was abundant with wonder and excitement, and they wanted to experience it all. Eternity provided ample time to accomplish that.

Questions filled their minds. Would they build houses and live in them? Would they work, be creative, invent new things, and grow food, or simply spend eternity worshiping Yahweh and Jesus? That would be okay with them! So many questions for which answers would come in time. After all, they had eternity to figure it out, yet doubted that was even possible.

They pondered another question, one which they would need to summon courage to ask. What about space? Would Yahweh allow them to explore the *entire* new universe? How they could do that, none of them knew, but they hoped to receive an answer soon. Endless possibilities lay ahead.

For now, the New Jerusalem beckoned them to return. They made their way back and approached the gate leading into the garden. After touring the city and experiencing all it offered, the new world would await them. Standing outside the wall, they gazed upon the glorious place Jesus built for them. When they walked inside, his glory overwhelmed them again, and they stared in wonder.

"It was worth it all," said Blake. "It was definitely worth it all."

Every Smyrnian agreed.

CONCLUSION

Thank you for reading my series. The stories are fictional, but the truths behind them are fact. Only true followers of Jesus will experience the eternal blessings which occur when he returns. If that includes you, one day we will live together forever! You and I may not meet on this side of eternity, but what do you say we look each other up then? I look forward to getting to know you!

If you have not put your faith in Jesus and received him as your Savior, please do that right now as you finish Episode Five. While September 11, 2029 is only a speculative date, I do believe the Rapture of his church will occur soon. Whatever you do, don't miss it and be left behind to endure the horrors of the Tribulation. If you believe in Jesus and His death and resurrection, pray this simple prayer, and commit your life to Him.

Jesus, I confess with my mouth, you are Lord, and believe in my heart God raised you from the dead. Please forgive my sin and come into my life. I receive you as my personal Savior and commit my life to you as my Lord. Thank you, Jesus, for saving me. I will live the rest of my life expecting your return. Amen!

Welcome to the family of God! Find a good church and be baptized, symbolizing the death, burial, and resurrection of Jesus, and the death of your own old life, and resurrection to your new life in him. Tell others what he did for you and live for him. Following Jesus truly is the good life!

If you prayed that prayer, please email me at davidobullockwriting@gmail.com and let me know. I would love to celebrate with you! If you enjoyed this series, email me and share that, too. Then tell others about these books and leave a review everywhere you can. God bless you!

ABOUT THE AUTHOR

David O. Bullock is a pastor, teacher, and author of seven novels. He loves hurling people into spell-binding stories that captivate their imagination and bring future events to life, leaving them caught in the middle of the action. David thrives on writing fictional novels that open readers' minds to truths they never imagined. He lives in Somerset, Kentucky, cherishes his wife, and treasures his daughters and grandchildren. Despite his dramatic writing style, David is a fun-loving guy who considers himself somewhat weird and never plans on growing up. The search for his beloved and often hard-to-find Diet Rite is an ongoing family affair. In the car traveling anywhere while cranking 70s rock or contemporary Christian music is his favorite place to be.

NOTE FROM THE AUTHOR

Word-of-mouth is crucial for any author to succeed. If you enjoyed *Dawn of Deliverance*, please leave a review online—anywhere you are able. Even if it's just a sentence or two. It would make all the difference and would be very much appreciated.

Thanks!
David O. Bullock

We hope you enjoyed reading this title from:

BLACK ROSE
writing™

www.blackrosewriting.com

Subscribe to our mailing list – *The Rosevine* – and receive **FREE** books, daily deals, and stay current with news about upcoming releases and our hottest authors.
Scan the QR code below to sign up.

Already a subscriber? Please accept a sincere thank you for being a fan of Black Rose Writing authors.

View other Black Rose Writing titles at
www.blackrosewriting.com/books and use promo code
PRINT to receive a **20% discount** when purchasing.